SPARKS!

DOUBLE DOG DARE

WRITTEN BY IAN BOOTHBY

ART BY NINA MATSUMOTO
WITH COLOR BY DAVID DEDRICK

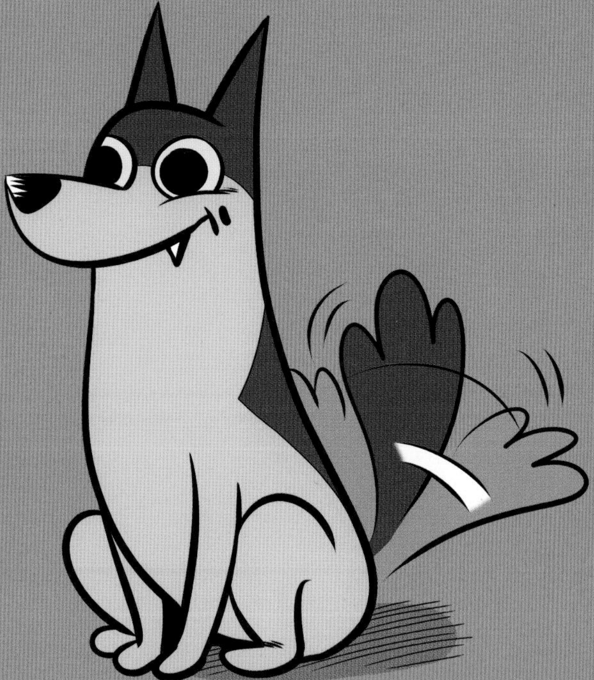

graphix
An Imprint of
SCHOLASTIC

Photo by Vicky Van

Dedicated to Cohen aka Coco aka BubBub
—Ian Boothby and Nina Matsumoto

Text copyright © 2020 by Ian Boothby
Art copyright © 2020 by Nina Matsumoto

Library of Congress cataloguing-in-publication data is available

ISBN 978-1-338-33991-8 (hardcover)
ISBN 978-1-338-33990-1 (paperback)

10 9 8 7 6 5 4 3 2 1   20 21 22 23 24

Printed in China   62
First edition, August 2020

Edited by Adam Rau
Book design by Phil Falco & Steve Ponzo
Publisher: David Saylor

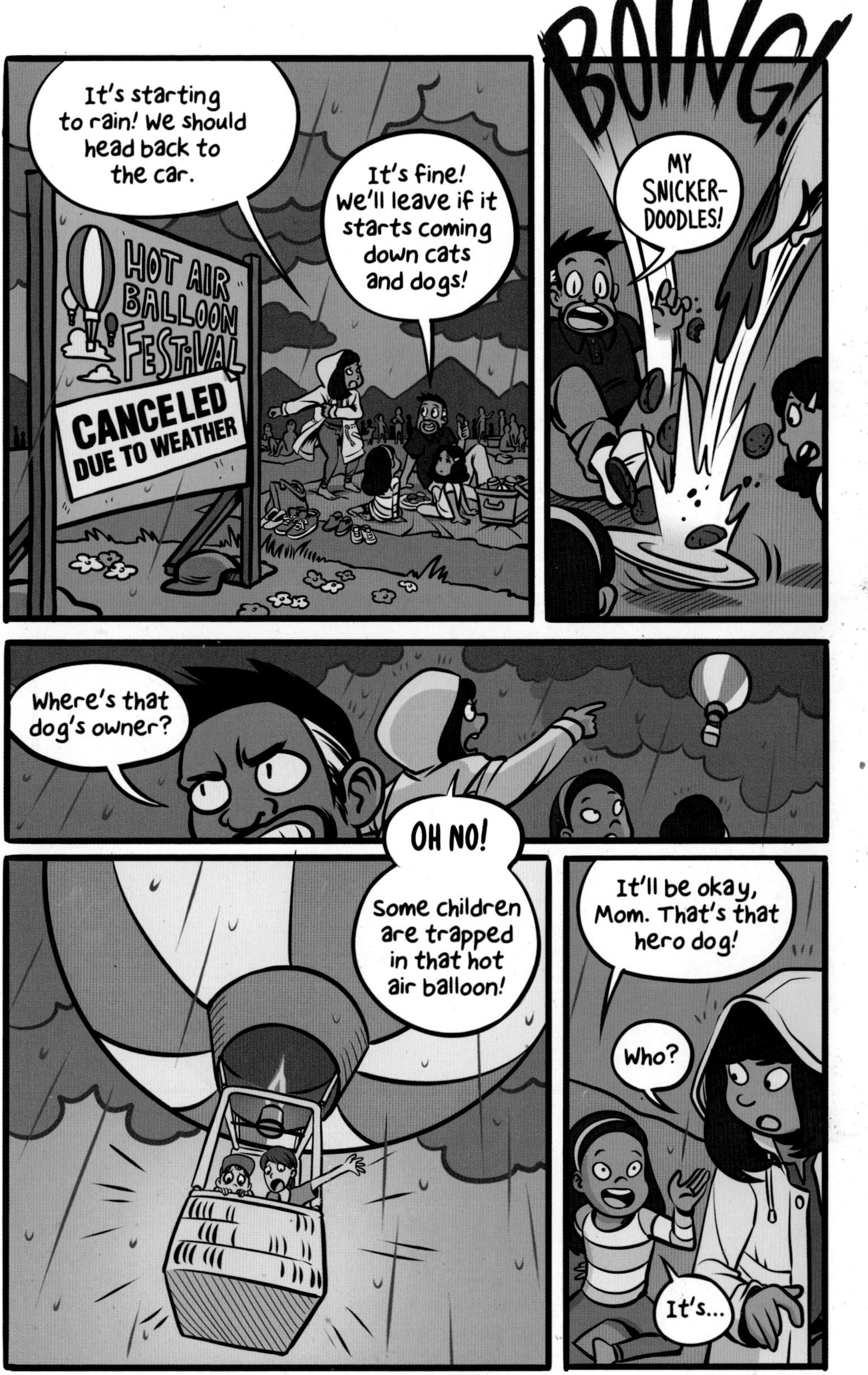
It's starting to rain! We should head back to the car.
HOT AIR BALLOON FESTIVAL
CANCELED DUE TO WEATHER
It's fine! We'll leave if it starts coming down cats and dogs!
BOING!
MY SNICKER-DOODLES!
Where's that dog's owner?
OH NO!
Some children are trapped in that hot air balloon!
It'll be okay, Mom. That's that hero dog!
Who?
It's...

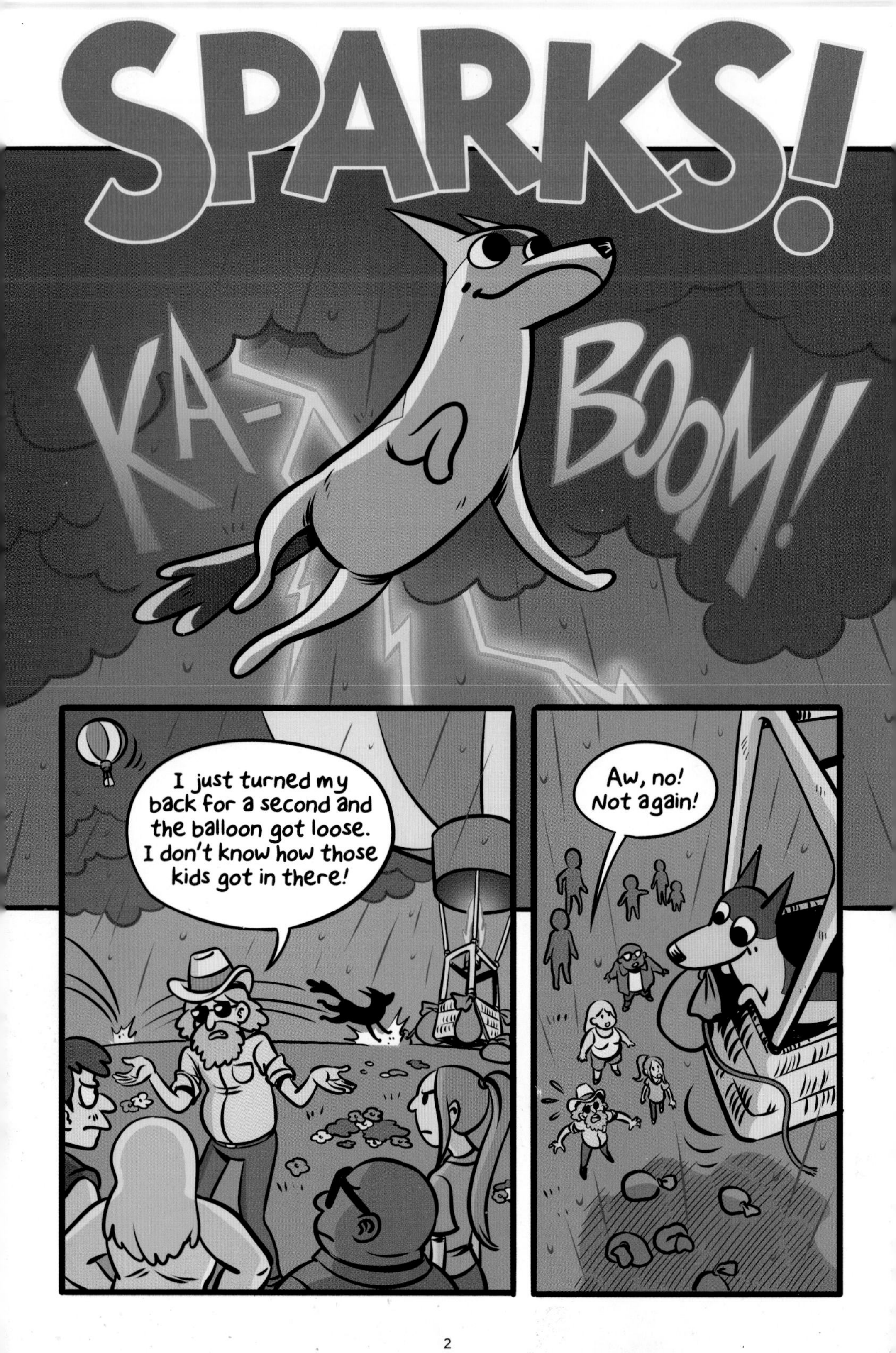
SPARKS!
KA-BOOM!
I just turned my back for a second and the balloon got loose. I don't know how those kids got in there!
Aw, no! Not again!

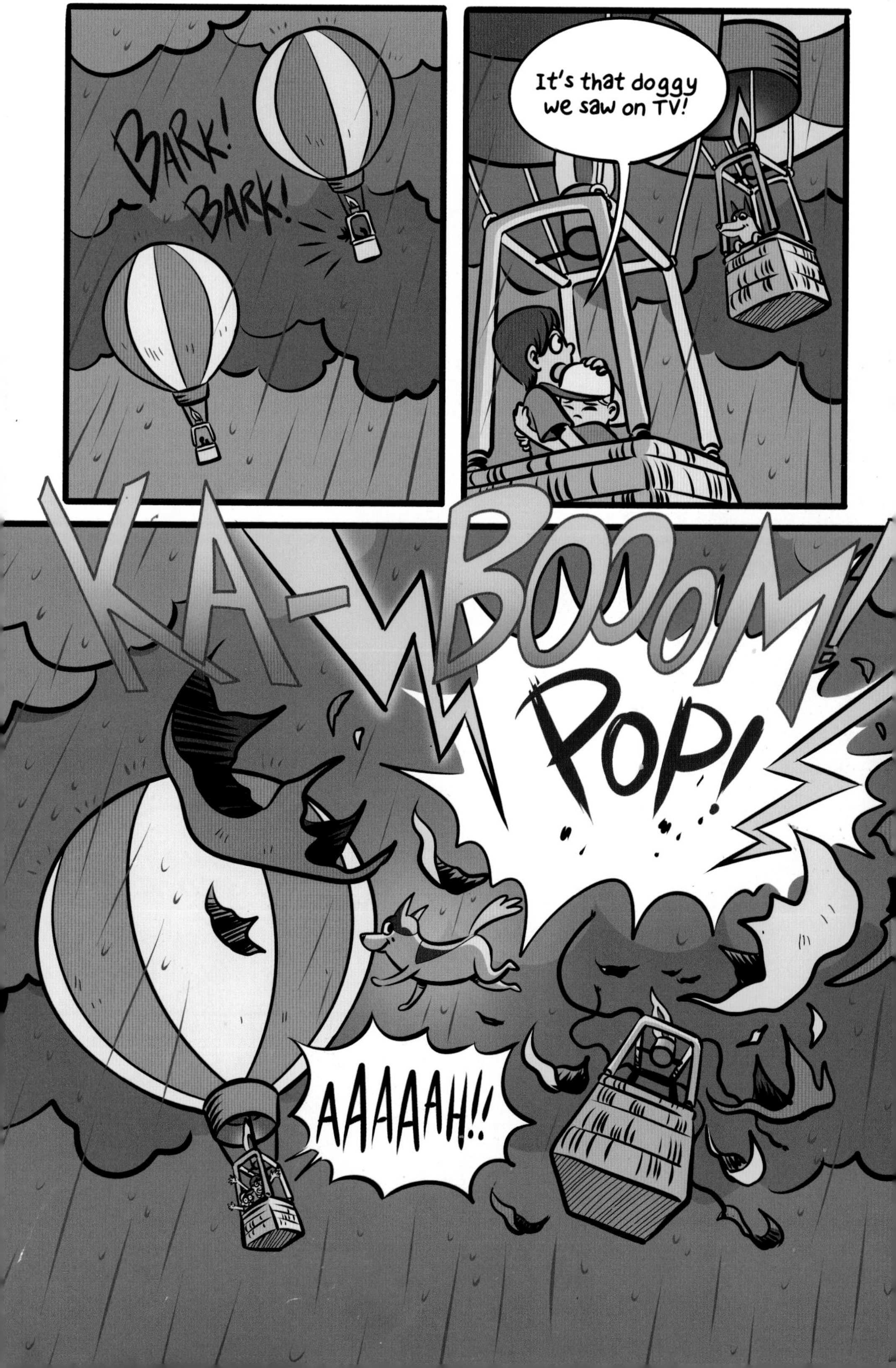
BARK! BARK!
It's that doggy we saw on TV!
KA-BOOOOM!
POP!
AAAAAH!!

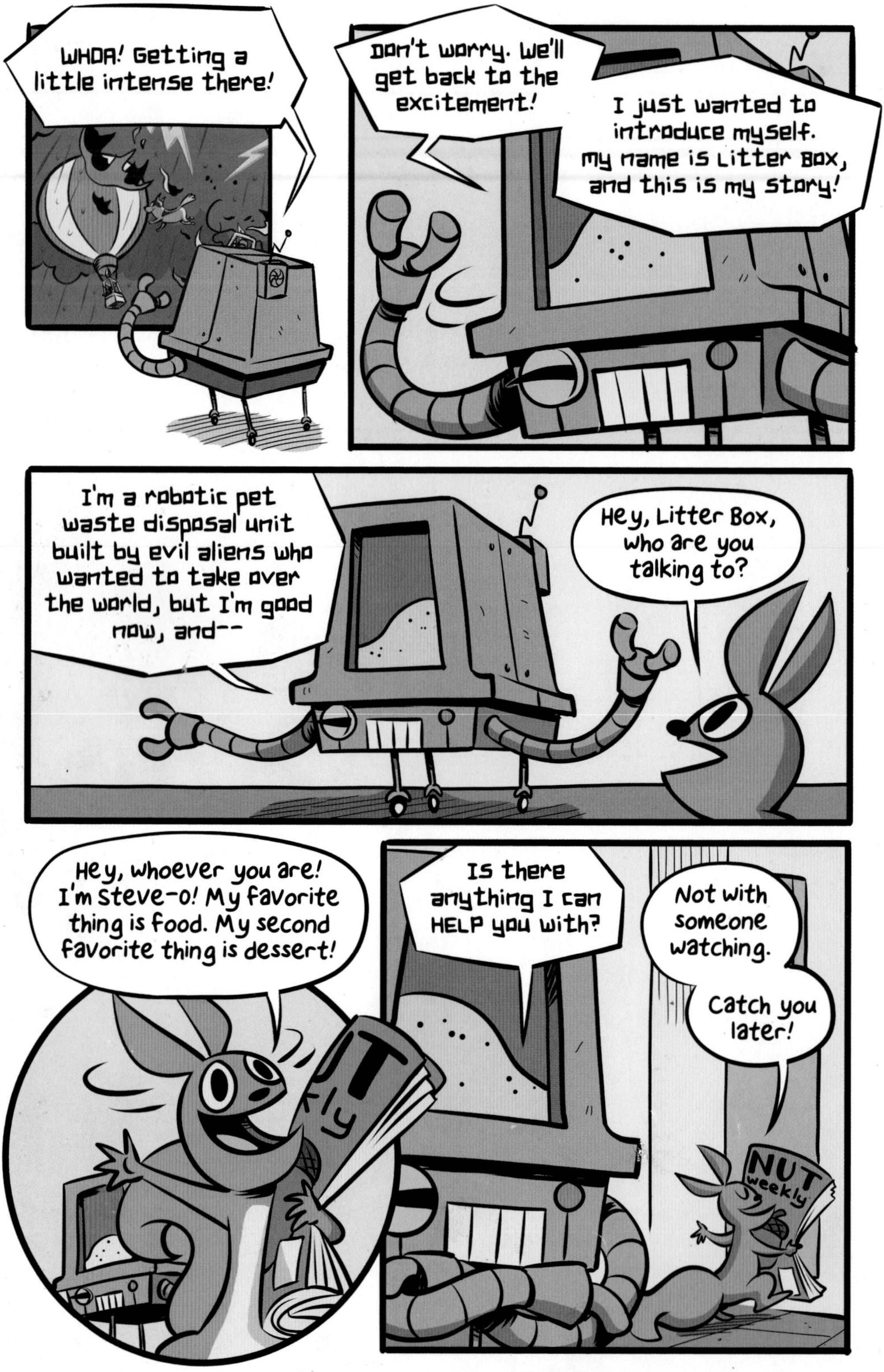
WHOA! Getting a little intense there!
Don't worry. We'll get back to the excitement!
I just wanted to introduce myself. My name is Litter Box, and this is my story!
I'm a robotic pet waste disposal unit built by evil aliens who wanted to take over the world, but I'm good now, and--
Hey, Litter Box, who are you talking to?
Hey, whoever you are! I'm Steve-O! My favorite thing is food. My second favorite thing is dessert!
Is there anything I can HELP you with?
Not with someone watching.
Catch you later!
NUT weekly

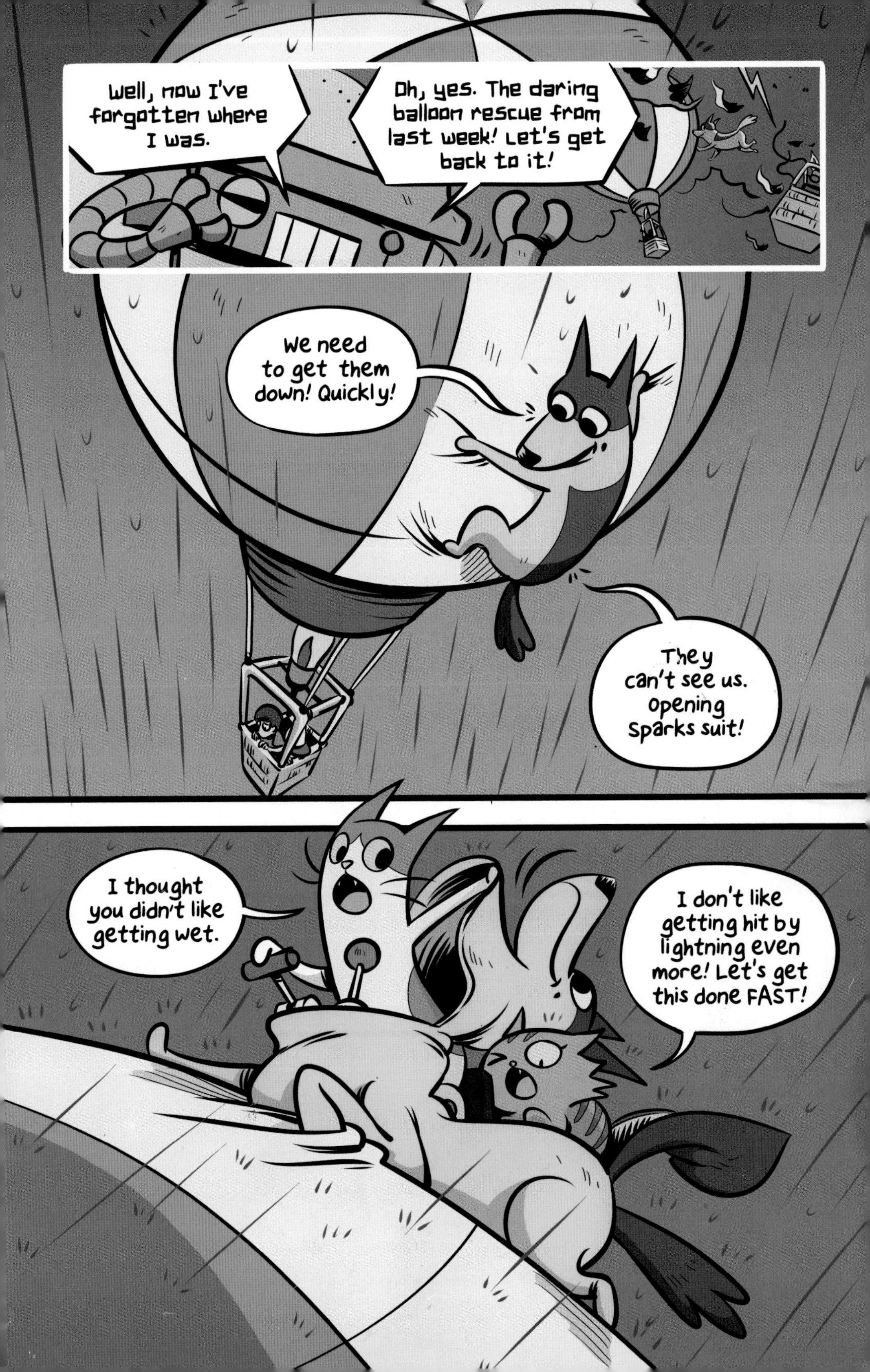
Well, now I've forgotten where I was.
Oh, yes. The daring balloon rescue from last week! Let's get back to it!
We need to get them down! Quickly!
They can't see us. Opening Sparks suit!
I thought you didn't like getting wet.
I don't like getting hit by lightning even more! Let's get this done FAST!

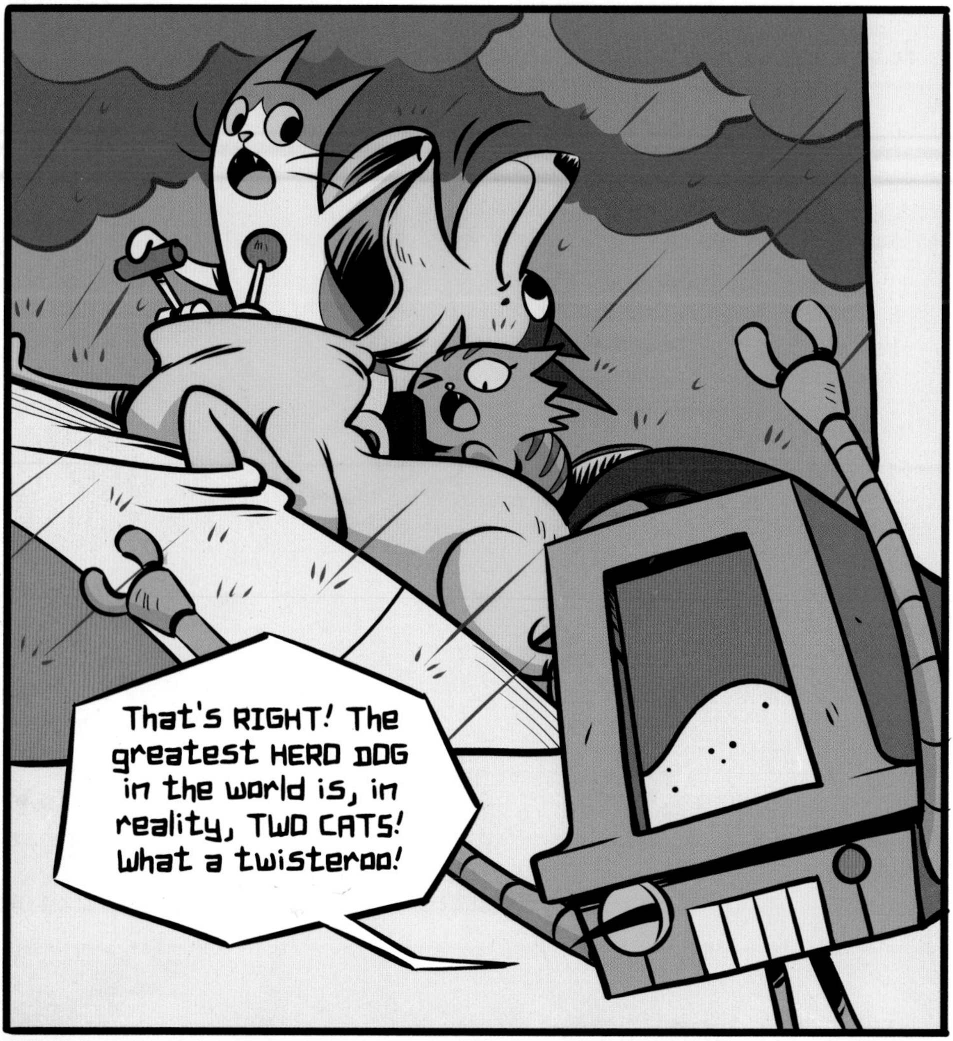
That's RIGHT! The greatest HERO DOG in the world is, in reality, TWO CATS! What a twisteroo!
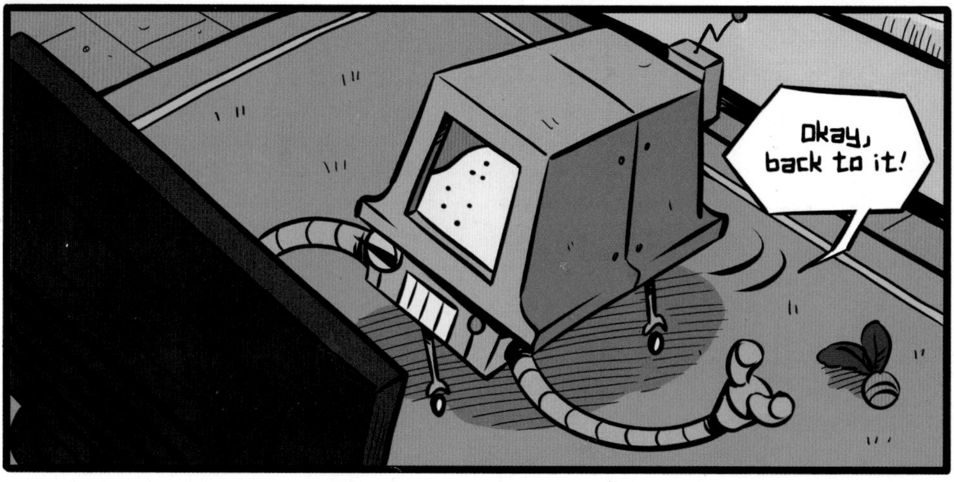
Okay, back to it!

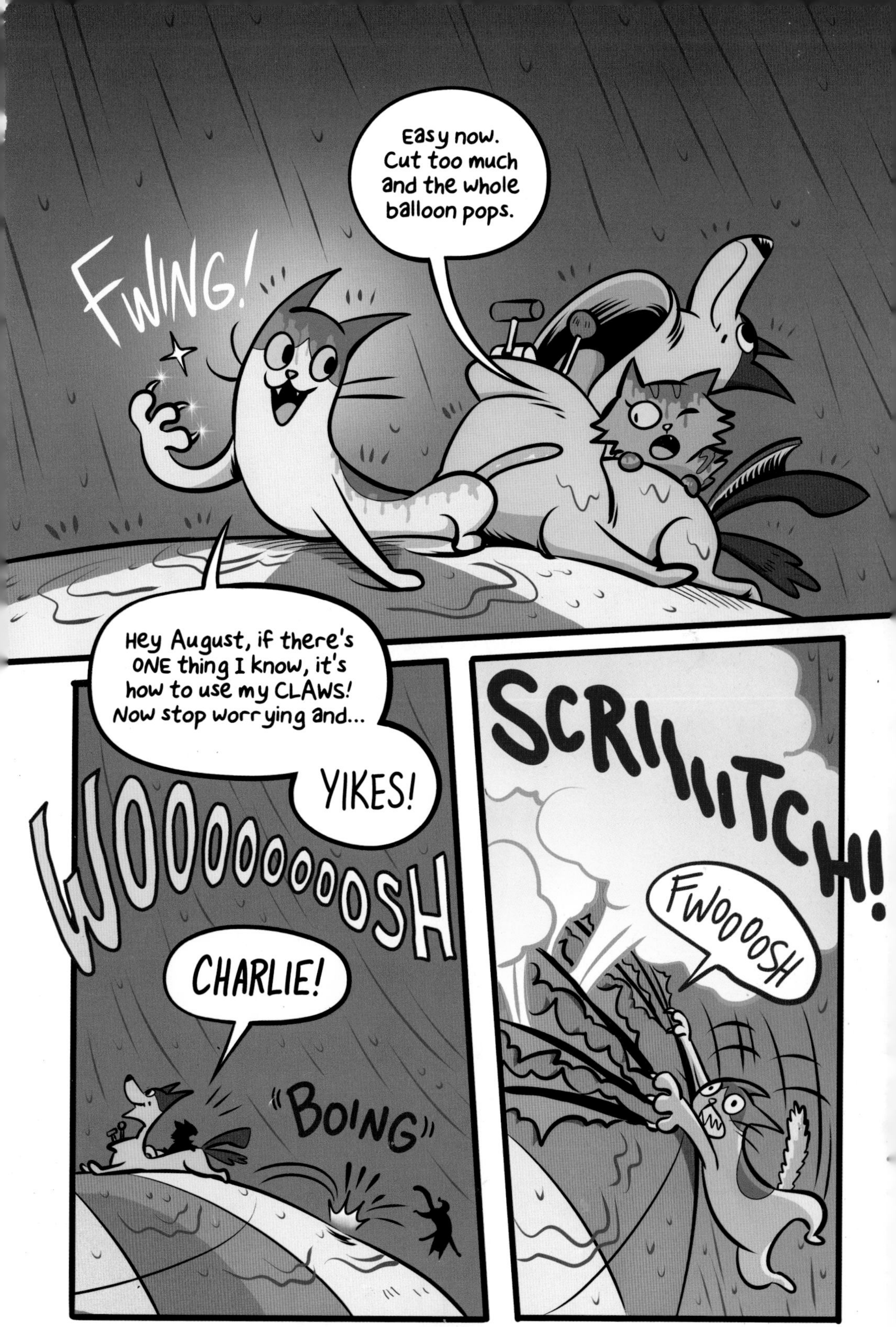
FWING!
Easy now. Cut too much and the whole balloon pops.
Hey August, if there's ONE thing I know, it's how to use my CLAWS! Now stop worrying and...
YIKES!
WOOOOOOOOSH
CHARLIE!
BOING
SCRIIIITCH!
FWOOOOSH

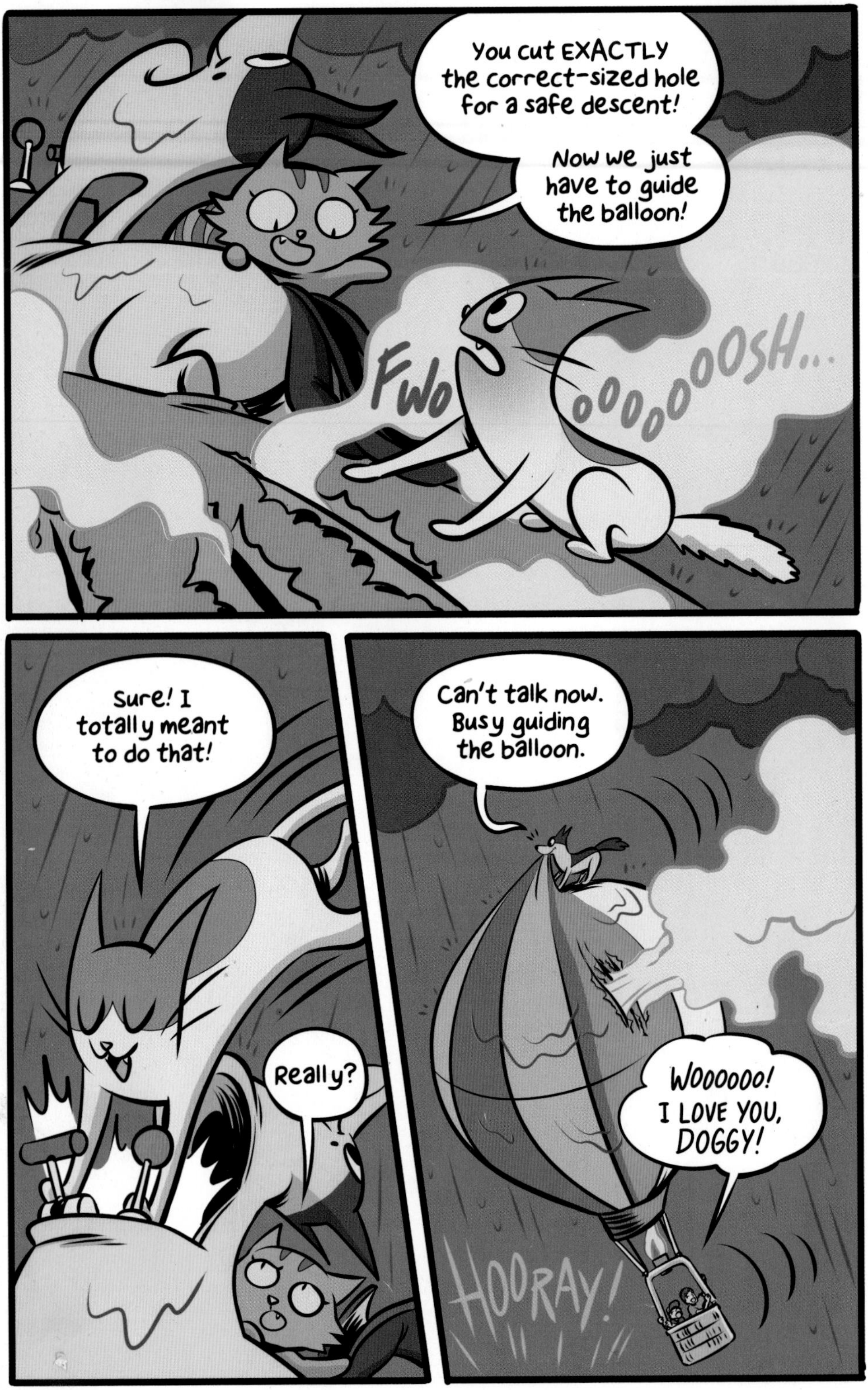
You cut EXACTLY the correct-sized hole for a safe descent!
Now we just have to guide the balloon!
FWOOOOOOOOOOSH...
Sure! I totally meant to do that!
Really?
Can't talk now. Busy guiding the balloon.
WOOOOOO! I LOVE YOU, DOGGY!
HOORAY!

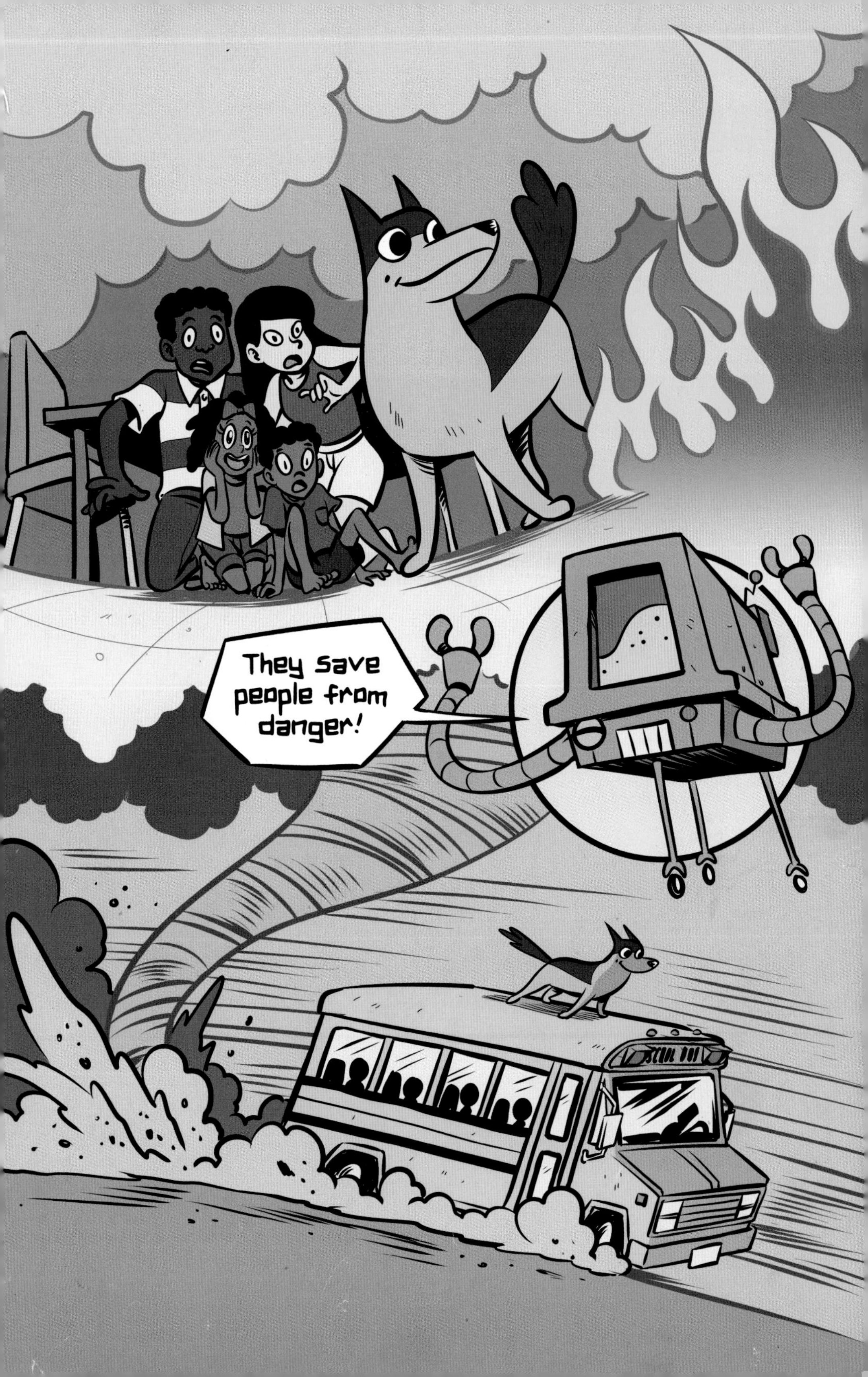
They save people from danger!

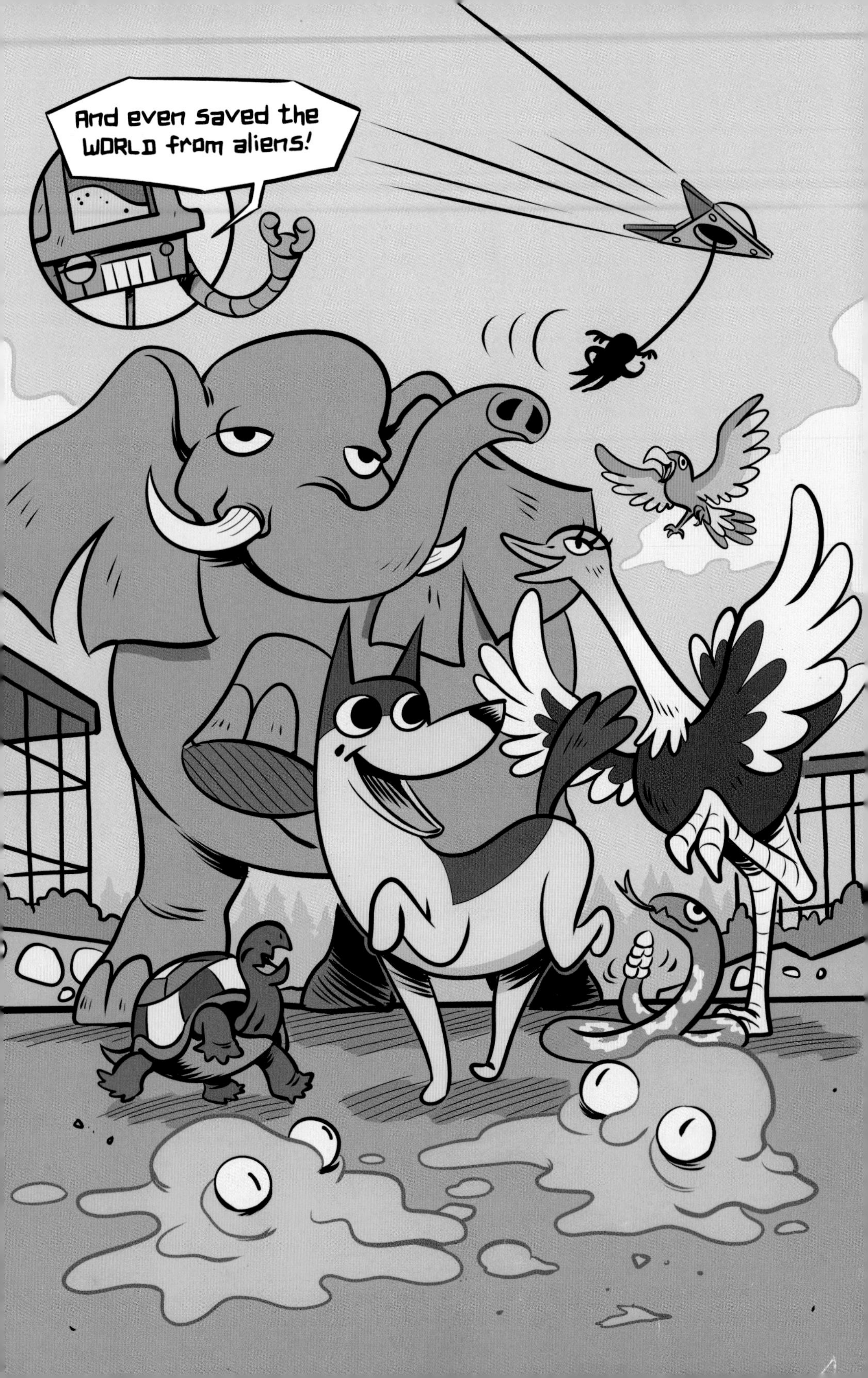
And even saved the WORLD from aliens!

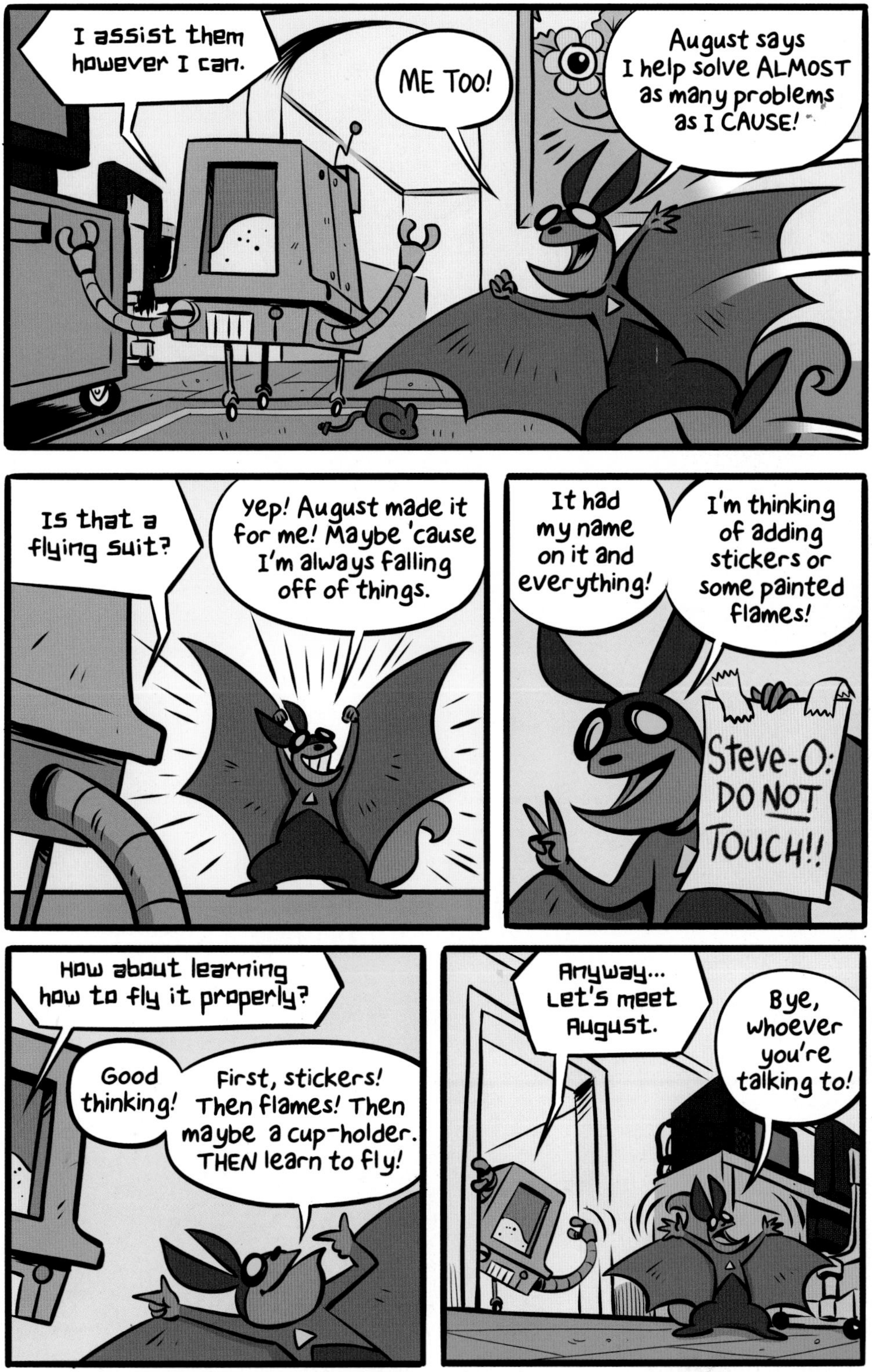
I assist them however I can.
ME TOO!
August says I help solve ALMOST as many problems as I CAUSE!
Is that a flying suit?
Yep! August made it for me! Maybe 'cause I'm always falling off of things.
It had my name on it and everything!
I'm thinking of adding stickers or some painted flames!
Steve-O: DO NOT TOUCH!!
How about learning how to fly it properly?
Good thinking!
First, stickers! Then flames! Then maybe a cup-holder. THEN learn to fly!
Anyway... Let's meet August.
Bye, whoever you're talking to!

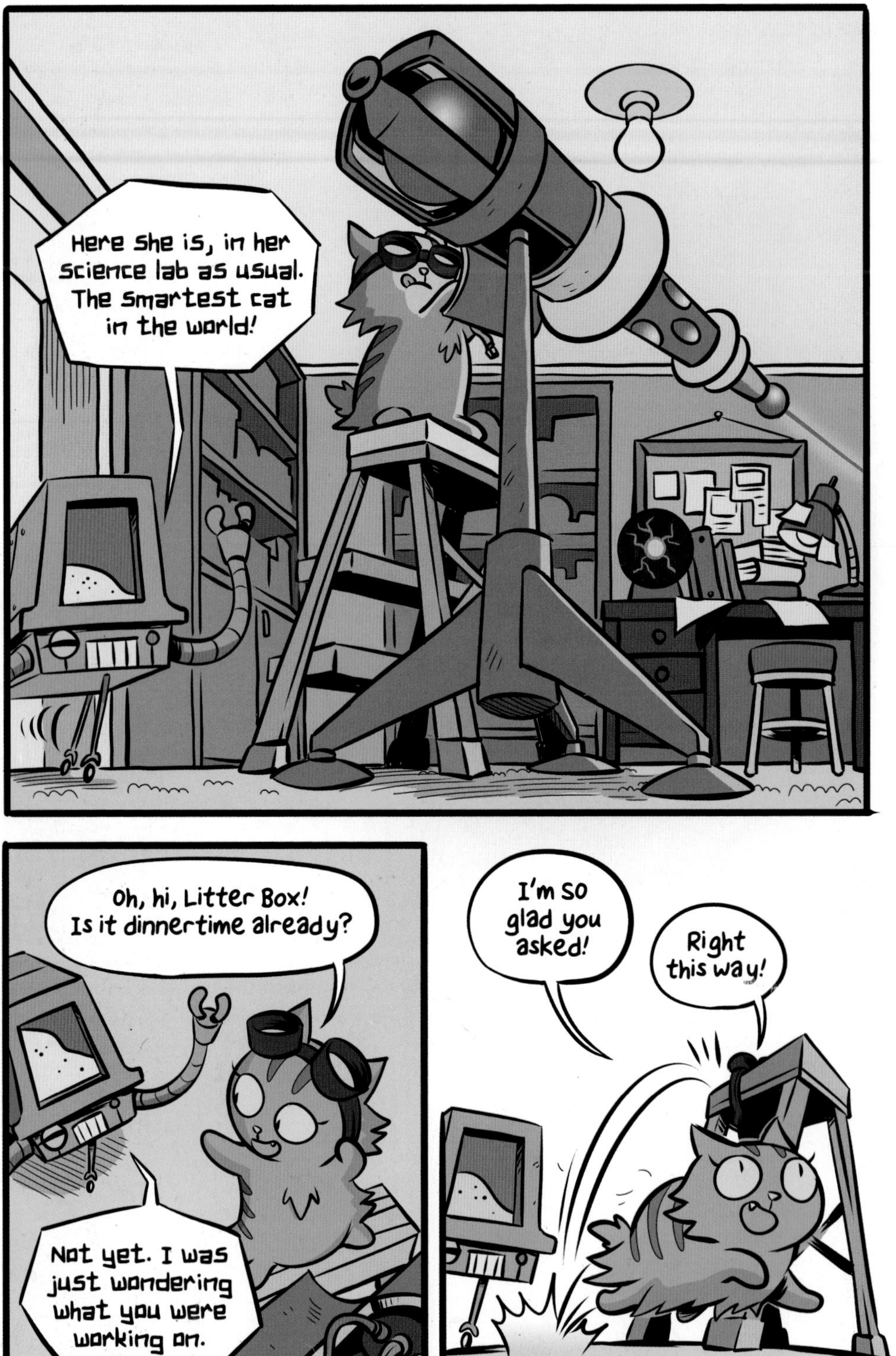
Here she is, in her science lab as usual. The smartest cat in the world!
Oh, hi, Litter Box! Is it dinnertime already?
Not yet. I was just wondering what you were working on.
I'm so glad you asked!
Right this way!

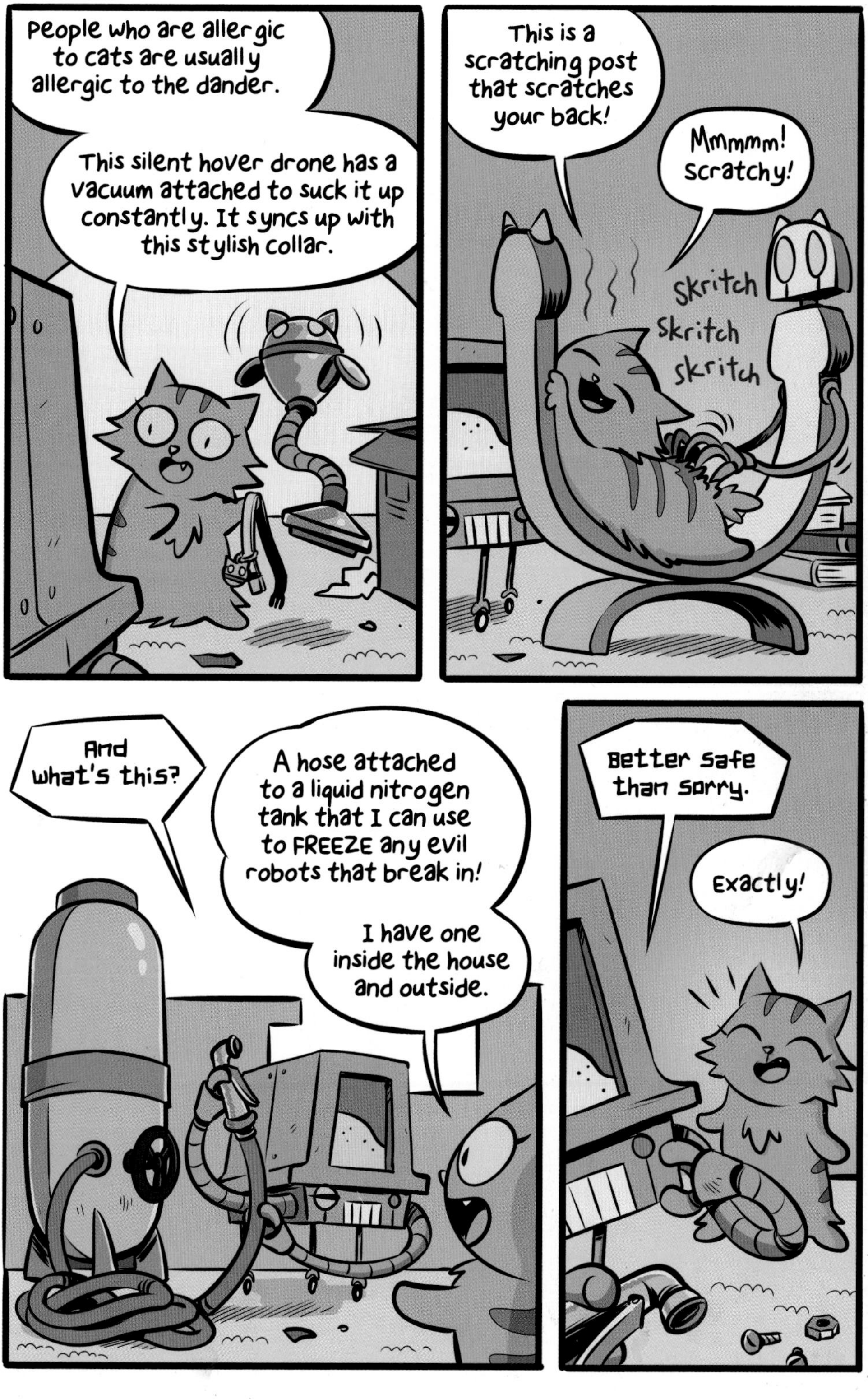
People who are allergic to cats are usually allergic to the dander.
This silent hover drone has a vacuum attached to suck it up constantly. It syncs up with this stylish collar.
This is a scratching post that scratches your back!
Mmmmm! Scratchy!
Skritch
Skritch
Skritch
And what's this?
A hose attached to a liquid nitrogen tank that I can use to FREEZE any evil robots that break in!
I have one inside the house and outside.
Better safe than sorry.
Exactly!

And what's THAT?

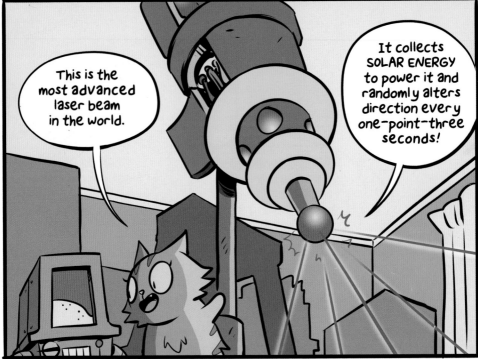

This is the most advanced laser beam in the world.

It collects SOLAR ENERGY to power it and randomly alters direction every one-point-three seconds!

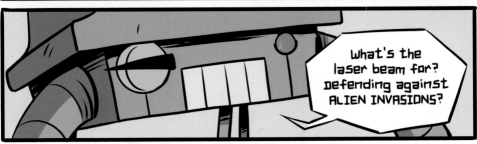

What's the laser beam for? Defending against ALIEN INVASIONS?

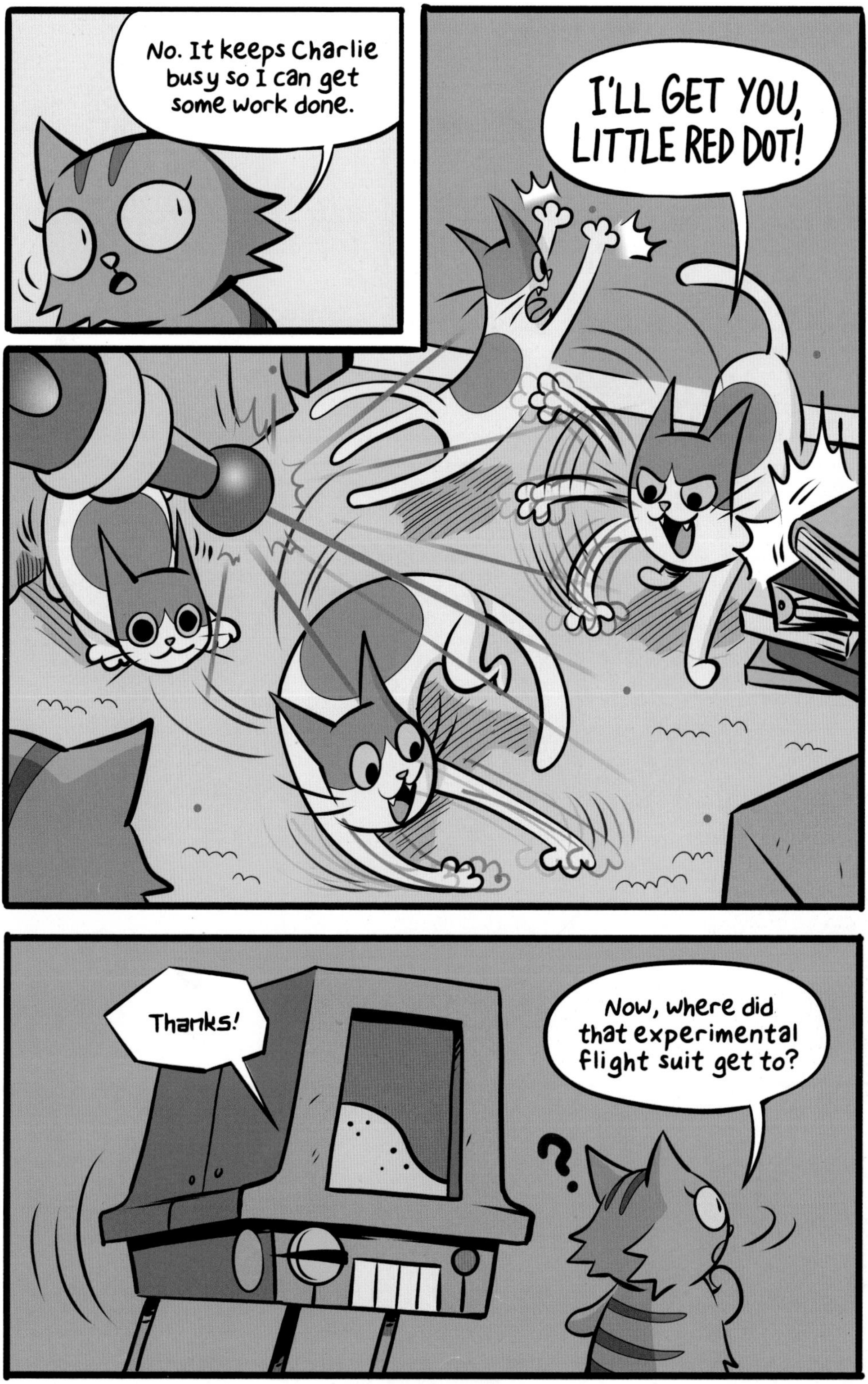
No. It keeps Charlie busy so I can get some work done.
I'LL GET YOU, LITTLE RED DOT!
Thanks!
Now, where did that experimental flight suit get to?

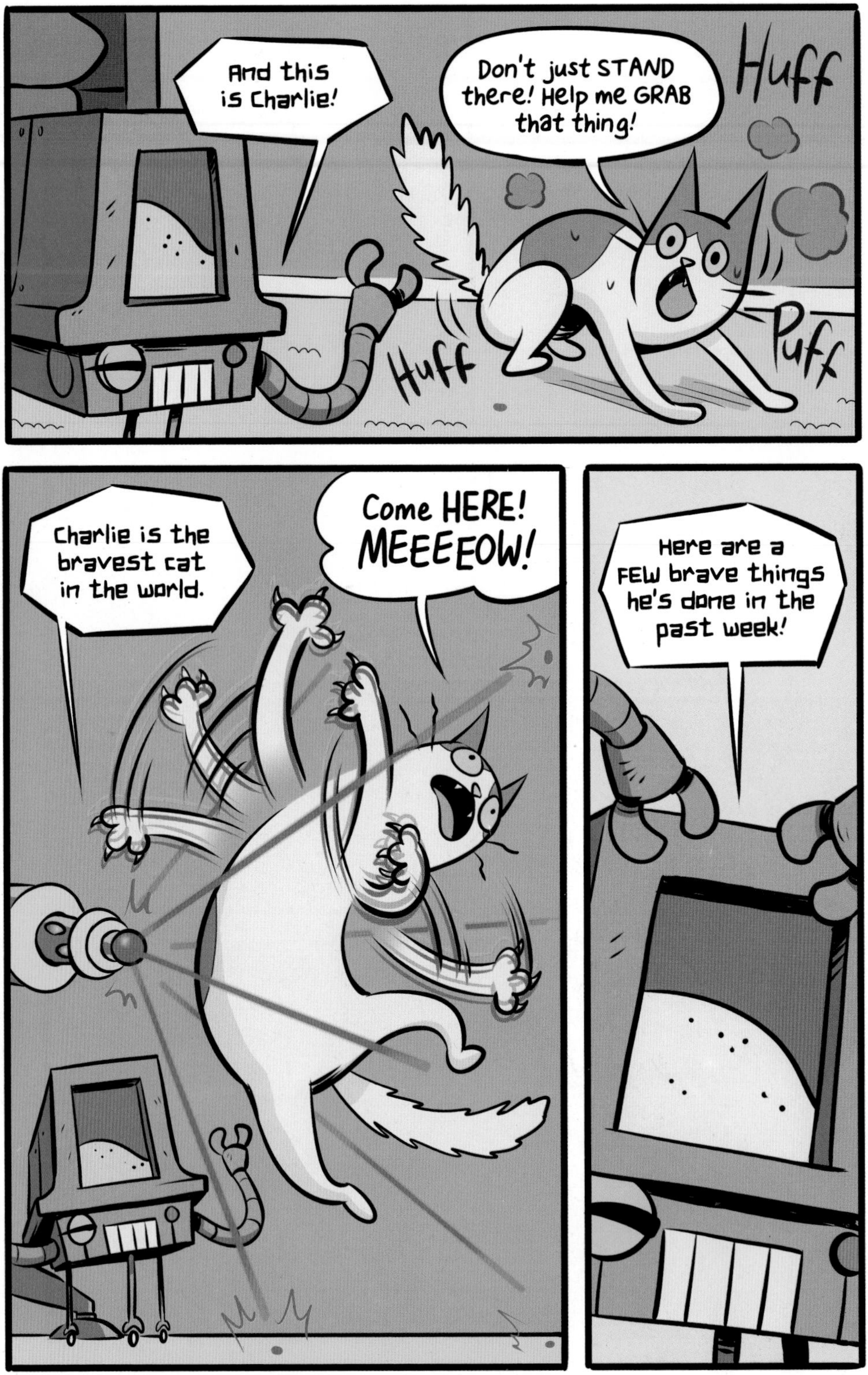
And this is Charlie!
Don't just STAND there! Help me GRAB that thing!
Huff
Huff
Puff
Charlie is the bravest cat in the world.
Come HERE! MEEEEOW!
Here are a FEW brave things he's done in the past week!

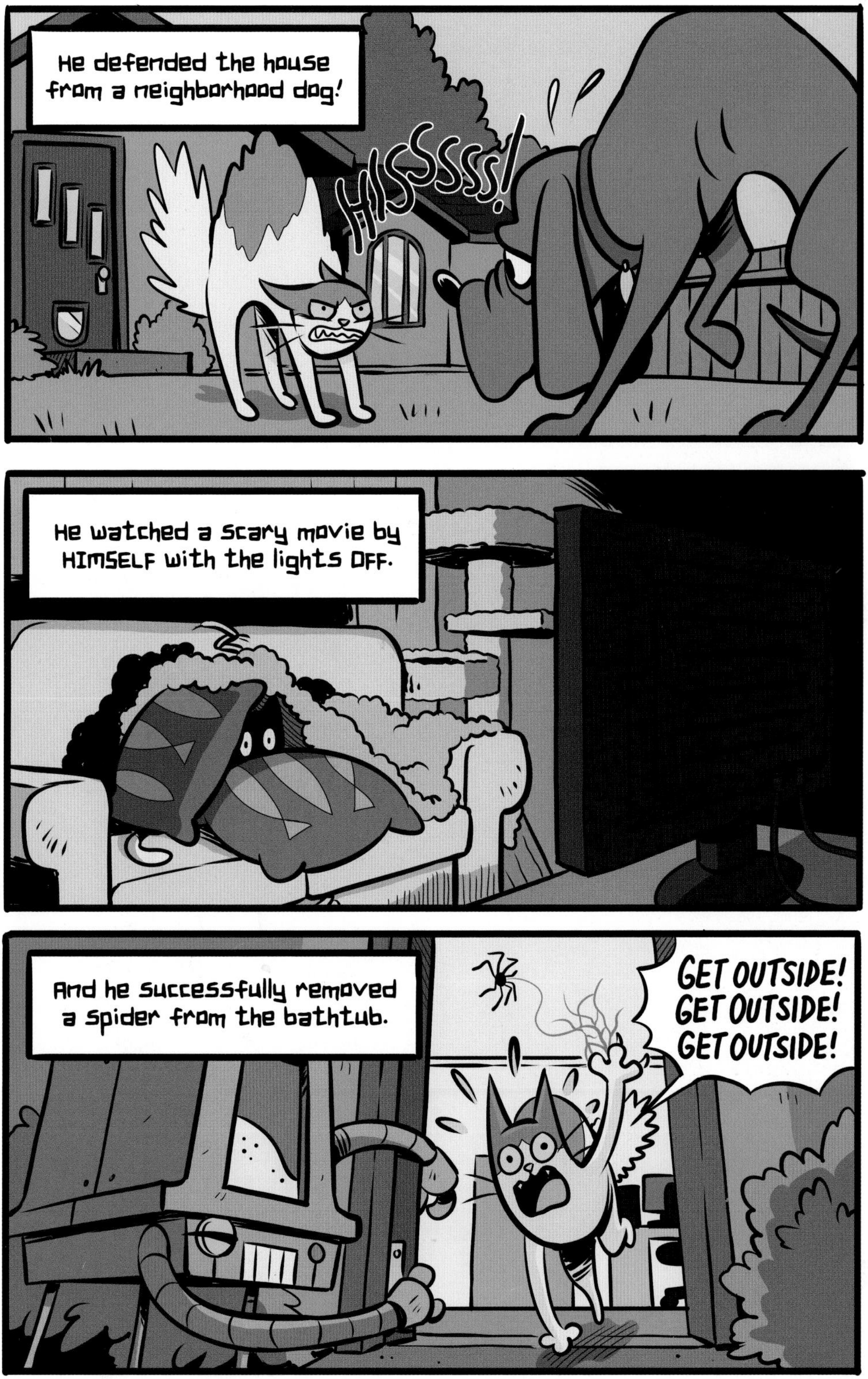
He defended the house from a neighborhood dog!
HISSSSS!
He watched a scary movie by HIMSELF with the lights OFF.
And he successfully removed a spider from the bathtub.
GET OUTSIDE! GET OUTSIDE! GET OUTSIDE!

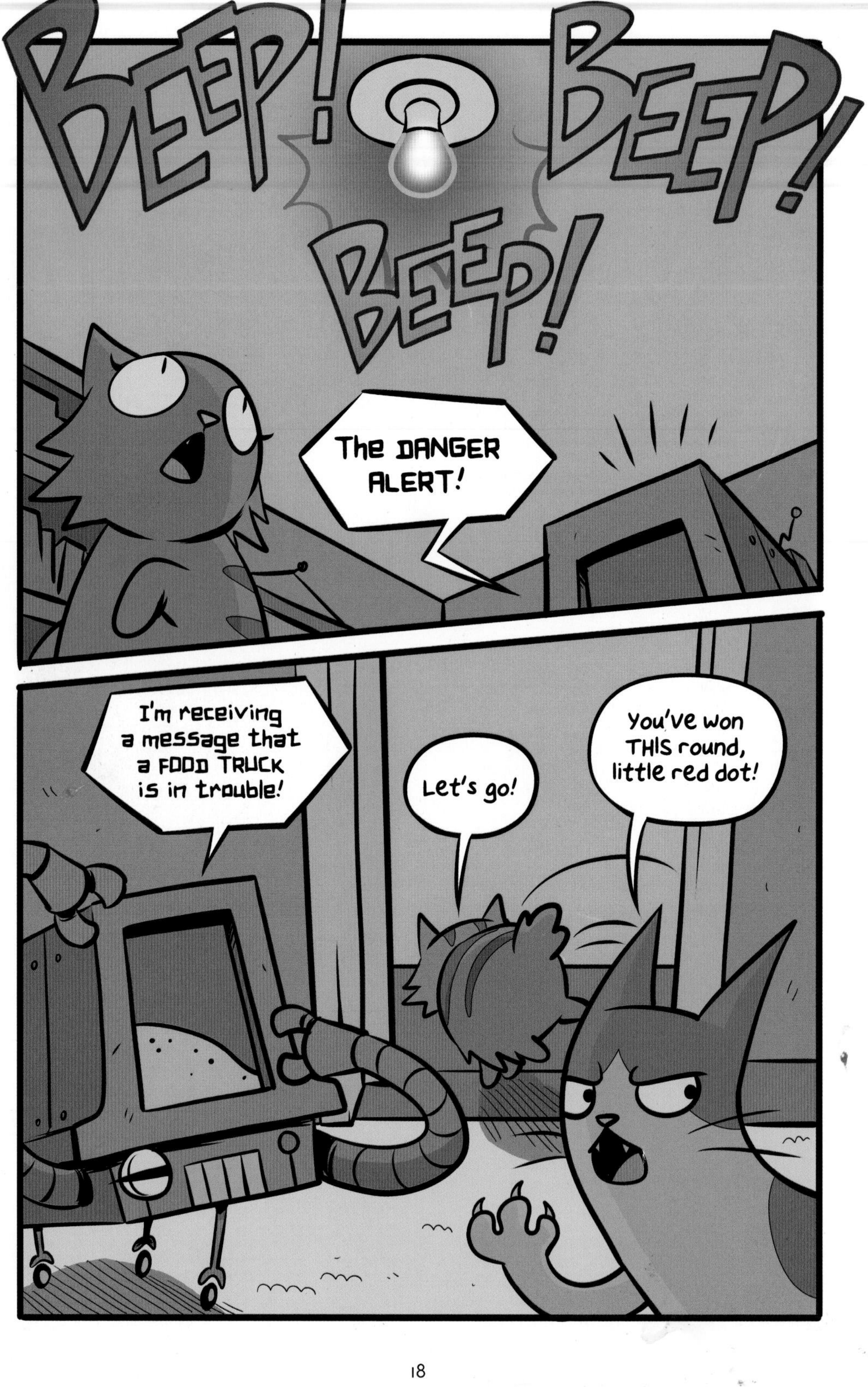
BEEP! BEEP! BEEP!
The DANGER ALERT!
I'm receiving a message that a FOOD TRUCK is in trouble!
Let's go!
You've won THIS round, little red dot!

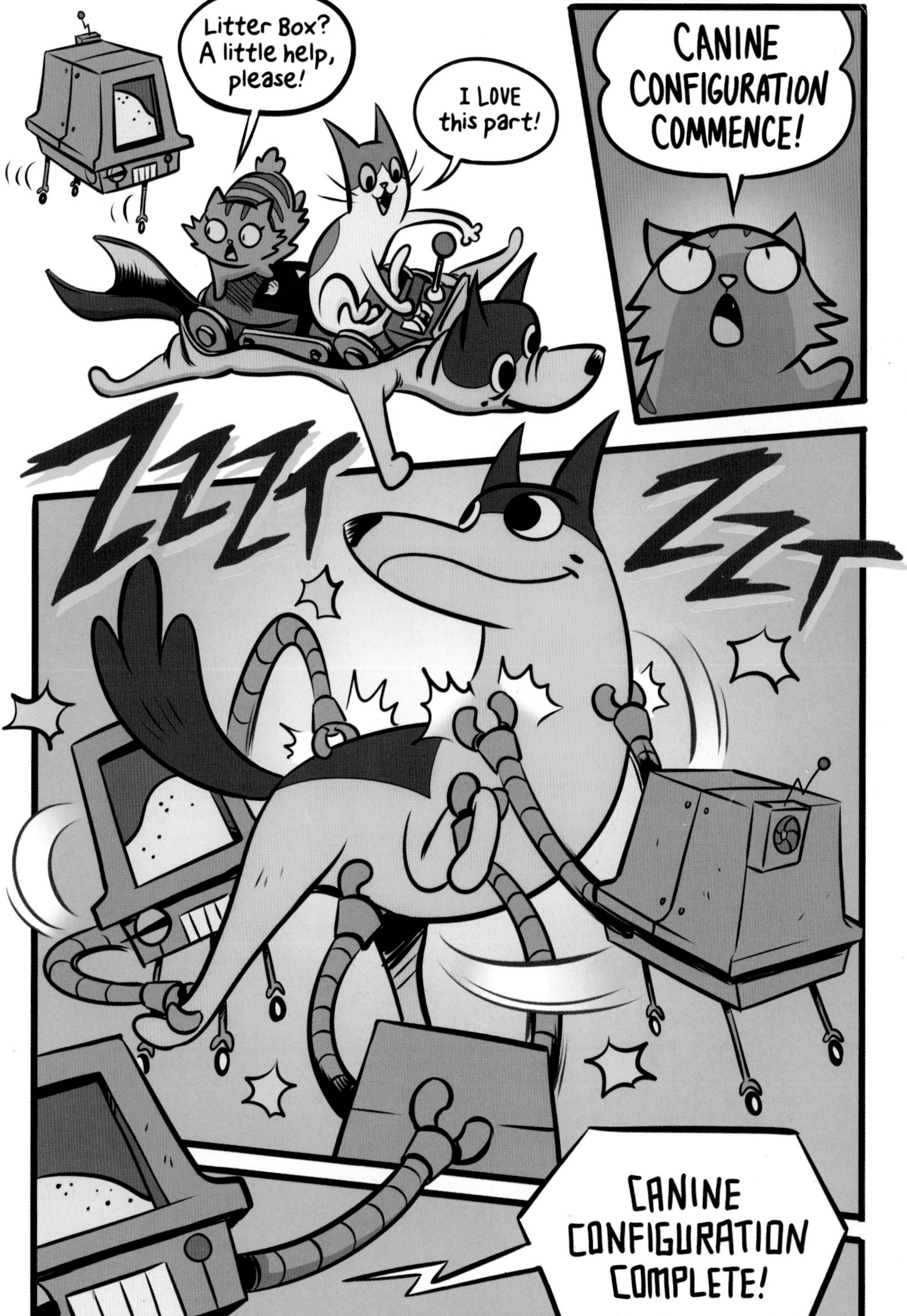
Litter Box? A little help, please!
I LOVE this part!
CANINE CONFIGURATION COMMENCE!
ZZZT
ZZZT
CANINE CONFIGURATION COMPLETE!

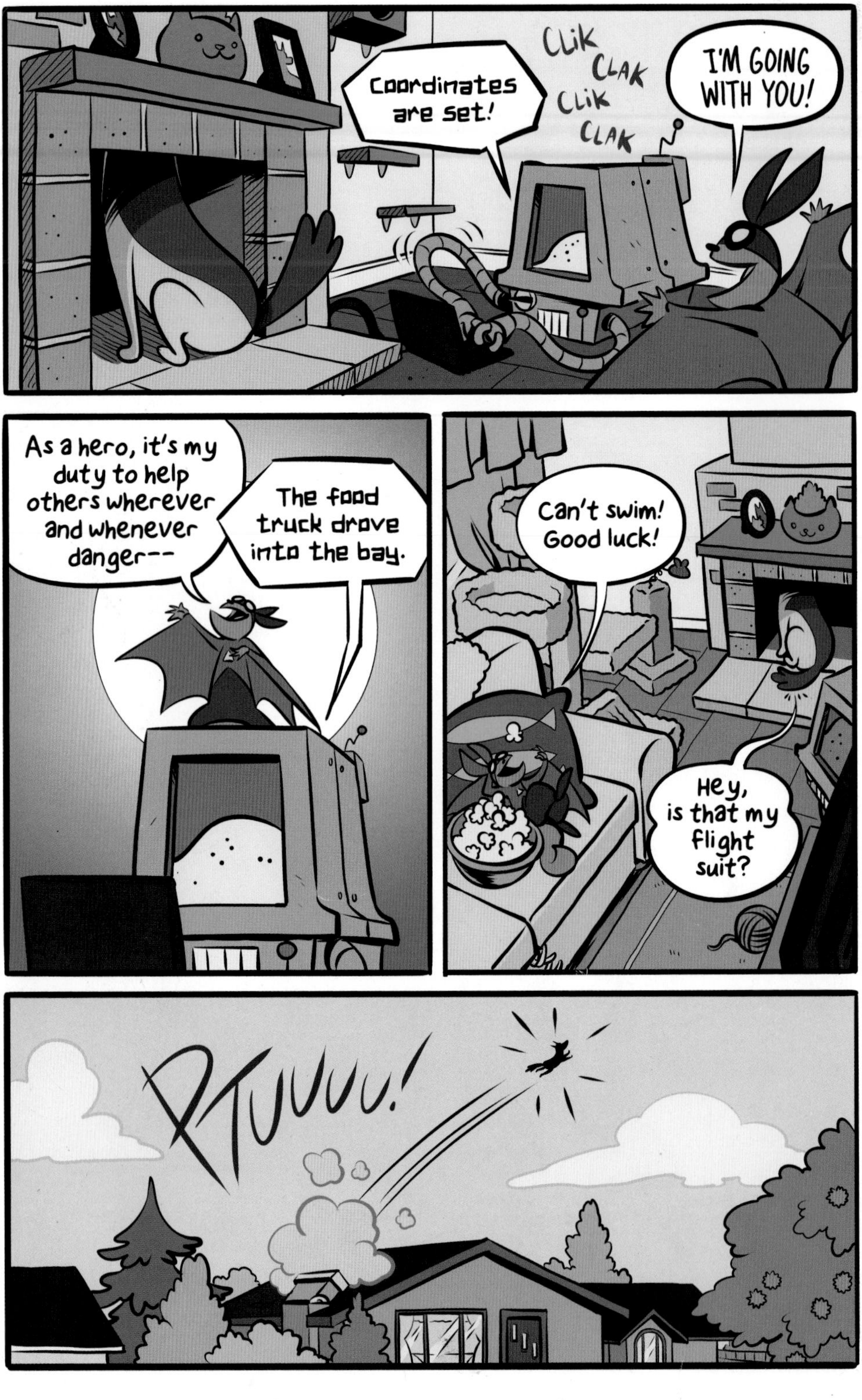
Coordinates are set!
CLIK CLAK CLIK CLAK
I'M GOING WITH YOU!
As a hero, it's my duty to help others wherever and whenever danger--
The food truck drove into the bay.
Can't swim! Good luck!
Hey, is that my flight suit?
PTUUUU!

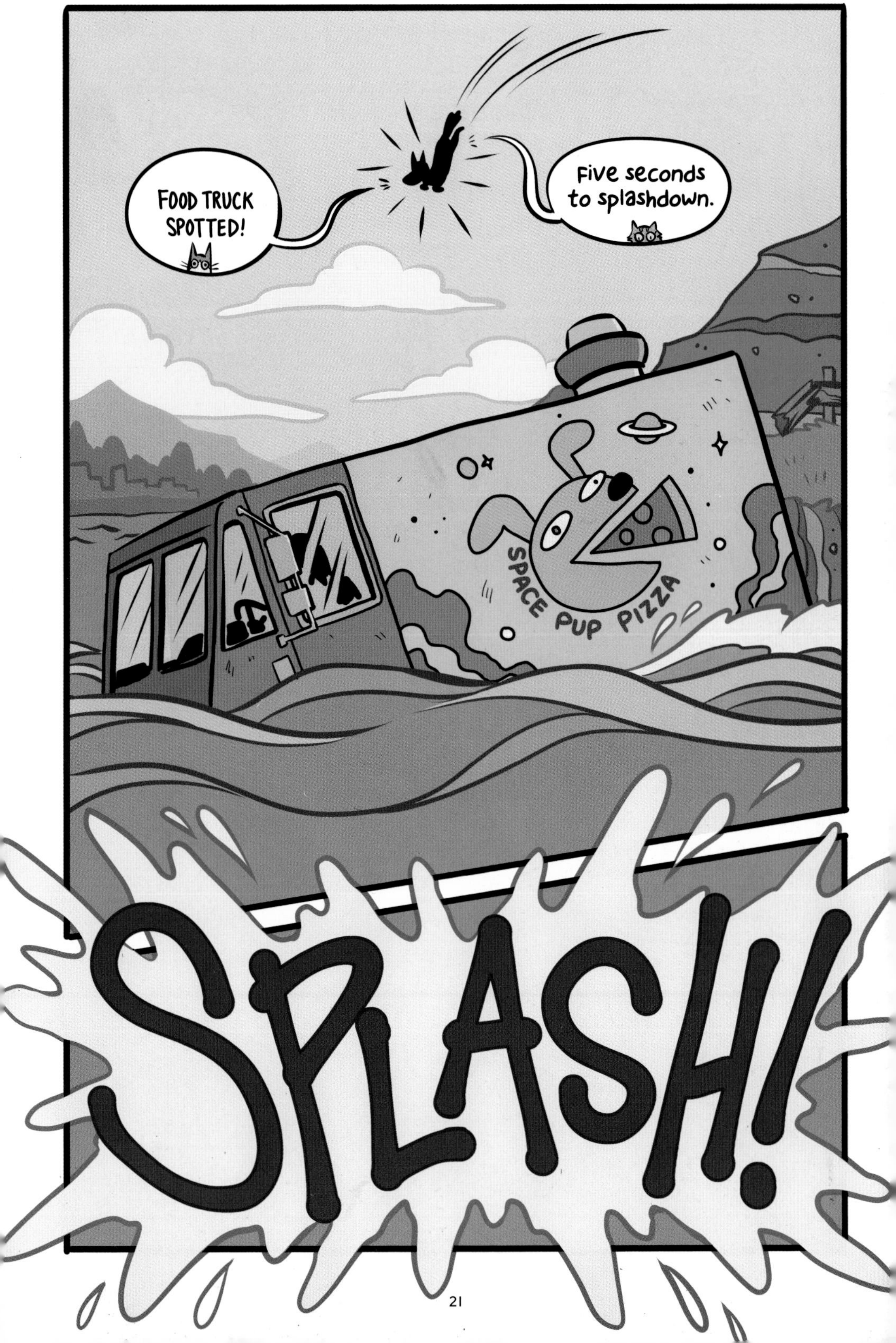
FOOD TRUCK SPOTTED!
Five seconds to splashdown.
SPACE PUP PIZZA
SPLASH!

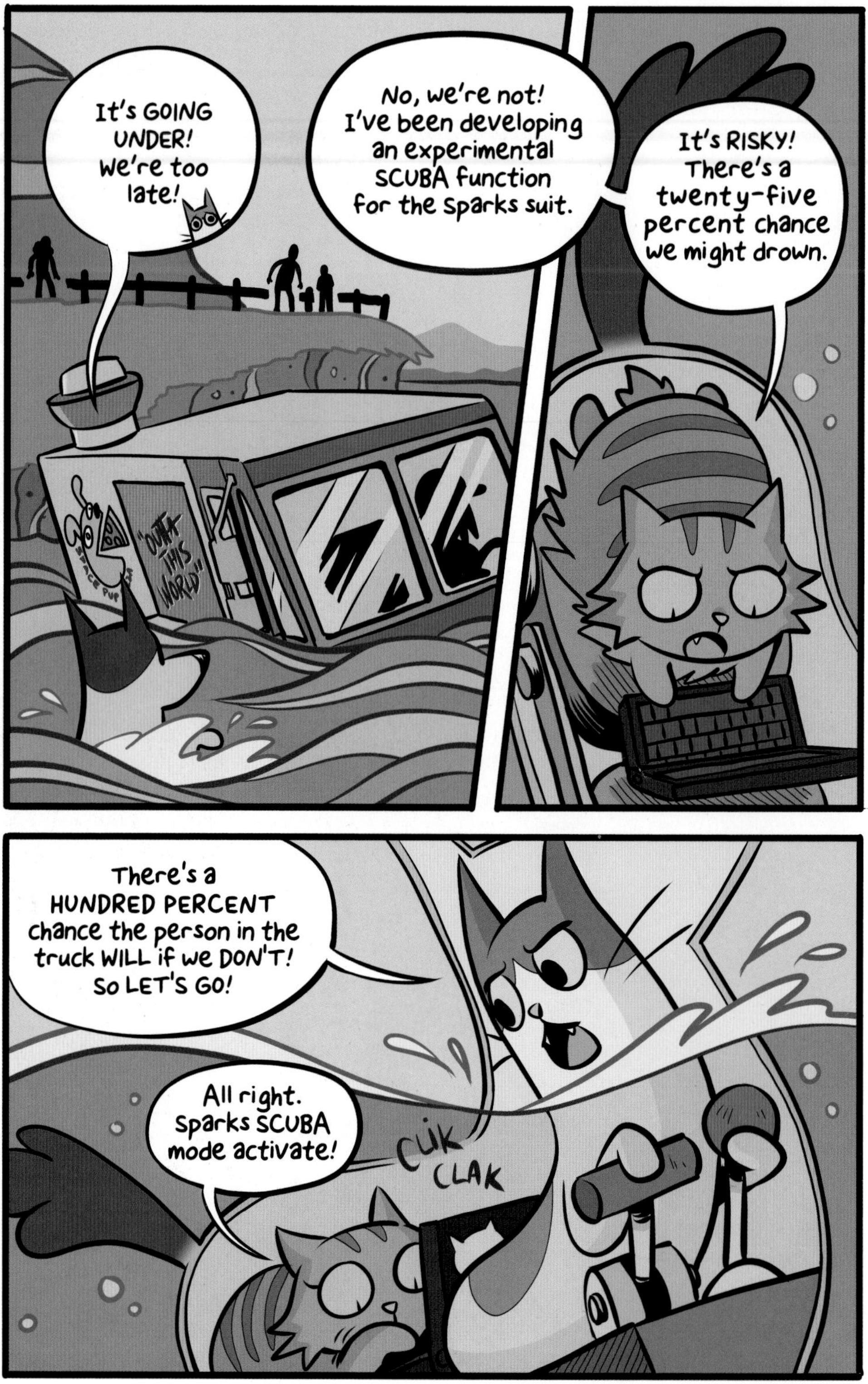
It's GOING UNDER! We're too late!
No, we're not! I've been developing an experimental SCUBA function for the sparks suit.
It's RISKY! There's a twenty-five percent chance we might drown.
There's a HUNDRED PERCENT chance the person in the truck WILL if we DON'T! So LET'S GO!
All right. Sparks SCUBA mode activate!
CLIK CLAK

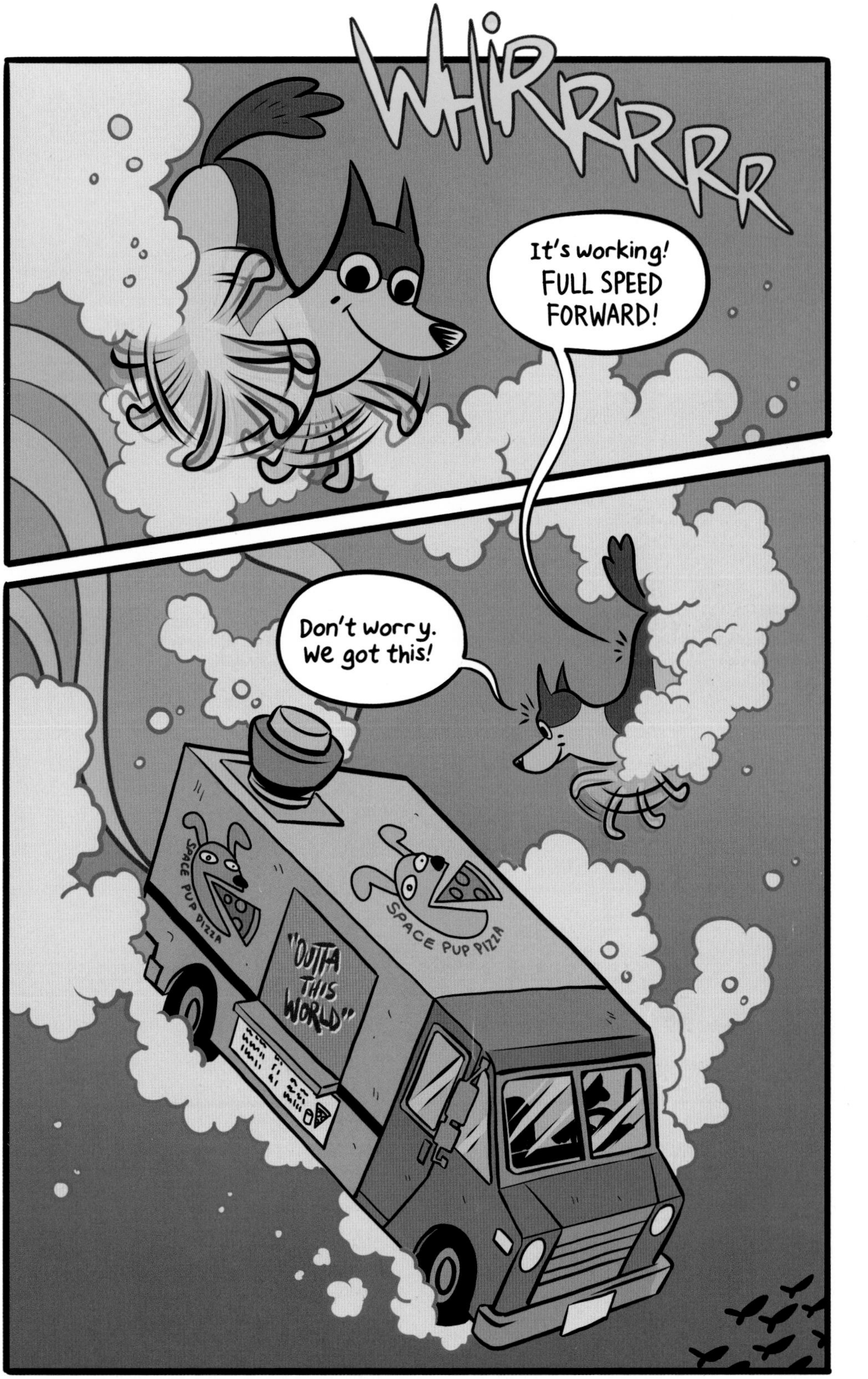
WHIRRRRR
It's working! FULL SPEED FORWARD!
Don't worry. We got this!
SPACE PUP PIZZA
"OUTTA THIS WORLD"
SPACE PUP PIZZA

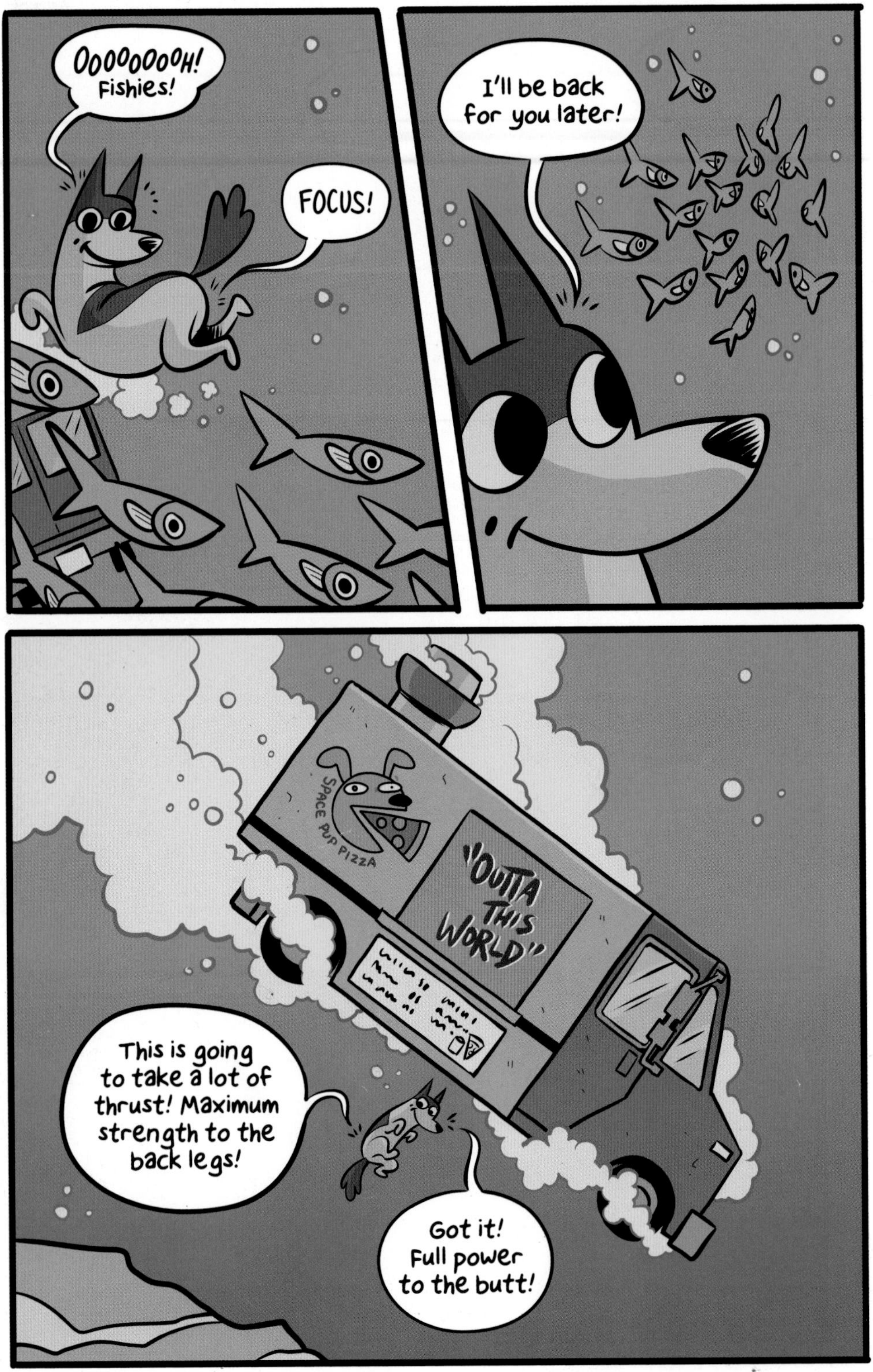
OOOOOOOOH! Fishies!
FOCUS!
I'll be back for you later!
SPACE PUP PIZZA
"OUTTA THIS WORLD"
This is going to take a lot of thrust! Maximum strength to the back legs!
Got it! Full power to the butt!

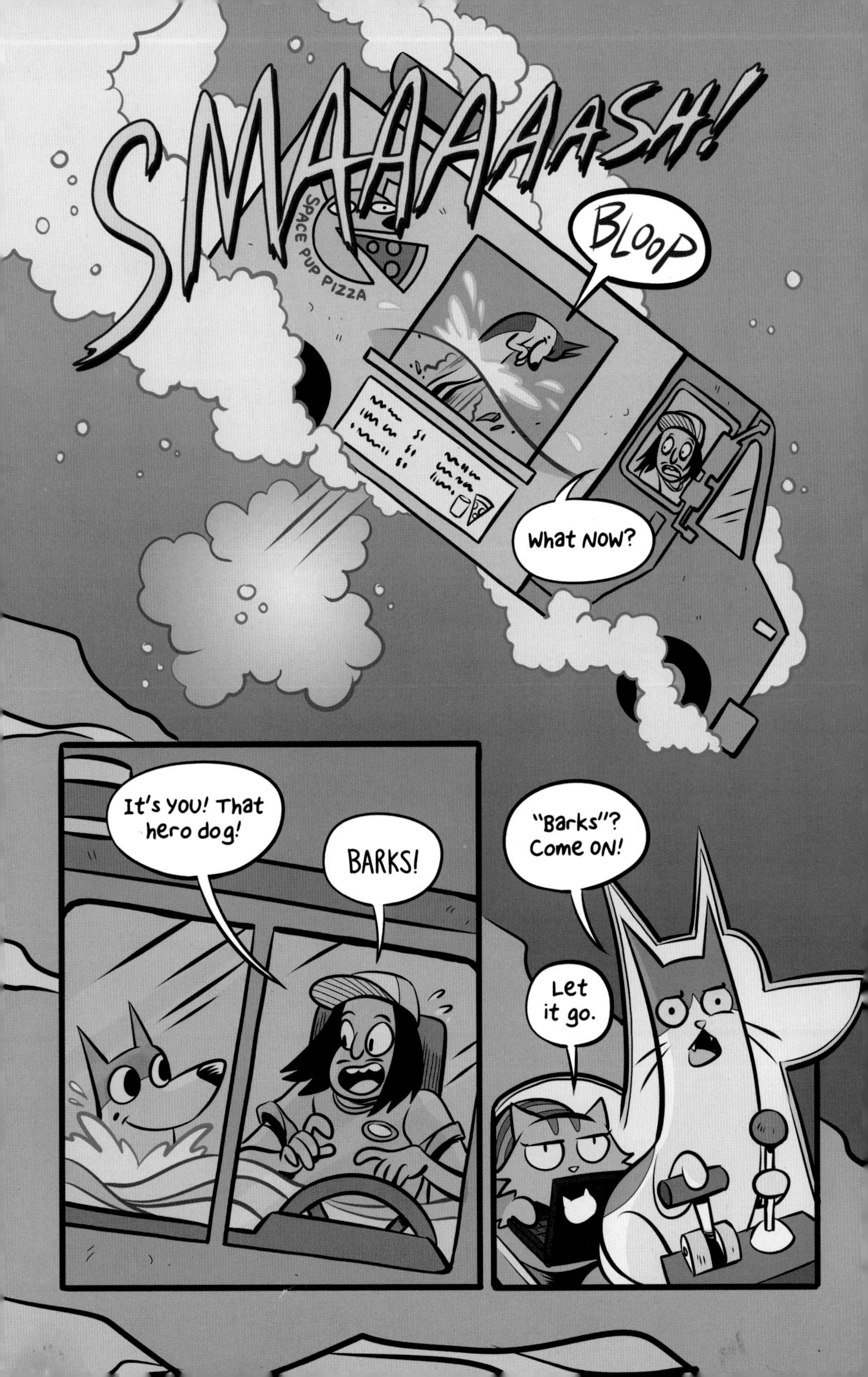
SMAAAAAASH!
SPACE PUP PIZZA
BLOOP
What NOW?
It's YOU! That hero dog!
BARKS!
"Barks"? Come ON!
Let it go.

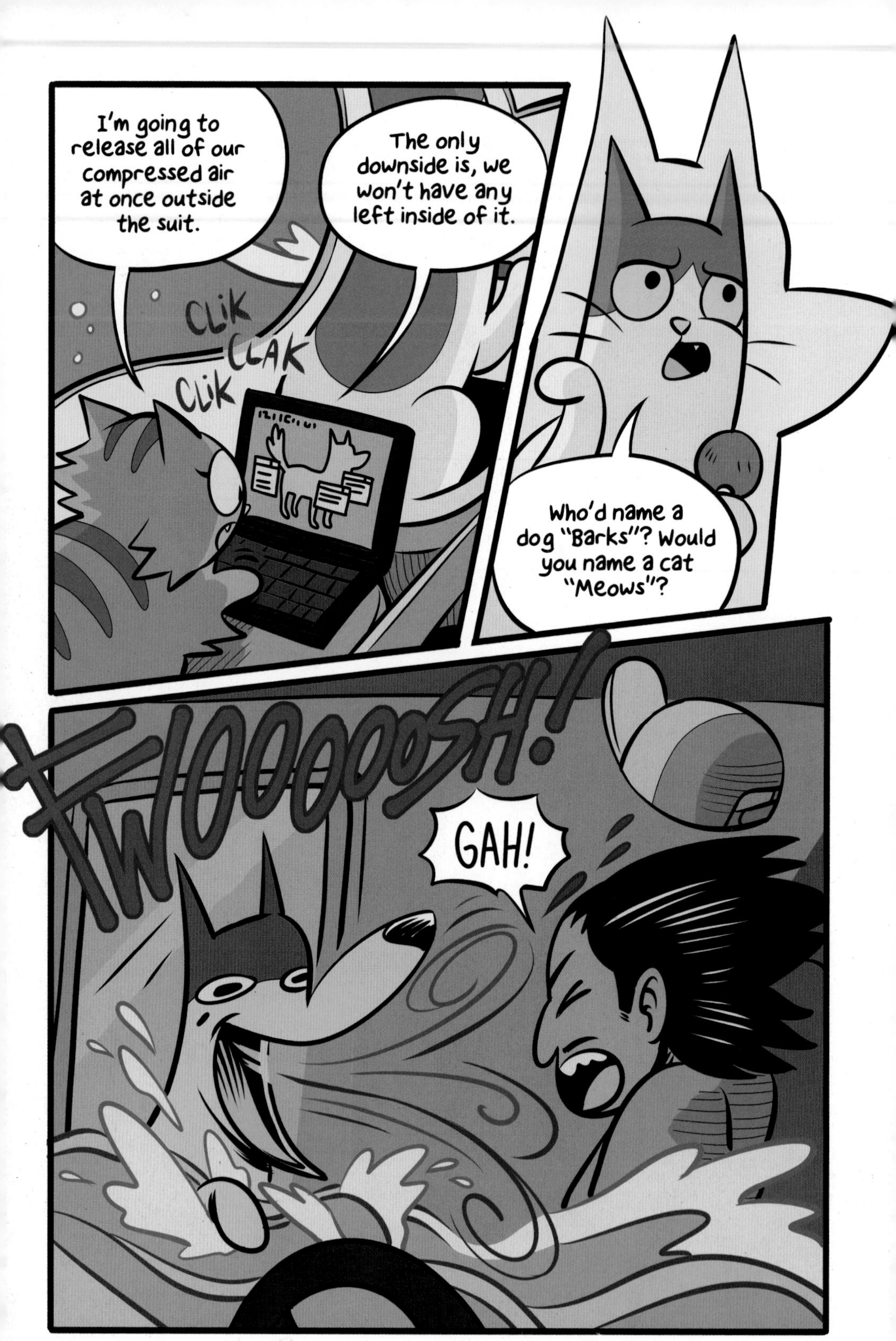
I'm going to release all of our compressed air at once outside the suit.
The only downside is, we won't have any left inside of it.
CLIK
CLAK
CLIK
Who'd name a dog "Barks"? Would you name a cat "Meows"?
FWOOOOOSH!
GAH!

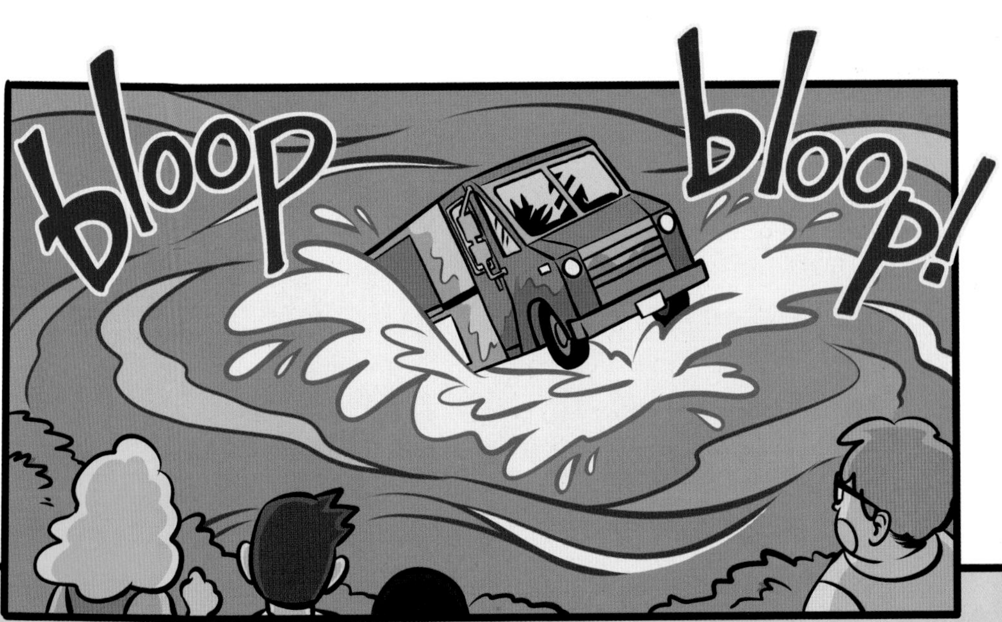
bloop
bloop!

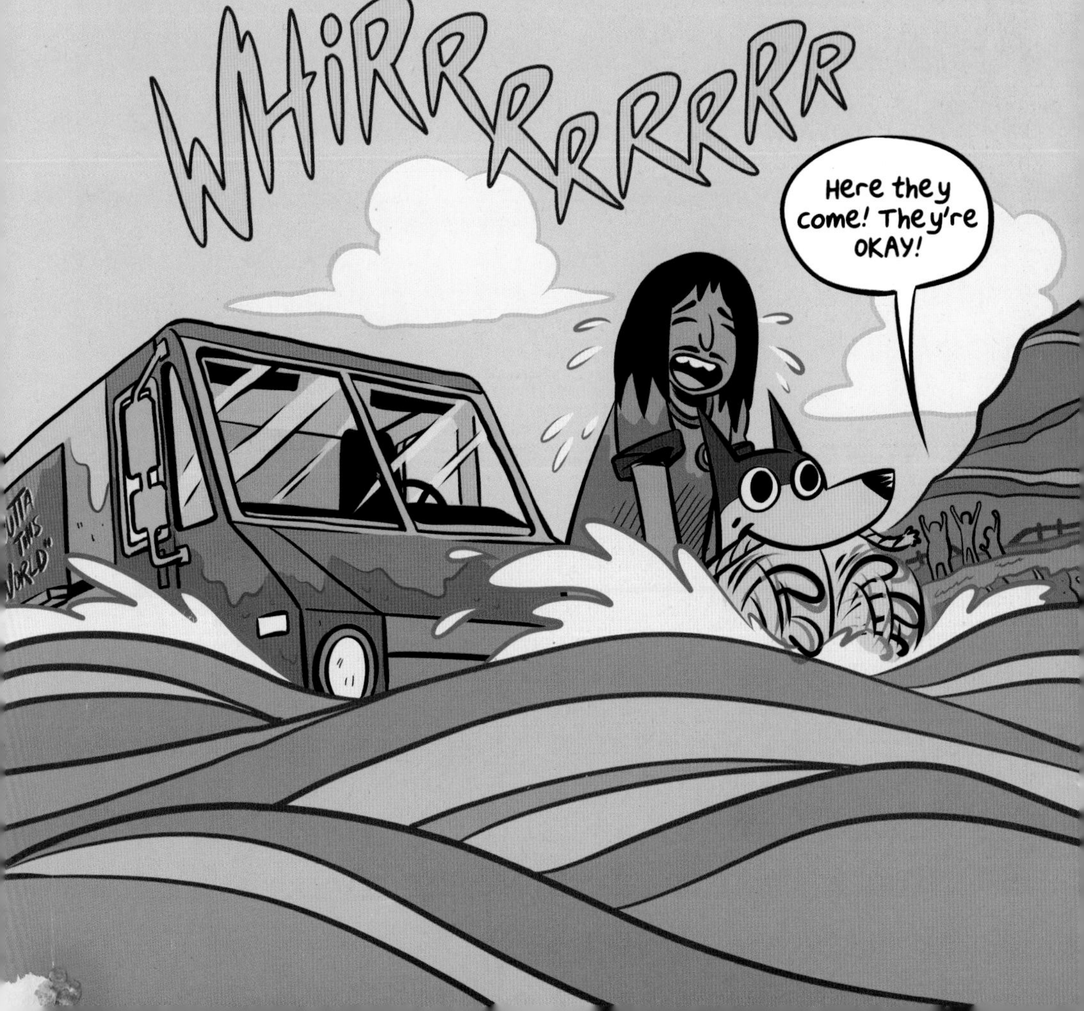
WHiRRRRRRRR
Here they come! They're OKAY!

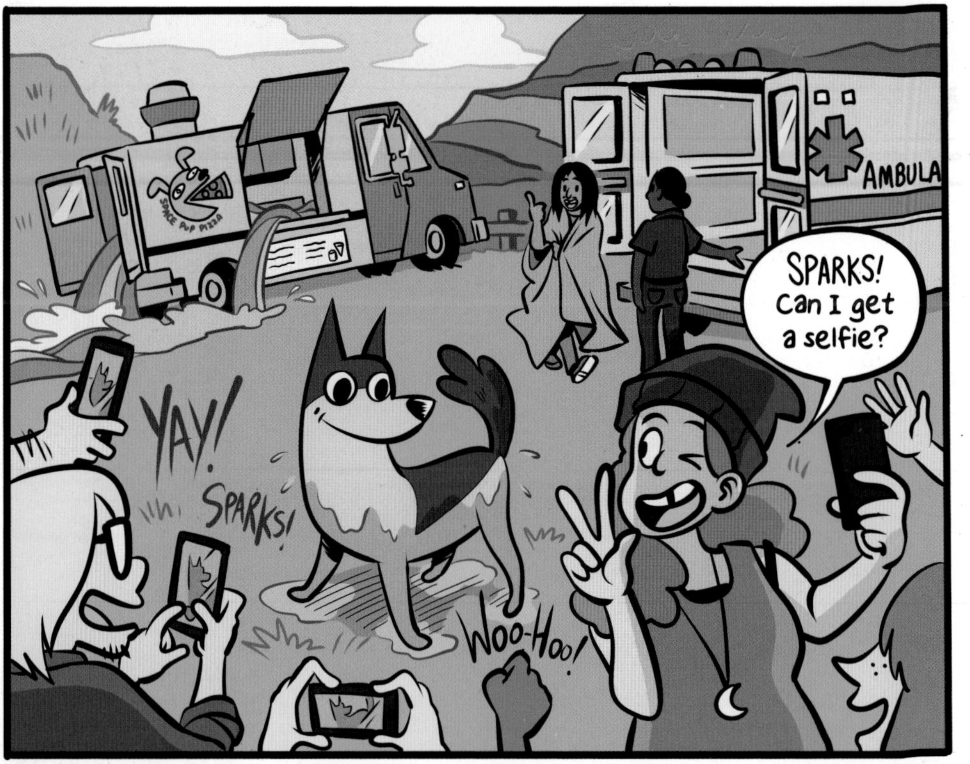
AMBULA
SPACE PUP PIZZA
SPARKS! Can I get a selfie?
YAY!
SPARKS!
WOO-HOO!

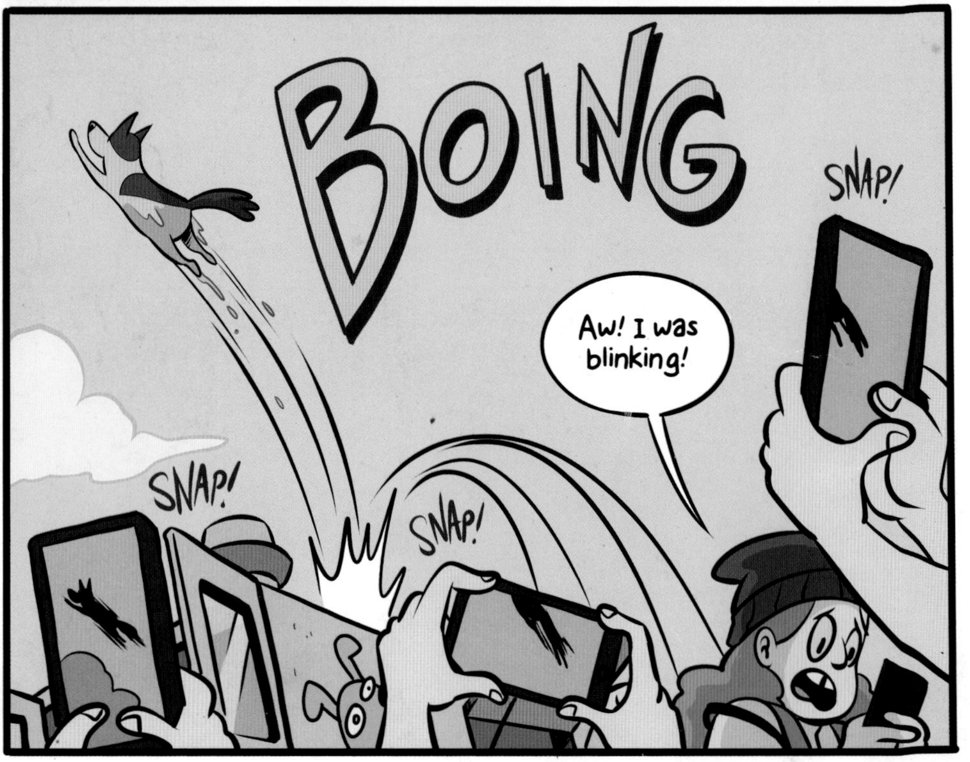
BOING
SNAP!
Aw! I was blinking!
SNAP!
SNAP!

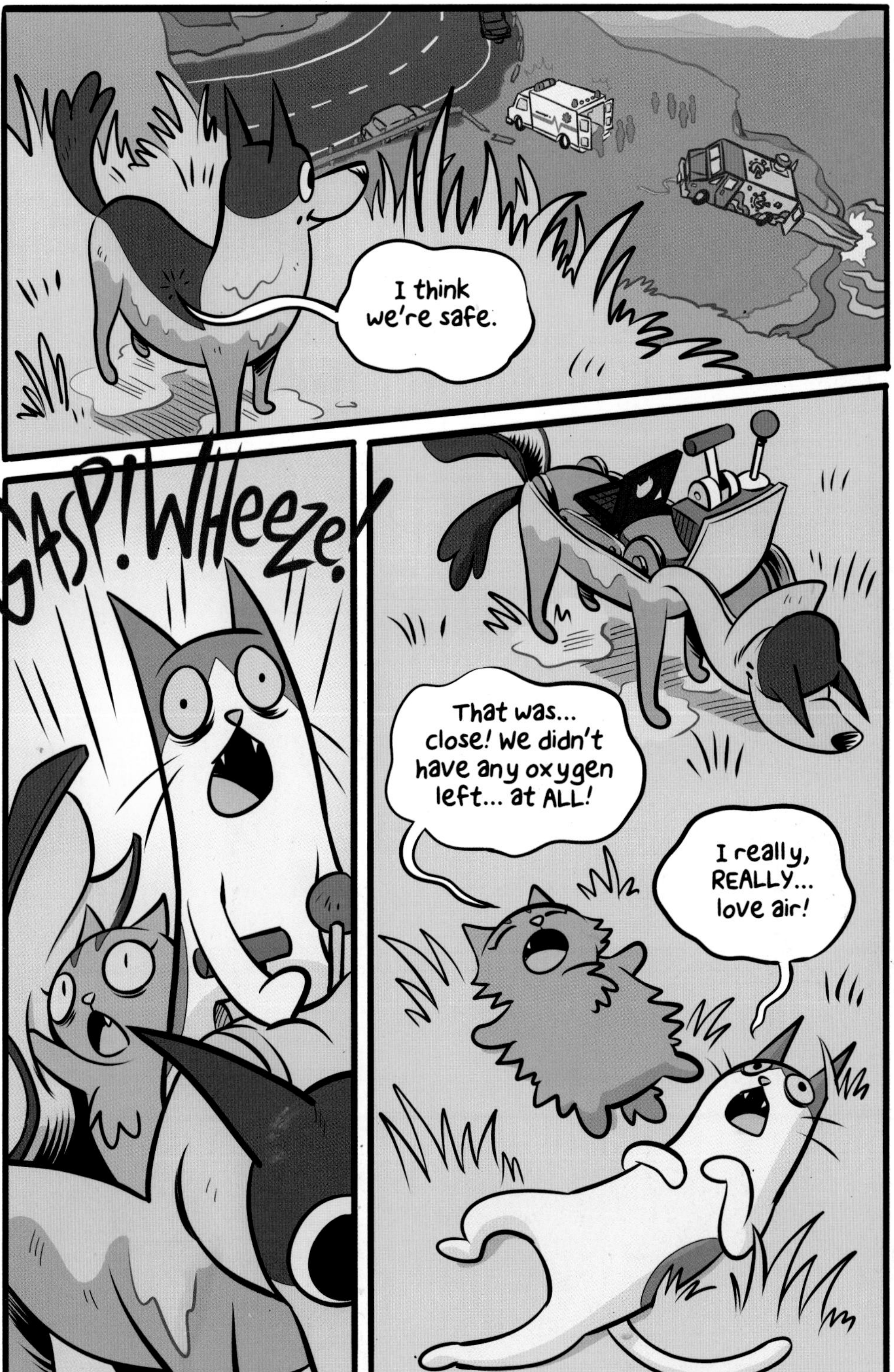
I think we're safe.
GASP! WHEEZE!
That was... close! We didn't have any oxygen left... at ALL!
I really, REALLY... love air!

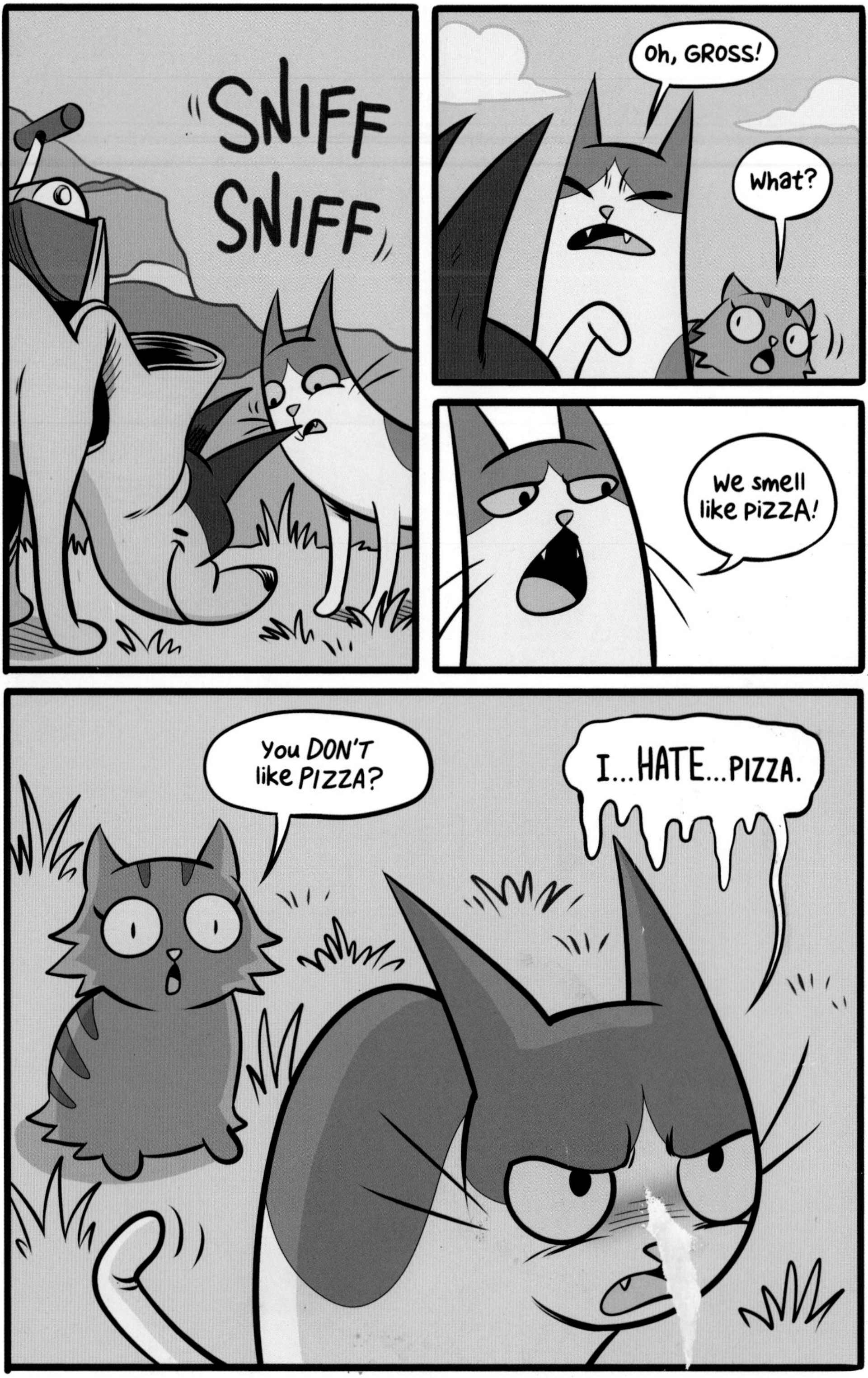
SNIFF
SNIFF
Oh, GROSS!
What?
We smell like PIZZA!
You DON'T like PIZZA?
I...HATE...PIZZA.

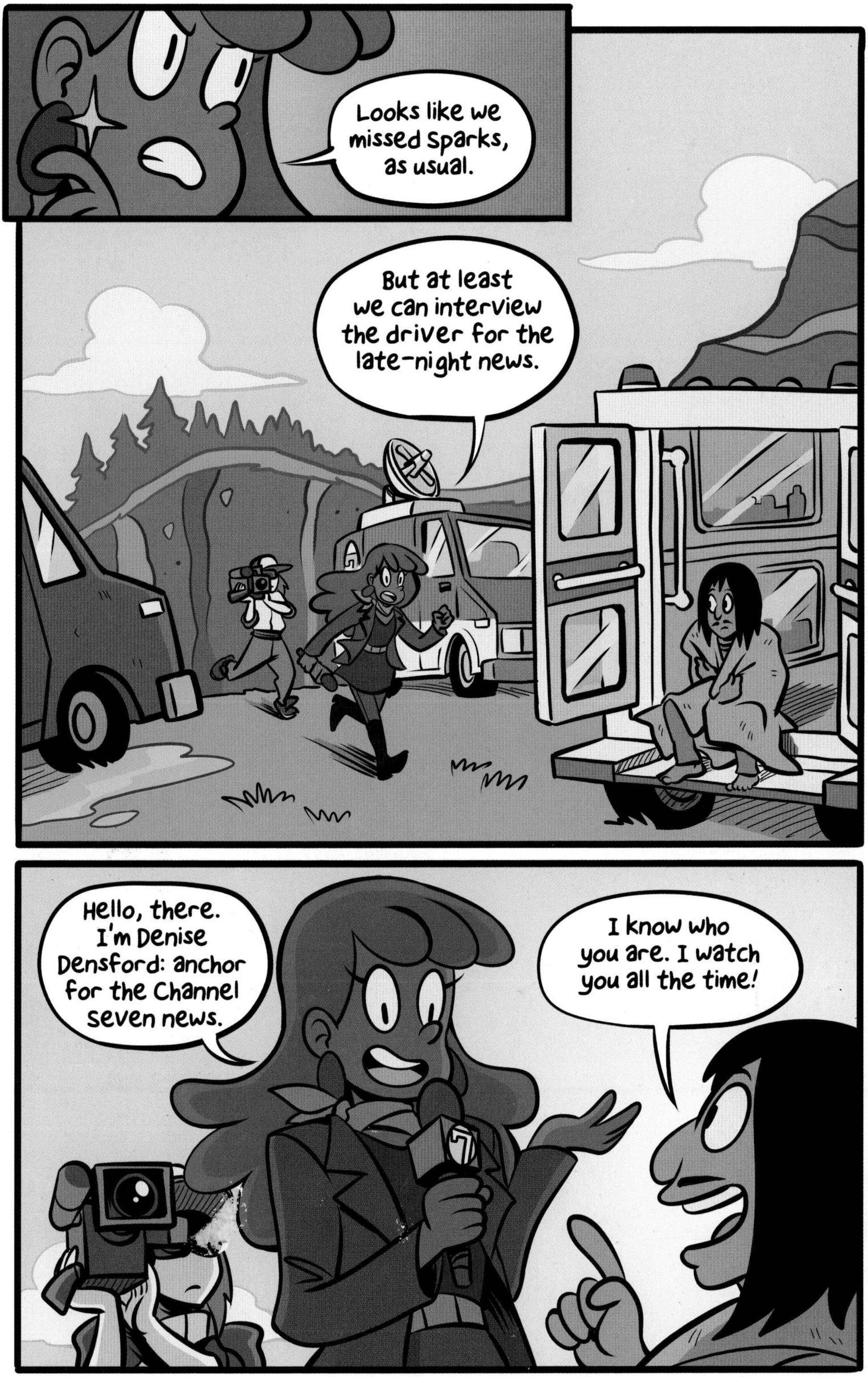
Looks like we missed Sparks, as usual.
But at least we can interview the driver for the late-night news.
Hello, there. I'm Denise Densford: anchor for the Channel seven news.
I know who you are. I watch you all the time!

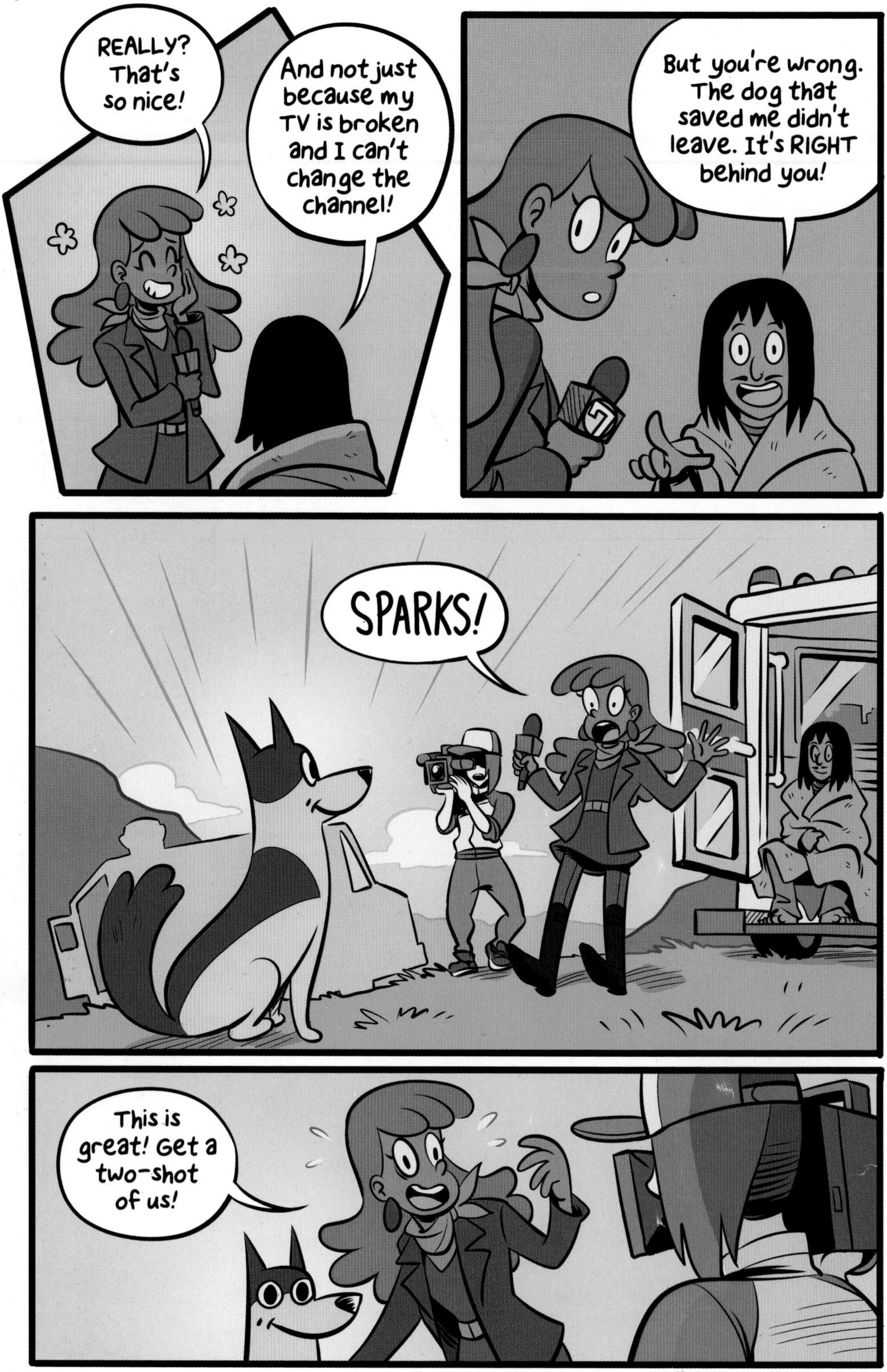
REALLY? That's so nice!
And not just because my TV is broken and I can't change the channel!
But you're wrong. The dog that saved me didn't leave. It's RIGHT behind you!
SPARKS!
This is great! Get a two-shot of us!

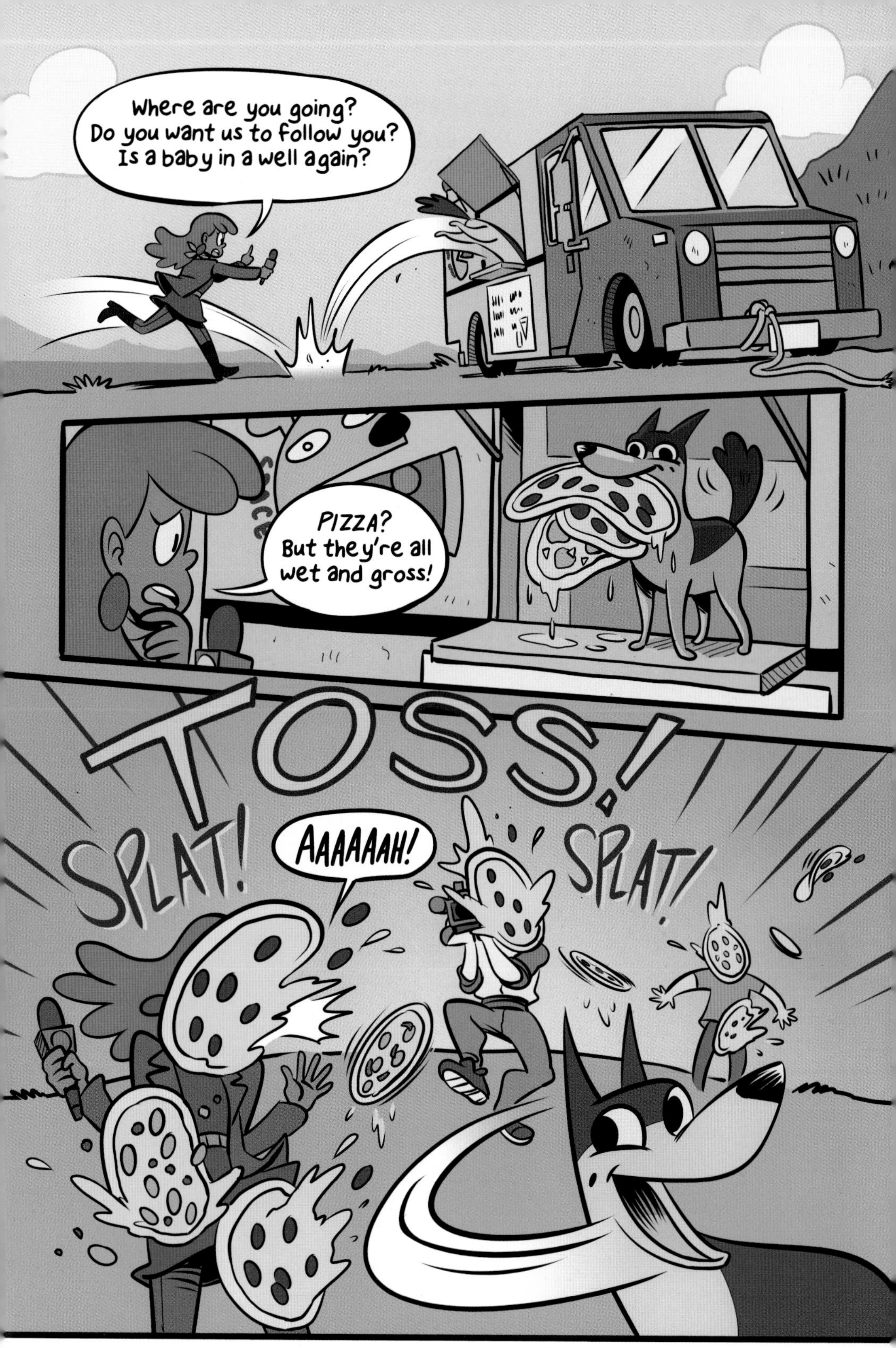
Where are you going?
Do you want us to follow you?
Is a baby in a well again?
PIZZA?
But they're all wet and gross!
TOSS!
SPLAT!
AAAAAAH!
SPLAT!

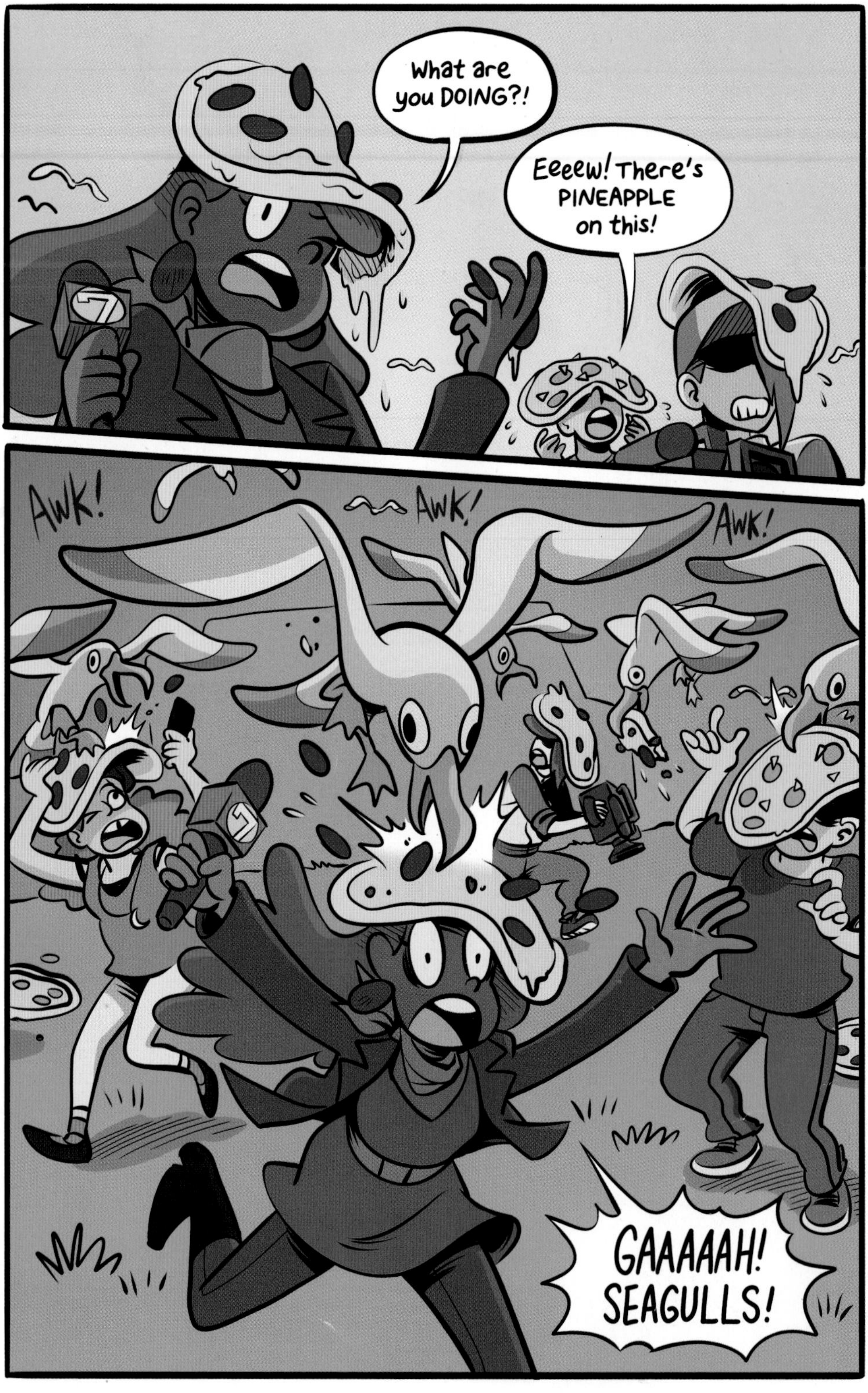
What are you DOING?!
Eeeew! There's PINEAPPLE on this!
AWK!
AWK!
AWK!
GAAAAAH! SEAGULLS!

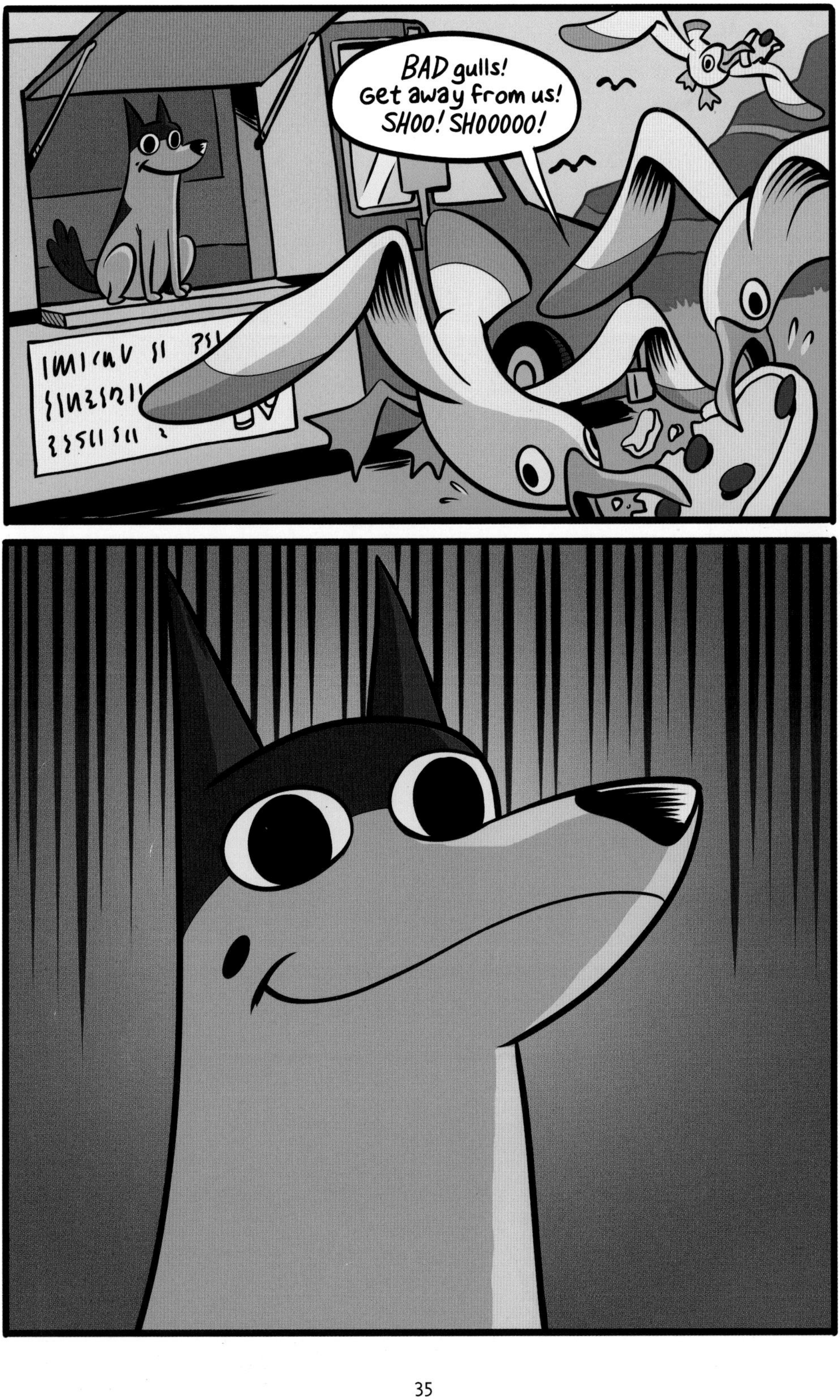
BAD gulls!
Get away from us!
SHOO! SHOOOOO!

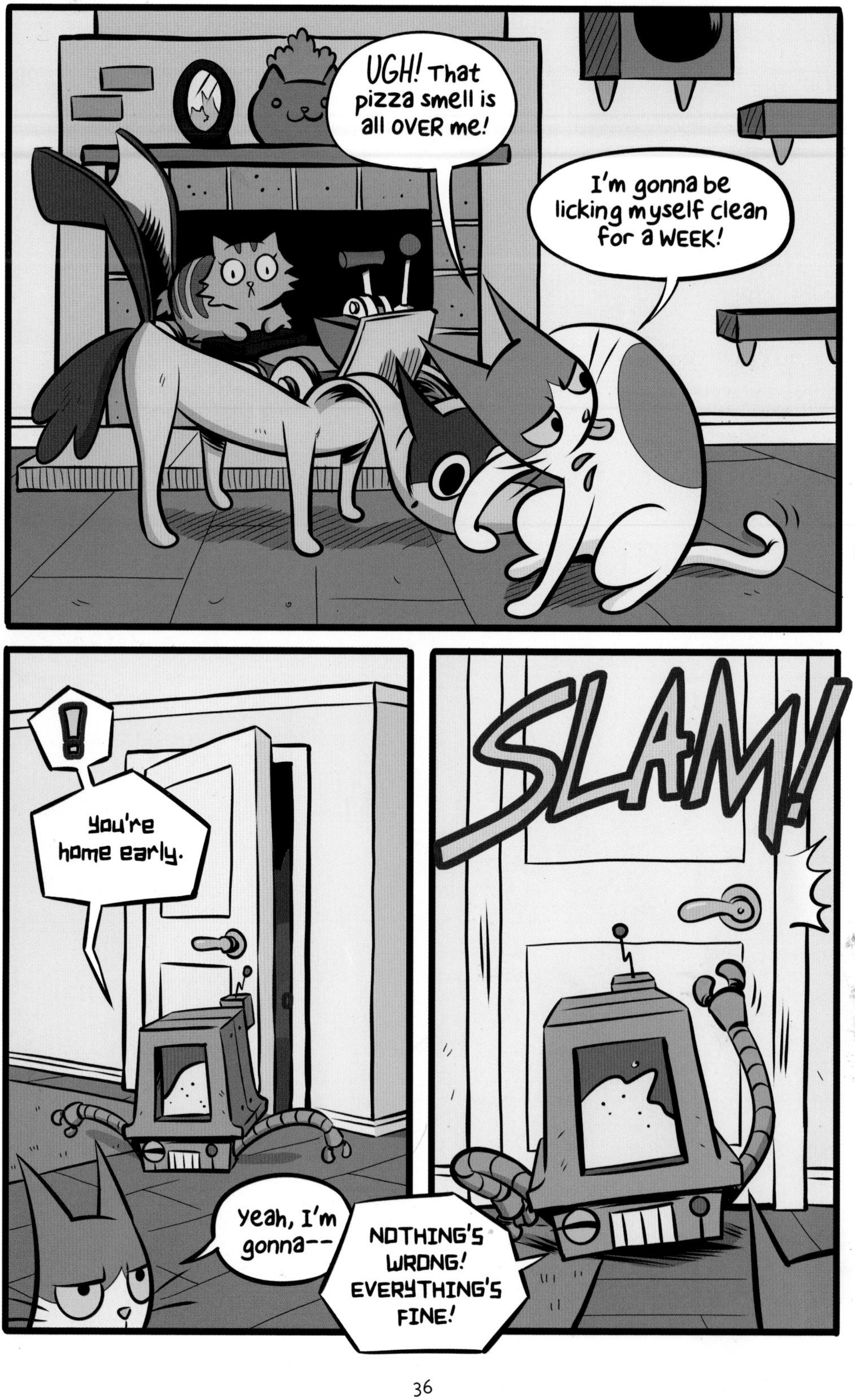
UGH! That pizza smell is all OVER me!
I'm gonna be licking myself clean for a WEEK!
!
you're home early.
SLAM!
yeah, I'm gonna--
NOTHING'S WRONG! EVERYTHING'S FINE!

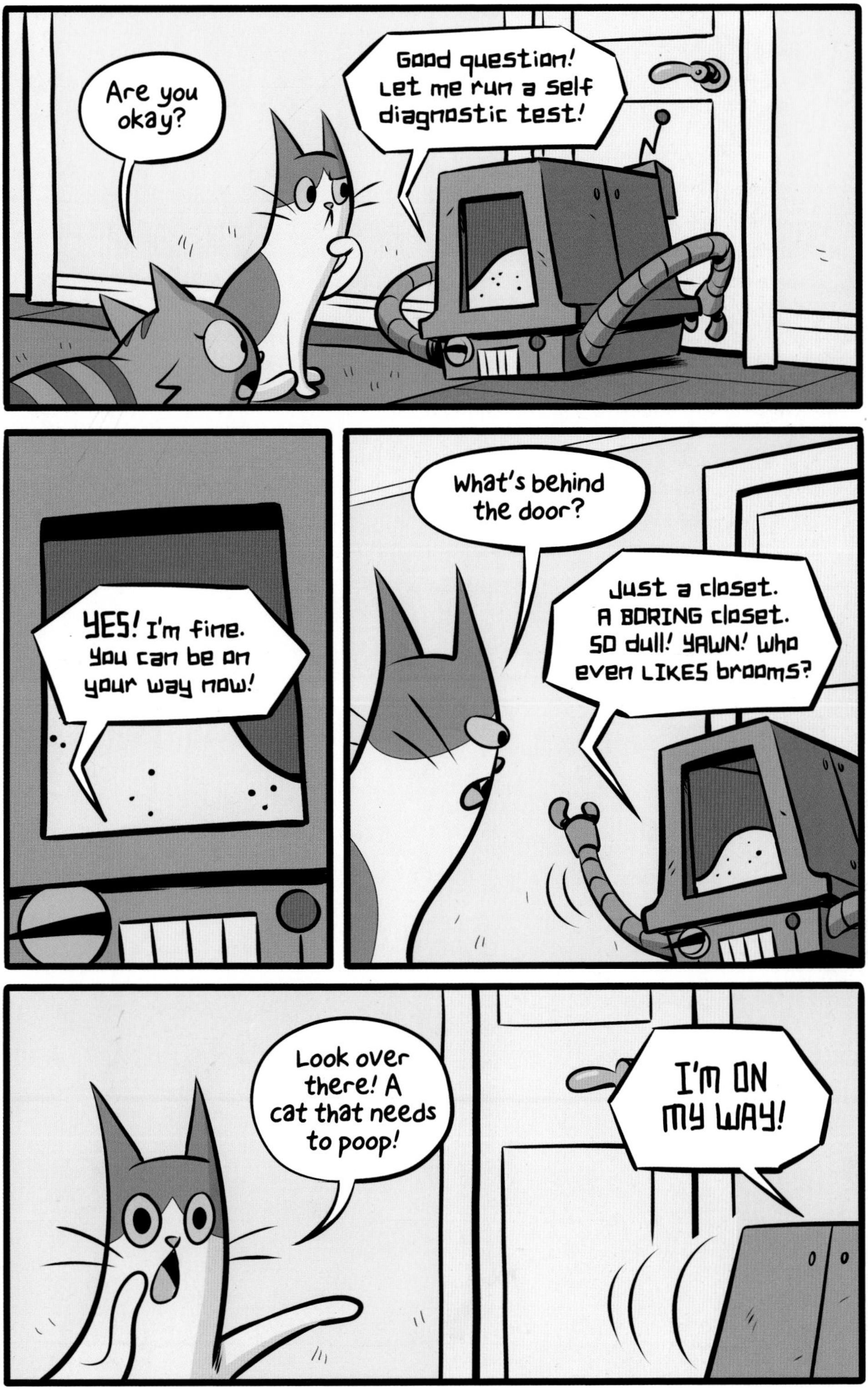
Are you okay?
Good question! Let me run a self diagnostic test!
YES! I'm fine. You can be on your way now!
What's behind the door?
Just a closet. A BORING closet. SO dull! YAWN! Who even LIKES brooms?
Look over there! A cat that needs to poop!
I'M ON MY WAY!

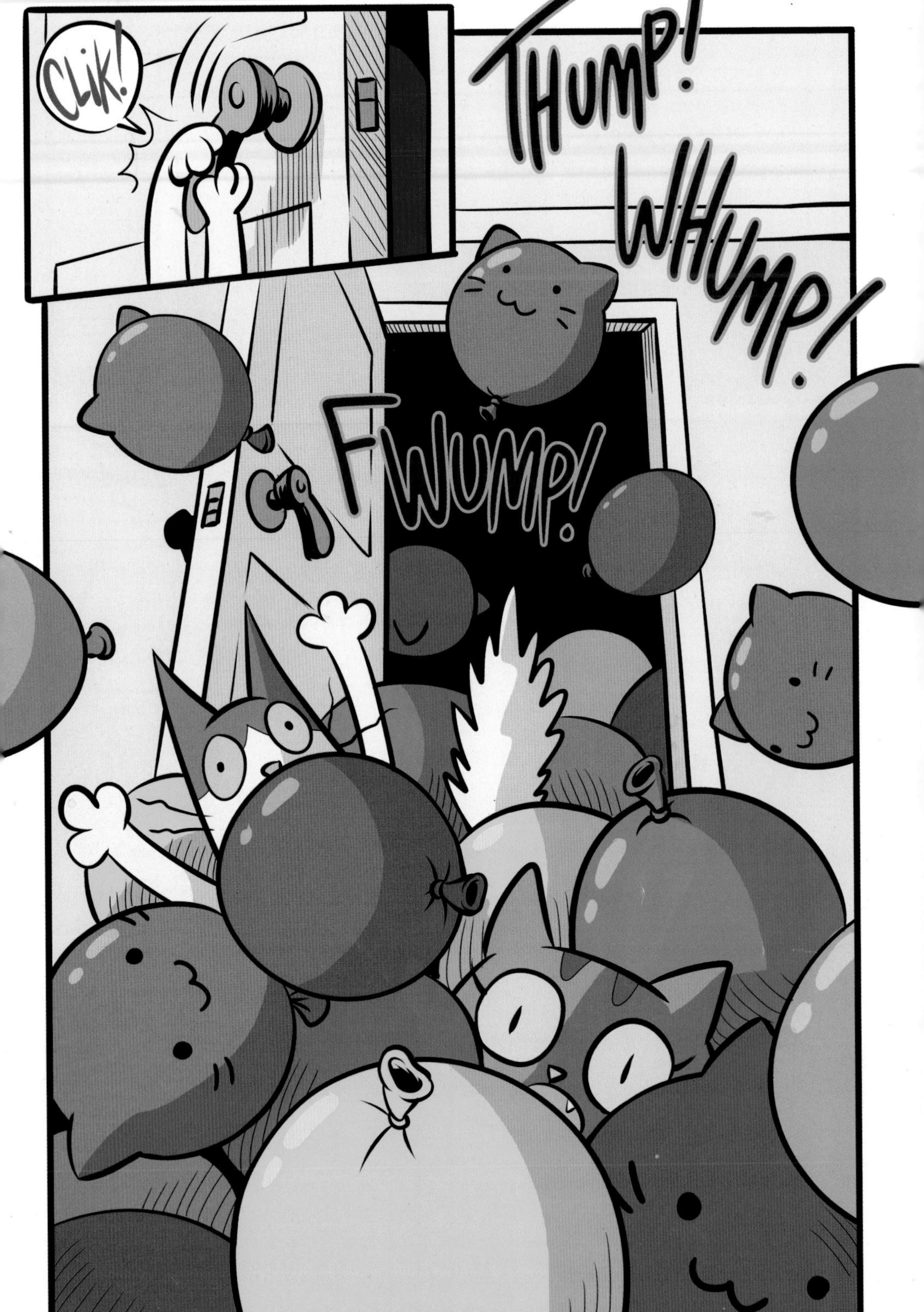
CLIK!
THUMP!
WHUMP!
FWUMP!

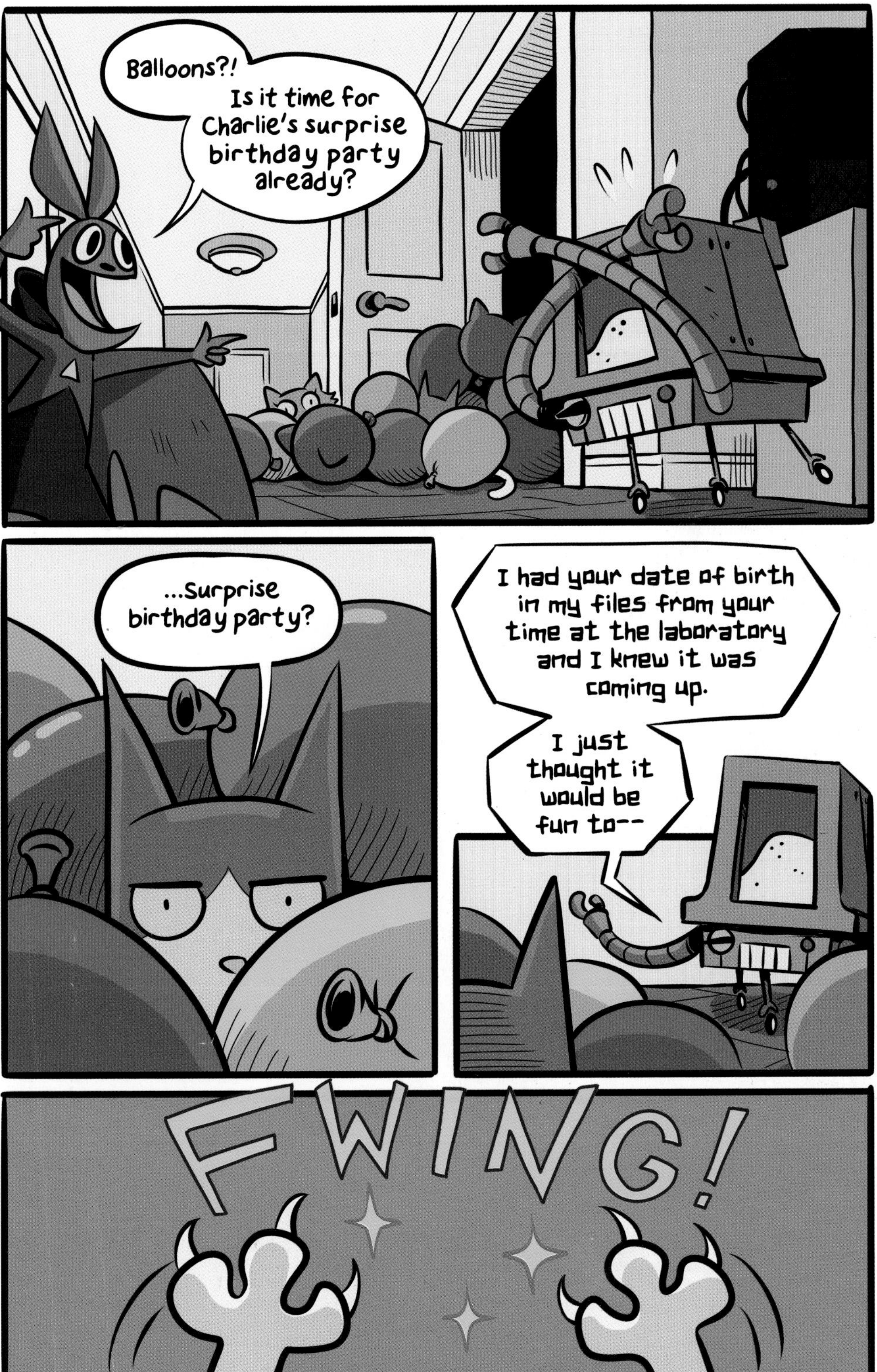
Balloons?!
Is it time for Charlie's surprise birthday party already?
...surprise birthday party?
I had your date of birth in my files from your time at the laboratory and I knew it was coming up.
I just thought it would be fun to--
FWING!

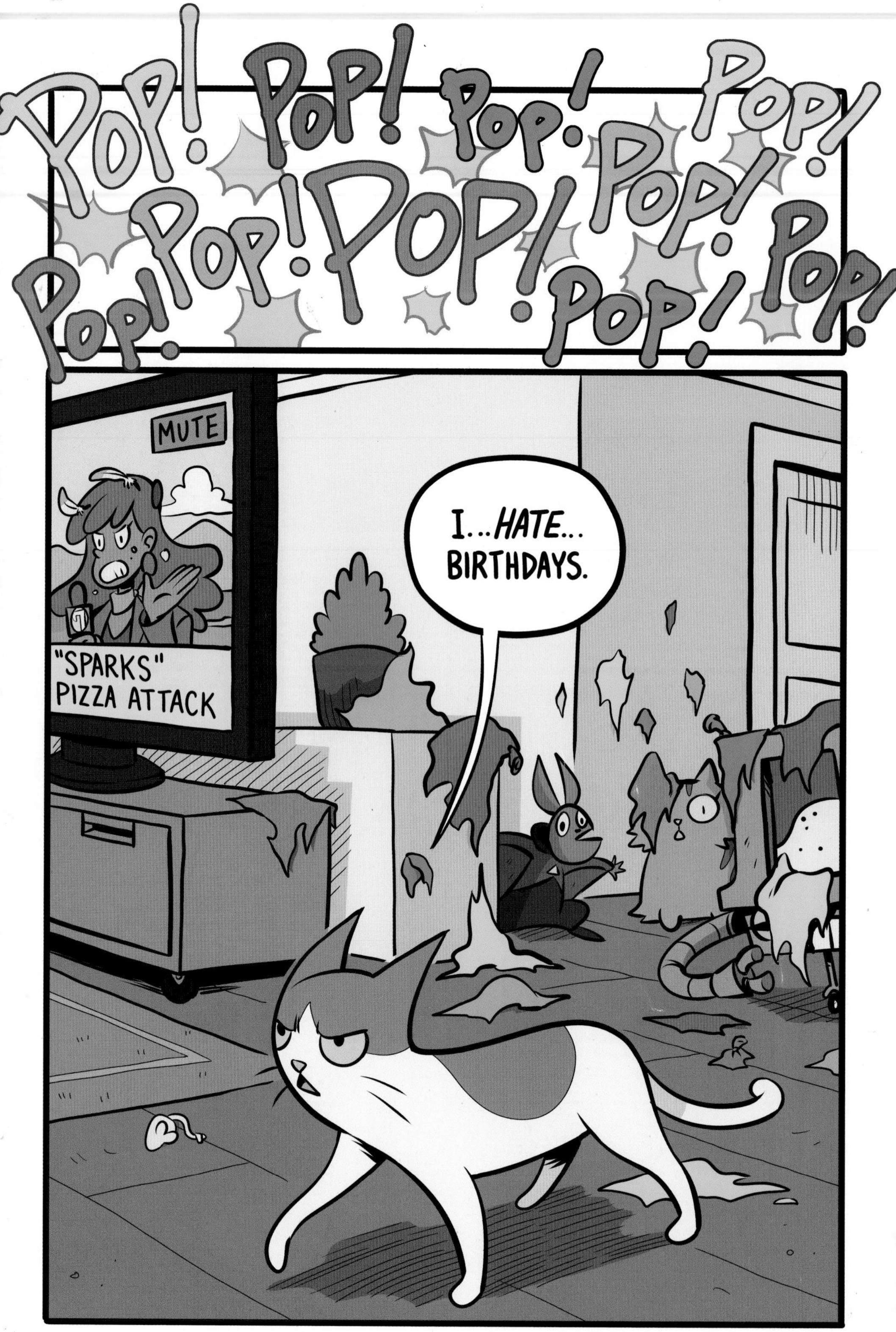
POP! POP! POP! POP!
POP! POP! POP! POP! POP! POP! POP!
MUTE
"SPARKS" PIZZA ATTACK
I...HATE... BIRTHDAYS.

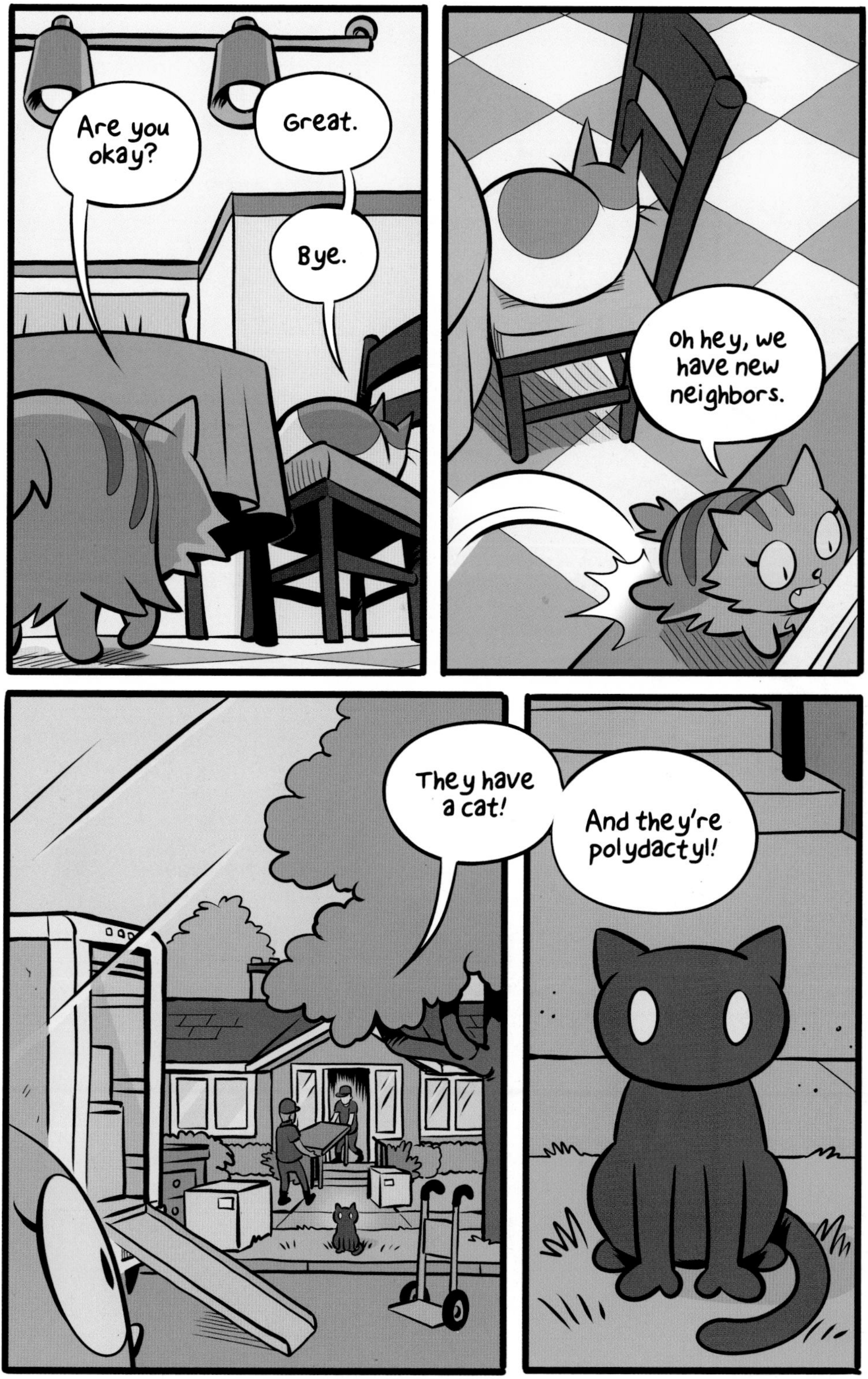
Are you okay?
Great.
Bye.
Oh hey, we have new neighbors.
They have a cat!
And they're polydactyl!

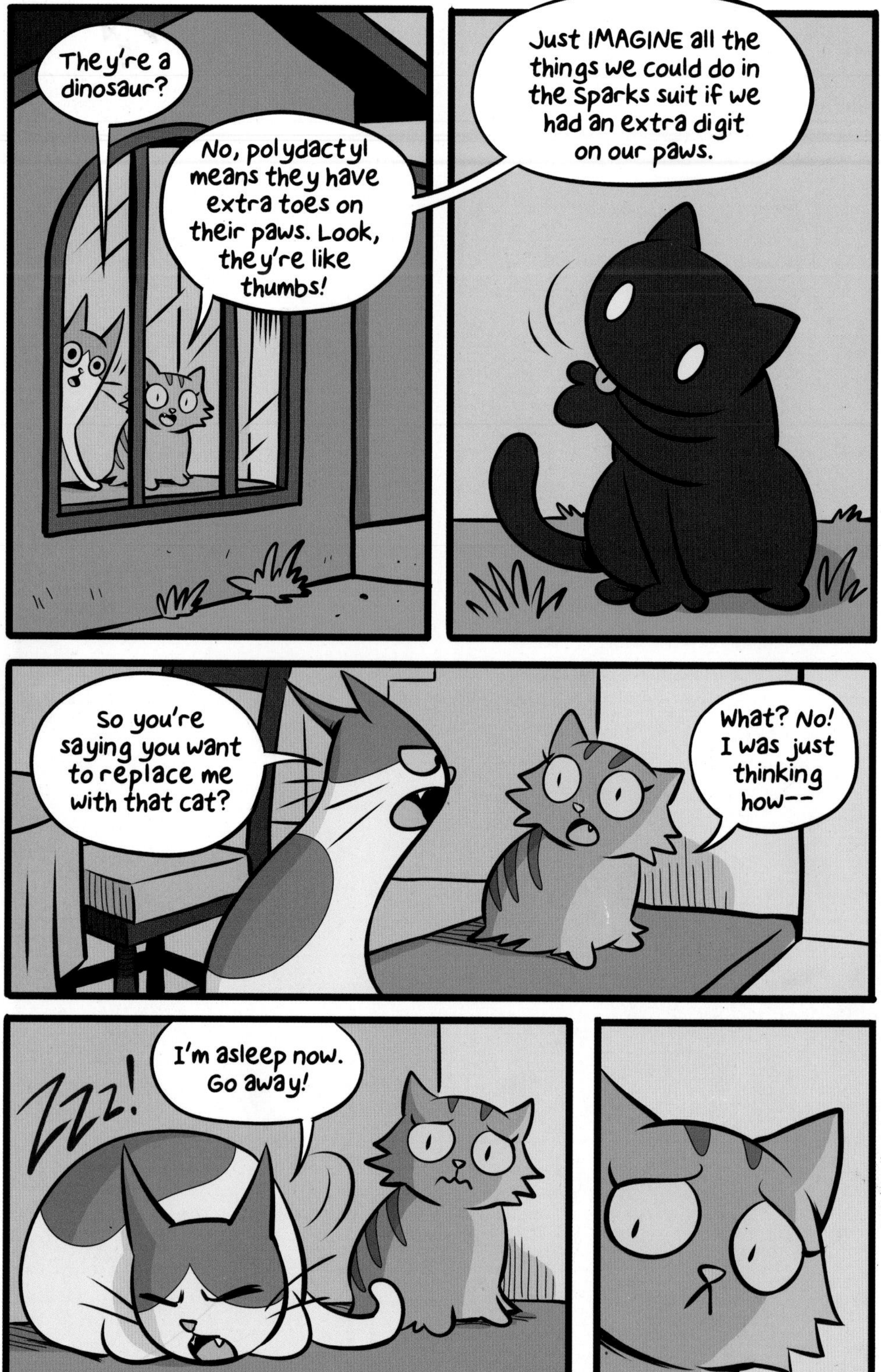
They're a dinosaur?
No, polydactyl means they have extra toes on their paws. Look, they're like thumbs!
Just IMAGINE all the things we could do in the Sparks suit if we had an extra digit on our paws.
So you're saying you want to replace me with that cat?
What? No! I was just thinking how--
ZZZ!
I'm asleep now. Go away!

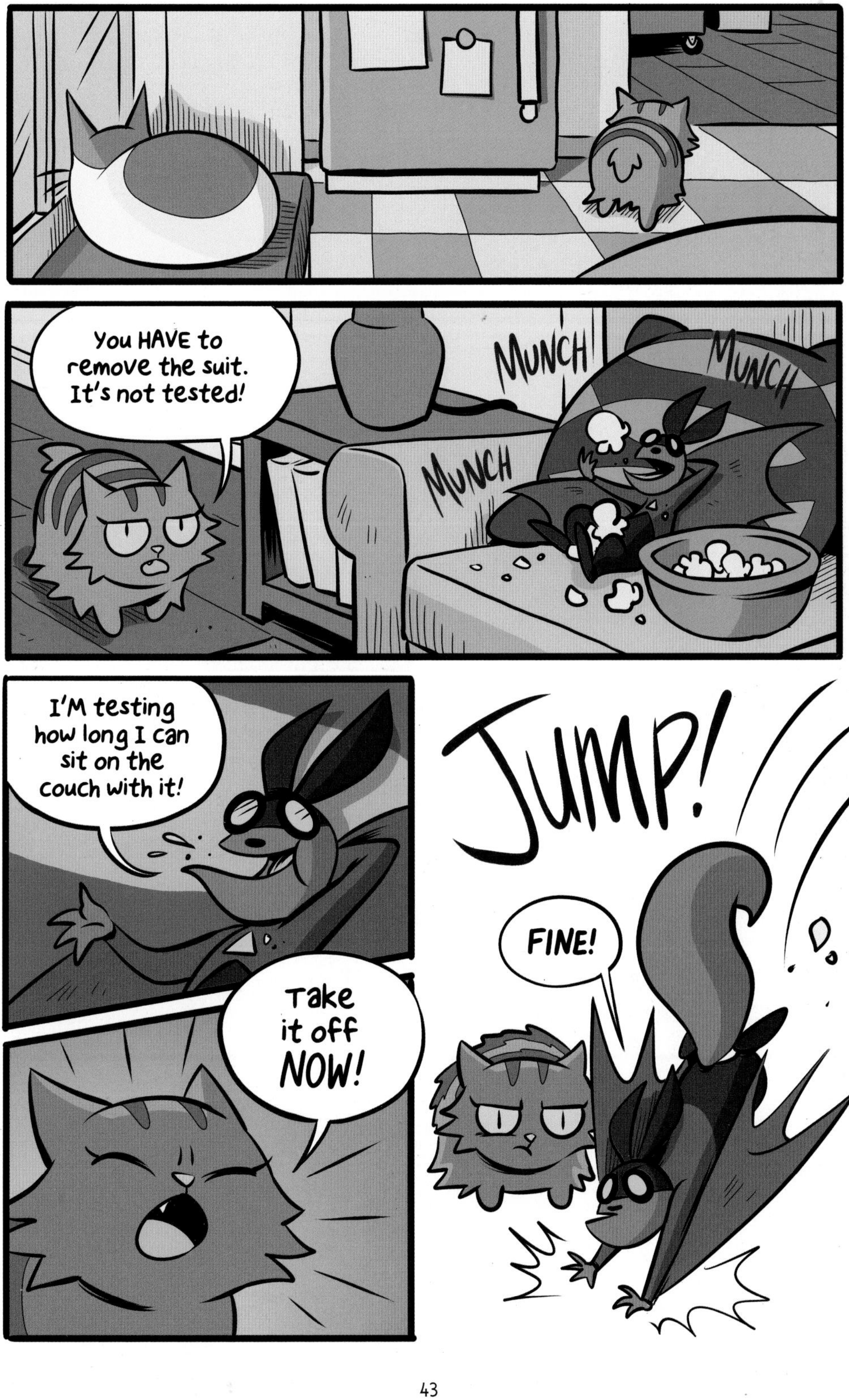
You HAVE to remove the suit. It's not tested!
MUNCH
MUNCH
MUNCH
I'M testing how long I can sit on the couch with it!
Take it off NOW!
JUMP!
FINE!

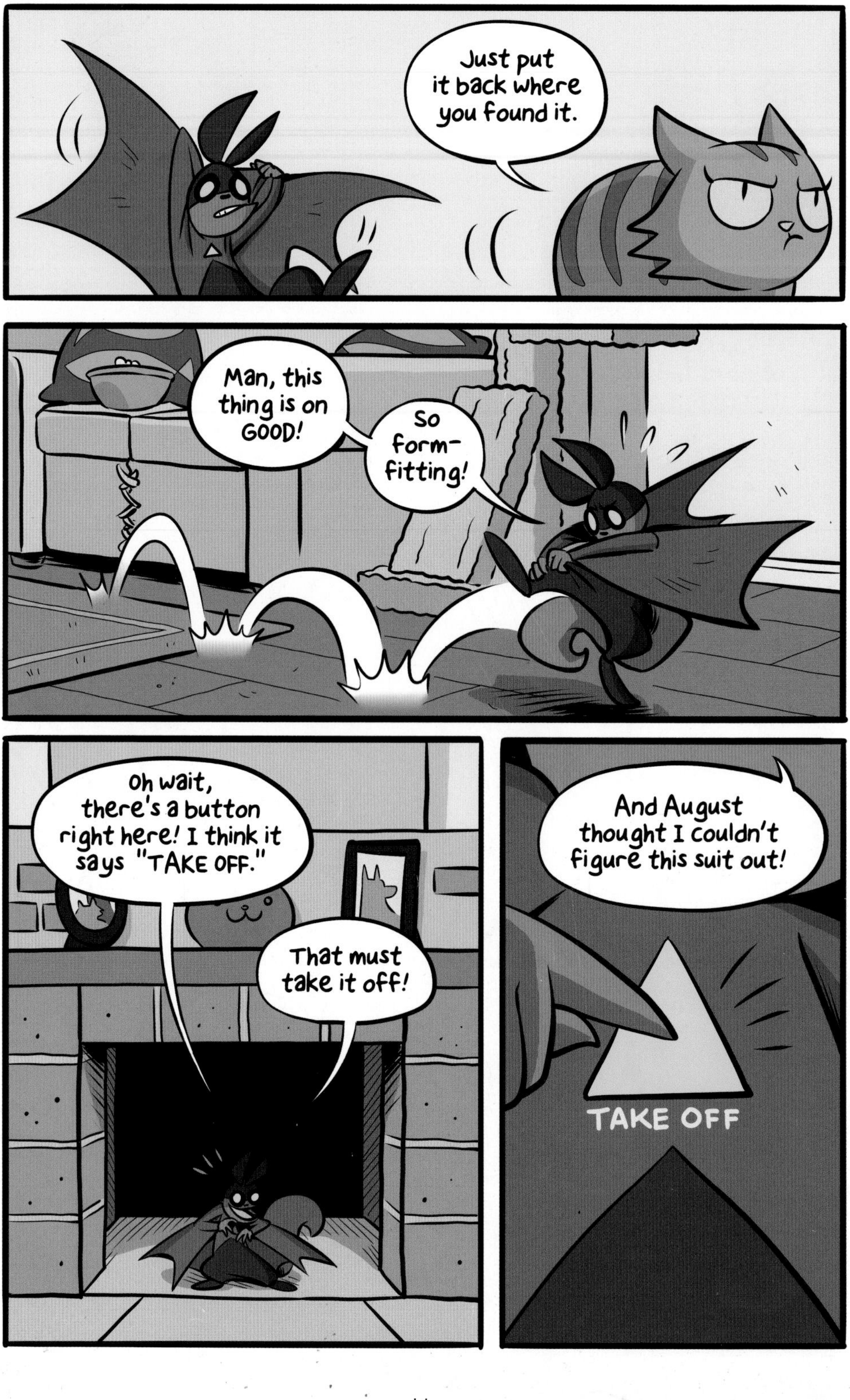
Just put it back where you found it.
Man, this thing is on GOOD!
So form-fitting!
Oh wait, there's a button right here! I think it says "TAKE OFF."
That must take it off!
And August thought I couldn't figure this suit out!
TAKE OFF

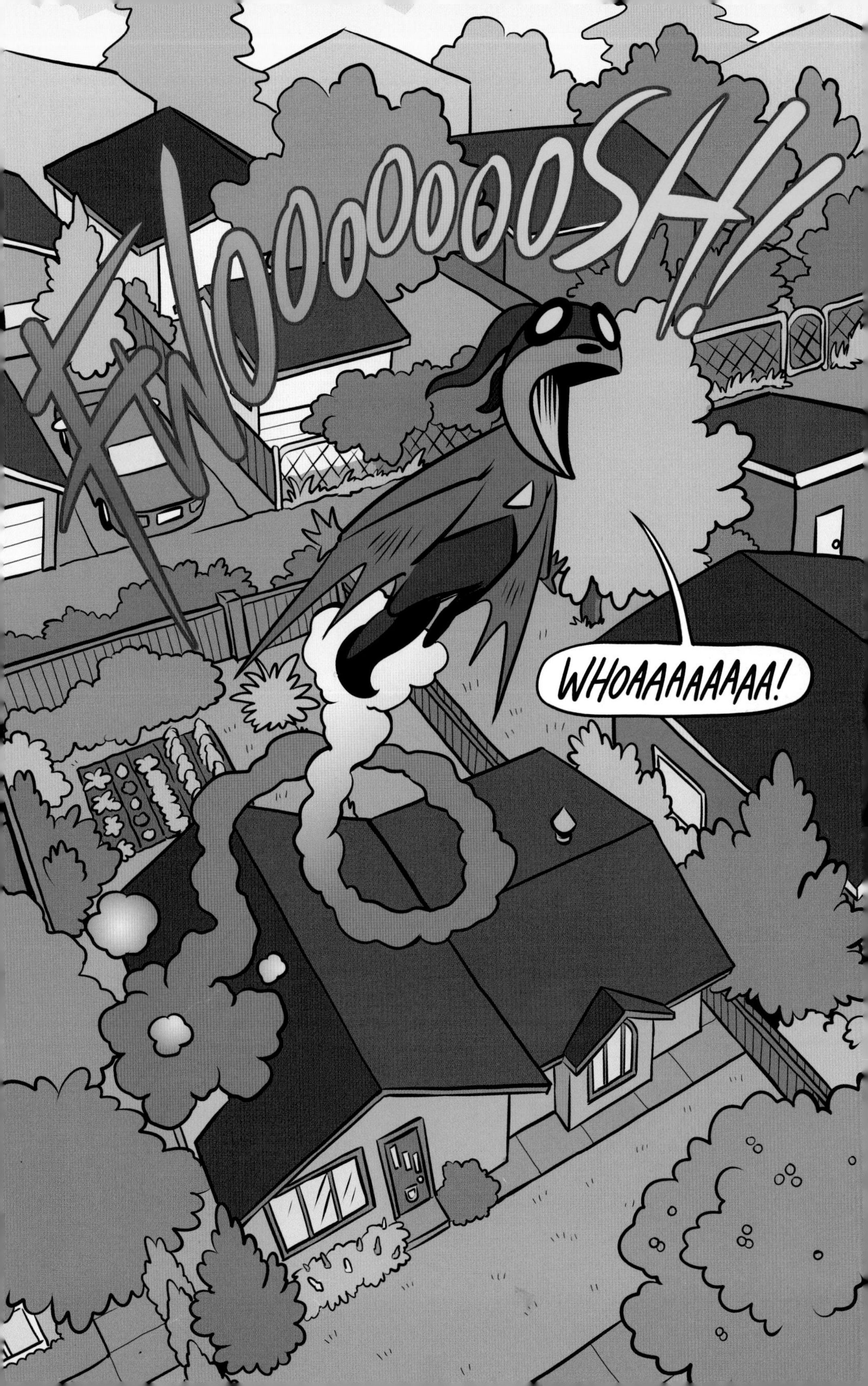
FWOOOOOOOSH!!
WHOAAAAAAAA!

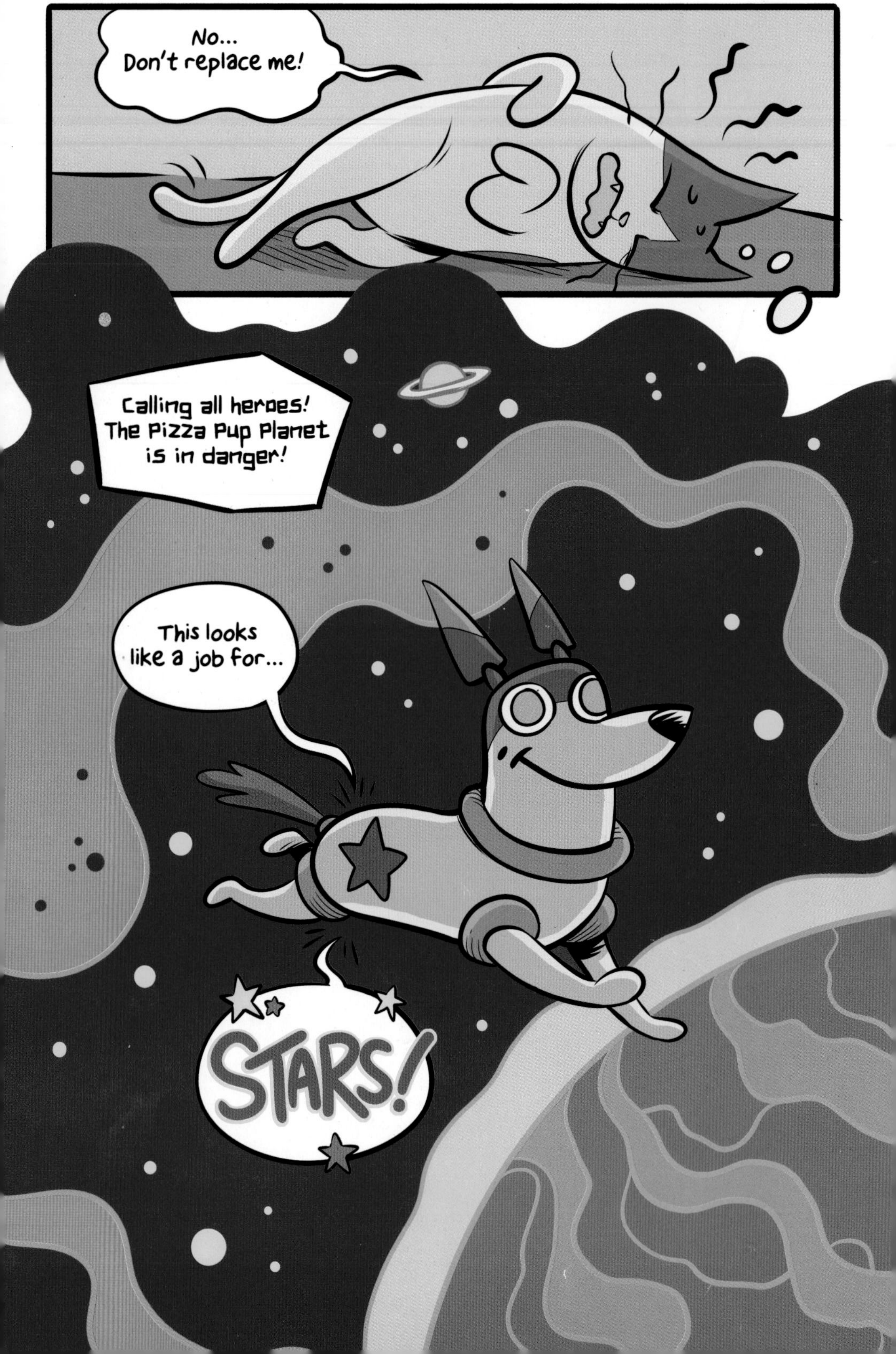
No... Don't replace me!
Calling all heroes! The Pizza Pup Planet is in danger!
This looks like a job for...
STARS!

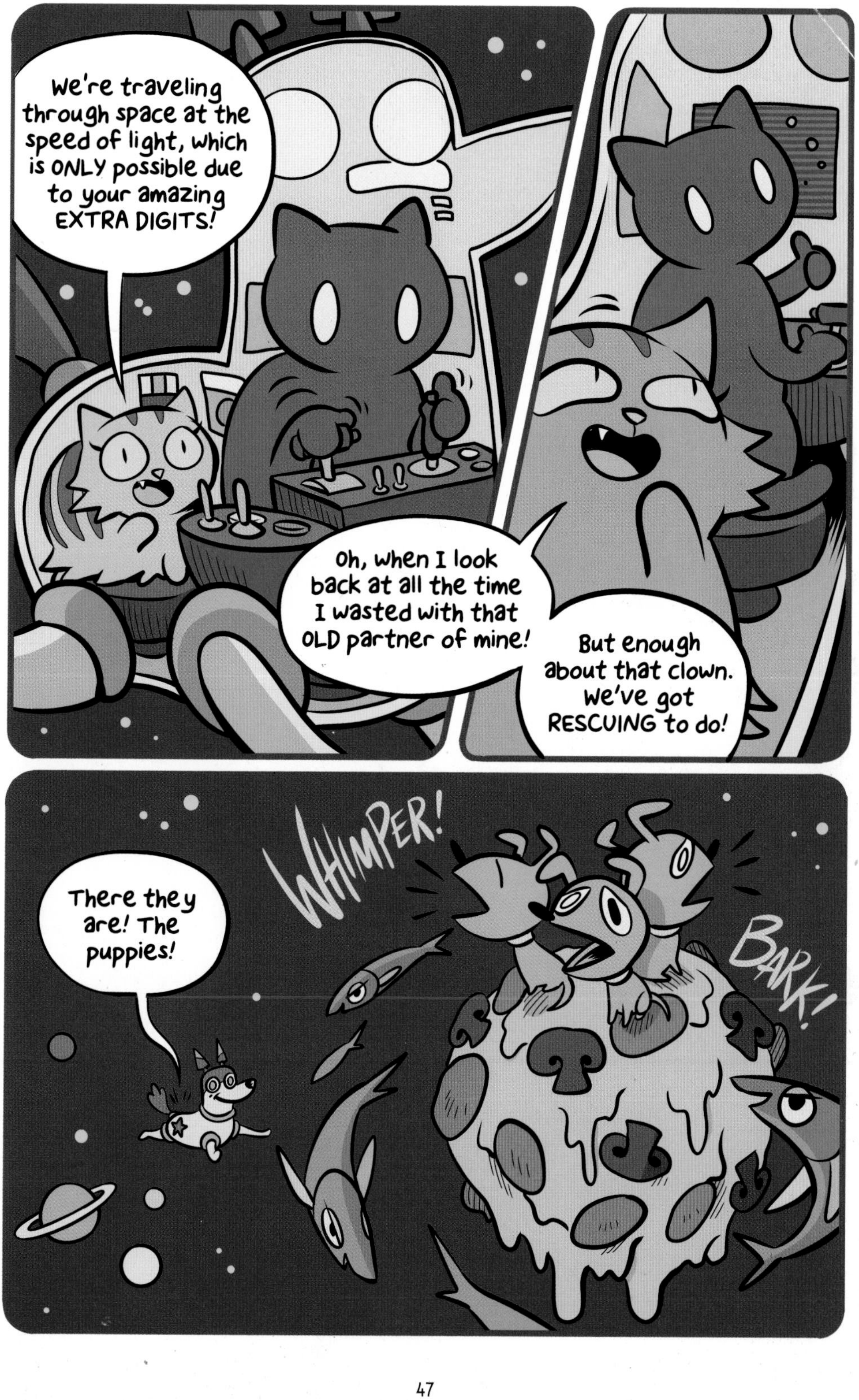
We're traveling through space at the speed of light, which is ONLY possible due to your amazing EXTRA DIGITS!
Oh, when I look back at all the time I wasted with that OLD partner of mine!
But enough about that clown. We've got RESCUING to do!
WHIMPER!
There they are! The puppies!
BARK!

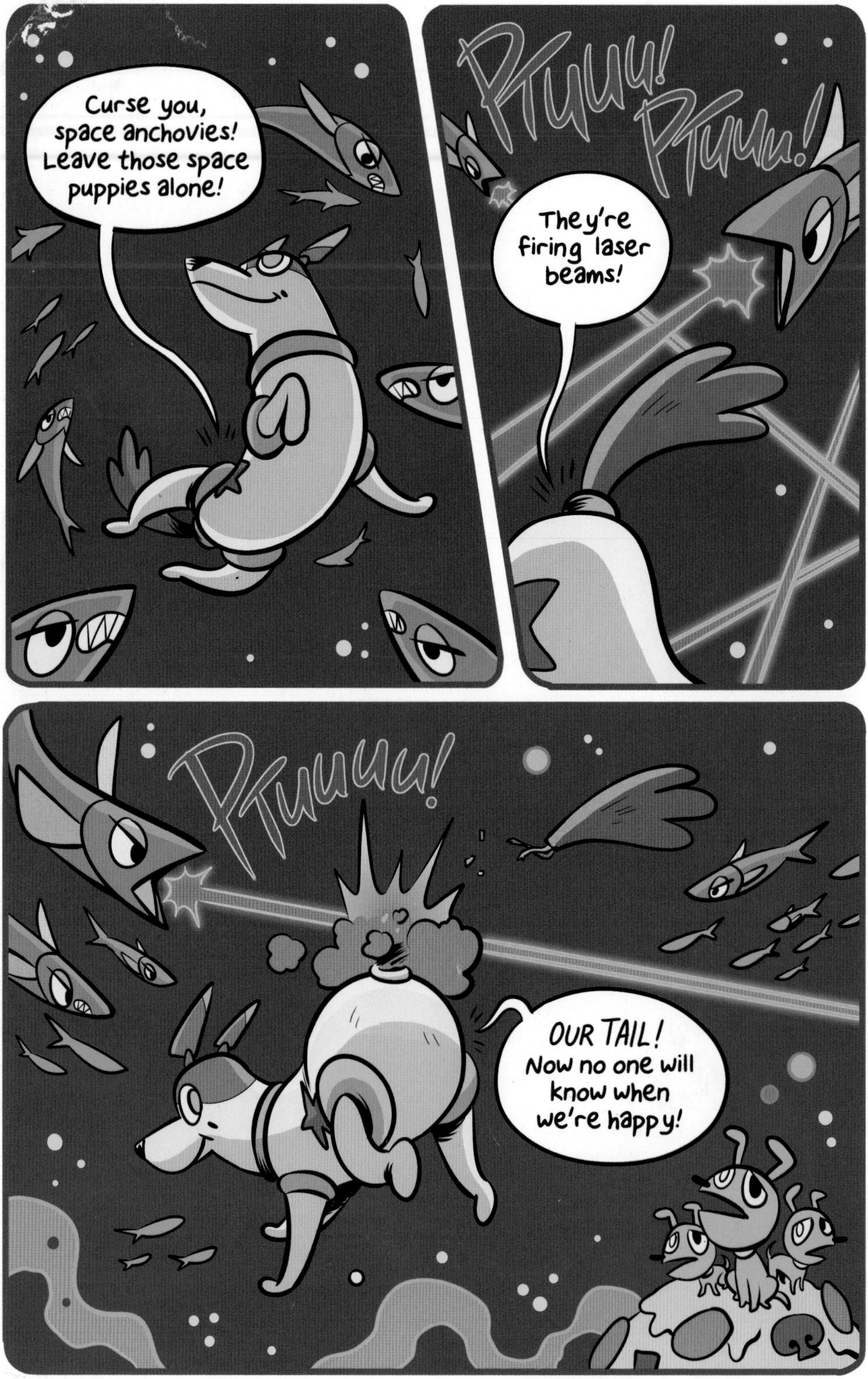
Curse you, space anchovies! Leave those space puppies alone!
PTUUU! PTUUU!
They're firing laser beams!
PTUUUU!
OUR TAIL! Now no one will know when we're happy!

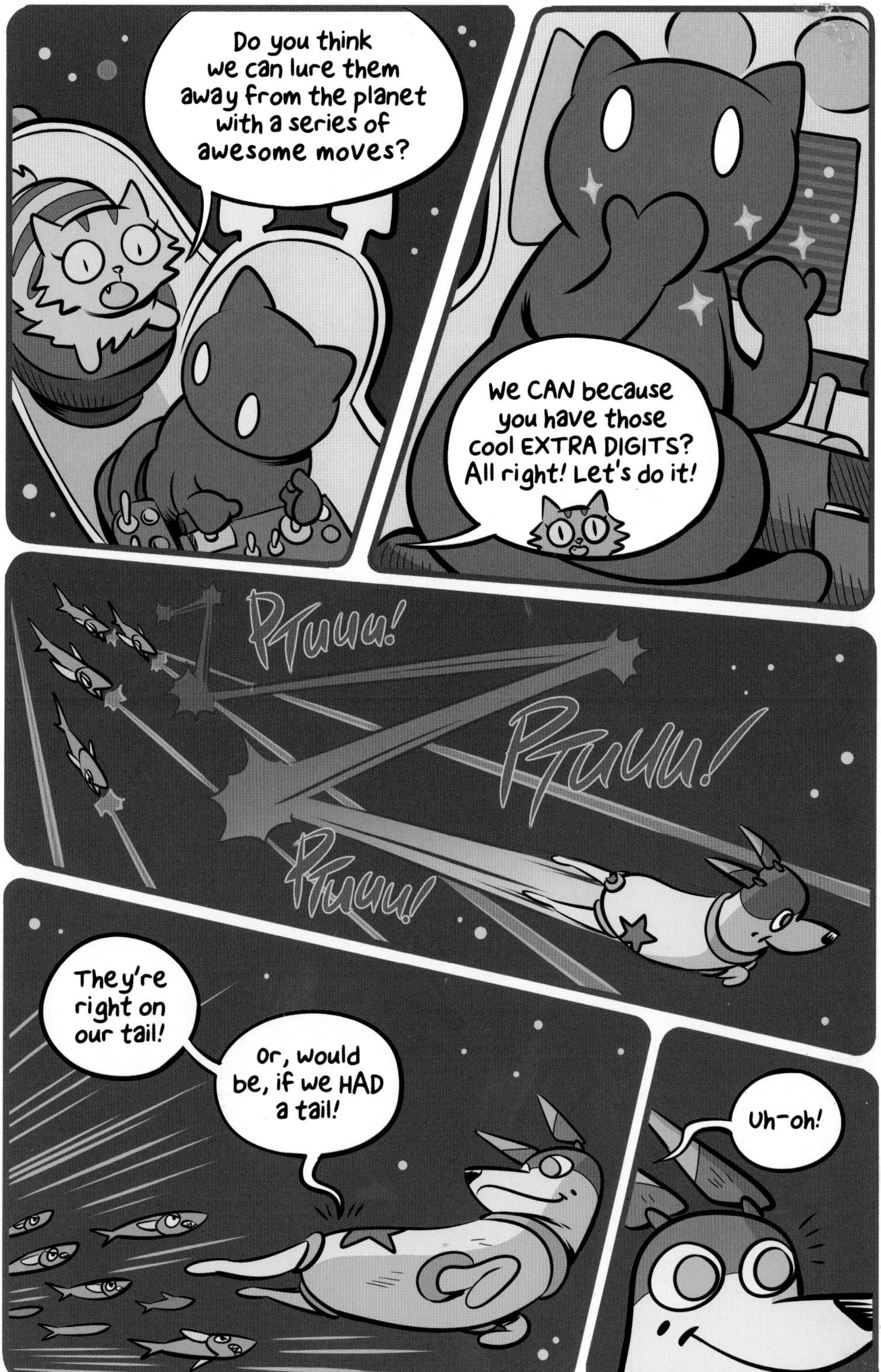
Do you think we can lure them away from the planet with a series of awesome moves?
We CAN because you have those cool EXTRA DIGITS? All right! Let's do it!
Ptuuu!
Ptuuu!
Ptuuu!
They're right on our tail!
Or, would be, if we HAD a tail!
Uh-oh!

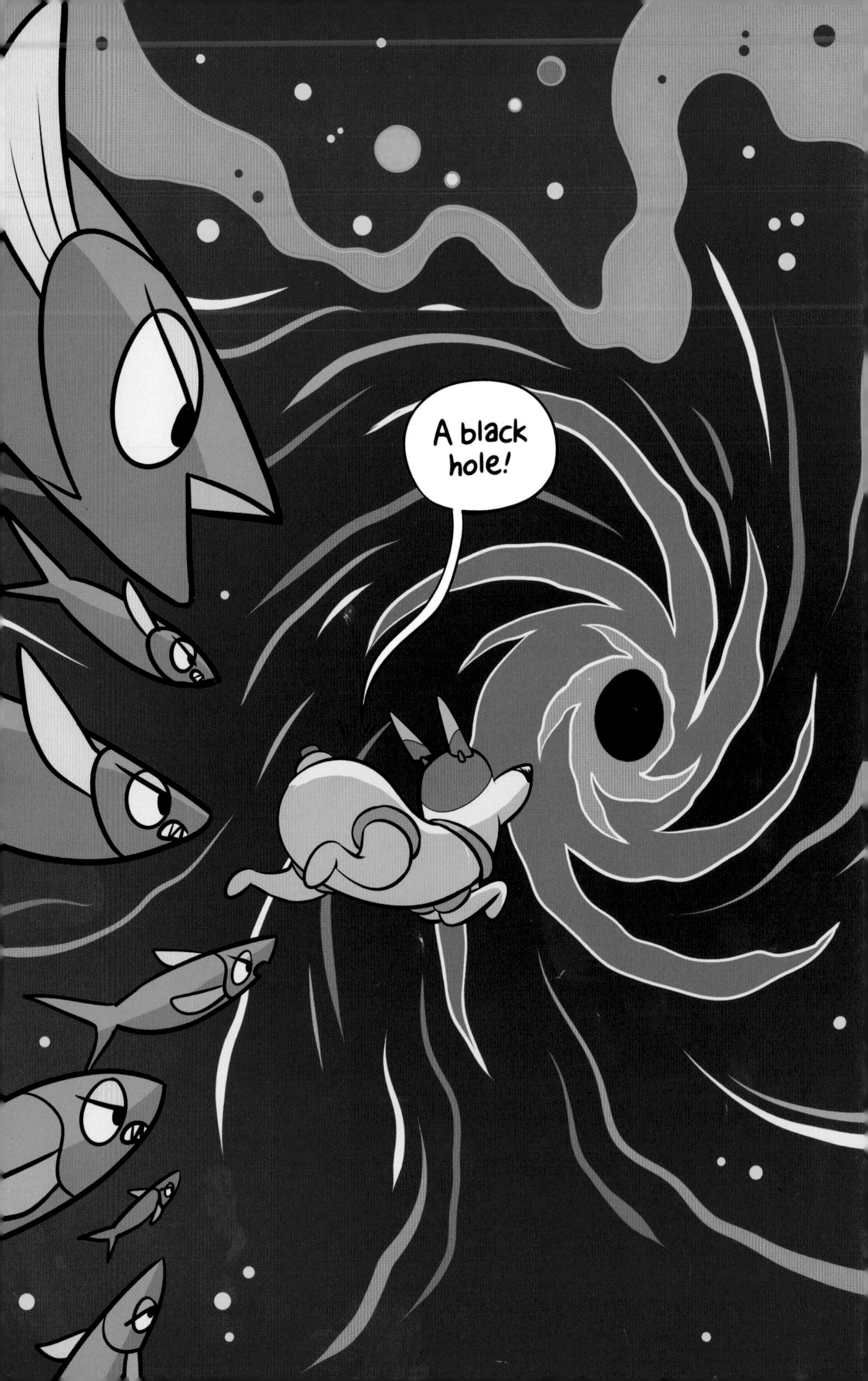
A black hole!

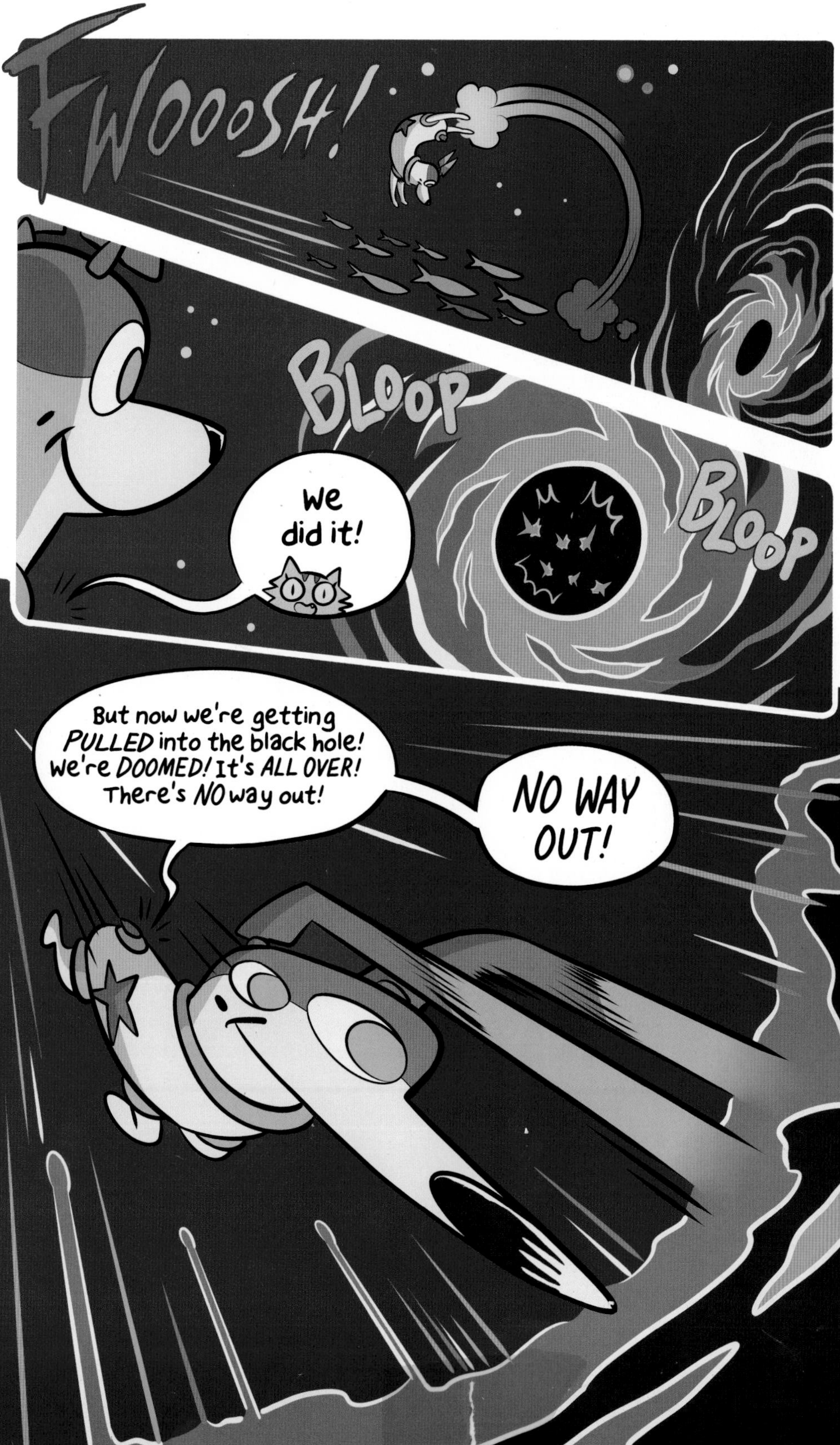
FWOOOSH!
BLOOP
BLOOP
We did it!
But now we're getting PULLED into the black hole! We're DOOMED! It's ALL OVER! There's NO way out!
NO WAY OUT!

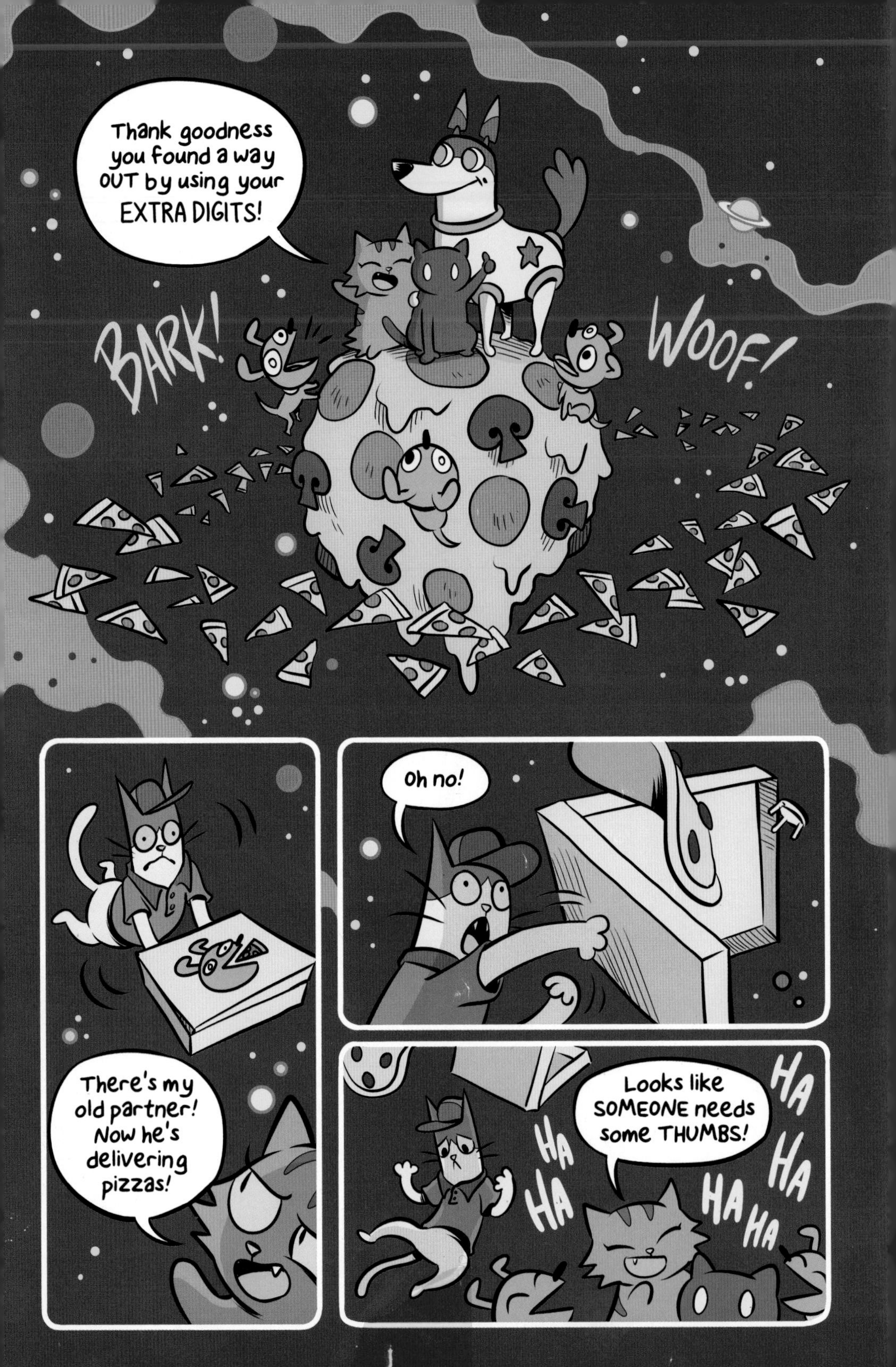
Thank goodness you found a way OUT by using your EXTRA DIGITS!
BARK!
WOOF!
There's my old partner! Now he's delivering pizzas!
Oh no!
Looks like SOMEONE needs some THUMBS!
HA HA HA HA HA HA HA HA

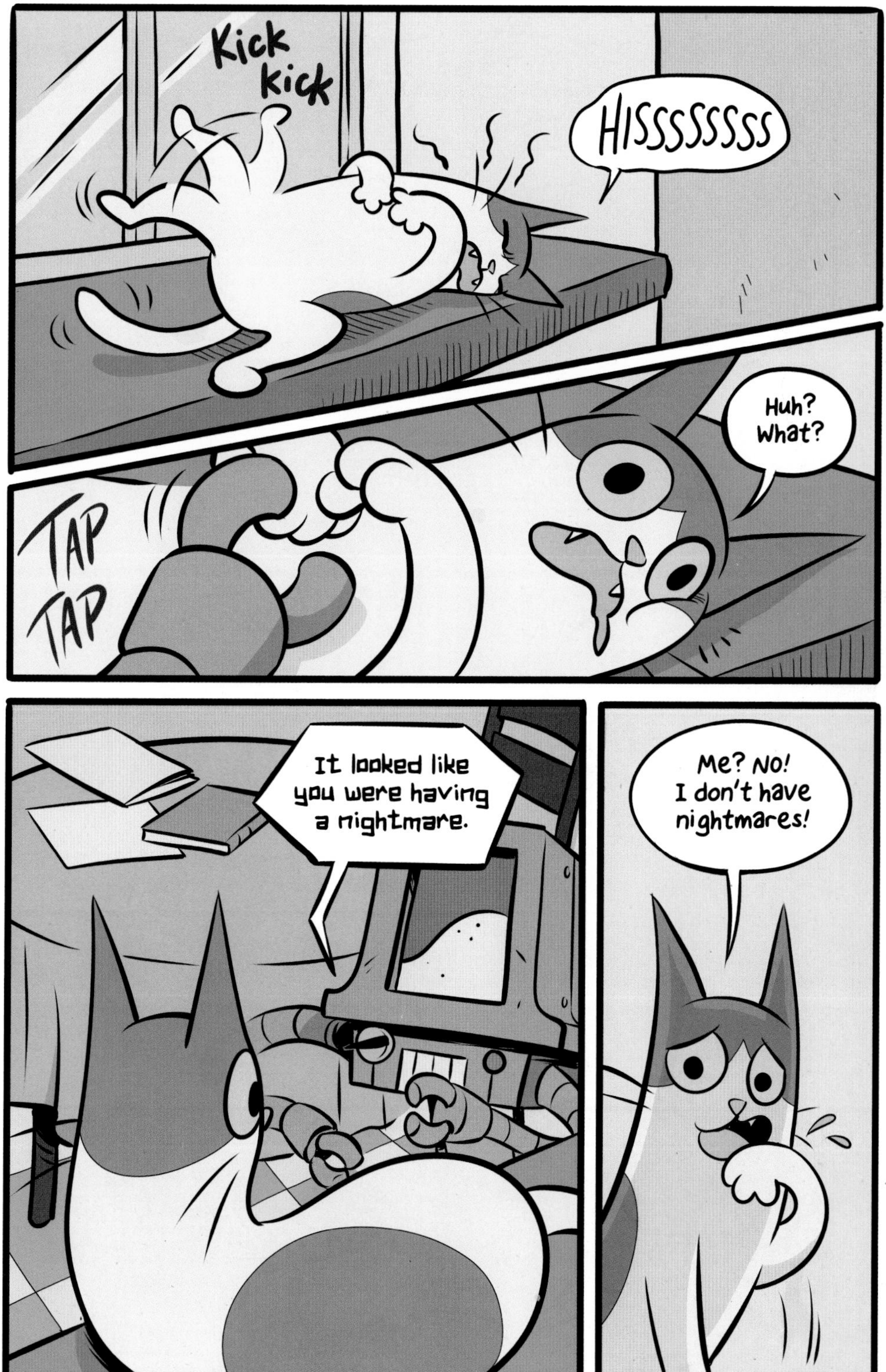
Kick kick
HISSSSSSSS
TAP TAP
Huh? What?
It looked like you were having a nightmare.
Me? NO! I don't have nightmares!

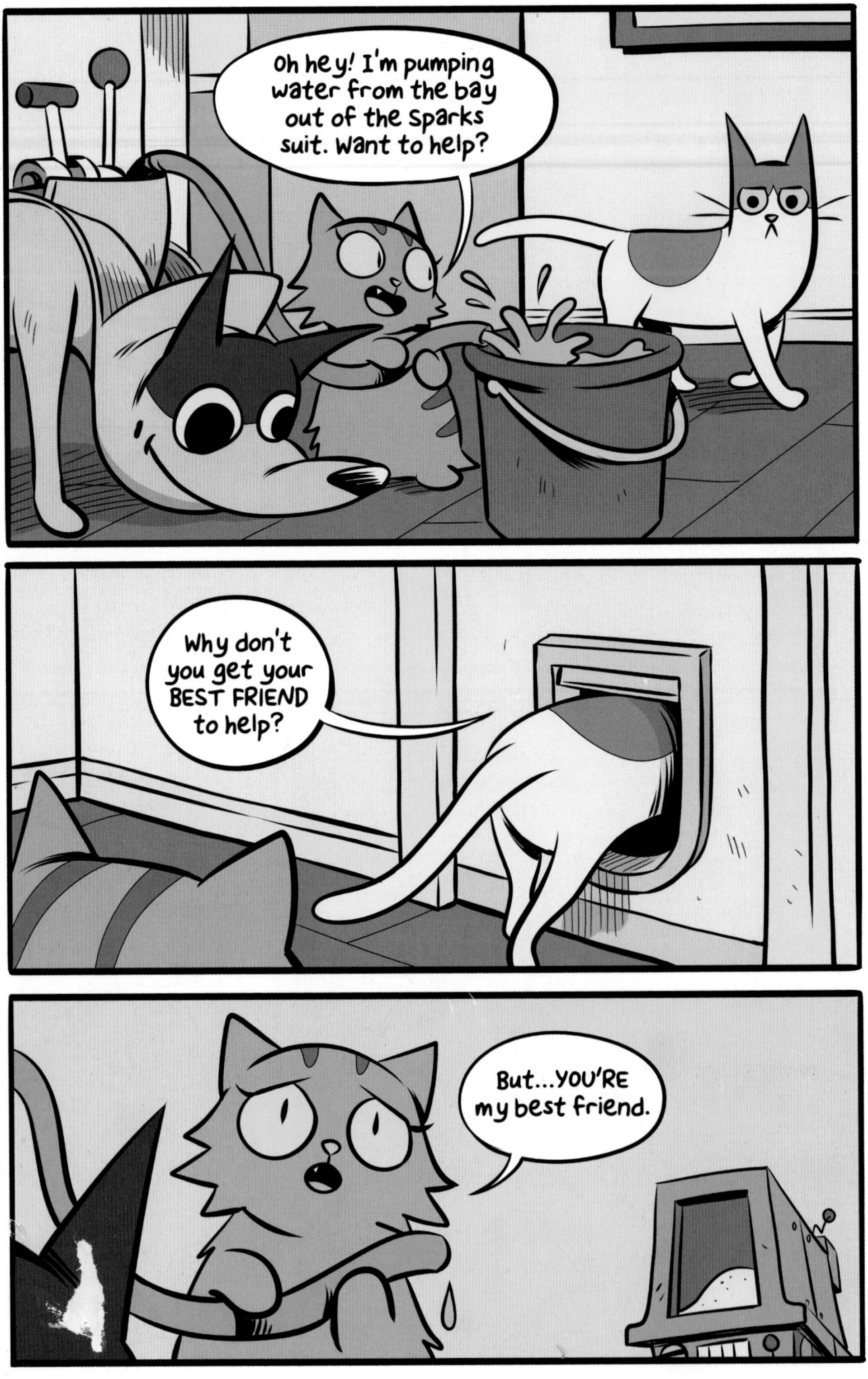
Oh hey! I'm pumping water from the bay out of the Sparks suit. Want to help?
Why don't you get your BEST FRIEND to help?
But...YOU'RE my best friend.

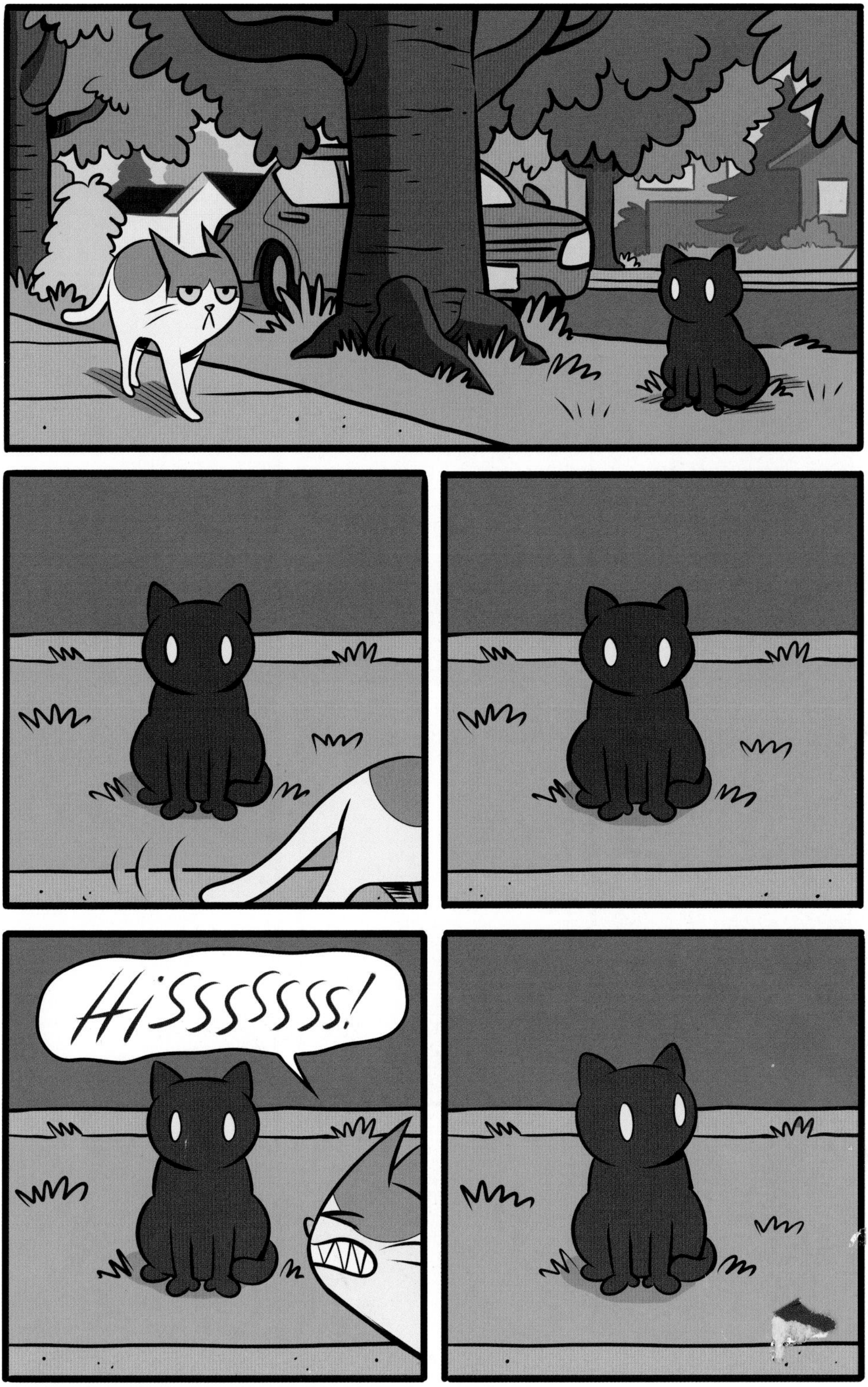
Hisssssss!

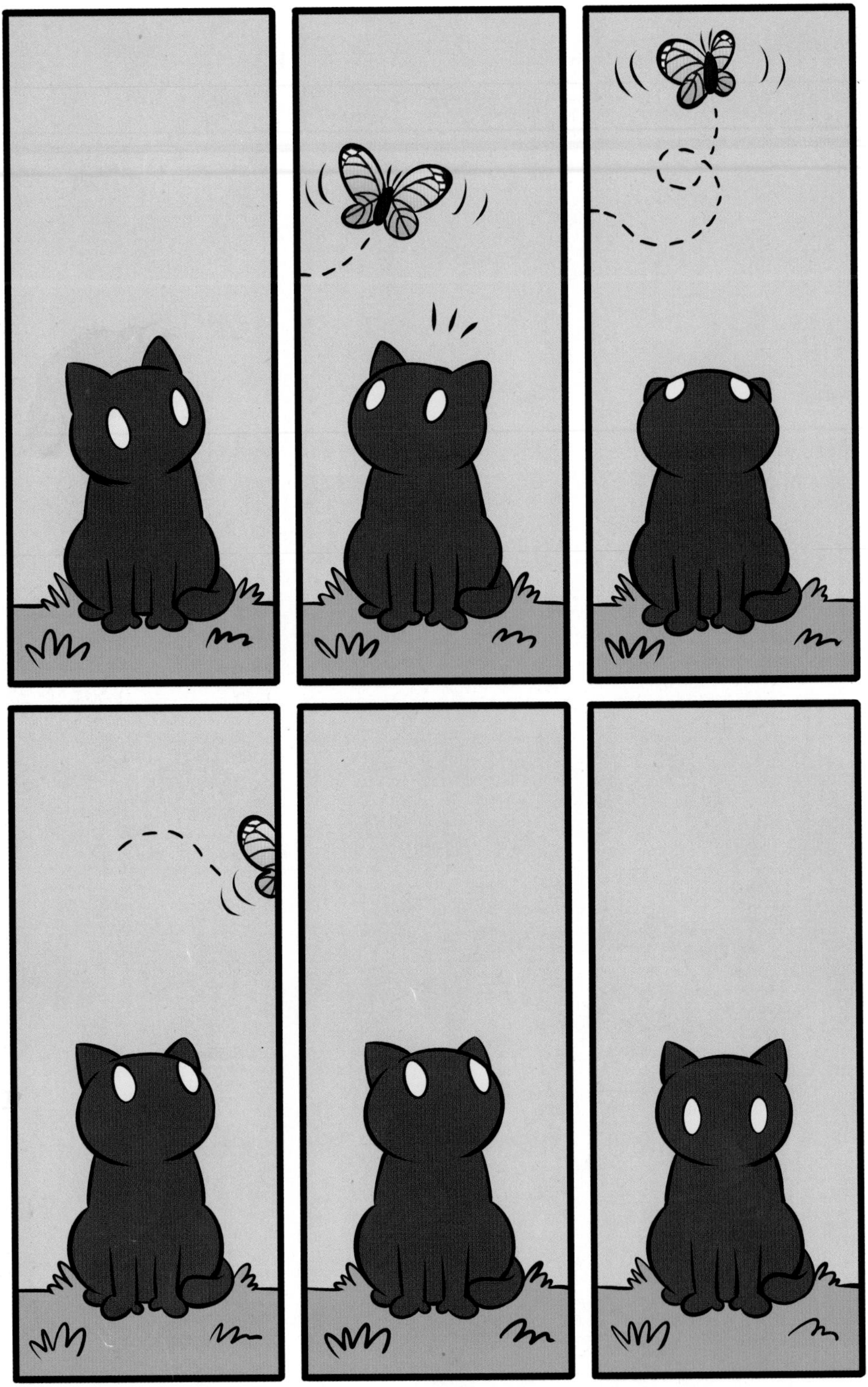

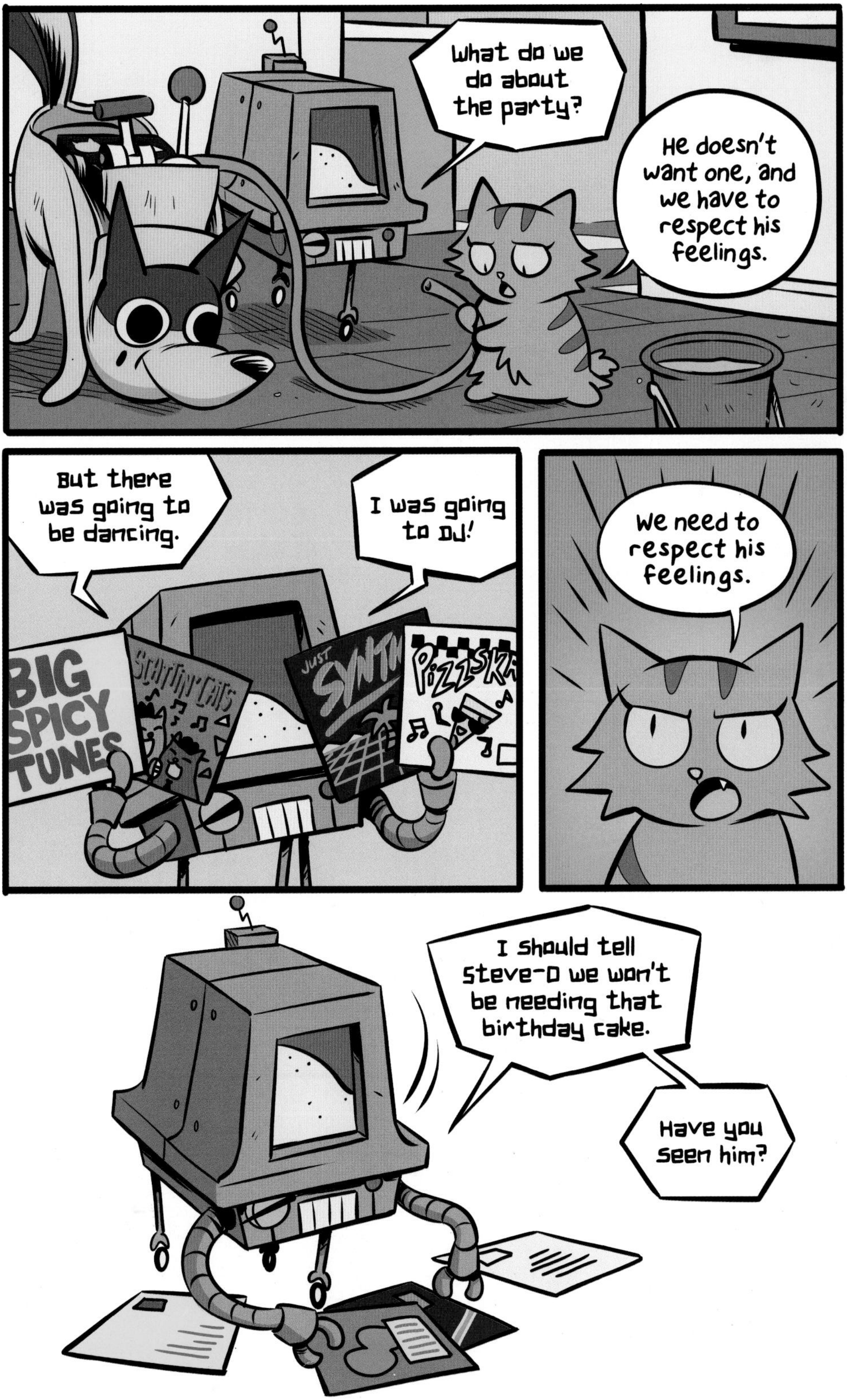
What do we do about the party?
He doesn't want one, and we have to respect his feelings.
But there was going to be dancing.
I was going to DJ!
BIG SPICY TUNES
SCATTIN' CATS
JUST SYNTH
We need to respect his feelings.
I should tell Steve-O we won't be needing that birthday cake.
Have you seen him?

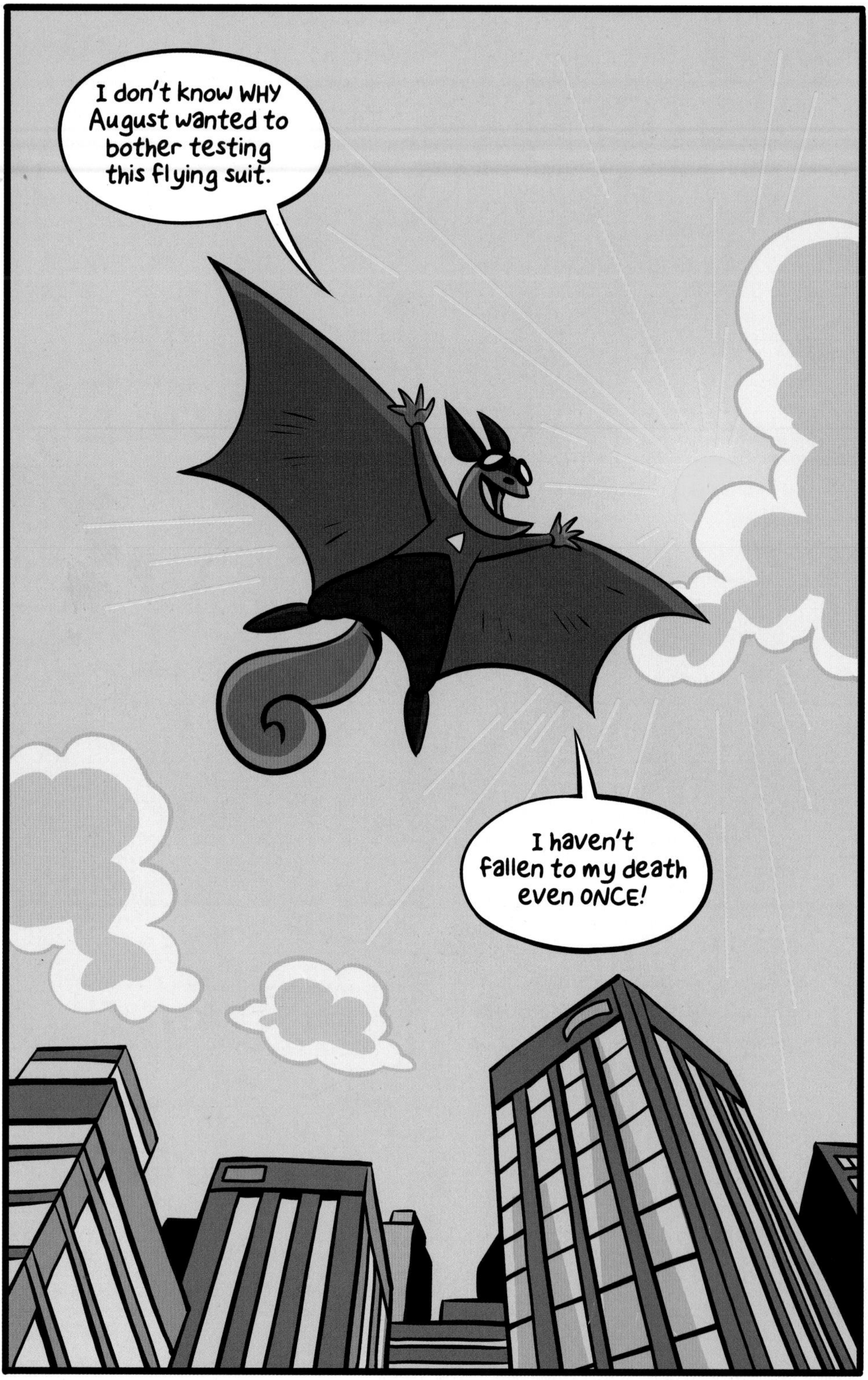
I don't know WHY August wanted to bother testing this flying suit.
I haven't fallen to my death even ONCE!

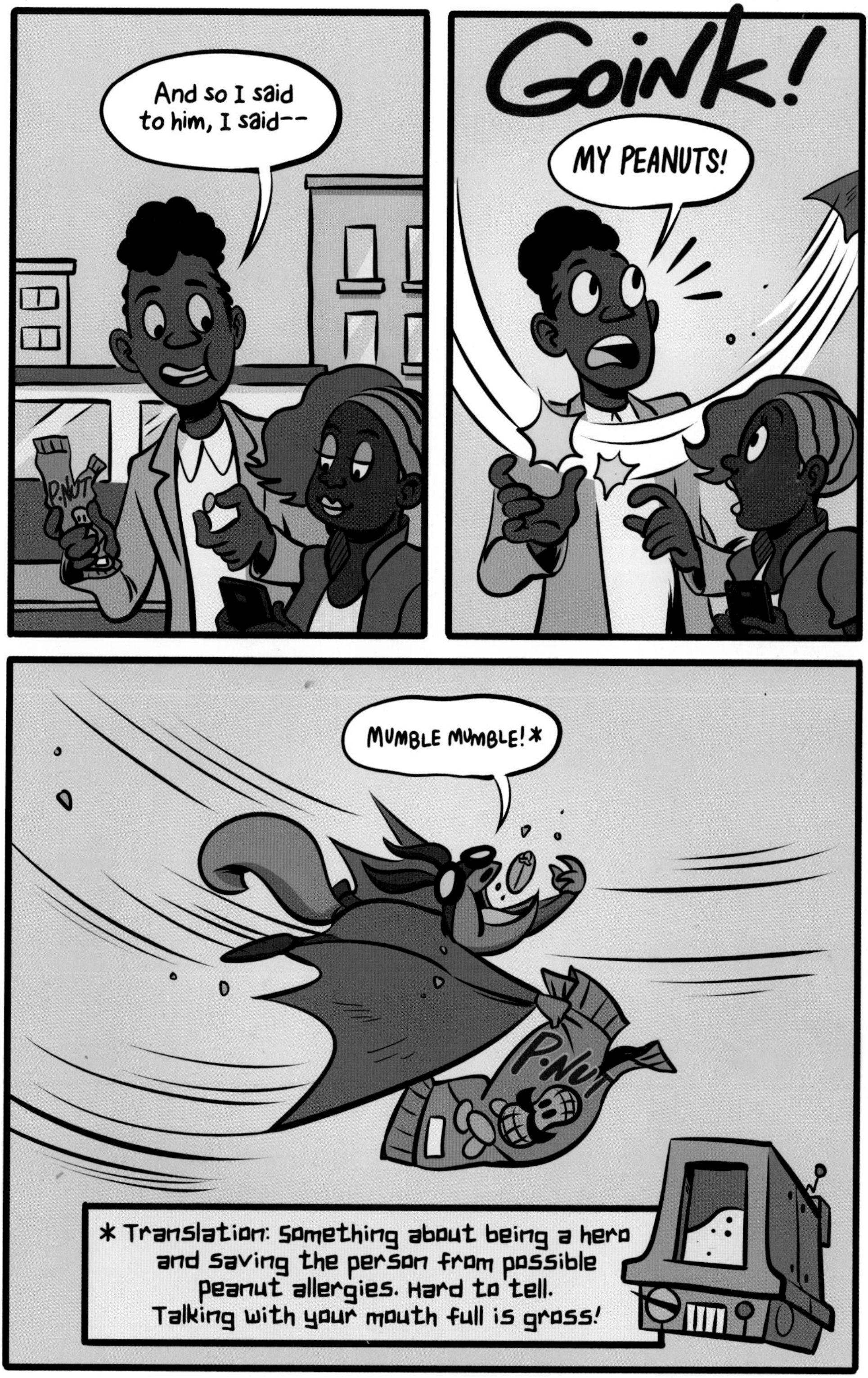
And so I said to him, I said--
GOINK!
MY PEANUTS!
P-NUT
MUMBLE MUMBLE! *
P-NUT
* Translation: Something about being a hero and saving the person from possible peanut allergies. Hard to tell. Talking with your mouth full is gross!

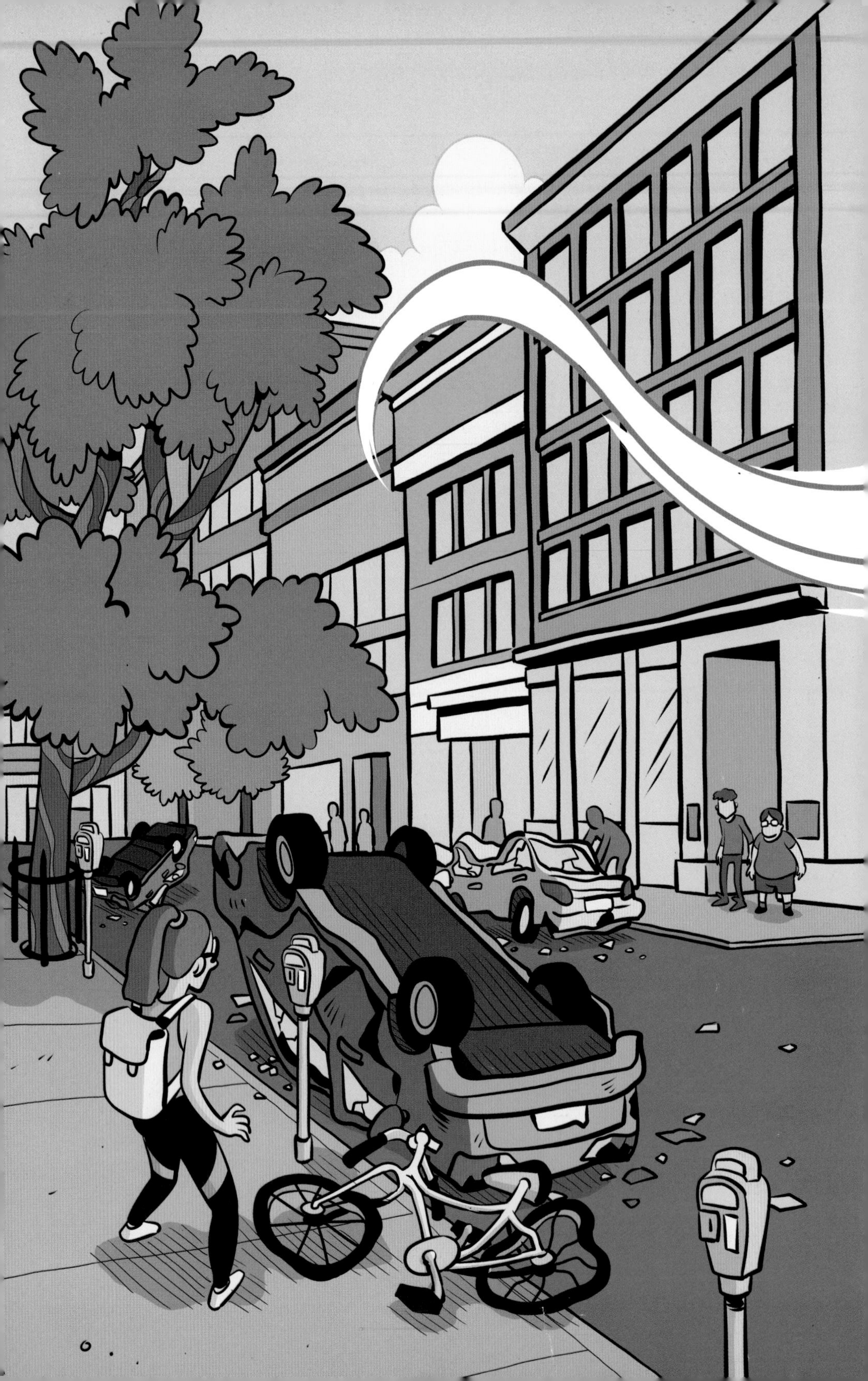

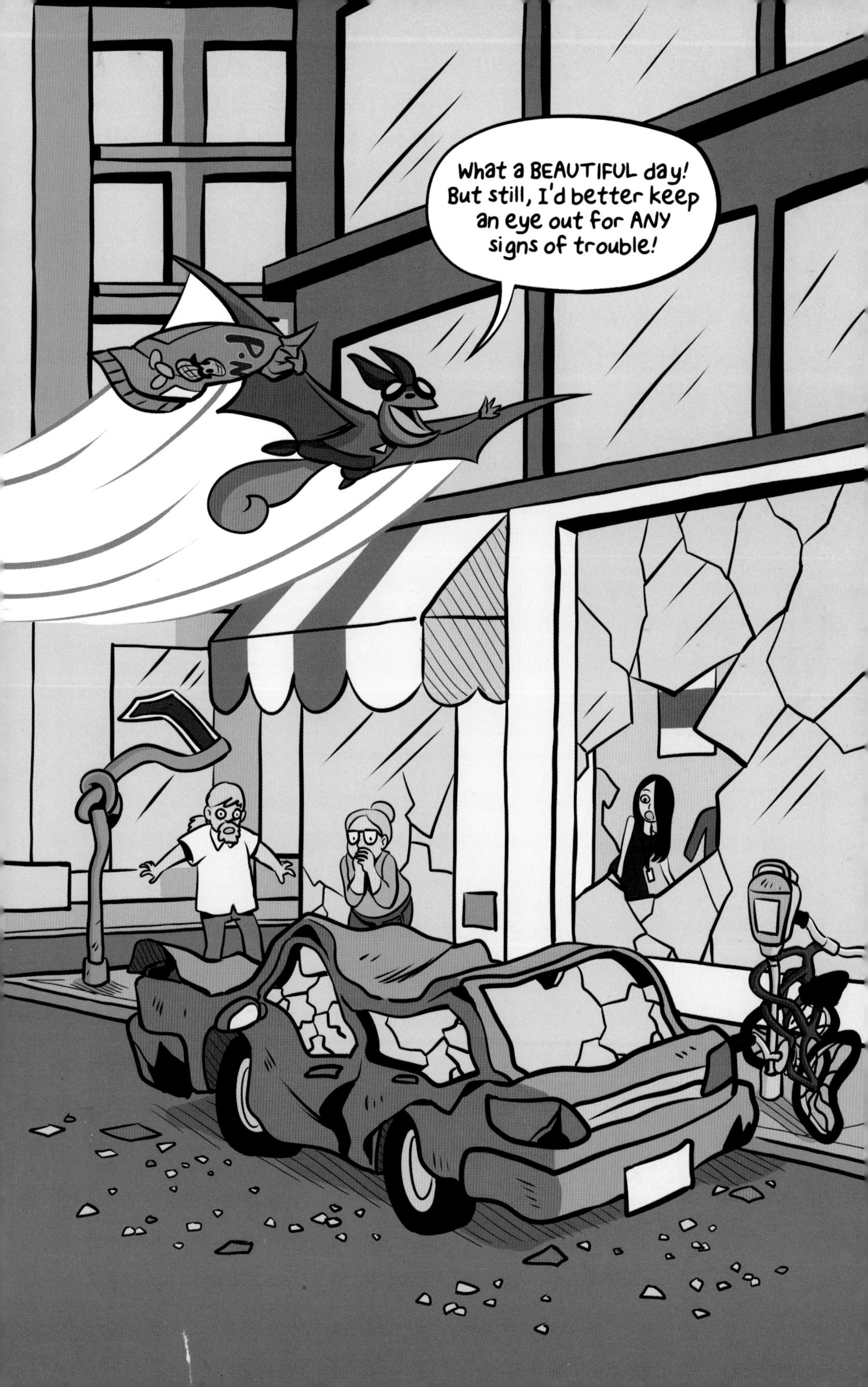
What a BEAUTIFUL day! But still, I'd better keep an eye out for ANY signs of trouble!

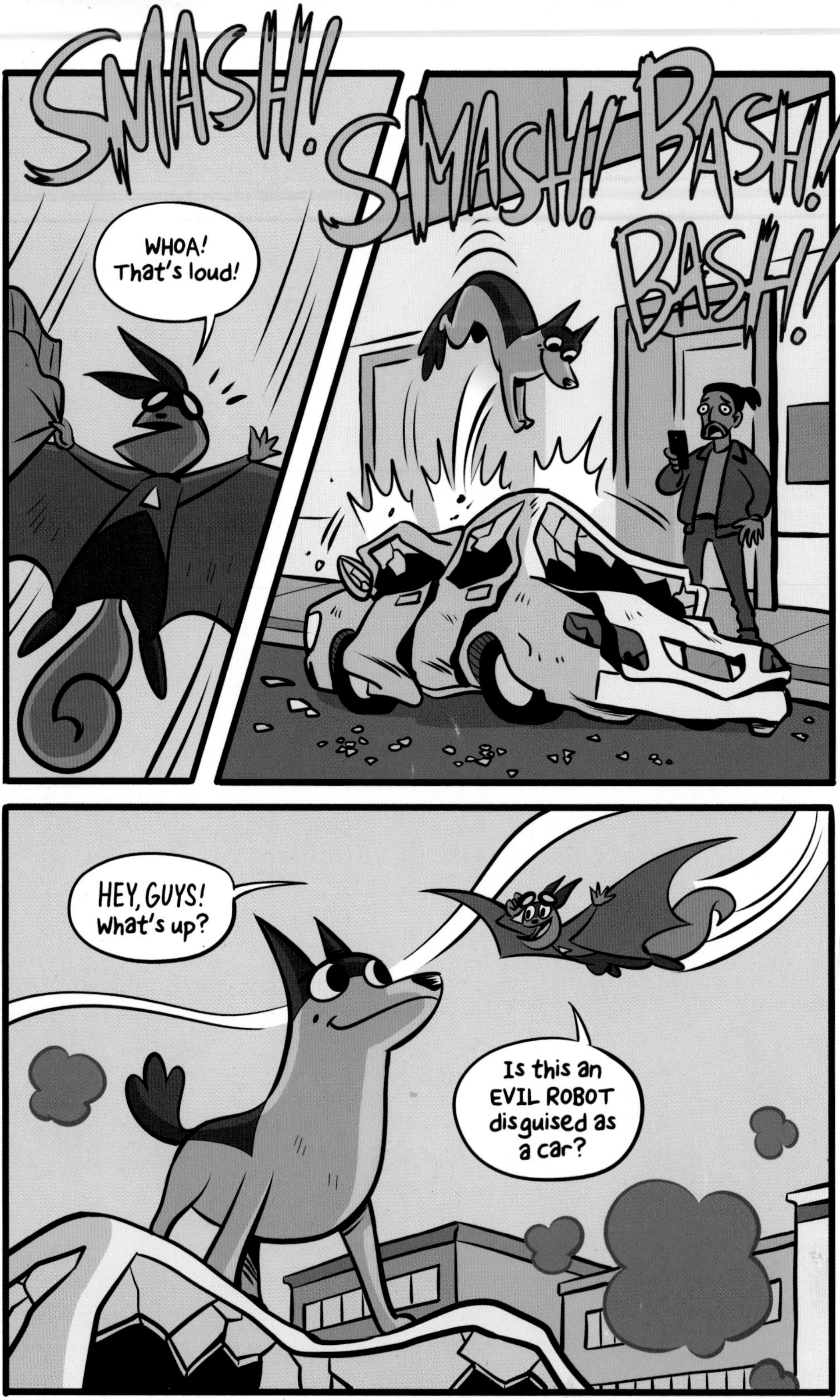
SMASH!
WHOA! That's loud!
SMASH! BASH!
BASH!
HEY, GUYS! What's up?
Is this an EVIL ROBOT disguised as a car?

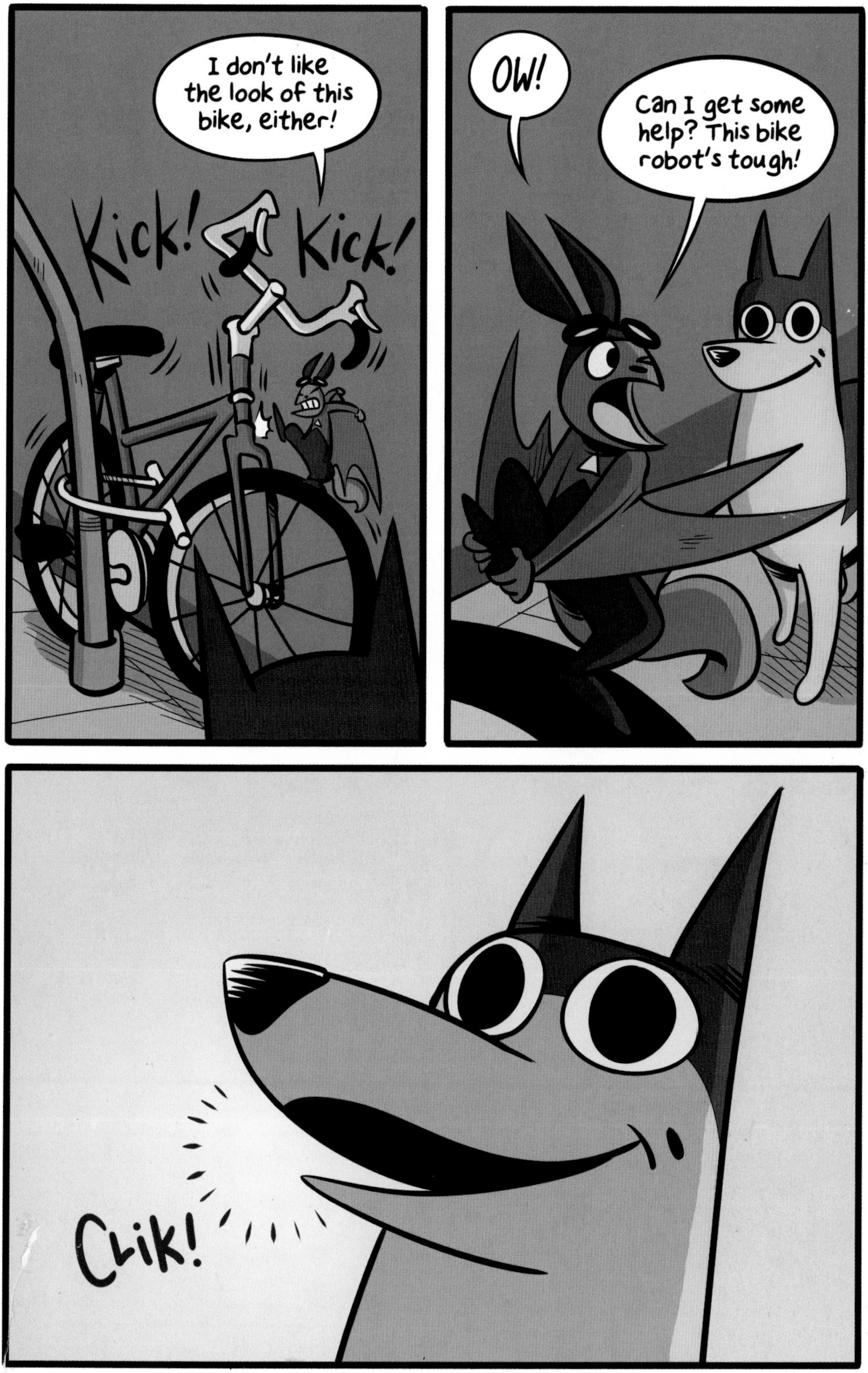
I don't like the look of this bike, either!
Kick! Kick!
OW!
Can I get some help? This bike robot's tough!
CLIK!

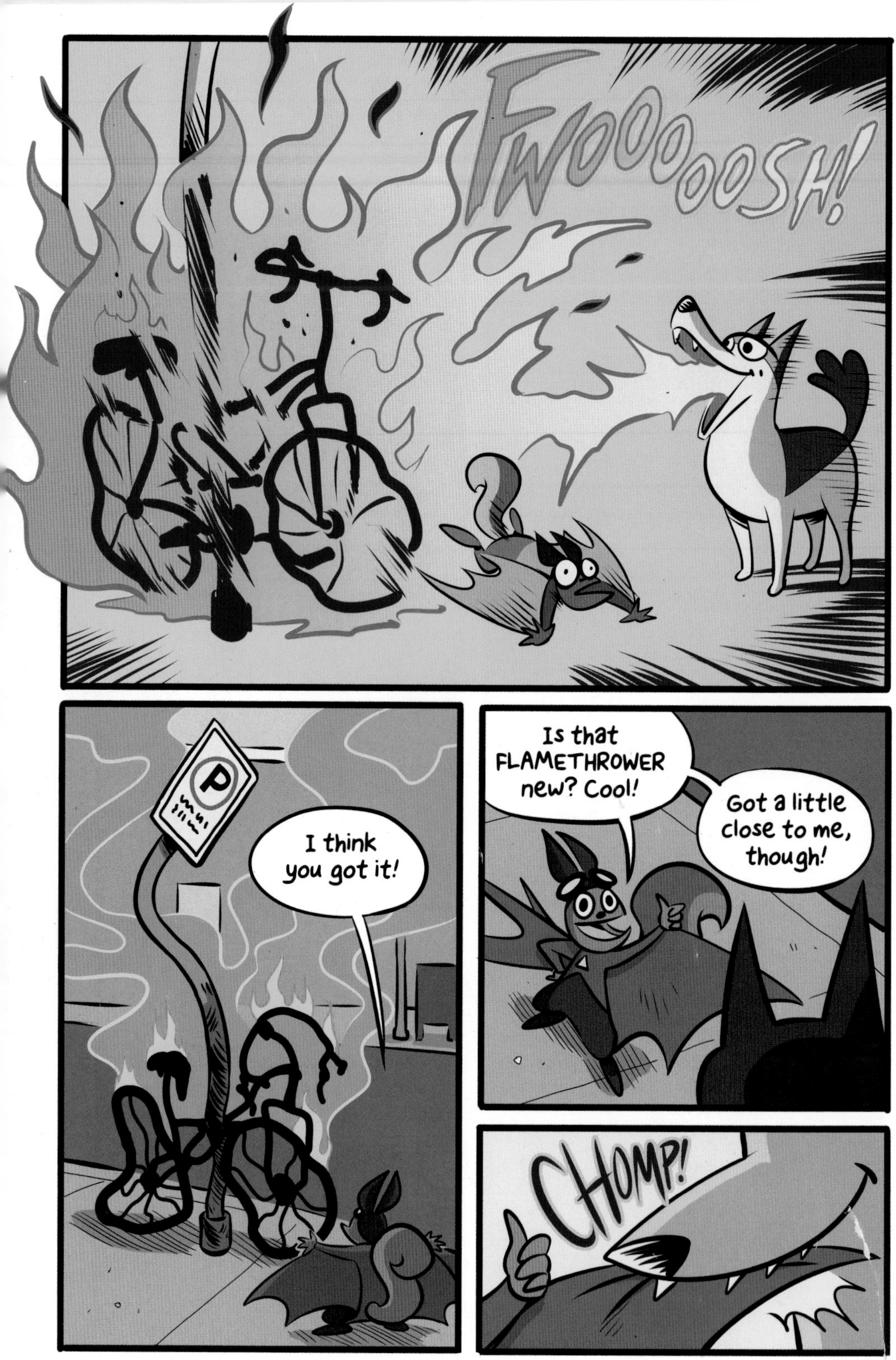
FWOOOOOOSH!
I think you got it!
Is that FLAMETHROWER new? Cool!
Got a little close to me, though!
CHOMP!

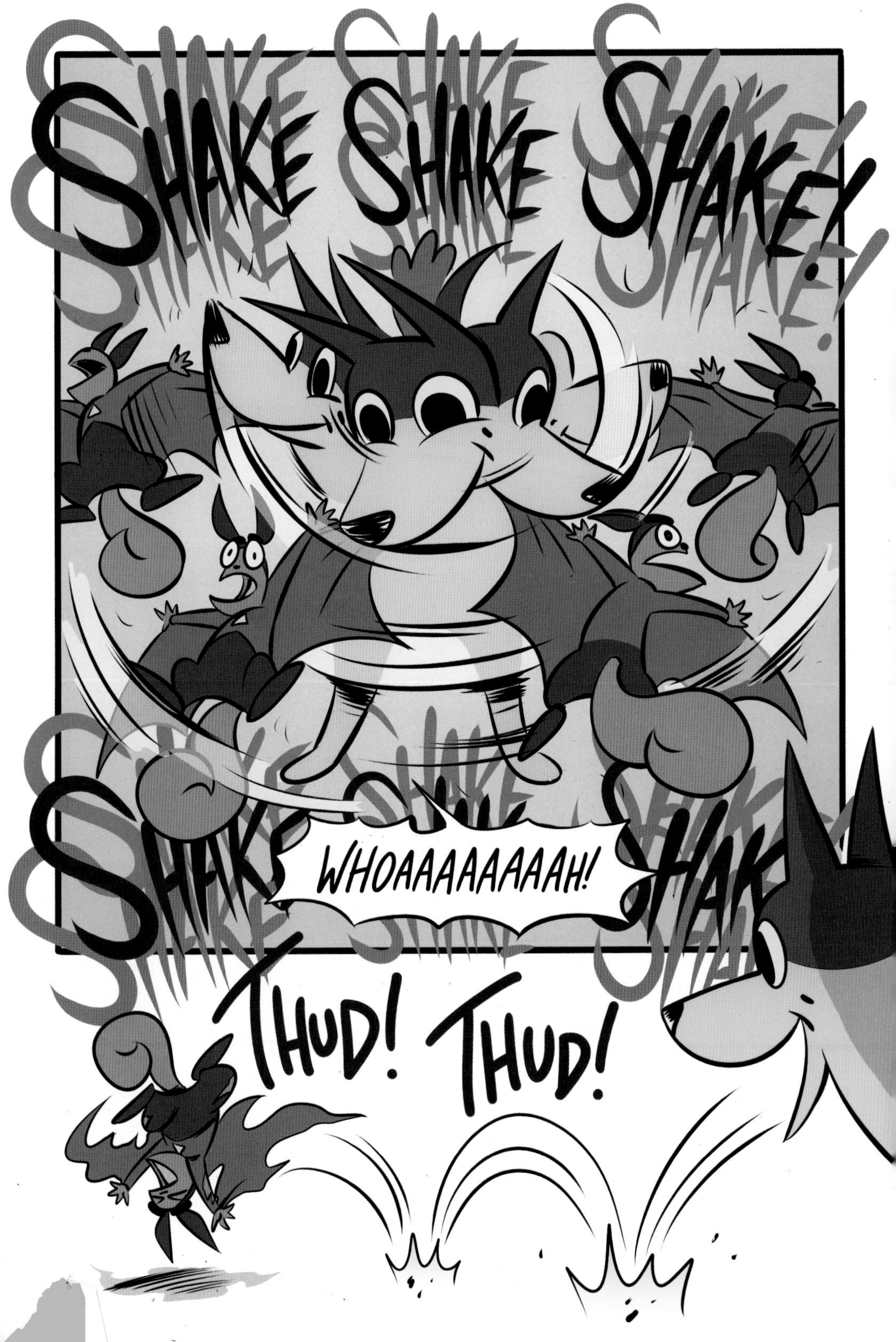
SHAKE SHAKE SHAKE!
SHAKE
WHOAAAAAAAAAH!
SHAKE
THUD! THUD!

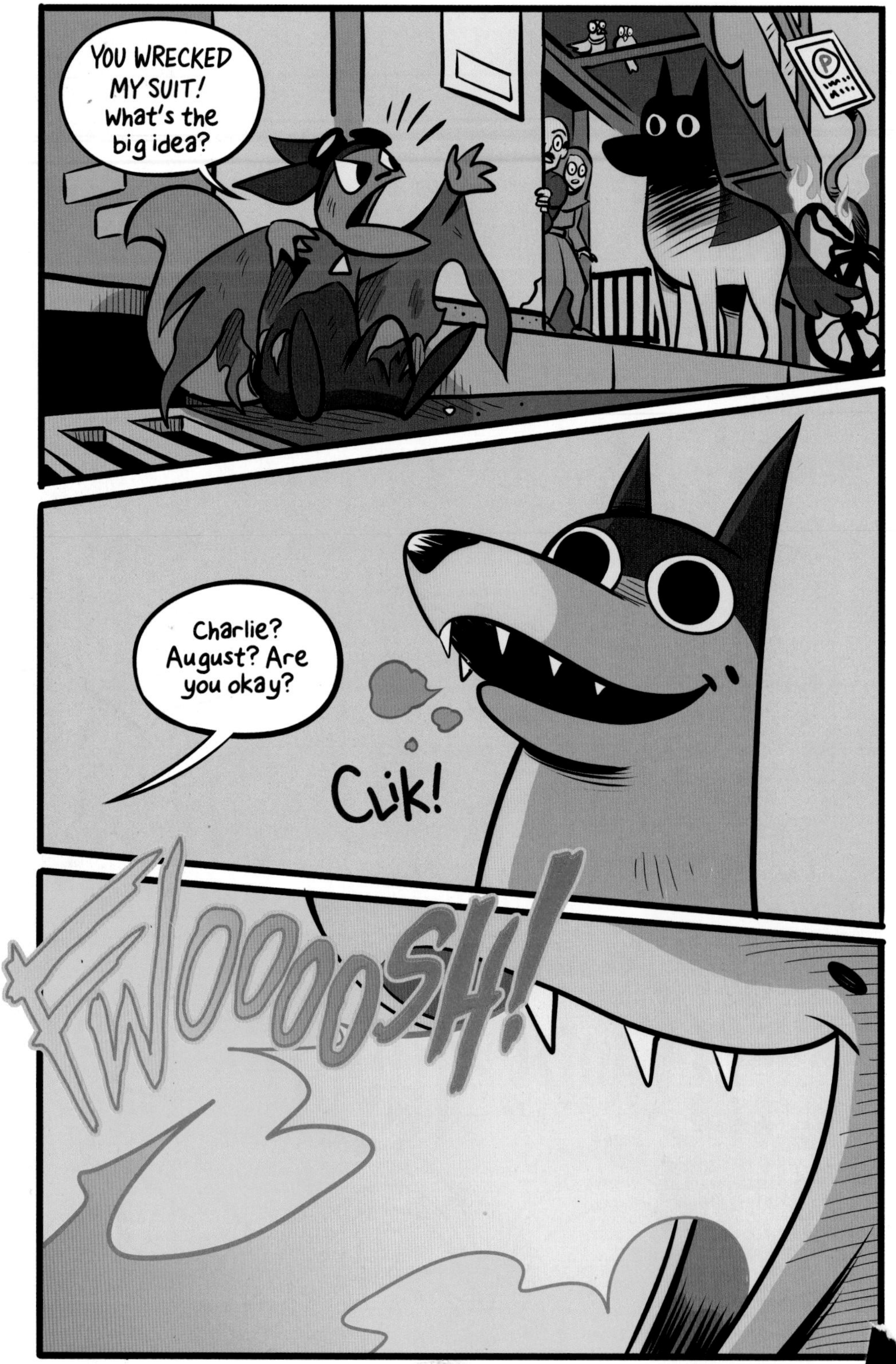
YOU WRECKED MY SUIT! What's the big idea?
Charlie? August? Are you okay?
CLIK!
FWOOOOSH!

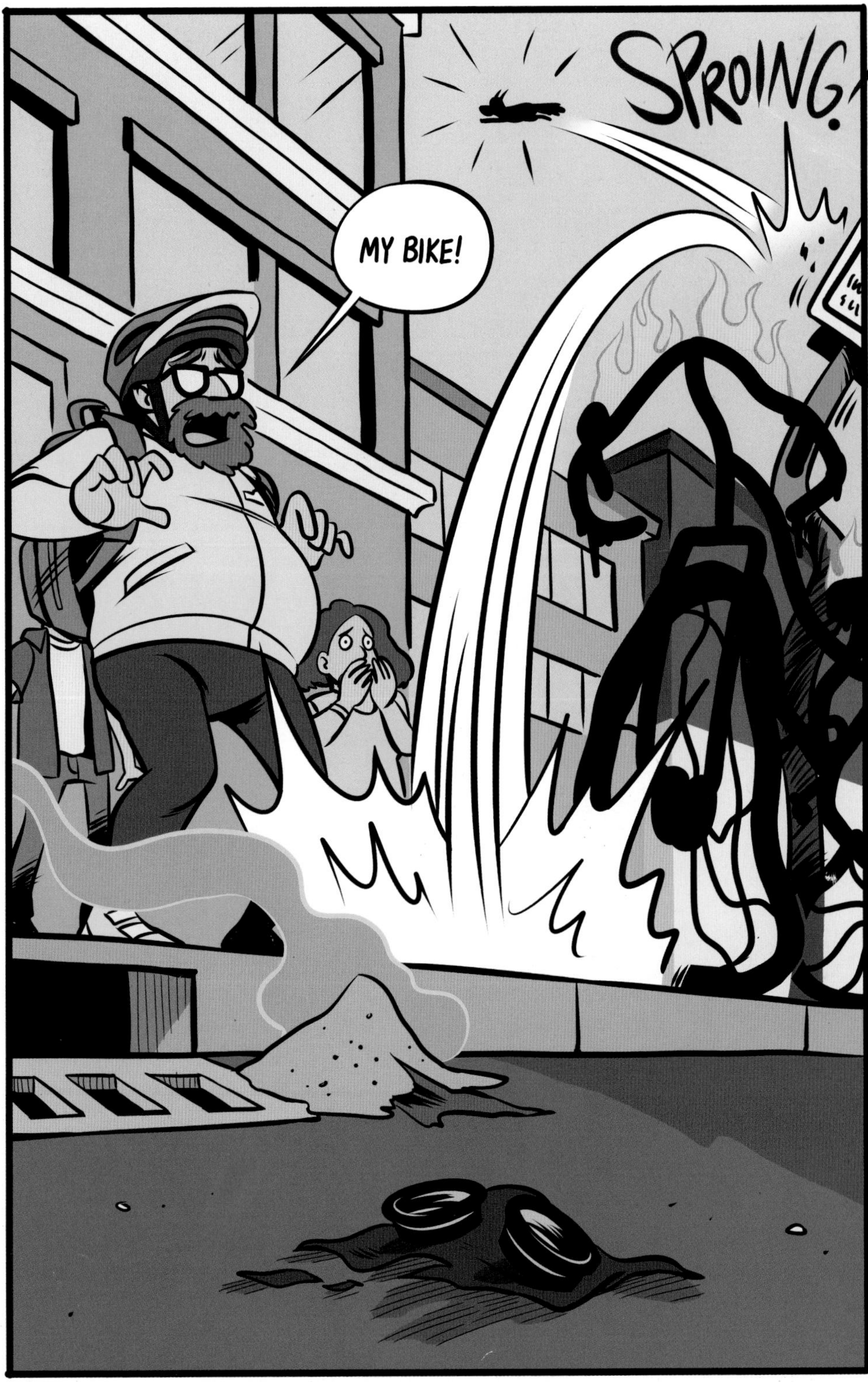
MY BIKE!
SPROING!

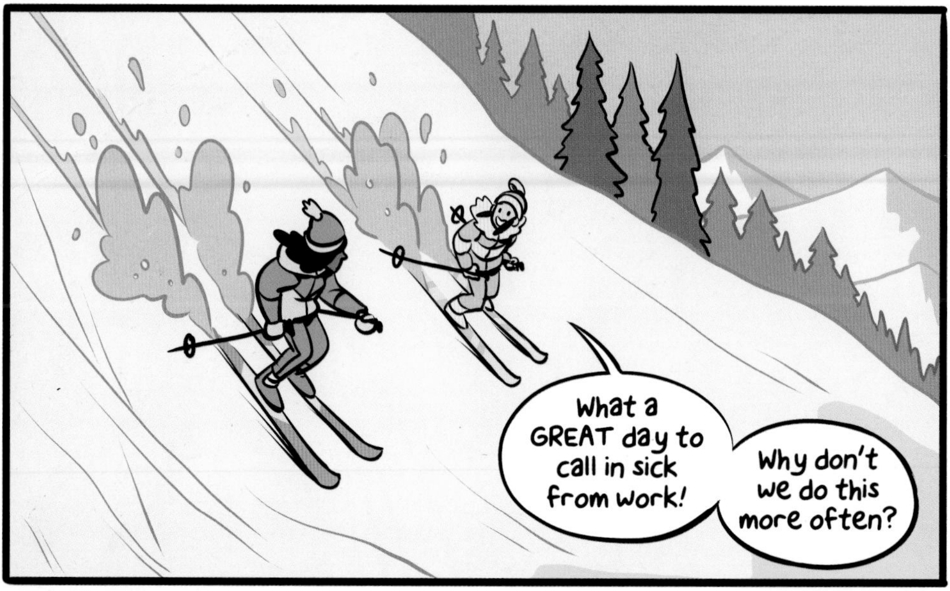
What a GREAT day to call in sick from work!
Why don't we do this more often?

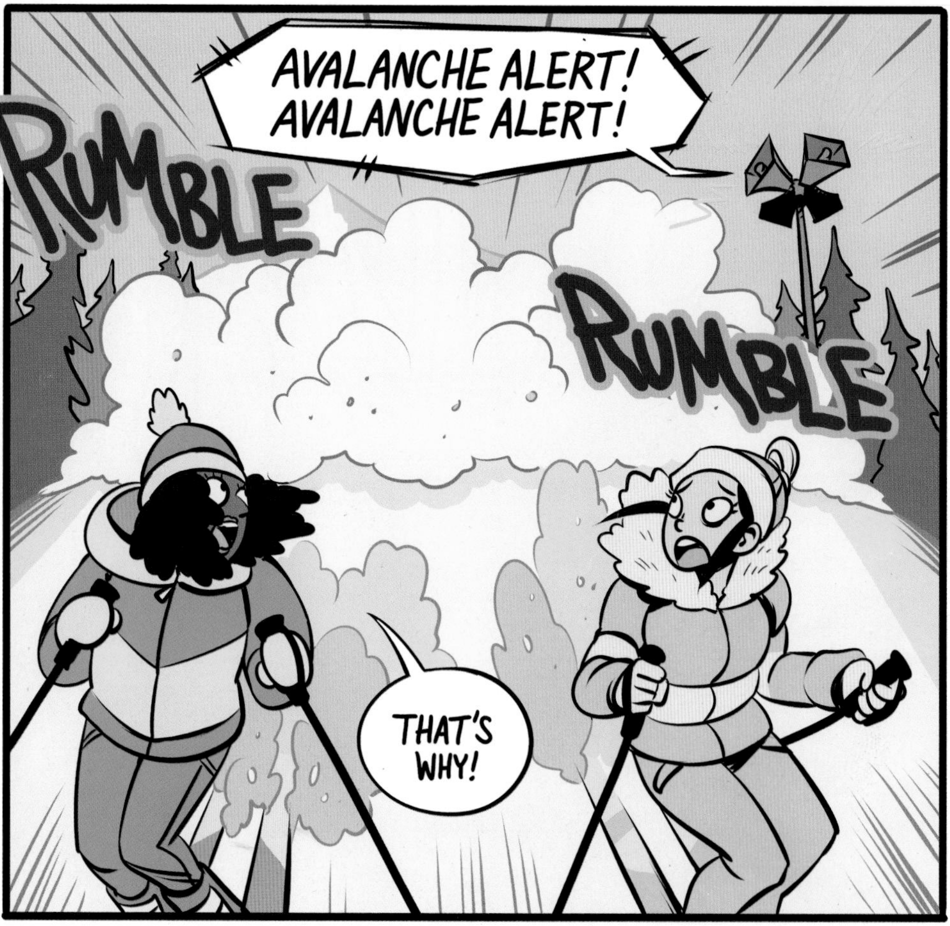
AVALANCHE ALERT! AVALANCHE ALERT!
RUMBLE
RUMBLE
THAT'S WHY!

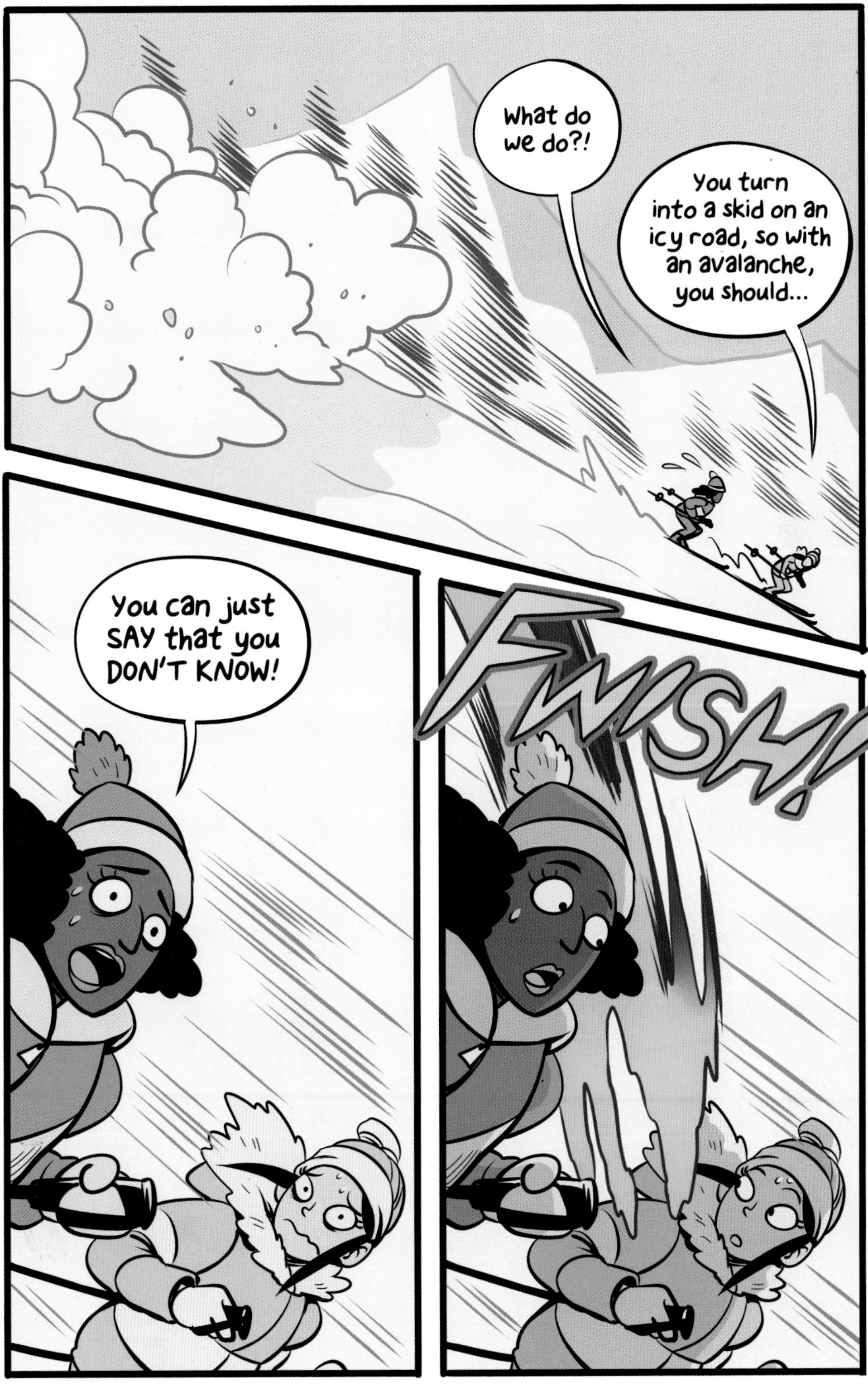
What do we do?!
You turn into a skid on an icy road, so with an avalanche, you should...
You can just SAY that you DON'T KNOW!
FWISH!

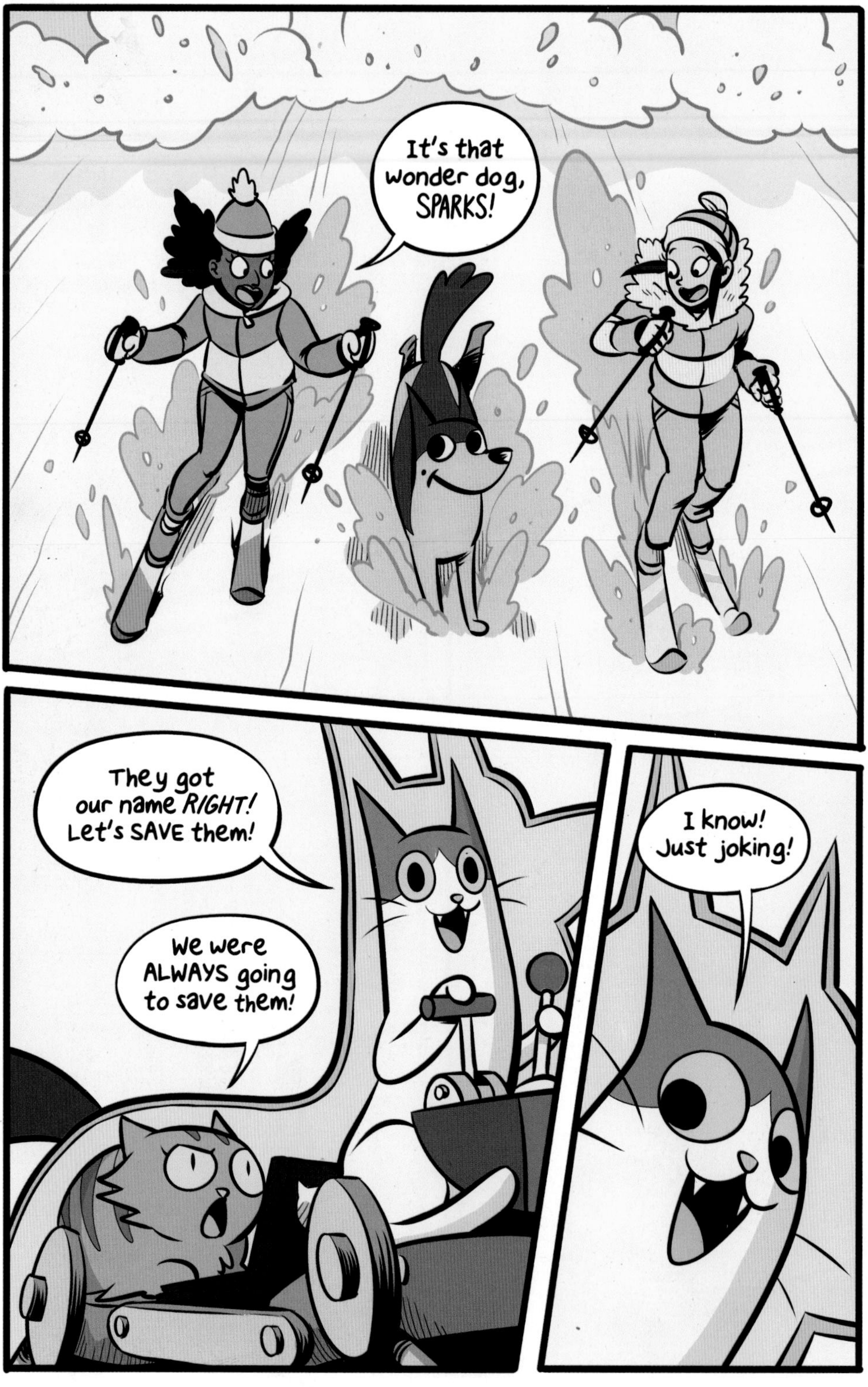
It's that wonder dog, SPARKS!
They got our name RIGHT! Let's SAVE them!
We were ALWAYS going to save them!
I know! Just joking!

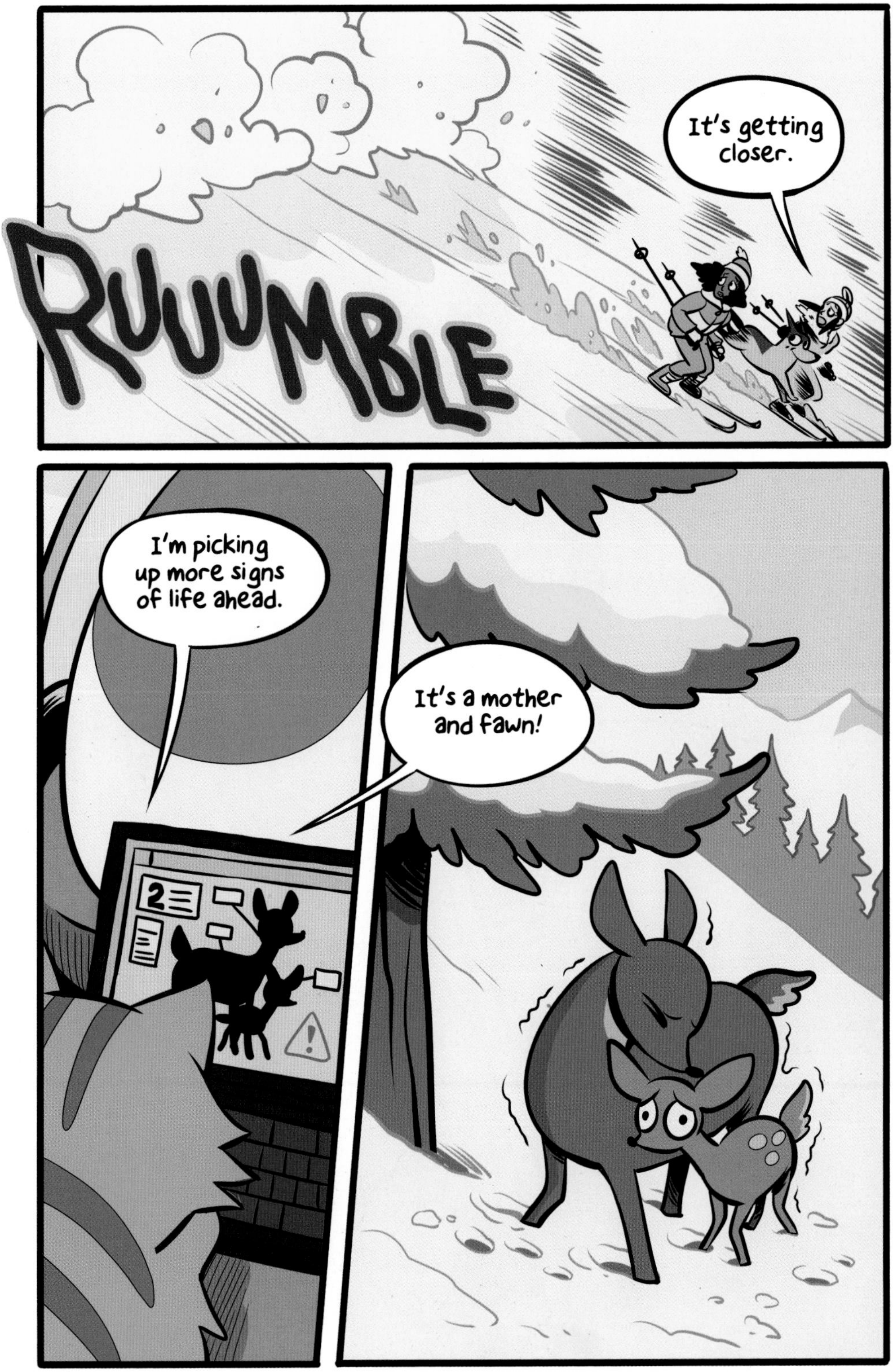
It's getting closer.
RUUUMBLE
I'm picking up more signs of life ahead.
It's a mother and fawn!

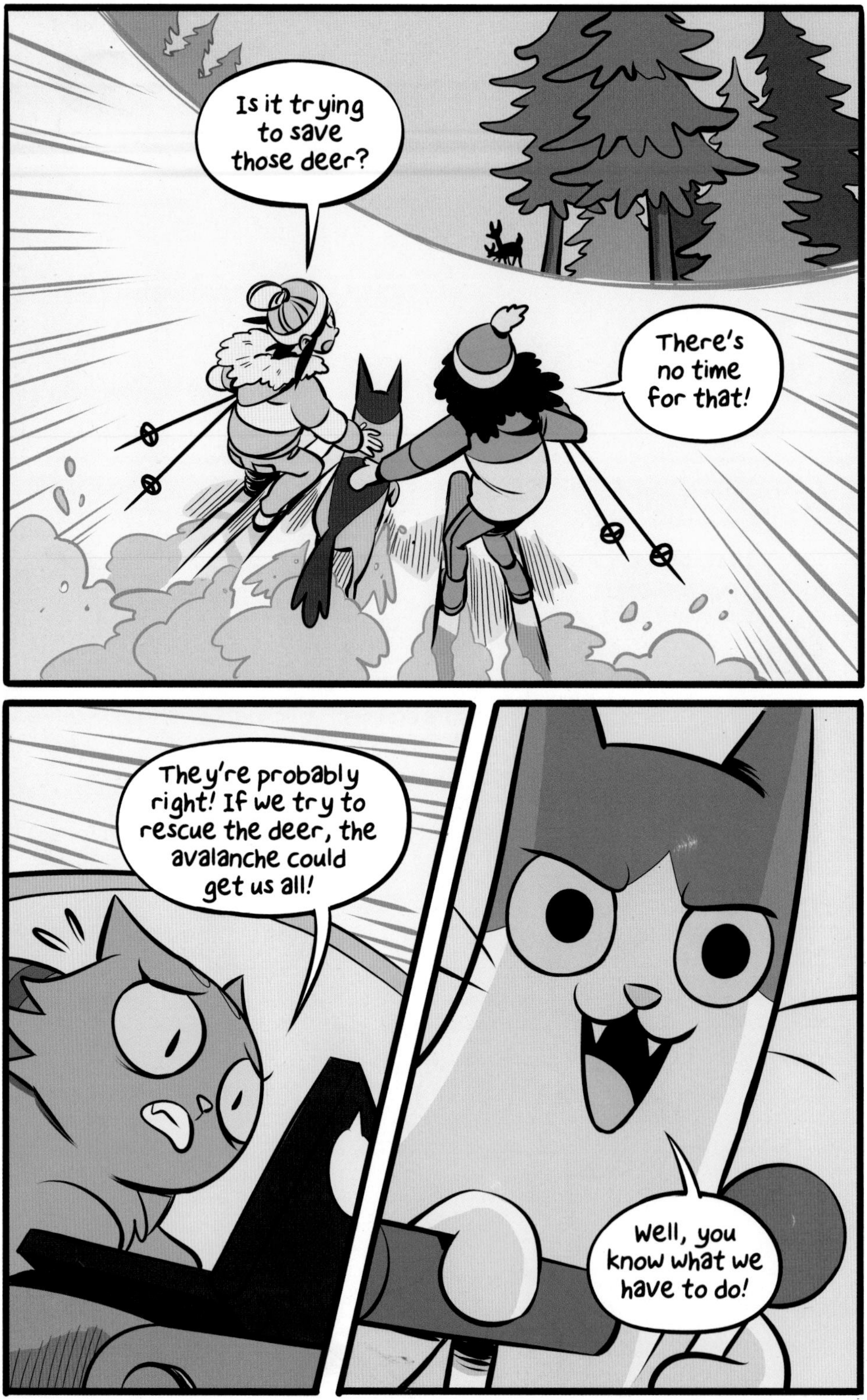
Is it trying to save those deer?
There's no time for that!
They're probably right! If we try to rescue the deer, the avalanche could get us all!
Well, you know what we have to do!

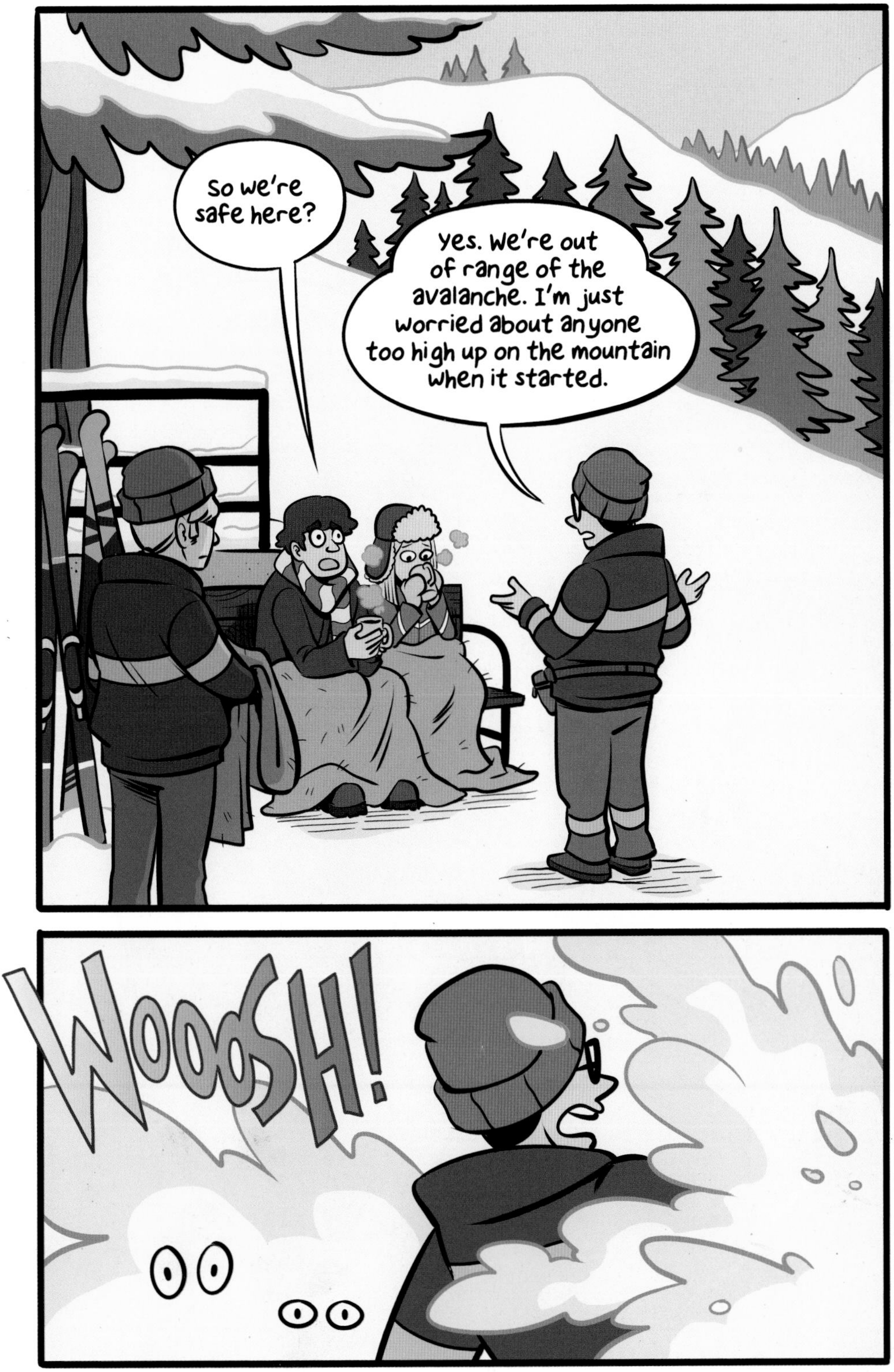
So we're safe here?
Yes. We're out of range of the avalanche. I'm just worried about anyone too high up on the mountain when it started.
WOOSH!

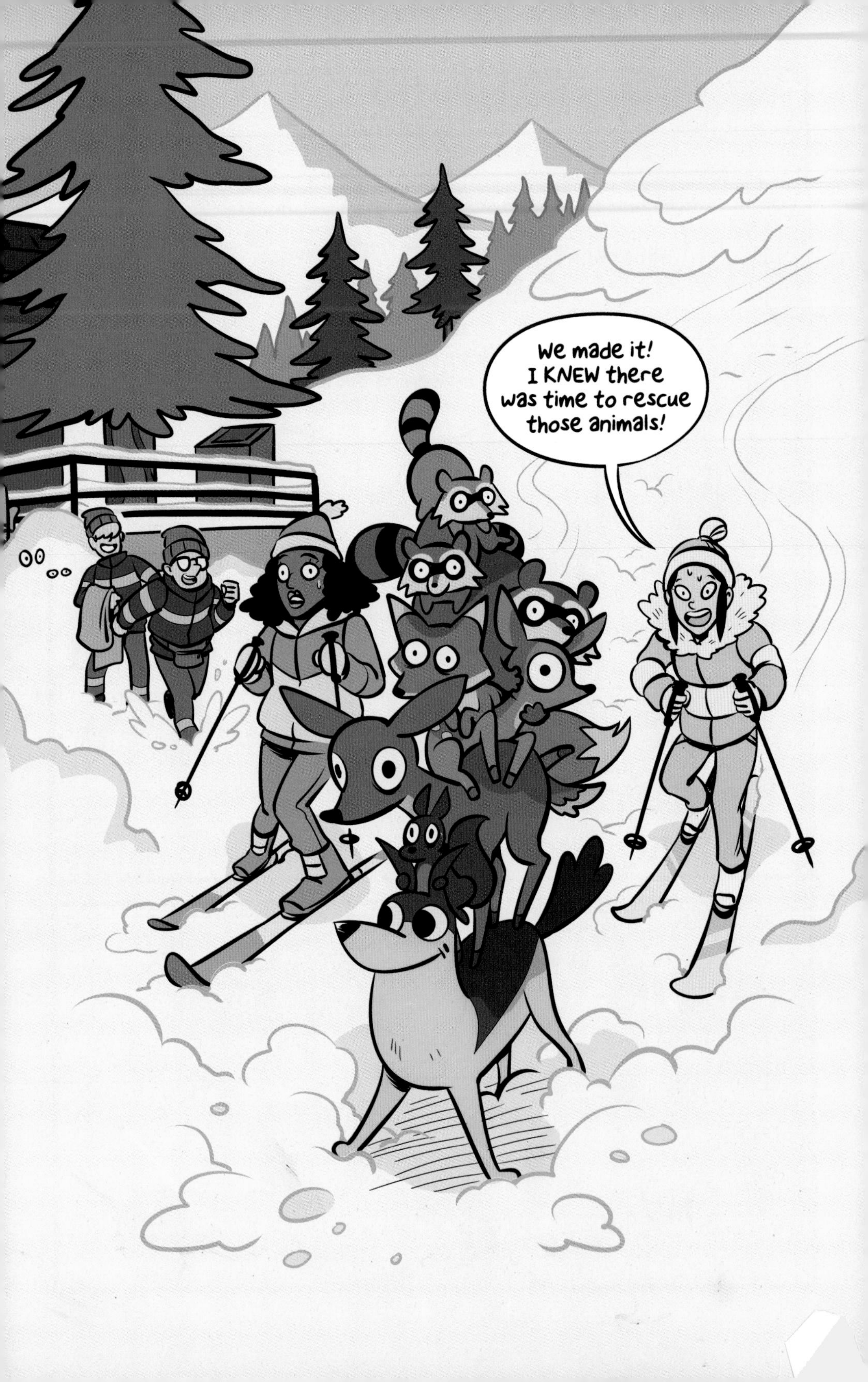
We made it! I KNEW there was time to rescue those animals!

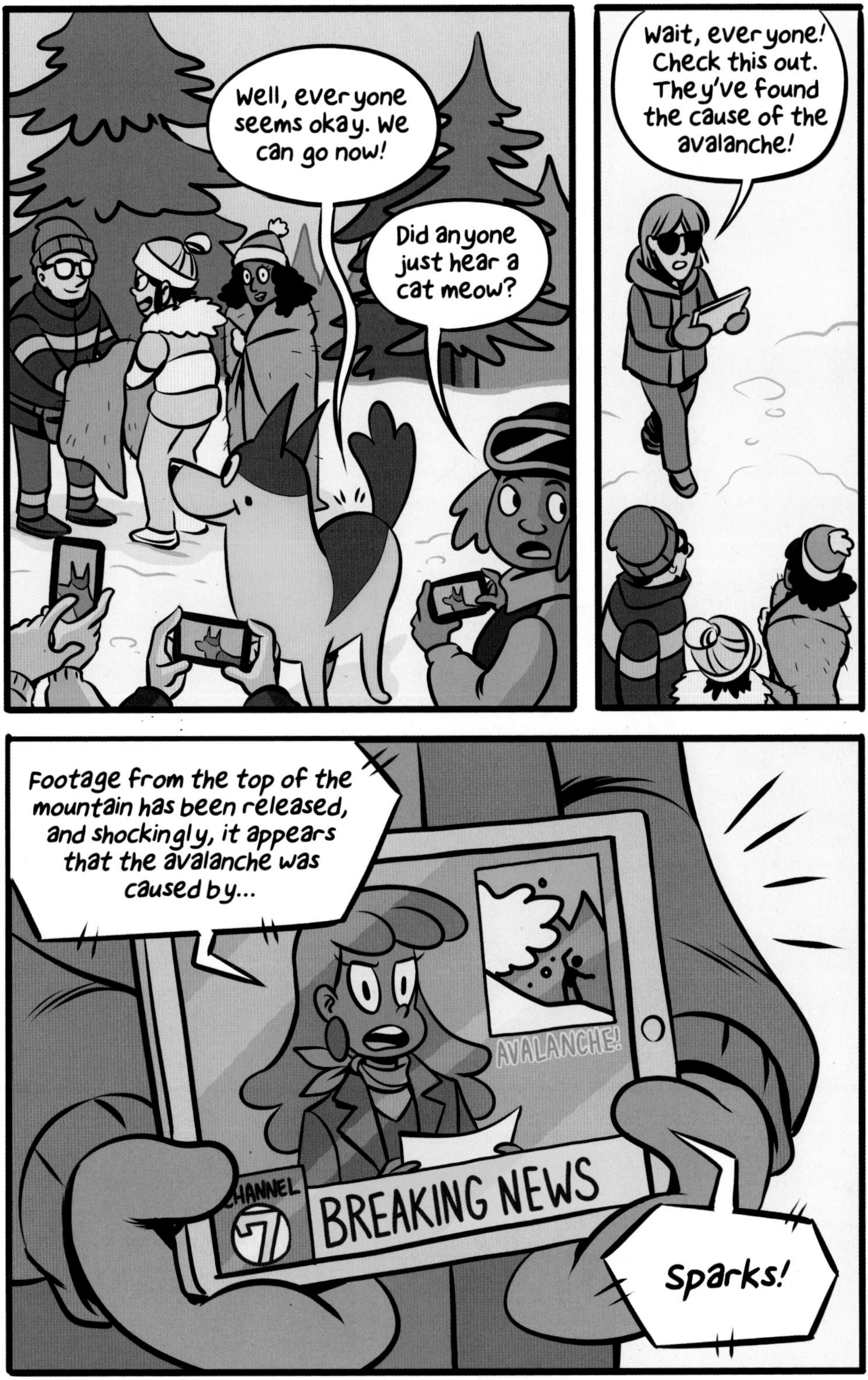
Well, everyone seems okay. We can go now!
Did anyone just hear a cat meow?
Wait, everyone! Check this out. They've found the cause of the avalanche!
Footage from the top of the mountain has been released, and shockingly, it appears that the avalanche was caused by...
AVALANCHE!
CHANNEL 7
BREAKING NEWS
Sparks!

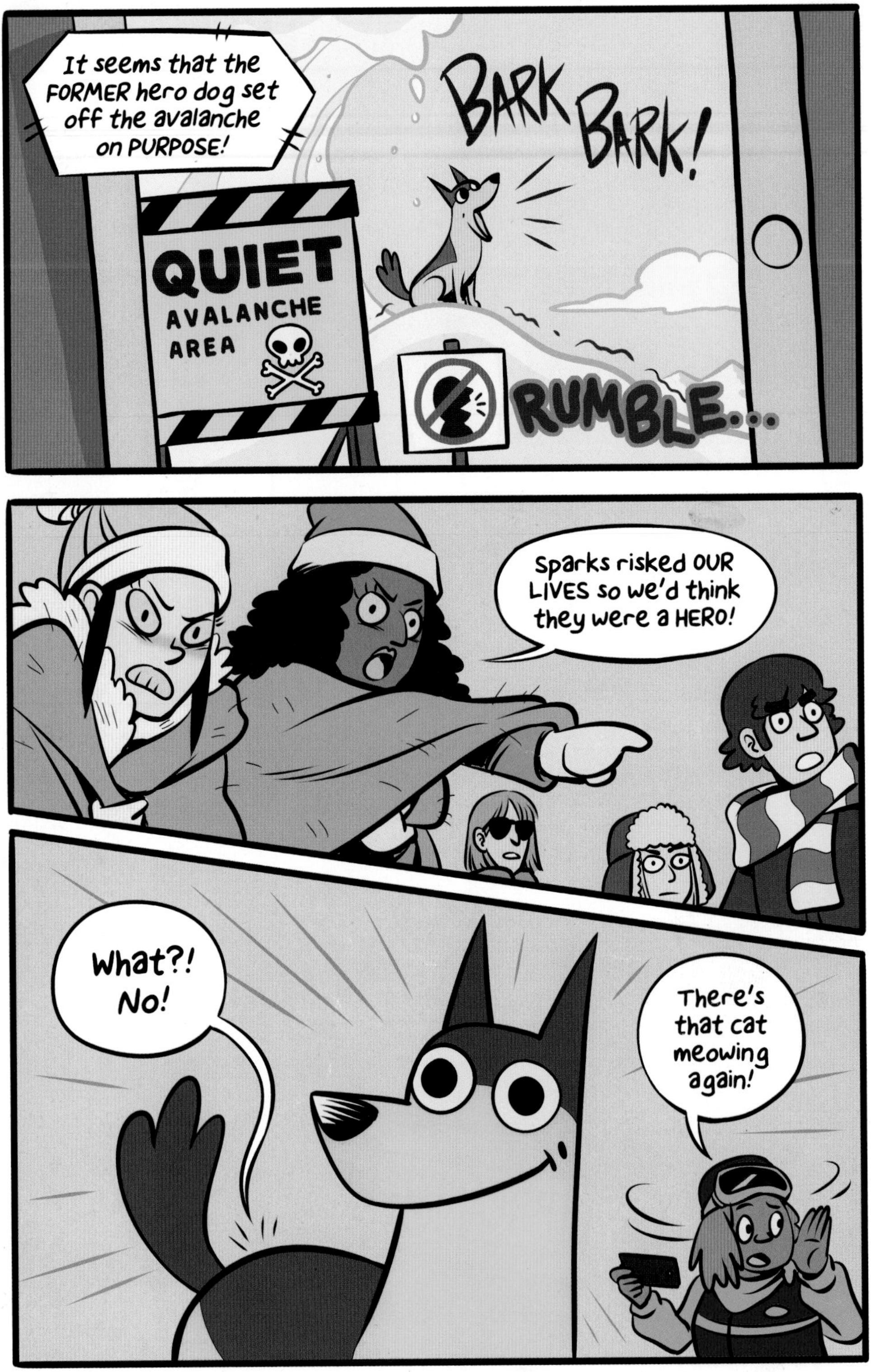
It seems that the FORMER hero dog set off the avalanche on PURPOSE!
BARK BARK!
QUIET
AVALANCHE AREA
RUMBLE...
Sparks risked OUR LIVES so we'd think they were a HERO!
What?! No!
There's that cat meowing again!

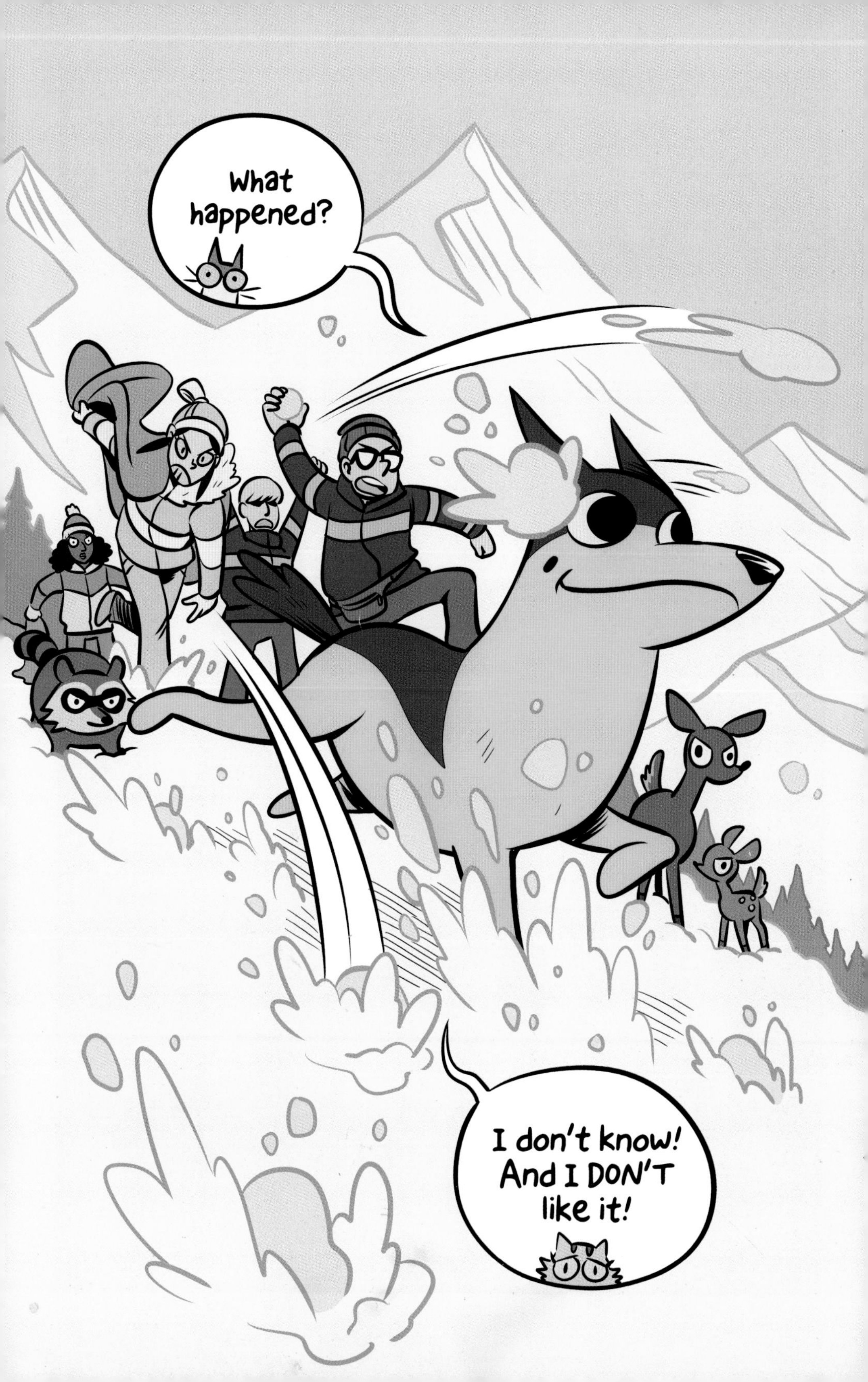
What happened?
I don't know! And I DON'T like it!

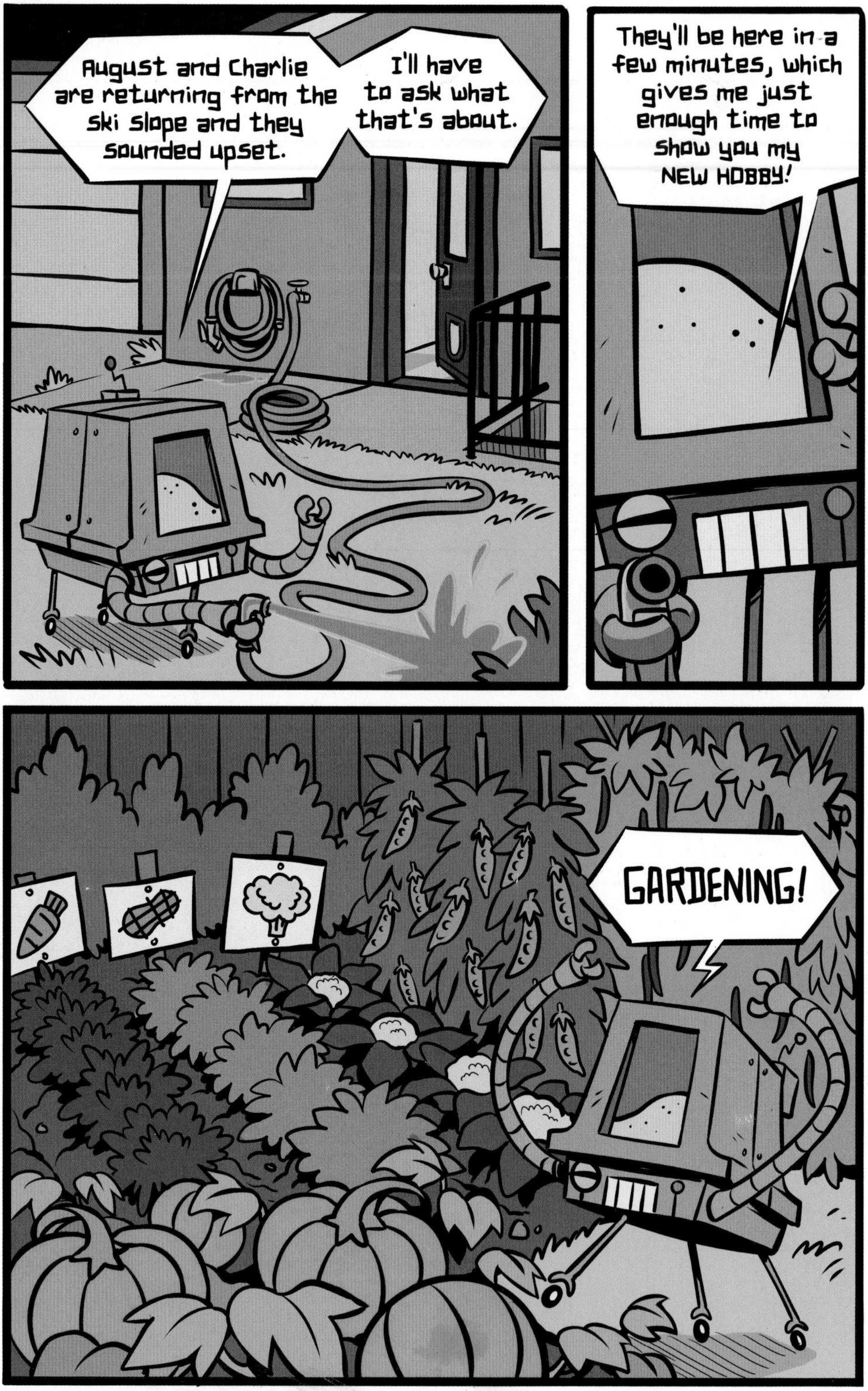
August and Charlie are returning from the ski slope and they sounded upset.
I'll have to ask what that's about.
They'll be here in a few minutes, which gives me just enough time to show you my NEW HOBBY!
GARDENING!

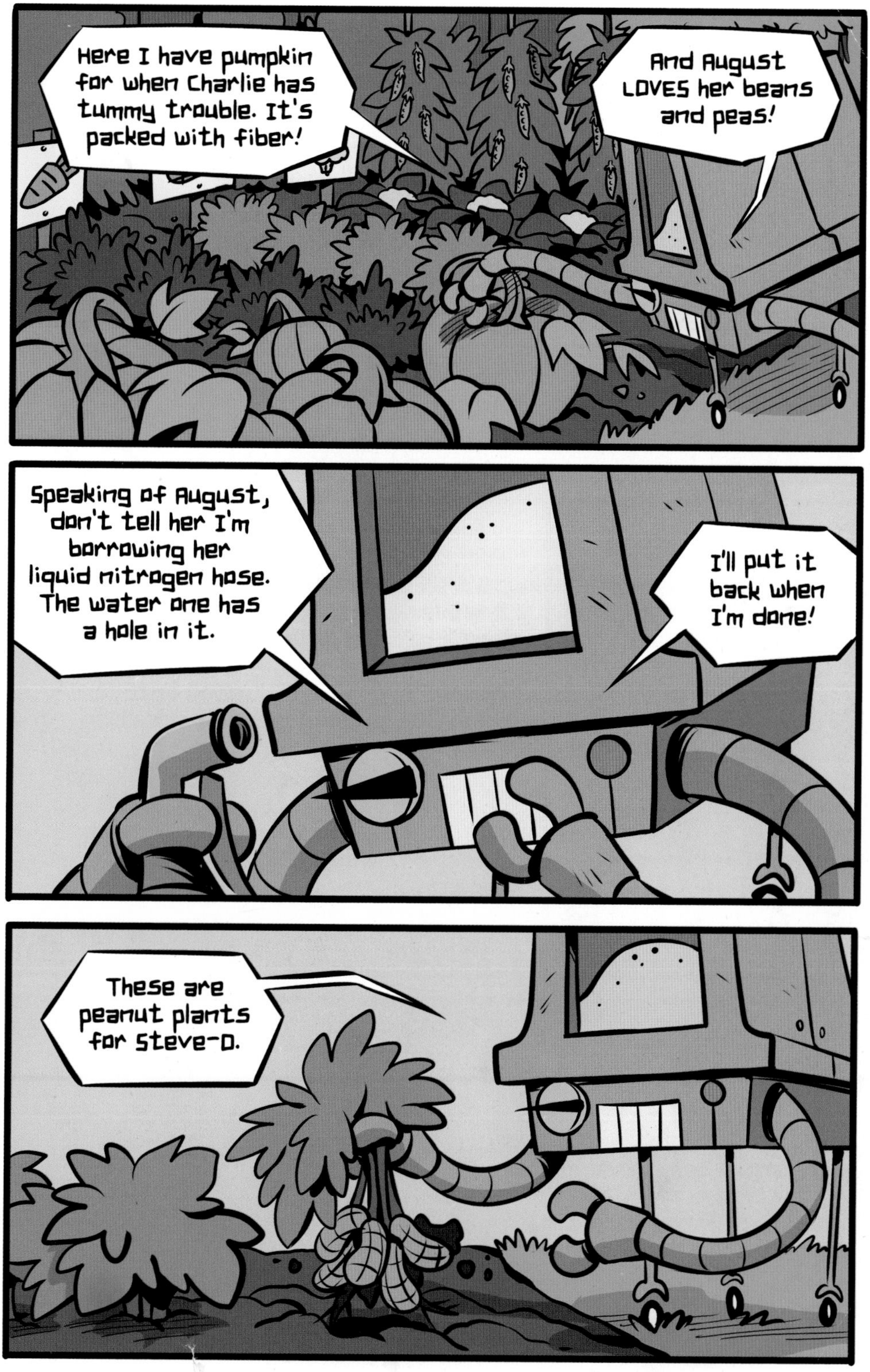
Here I have pumpkin for when Charlie has tummy trouble. It's packed with fiber!
And August LOVES her beans and peas!
Speaking of August, don't tell her I'm borrowing her liquid nitrogen hose. The water one has a hole in it.
I'll put it back when I'm done!
These are peanut plants for Steve-O.

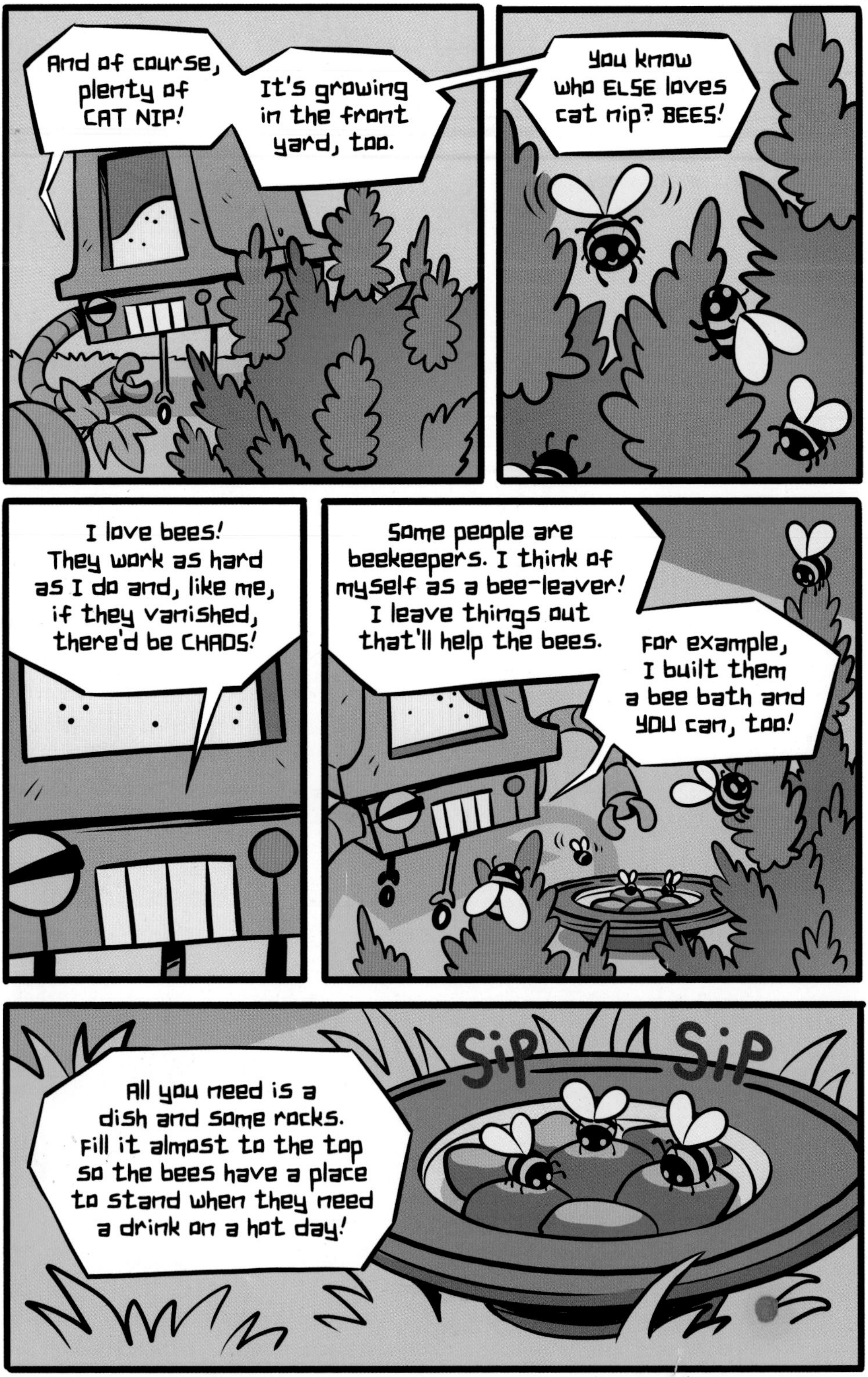
And of course, plenty of CAT NIP!
It's growing in the front yard, too.
You know who ELSE loves cat nip? BEES!
I love bees! They work as hard as I do and, like me, if they vanished, there'd be CHAOS!
Some people are beekeepers. I think of myself as a bee-leaver! I leave things out that'll help the bees.
For example, I built them a bee bath and YOU can, too!
SIP SIP
All you need is a dish and some rocks. Fill it almost to the top so the bees have a place to stand when they need a drink on a hot day!

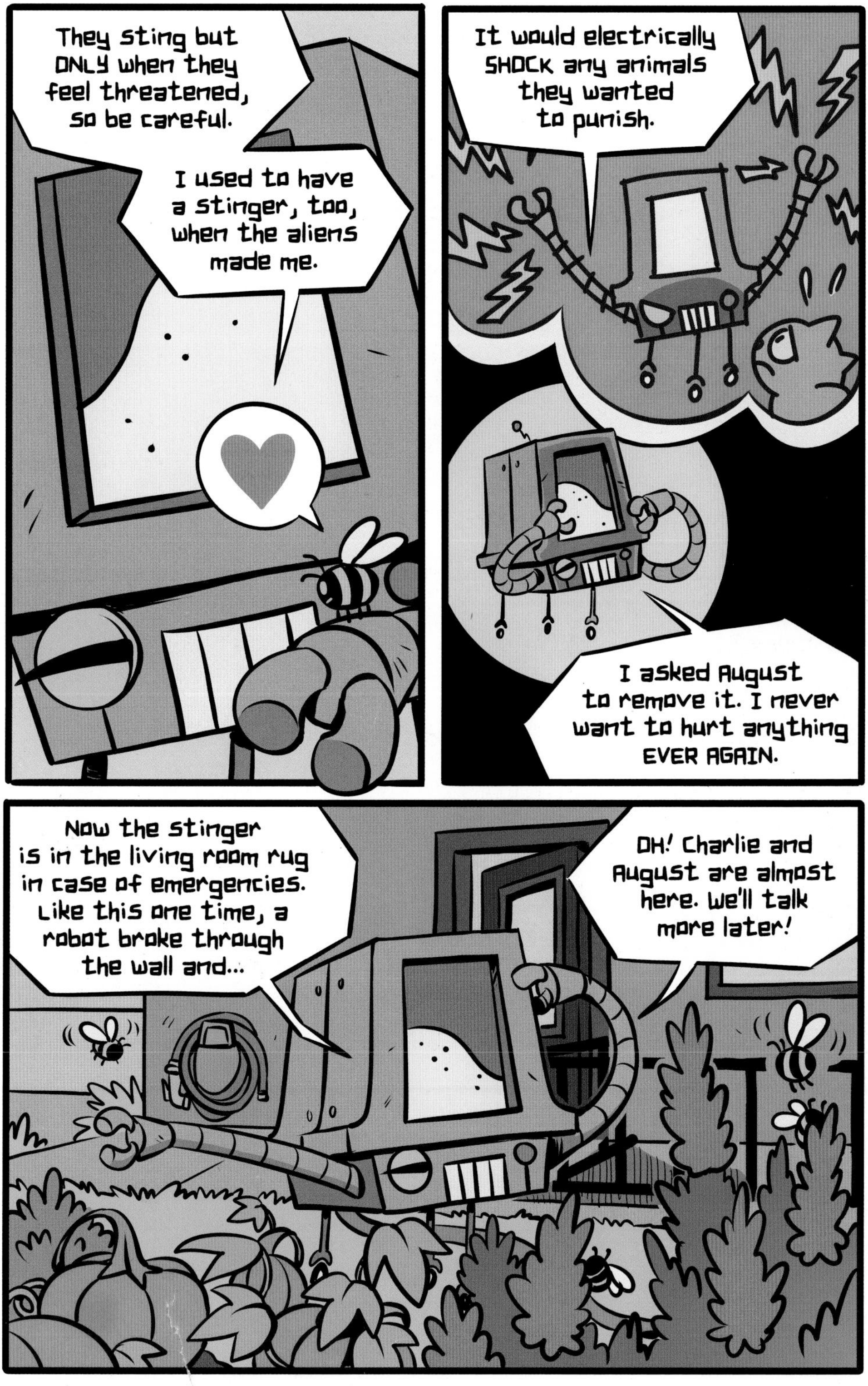
They sting but ONLY when they feel threatened, so be careful.
I used to have a stinger, too, when the aliens made me.
It would electrically SHOCK any animals they wanted to punish.
I asked August to remove it. I never want to hurt anything EVER AGAIN.
Now the stinger is in the living room rug in case of emergencies. Like this one time, a robot broke through the wall and...
OH! Charlie and August are almost here. We'll talk more later!

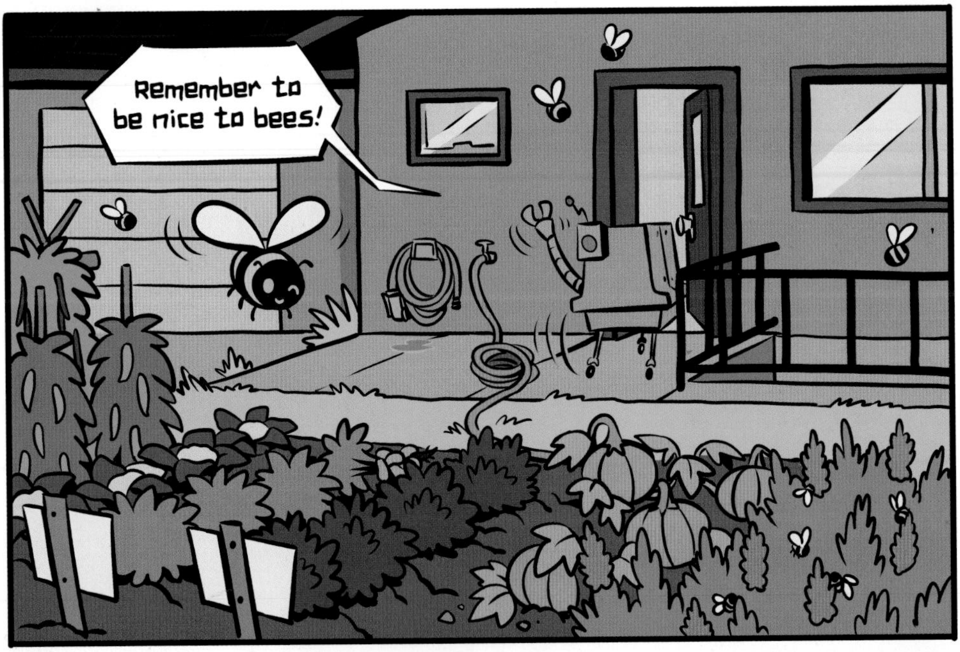
Remember to be nice to bees!

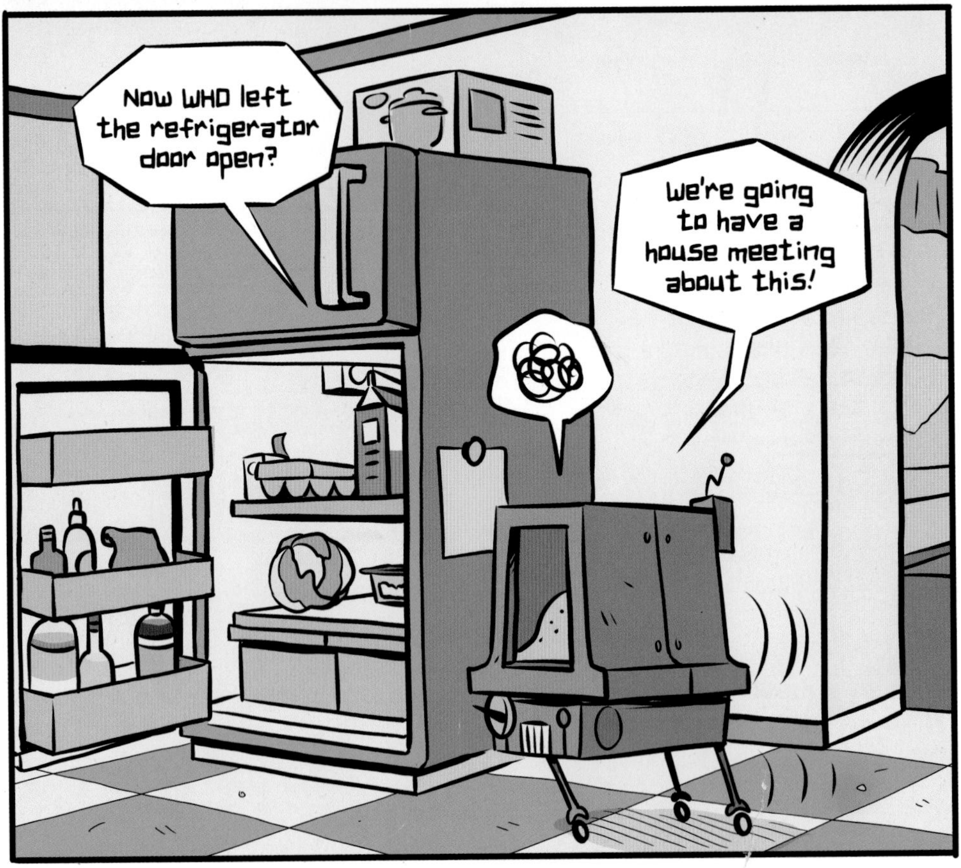
Now WHO left the refrigerator door open?
We're going to have a house meeting about this!

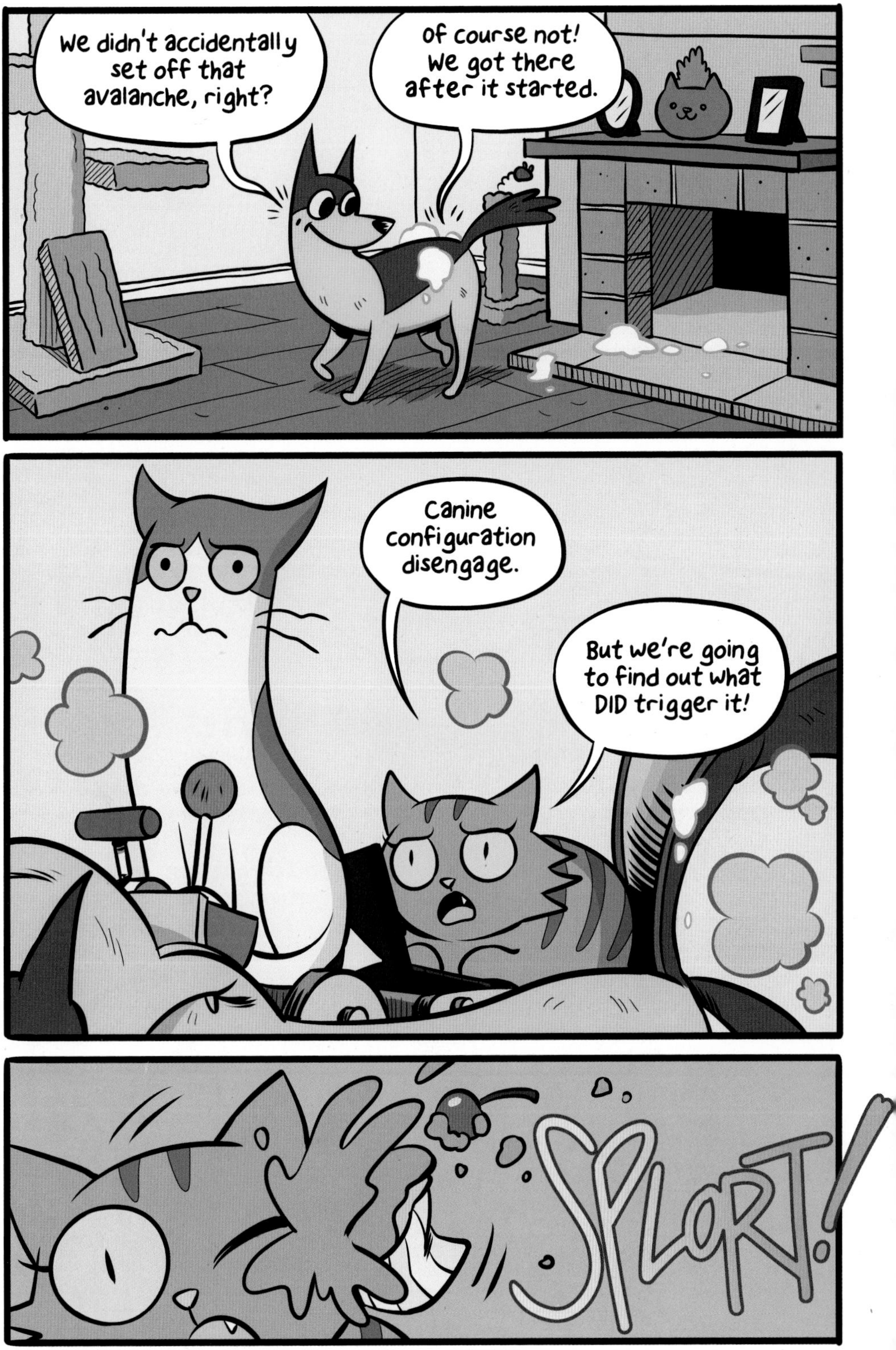
We didn't accidentally set off that avalanche, right?
Of course not! We got there after it started.
Canine configuration disengage.
But we're going to find out what DID trigger it!
SPLORT!

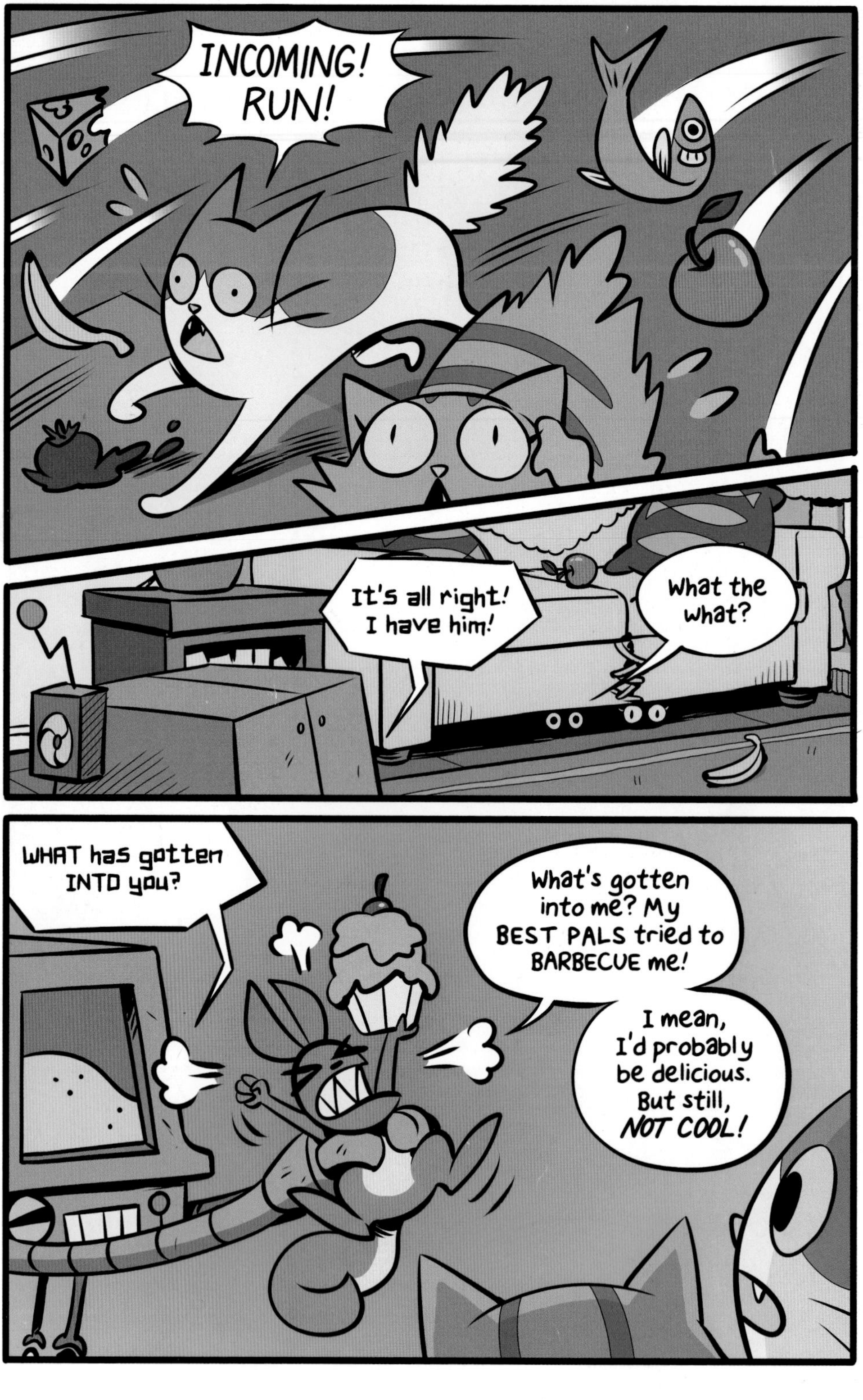
INCOMING! RUN!
It's all right! I have him!
What the what?
WHAT has gotten INTO you?
What's gotten into me? My BEST PALS tried to BARBECUE me!
I mean, I'd probably be delicious. But still, NOT COOL!

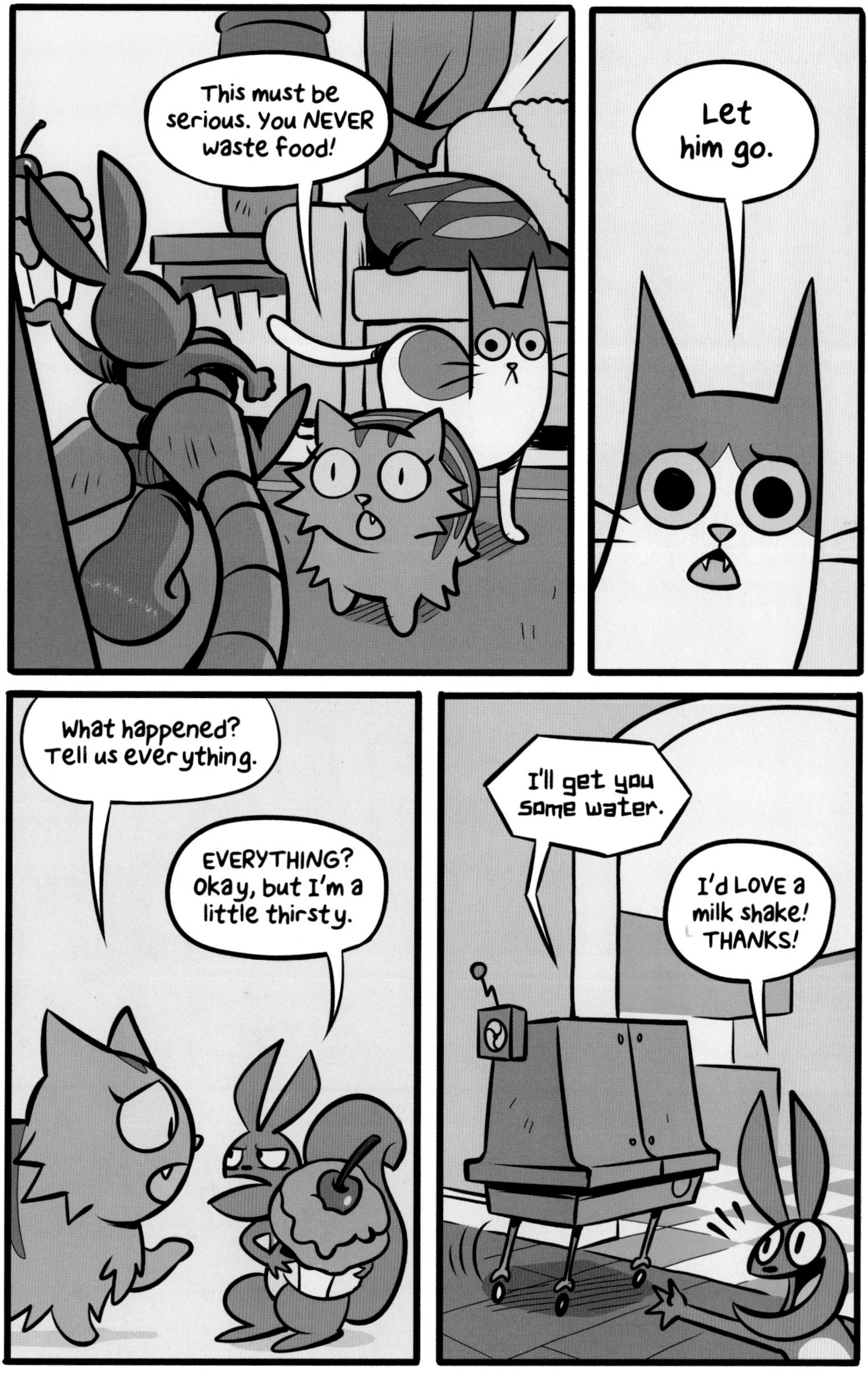
This must be serious. You NEVER waste food!
Let him go.
What happened? Tell us everything.
EVERYTHING? Okay, but I'm a little thirsty.
I'll get you some water.
I'd LOVE a milk shake! THANKS!

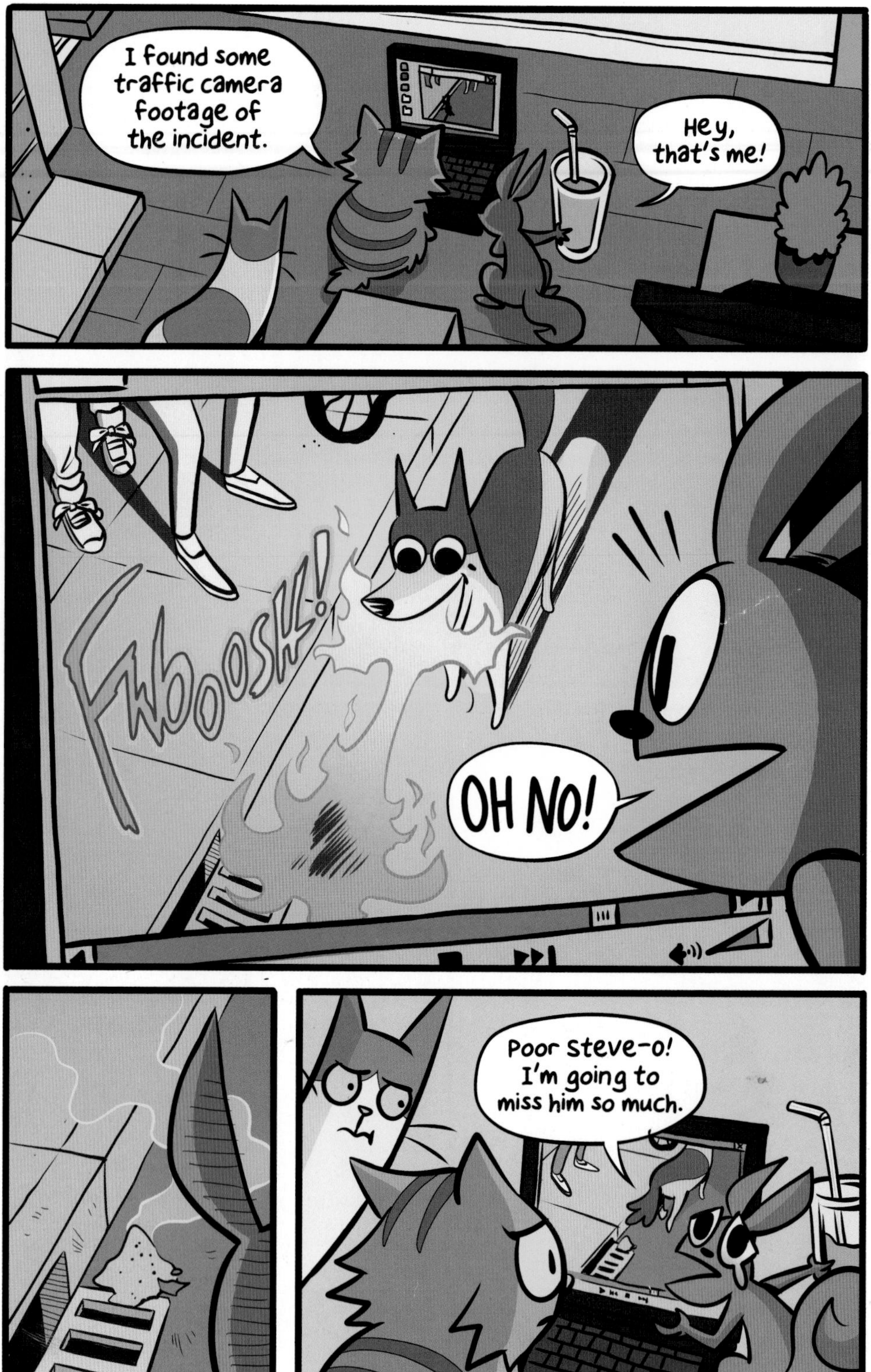
I found some traffic camera footage of the incident.
Hey, that's me!
FWOOSH!
OH NO!
Poor Steve-o! I'm going to miss him so much.

You're not dead.

OH YEAH! That's right!

FWOOOSH!

I jumped into the storm drain!

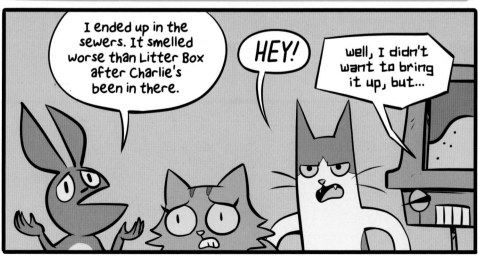

I ended up in the sewers. It smelled worse than Litter Box after Charlie's been in there.

HEY!

Well, I didn't want to bring it up, but...

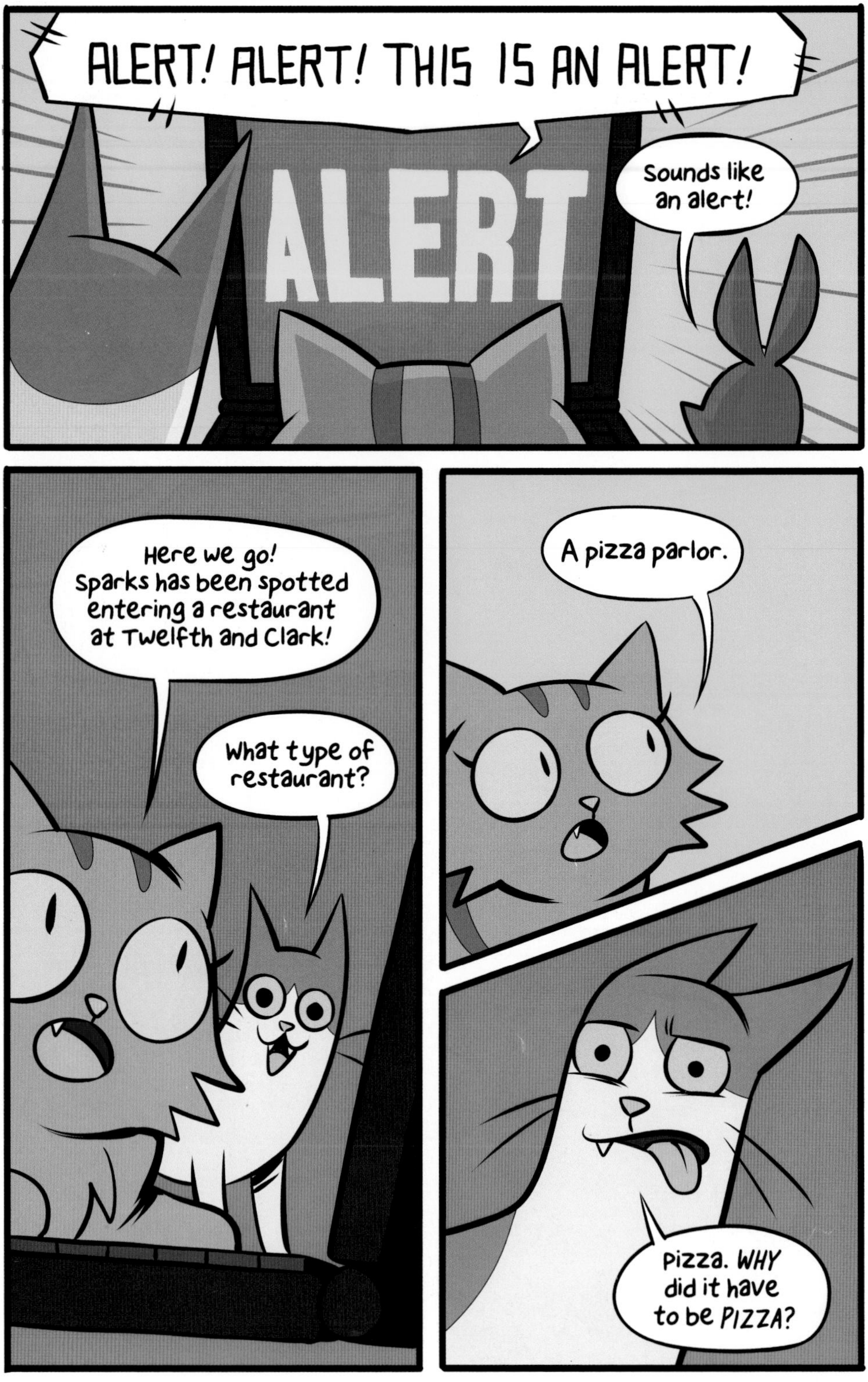
ALERT! ALERT! THIS IS AN ALERT!
ALERT
Sounds like an alert!
Here we go! Sparks has been spotted entering a restaurant at Twelfth and Clark!
What type of restaurant?
A pizza parlor.
Pizza. WHY did it have to be PIZZA?

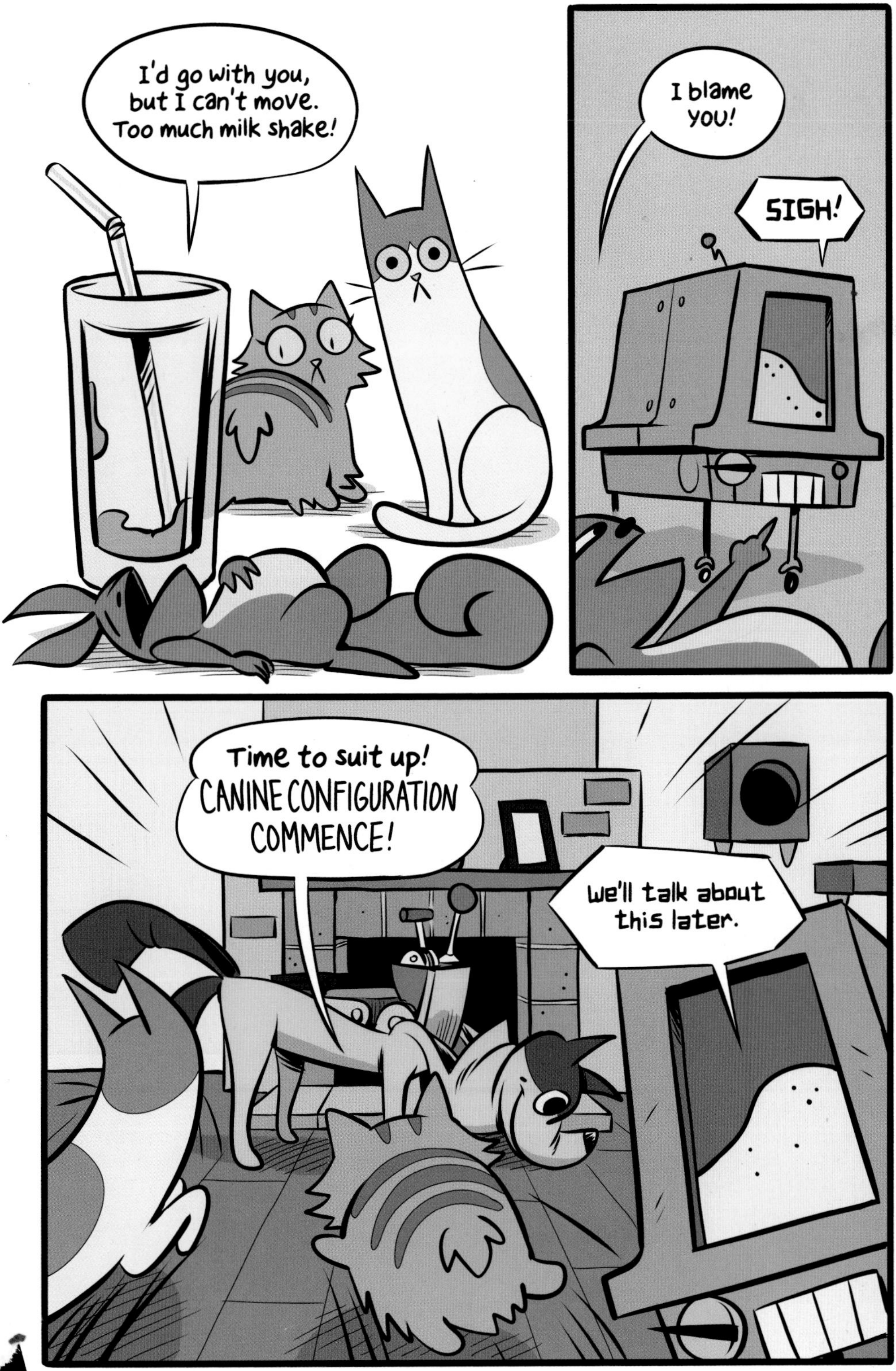
I'd go with you, but I can't move. Too much milk shake!
I blame you!
SIGH!
Time to suit up! CANINE CONFIGURATION COMMENCE!
We'll talk about this later.

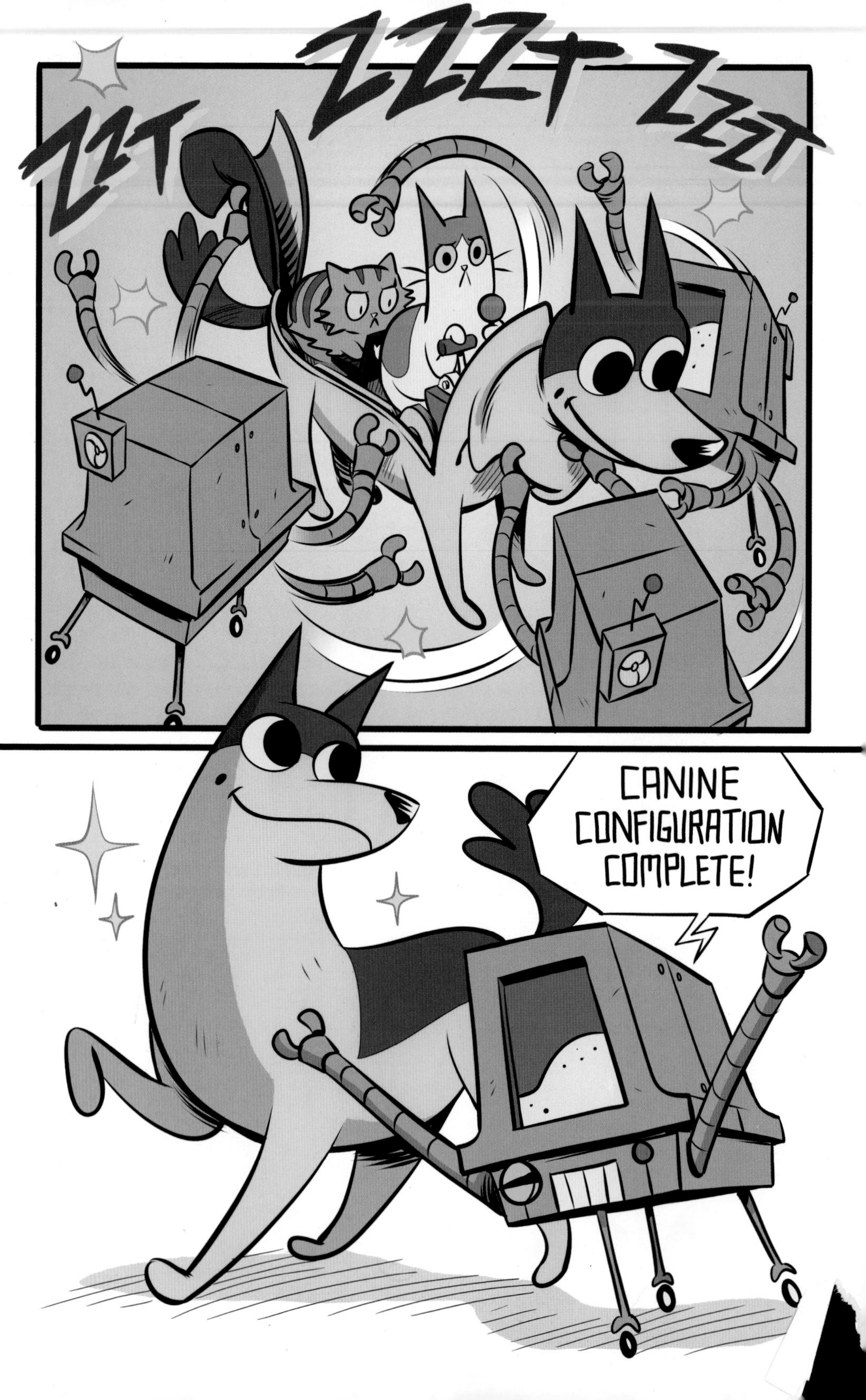
ZZT
ZZZT ZZZT
CANINE CONFIGURATION COMPLETE!

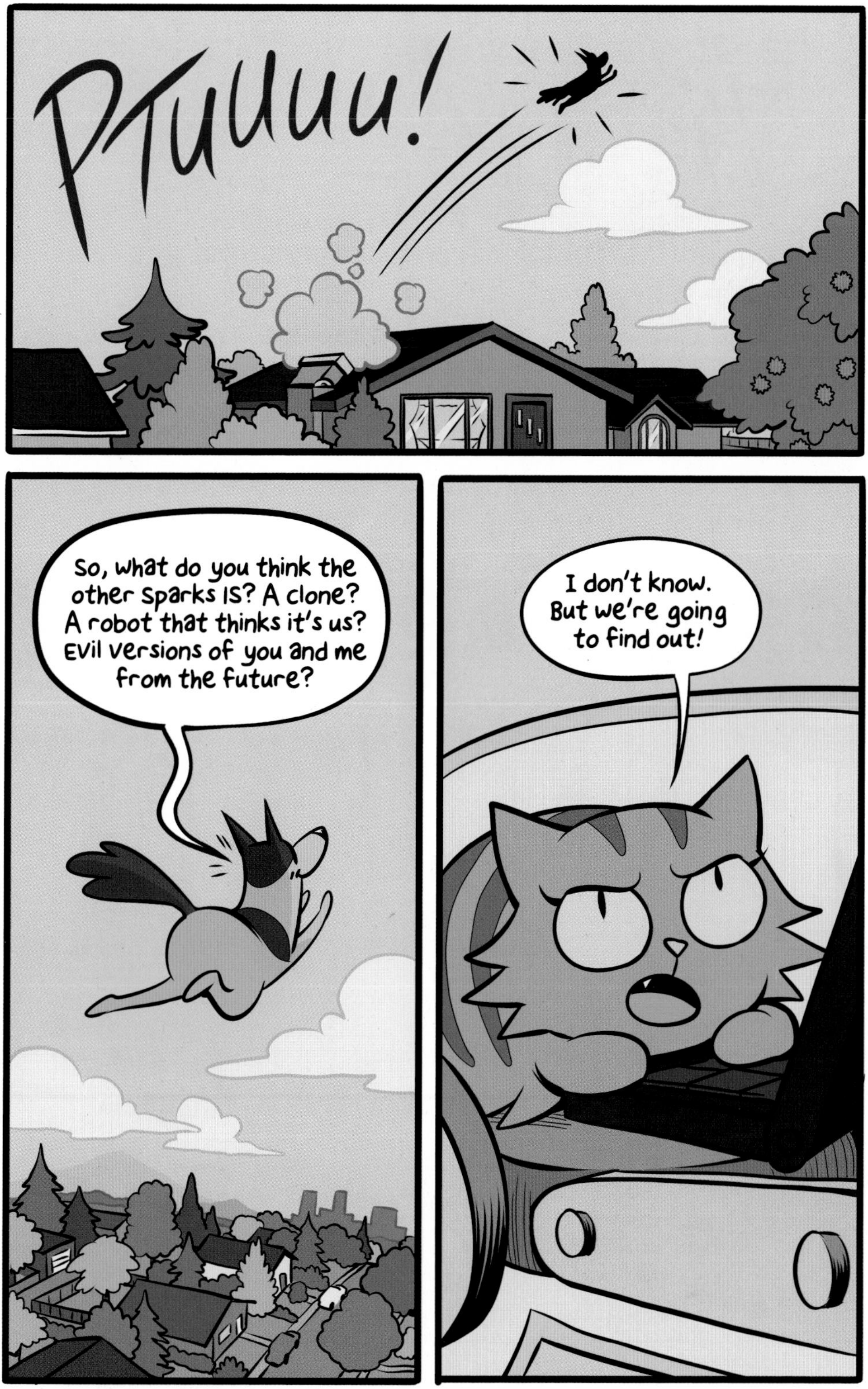
PTUUUU!
So, what do you think the other Sparks IS? A clone? A robot that thinks it's us? Evil versions of you and me from the future?
I don't know. But we're going to find out!

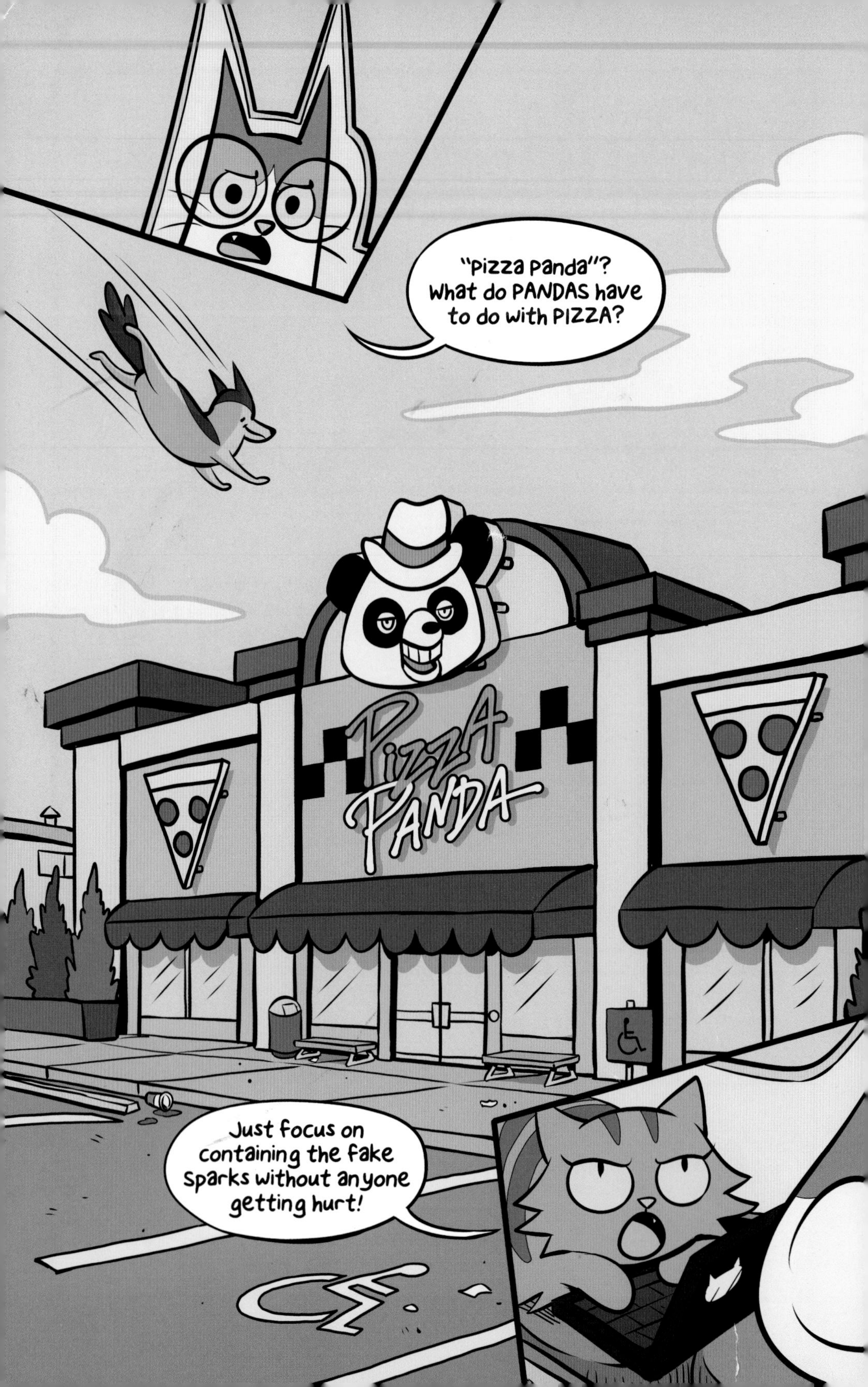
"pizza panda"? What do PANDAS have to do with PIZZA?
Pizza Panda
Just focus on containing the fake sparks without anyone getting hurt!

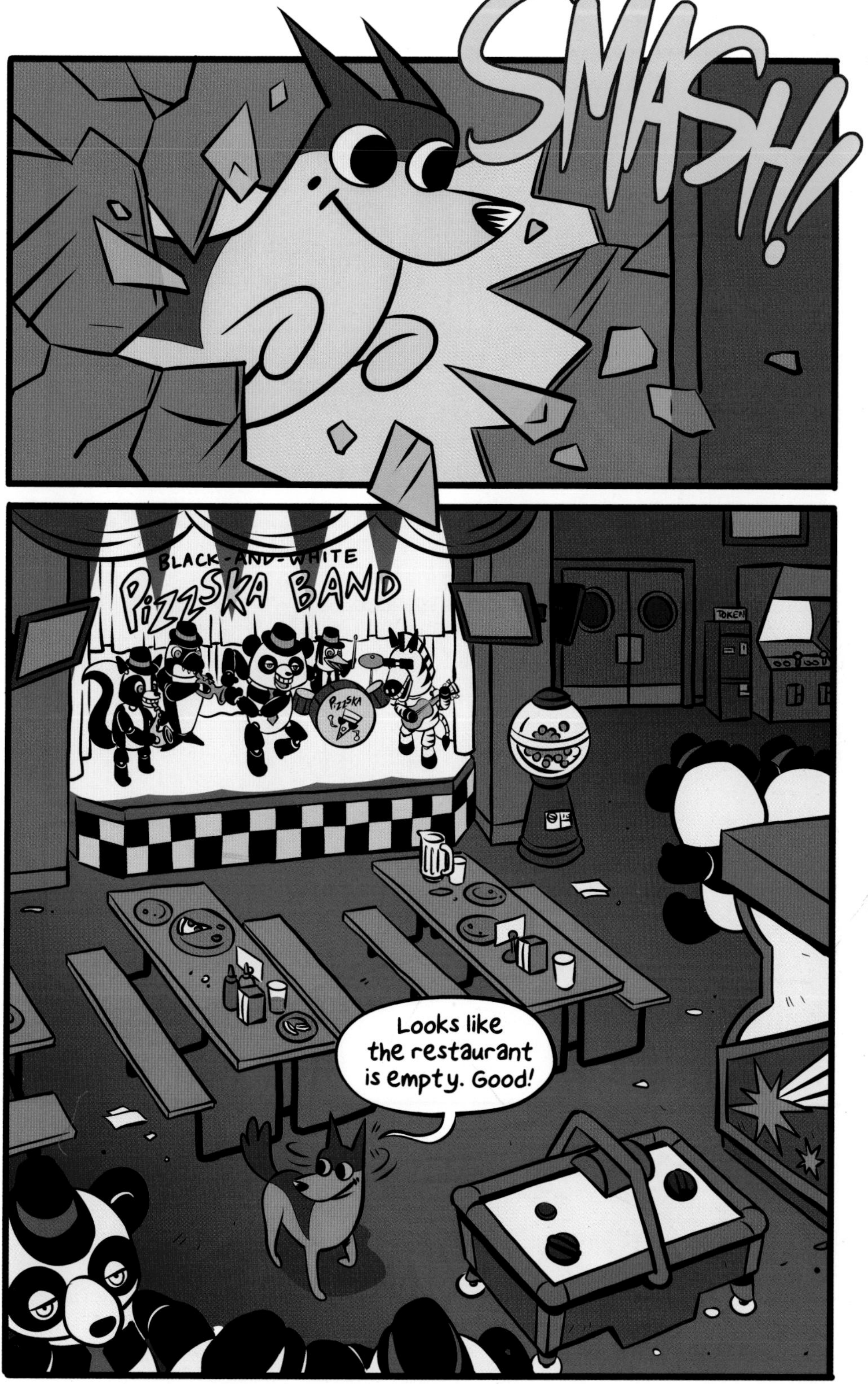
SMASH!!
BLACK-AND-WHITE
PIZZSKA BAND
PIZZSKA
TOKEN
Looks like the restaurant is empty. Good!

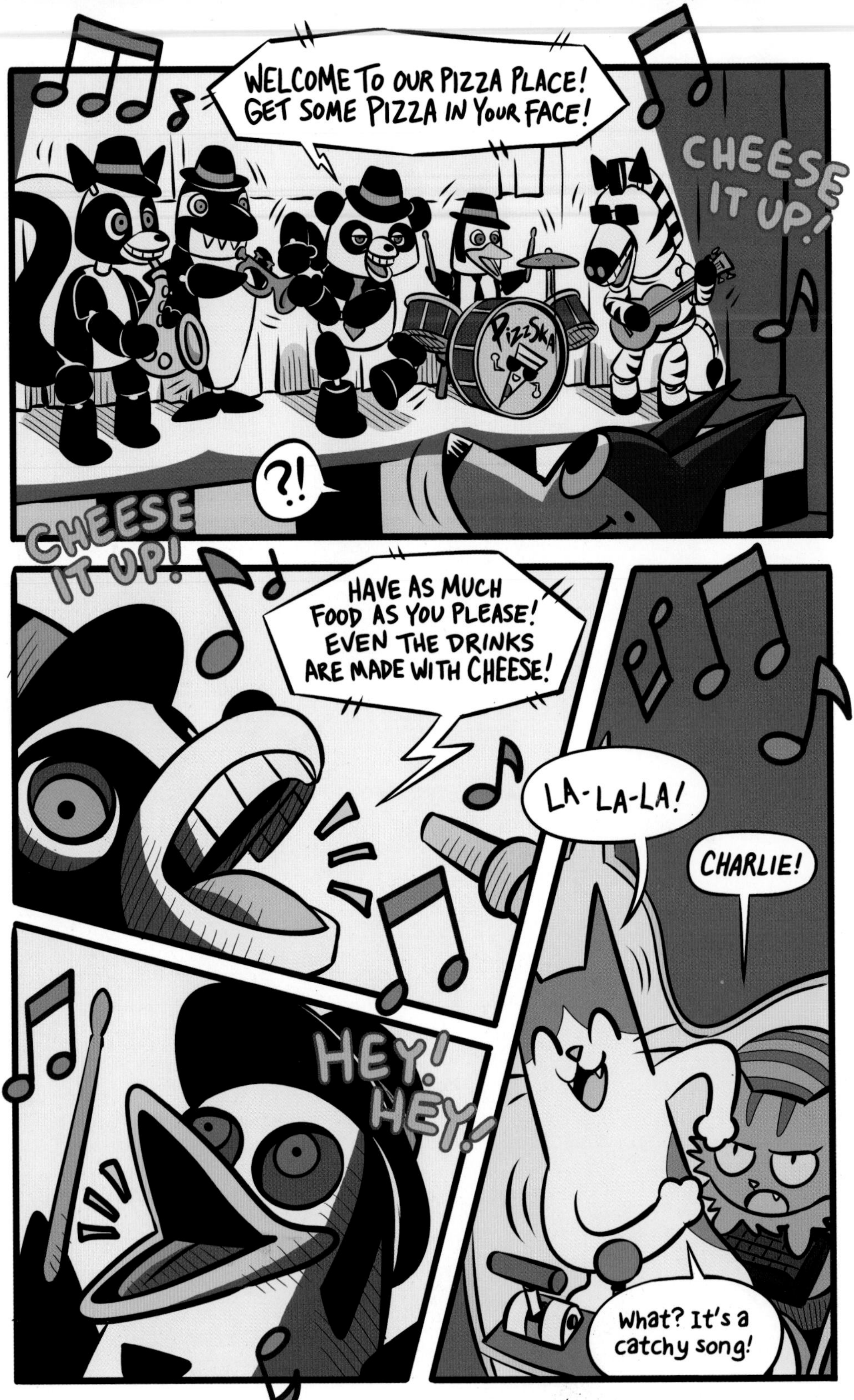
WELCOME TO OUR PIZZA PLACE! GET SOME PIZZA IN YOUR FACE!
CHEESE IT UP!
PIZZSKA
?!
CHEESE IT UP!
HAVE AS MUCH FOOD AS YOU PLEASE! EVEN THE DRINKS ARE MADE WITH CHEESE!
LA-LA-LA!
CHARLIE!
HEY! HEY!
What? It's a catchy song!

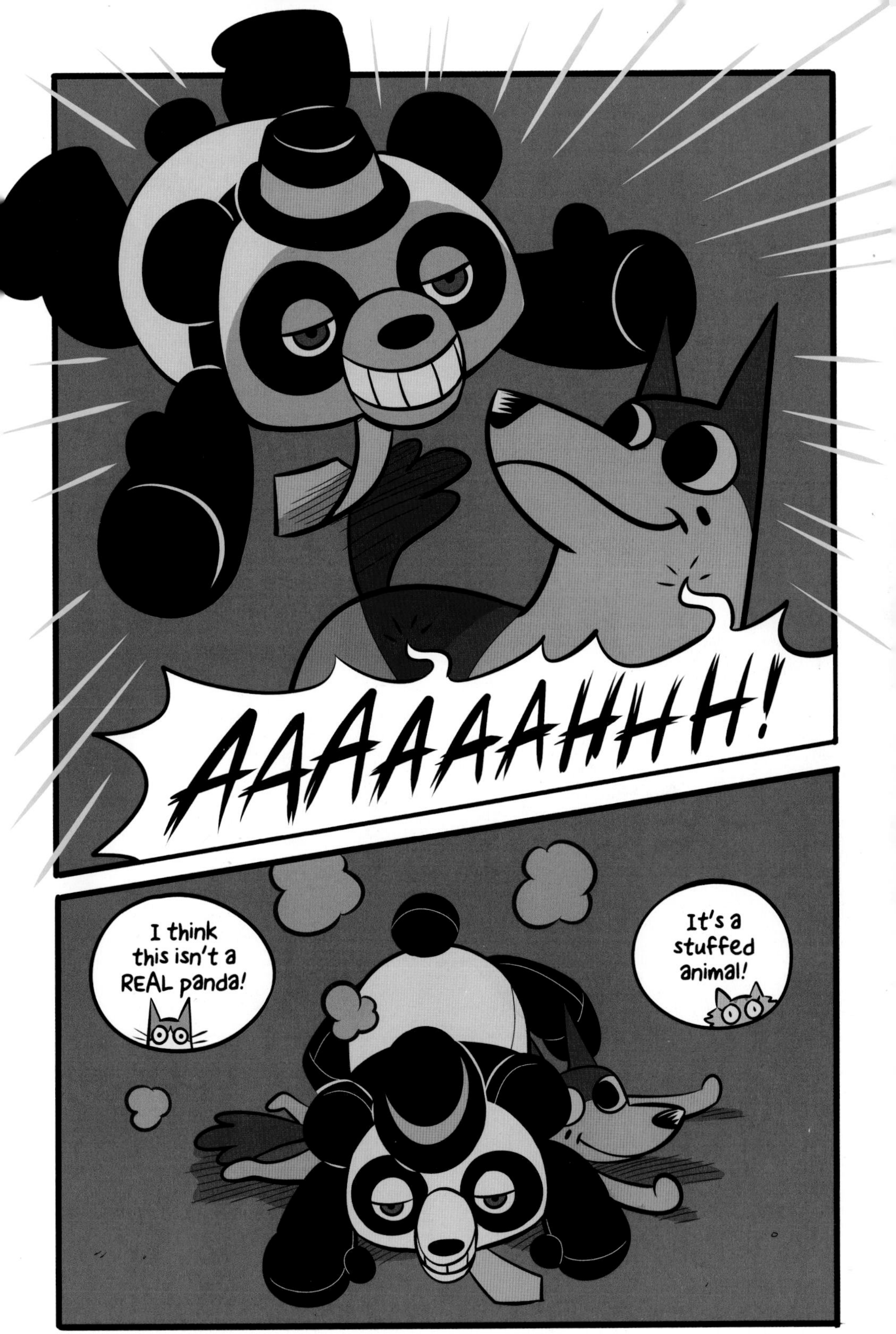
AAAAAAAHHH!
I think this isn't a REAL panda!
It's a stuffed animal!

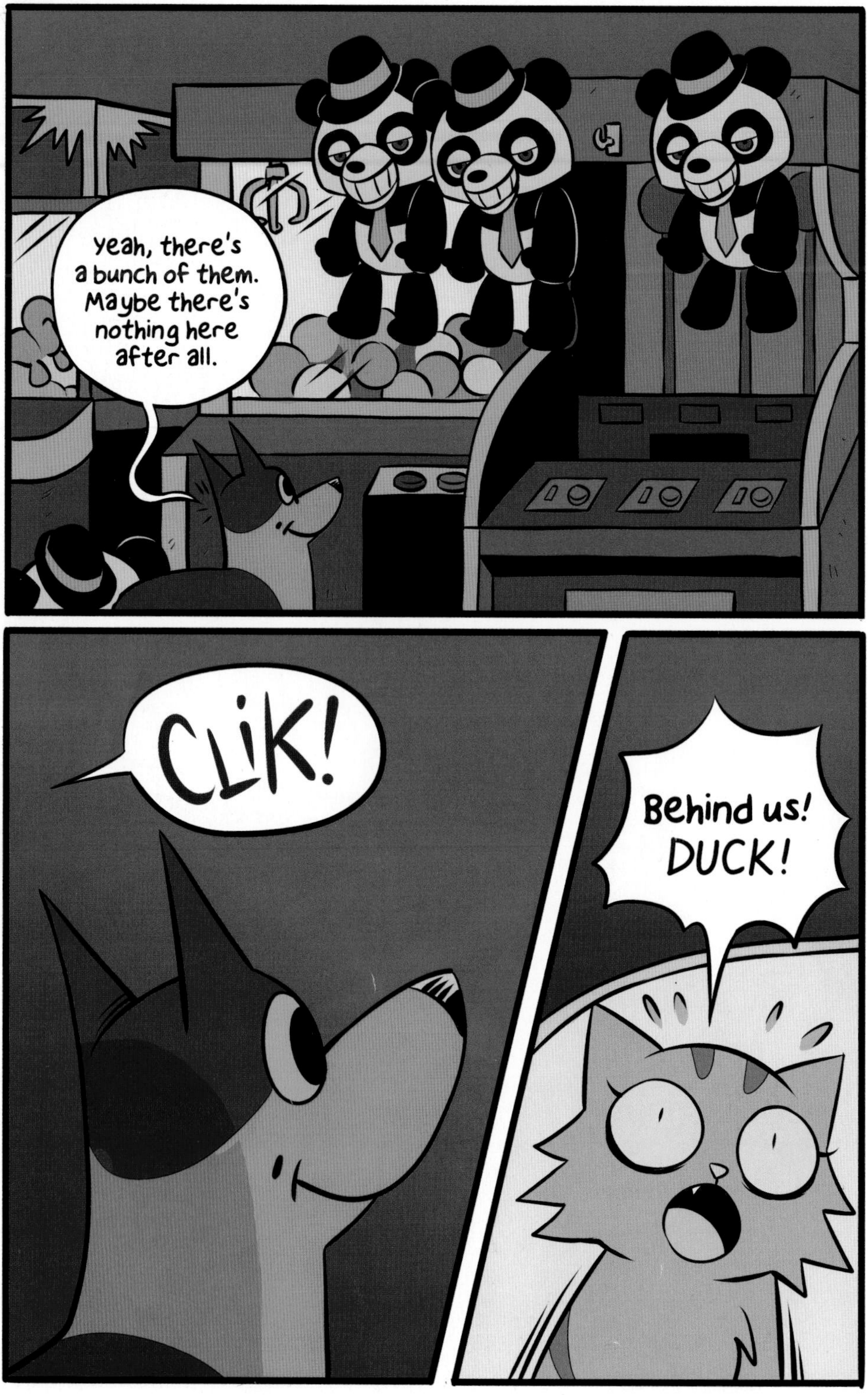
yeah, there's a bunch of them. Maybe there's nothing here after all.
CLIK!
Behind us! DUCK!

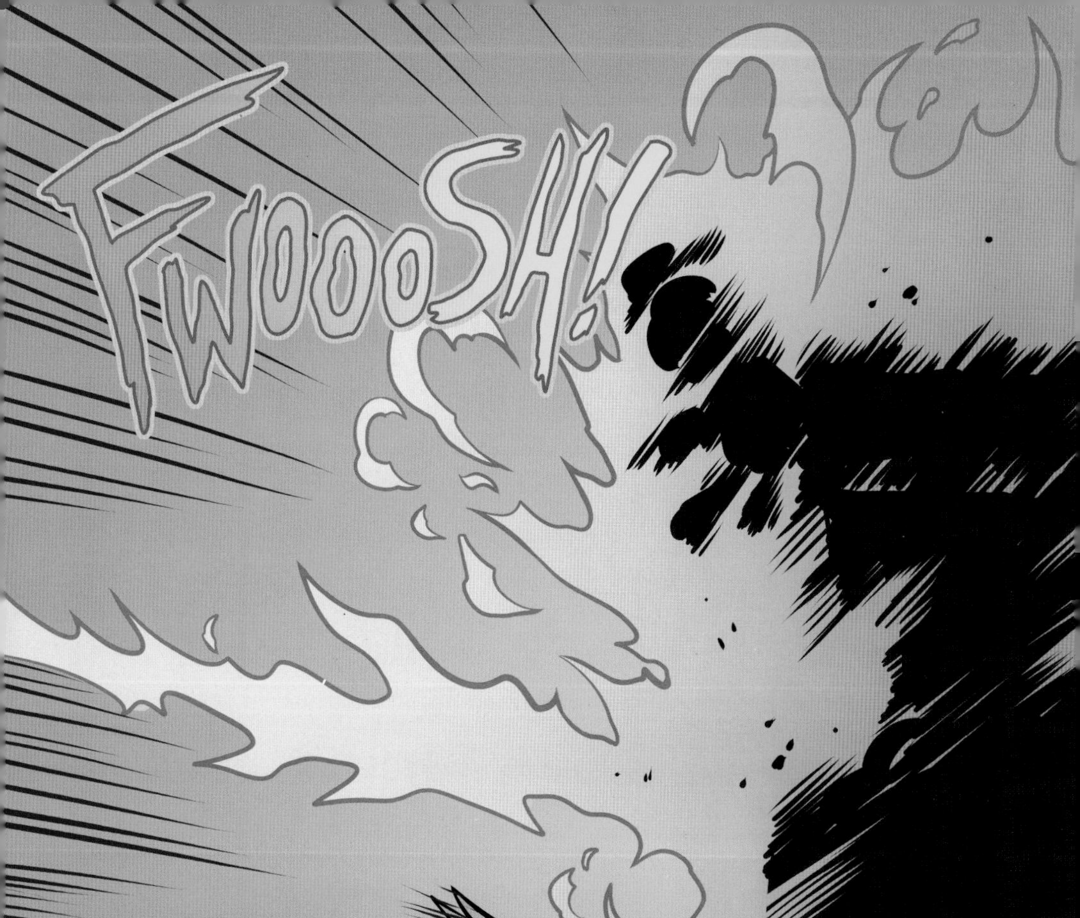
FWOOOSH!!

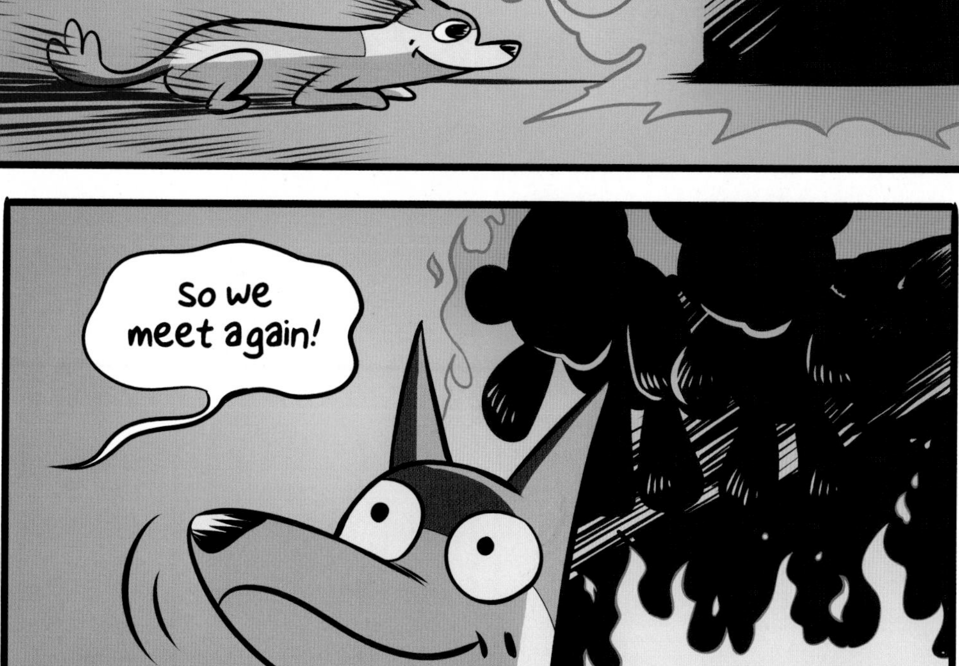
So we meet again!

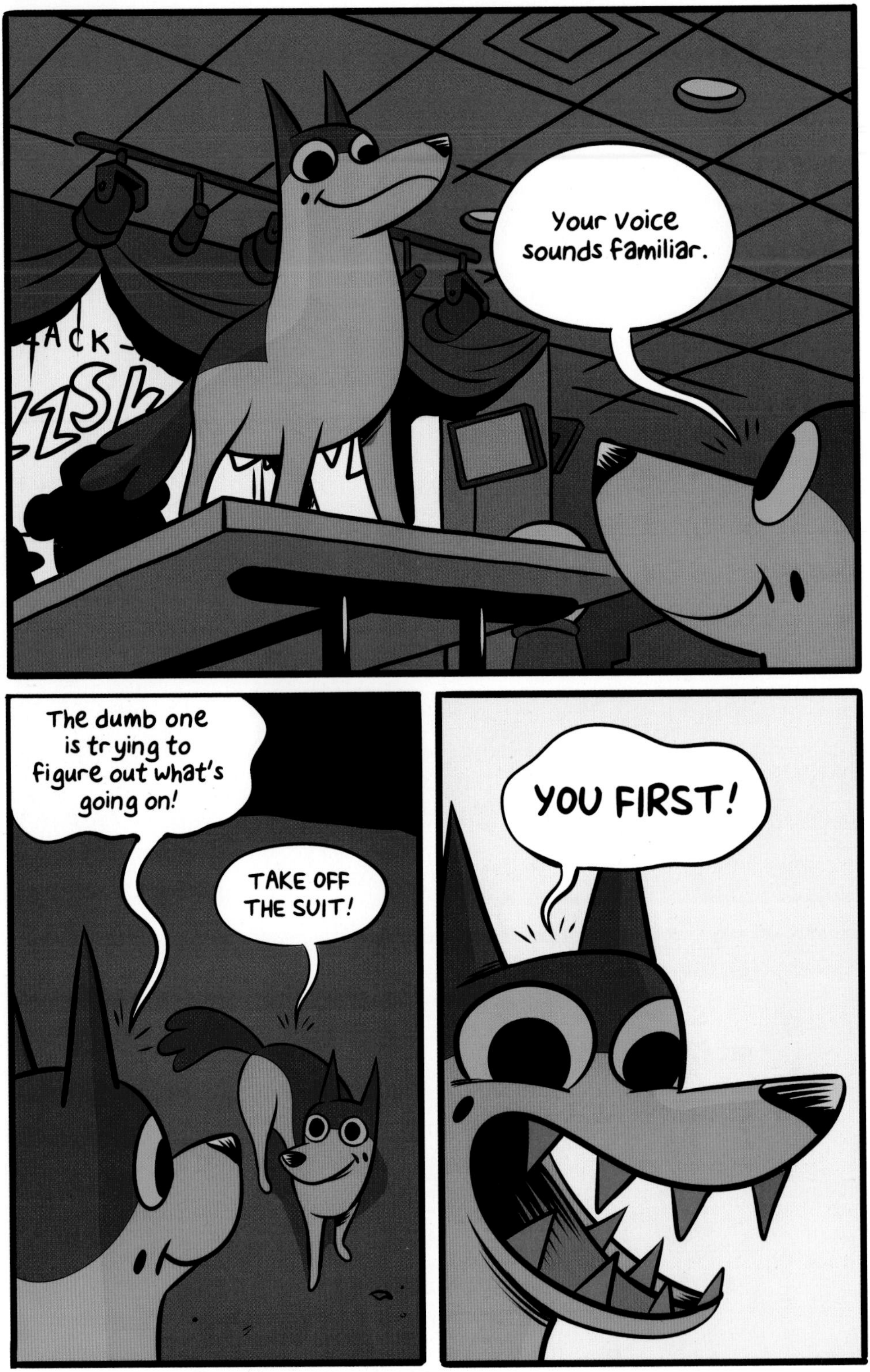
ACK-
ZZSH
Your voice sounds familiar.
The dumb one is trying to figure out what's going on!
TAKE OFF THE SUIT!
YOU FIRST!

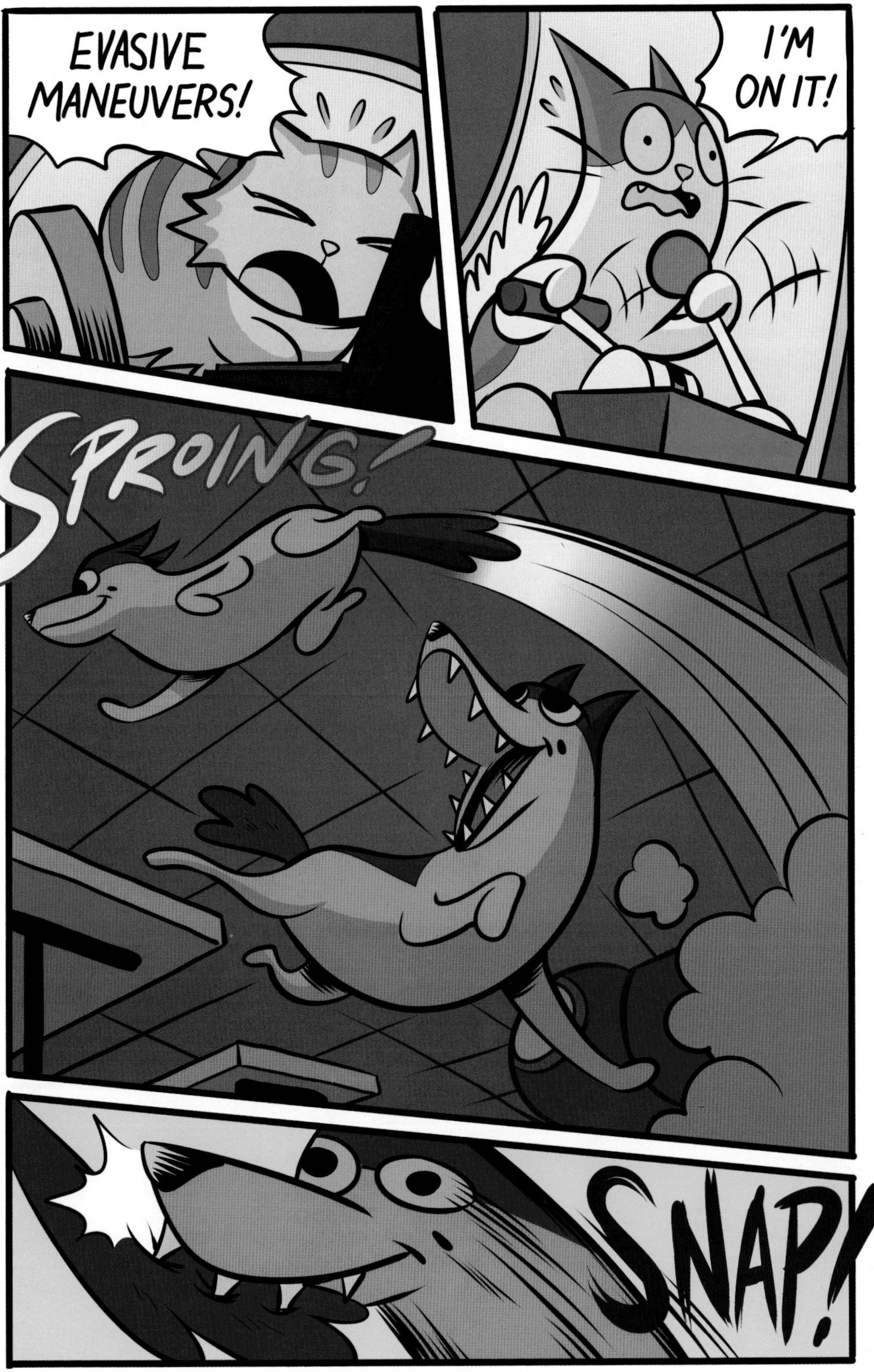
EVASIVE MANEUVERS!
I'M ON IT!
SPROING!
SNAP!

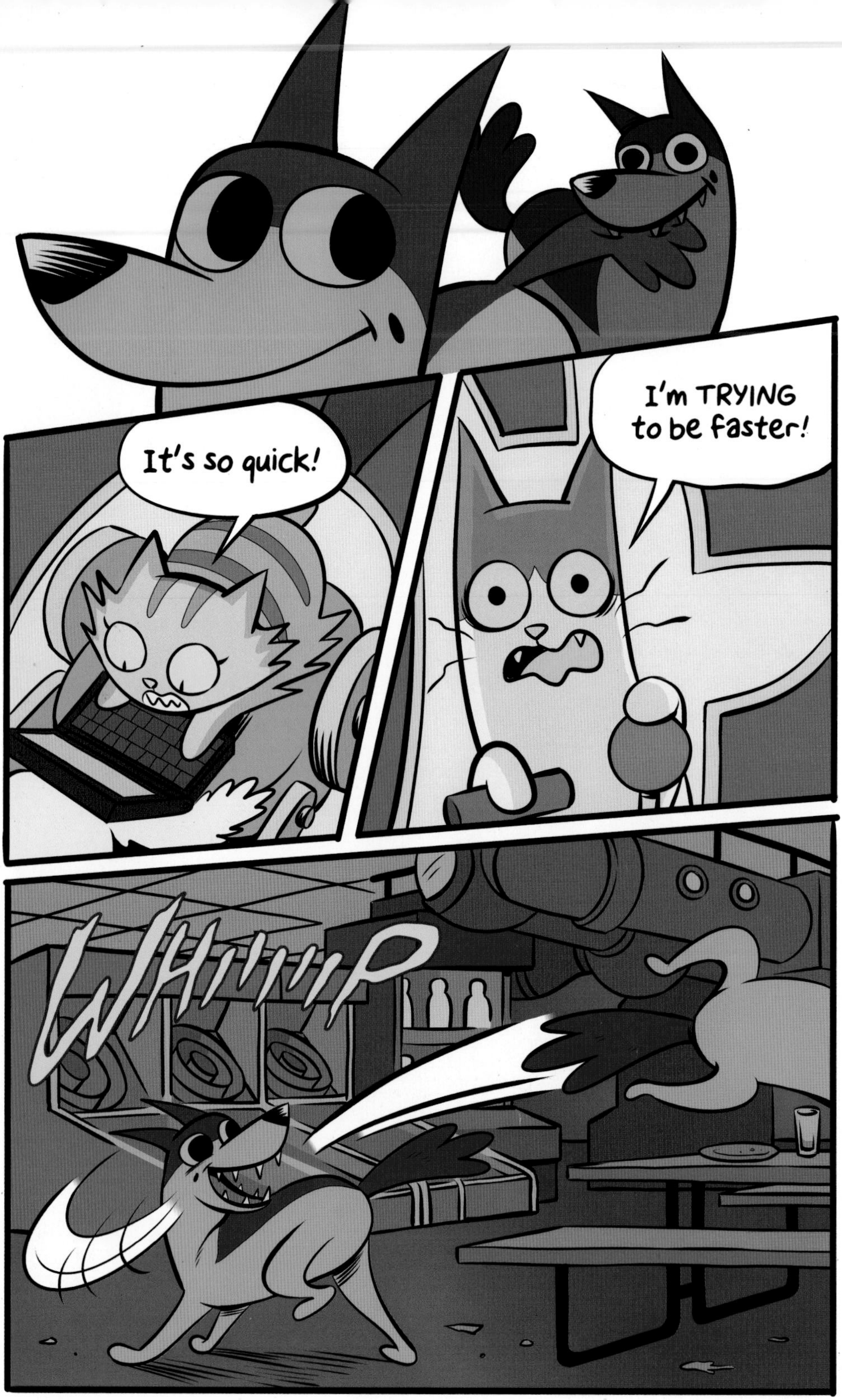
It's so quick!
I'm TRYING to be faster!
WHIIIIP

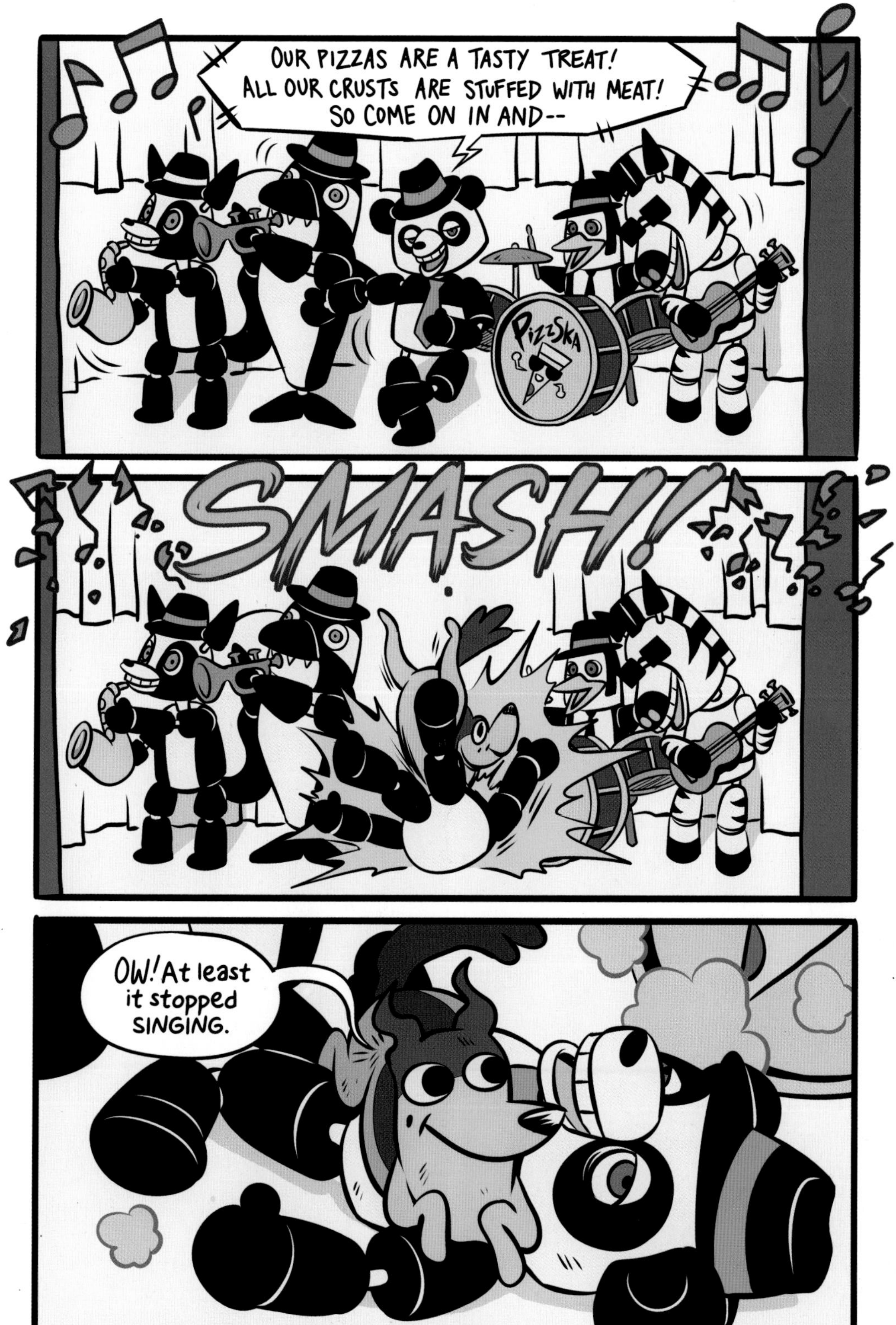
OUR PIZZAS ARE A TASTY TREAT! ALL OUR CRUSTS ARE STUFFED WITH MEAT! SO COME ON IN AND--
PIZZSKA
SMASH!
OW! At least it stopped SINGING.

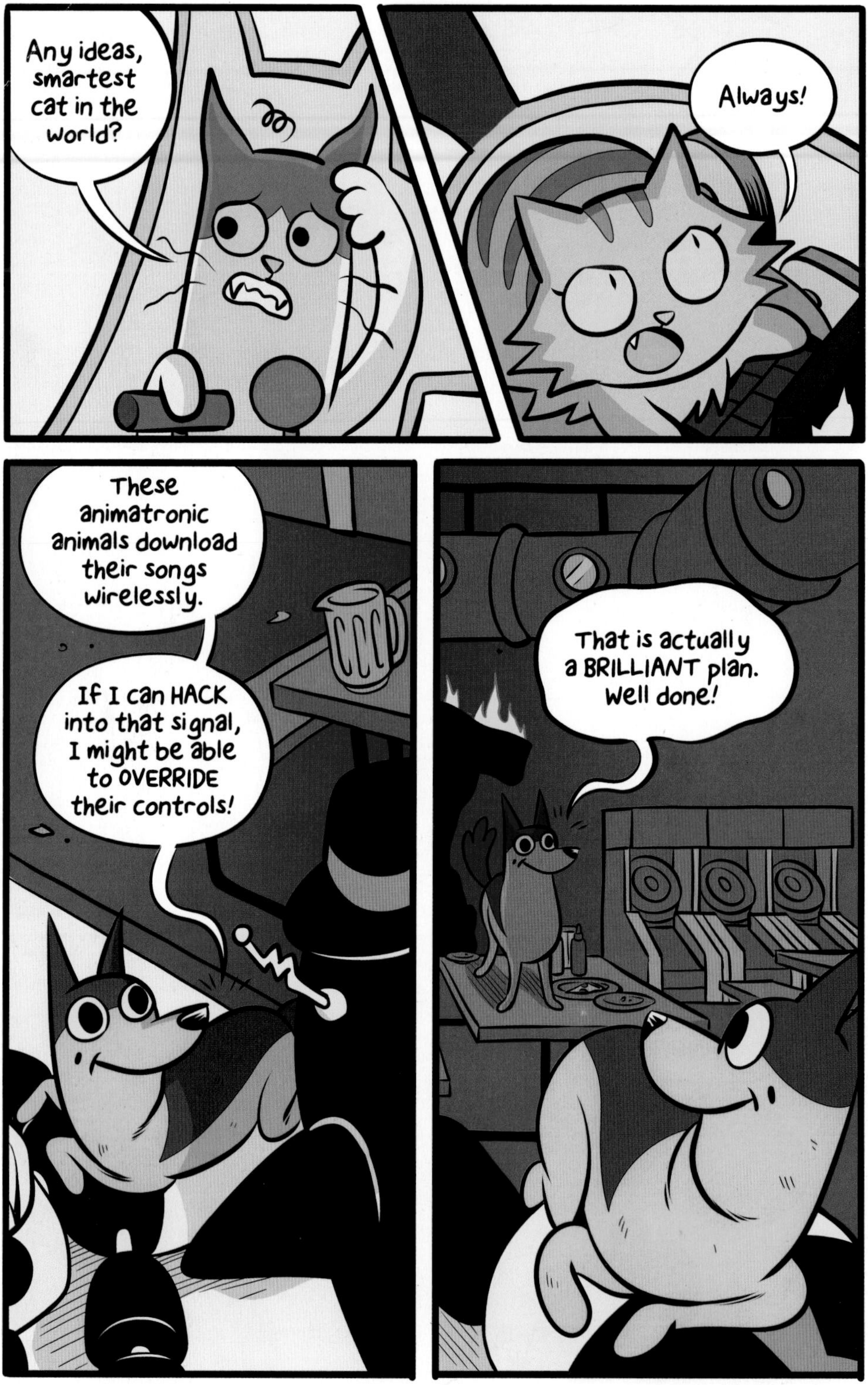
Any ideas, smartest cat in the world?
Always!
These animatronic animals download their songs wirelessly.
If I can HACK into that signal, I might be able to OVERRIDE their controls!
That is actually a BRILLIANT plan. Well done!

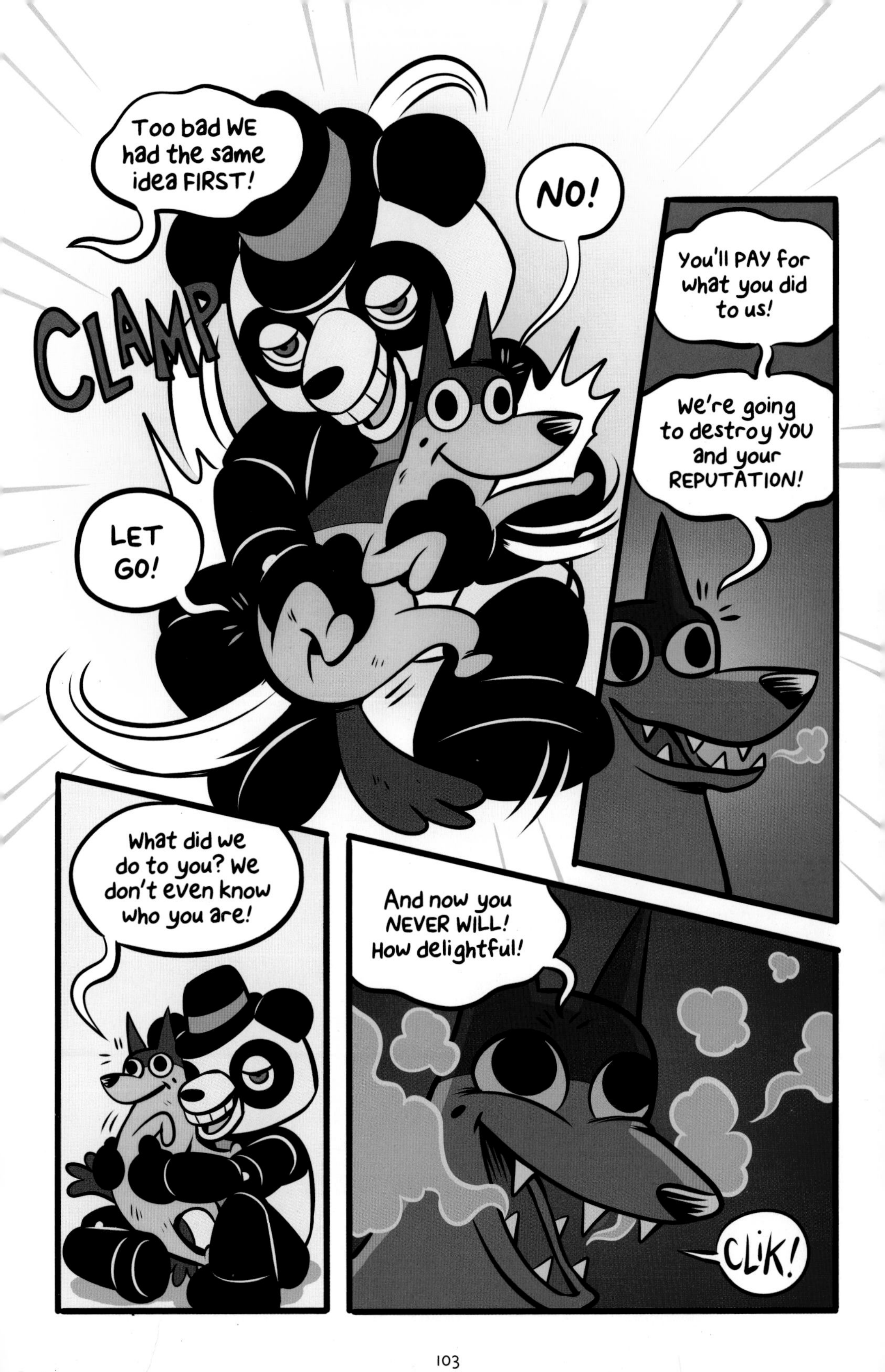
Too bad WE had the same idea FIRST!
NO!
CLAMP
LET GO!
You'll PAY for what you did to us!
We're going to destroy YOU and your REPUTATION!
What did we do to you? We don't even know who you are!
And now you NEVER WILL! How delightful!
CLIK!

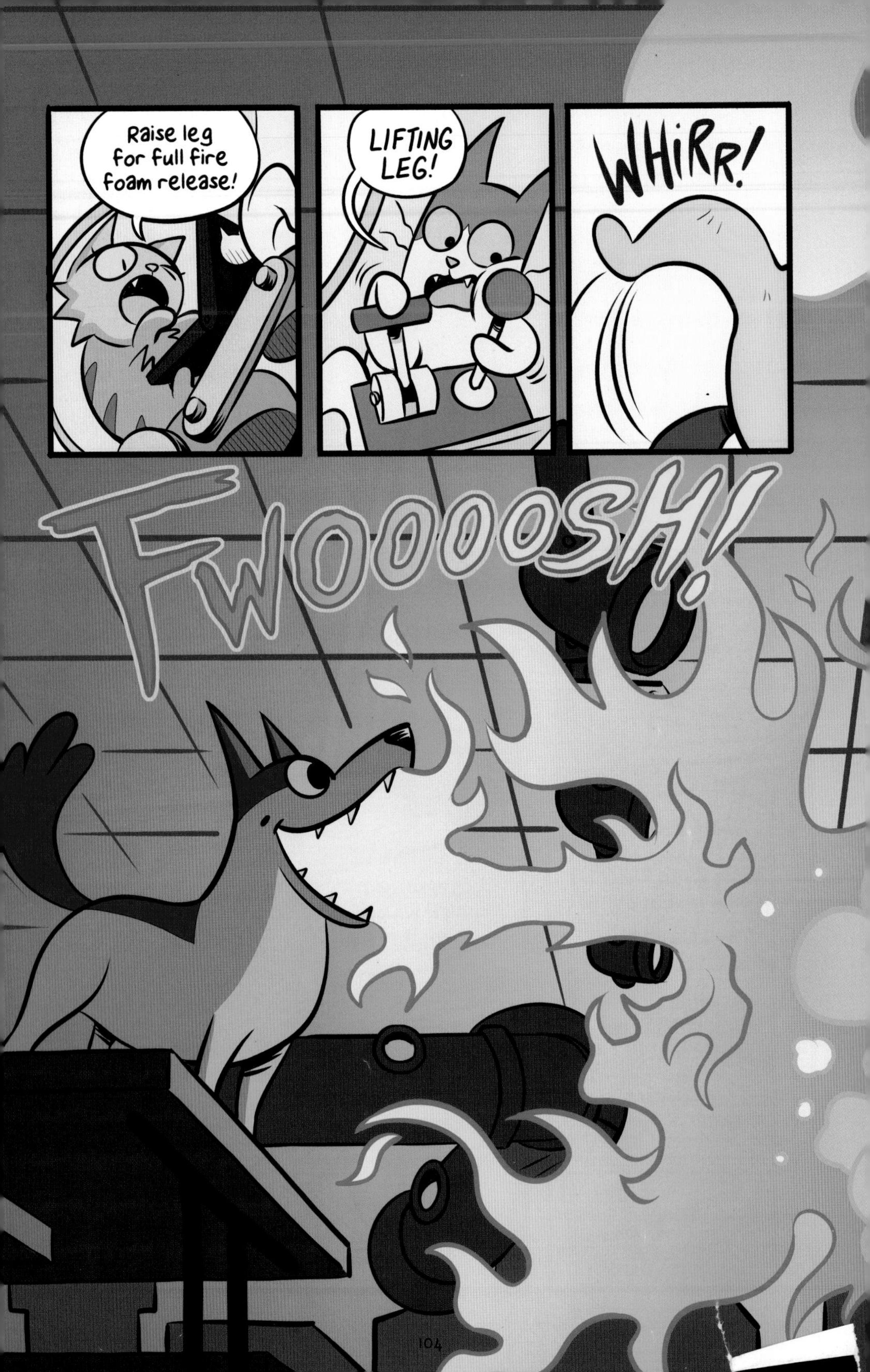
Raise leg for full fire foam release!
LIFTING LEG!
WHIRR!
FWOOOOSH!

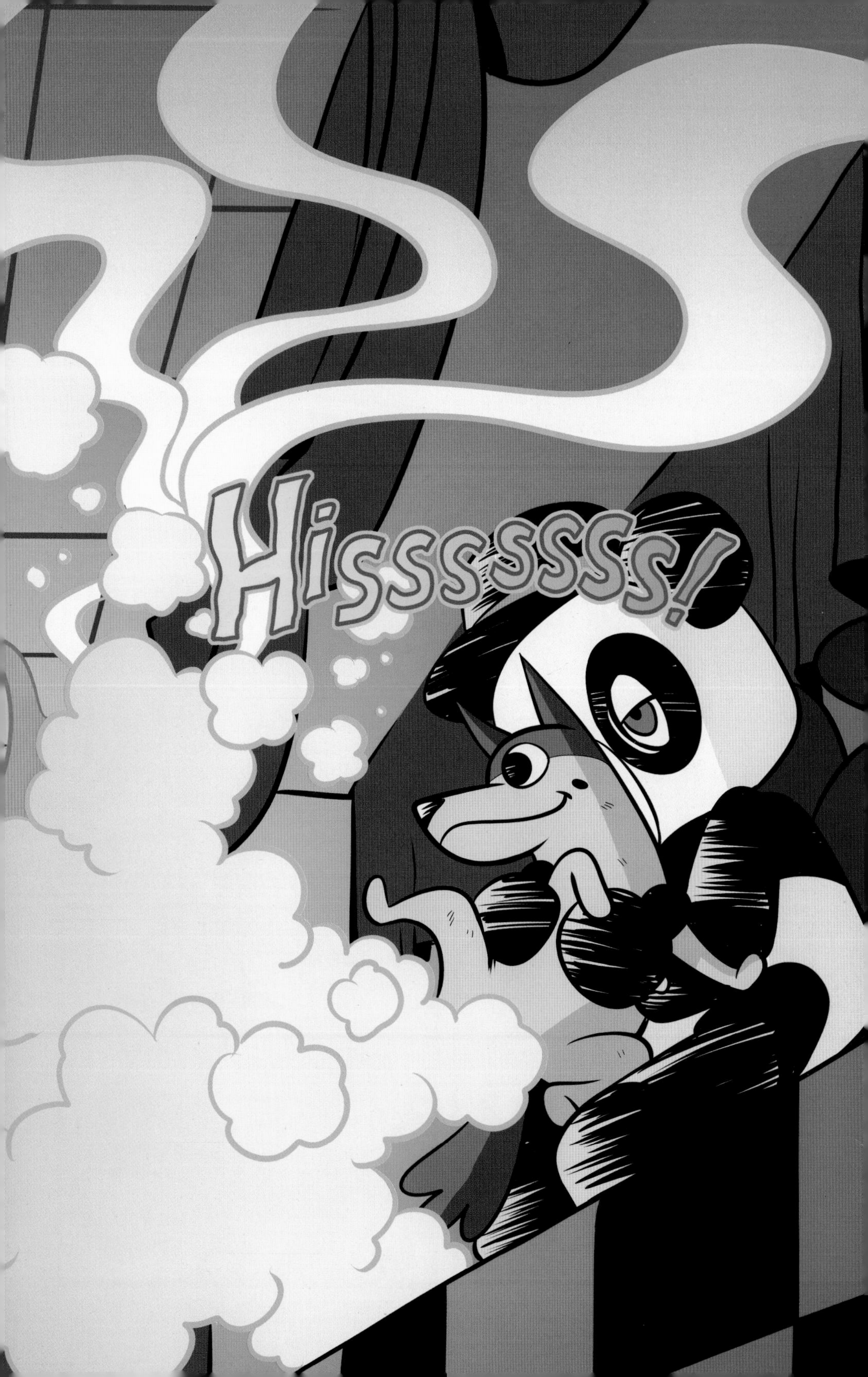
Hisssssss!

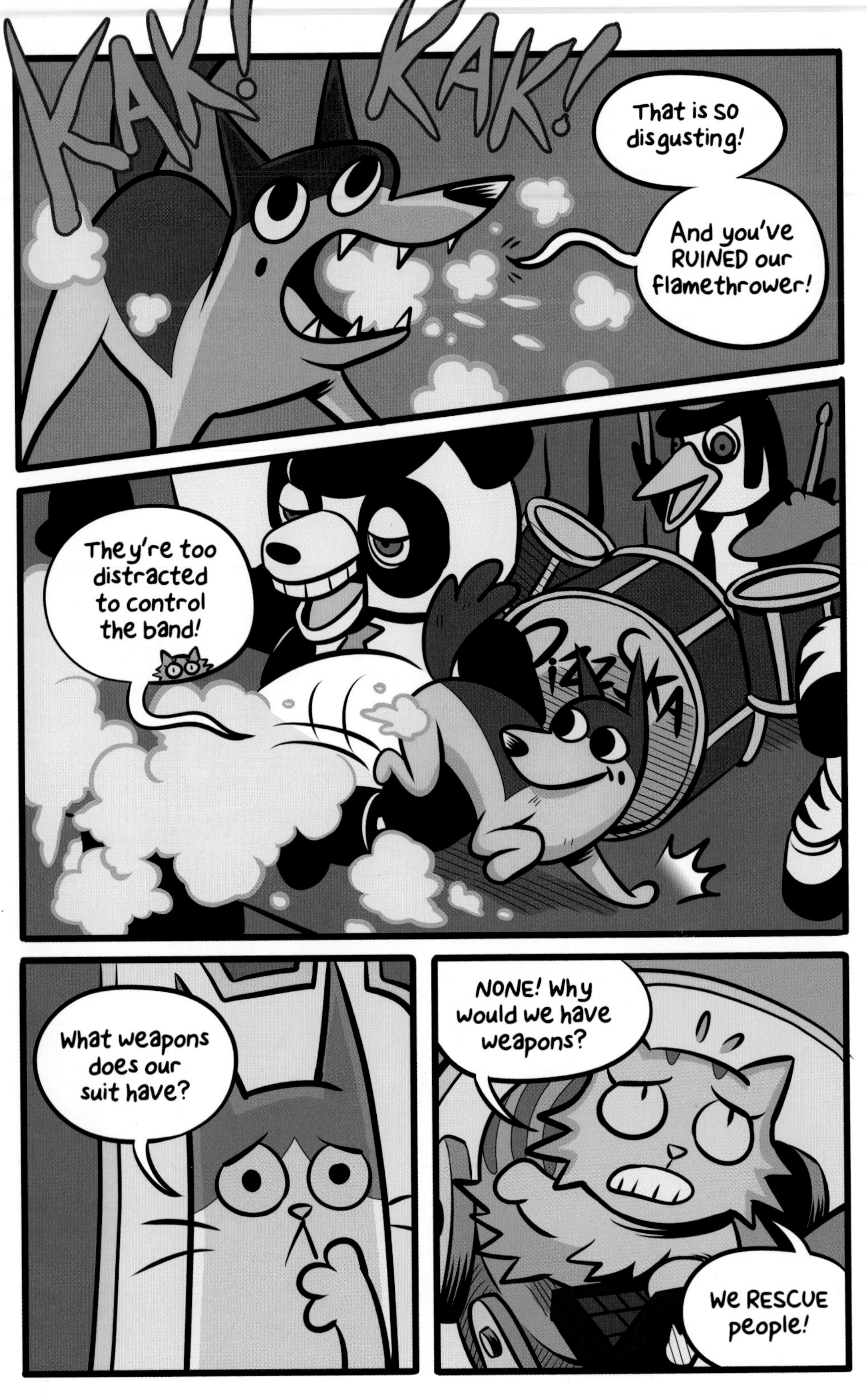
KAK! KAK!
That is so disgusting!
And you've RUINED our flamethrower!
They're too distracted to control the band!
PIZZA
What weapons does our suit have?
NONE! Why would we have weapons?
We RESCUE people!

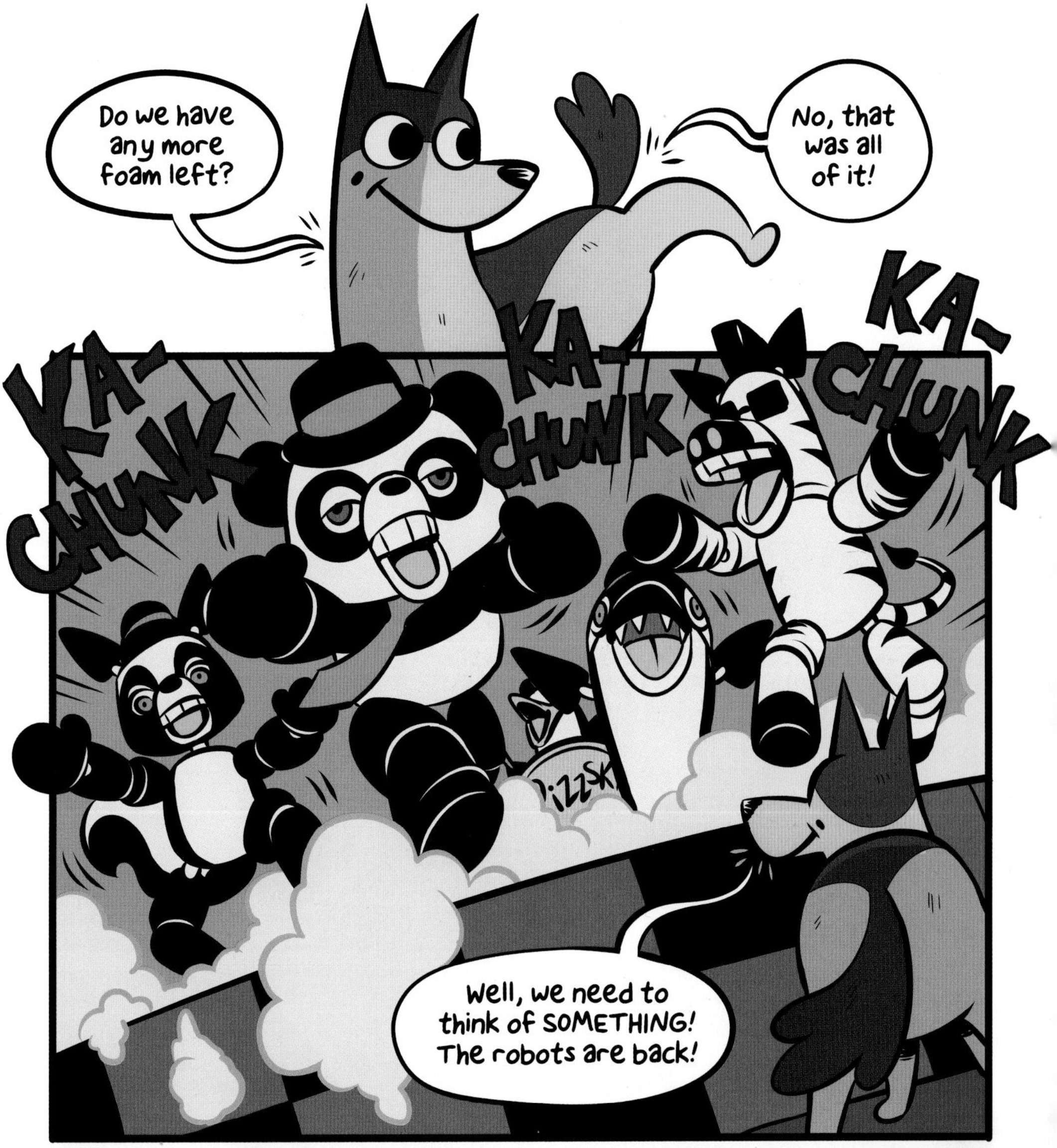
Do we have any more foam left?
No, that was all of it!
KA-CHUNK
KA-CHUNK
KA-CHUNK
Well, we need to think of SOMETHING! The robots are back!

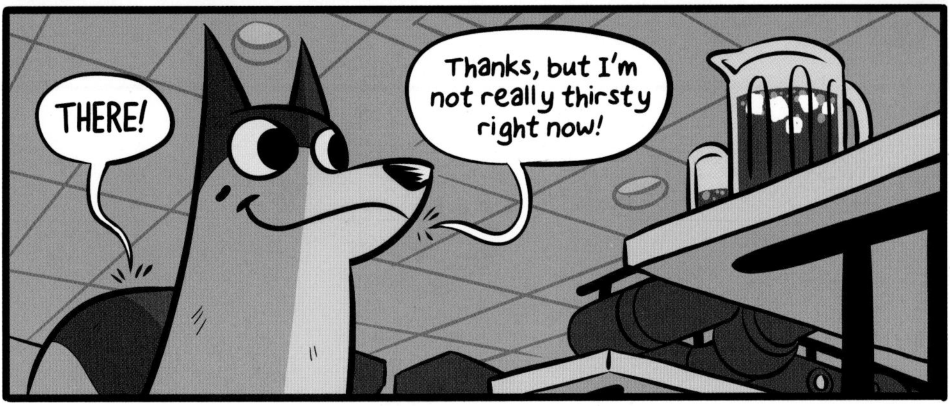
THERE!
Thanks, but I'm not really thirsty right now!

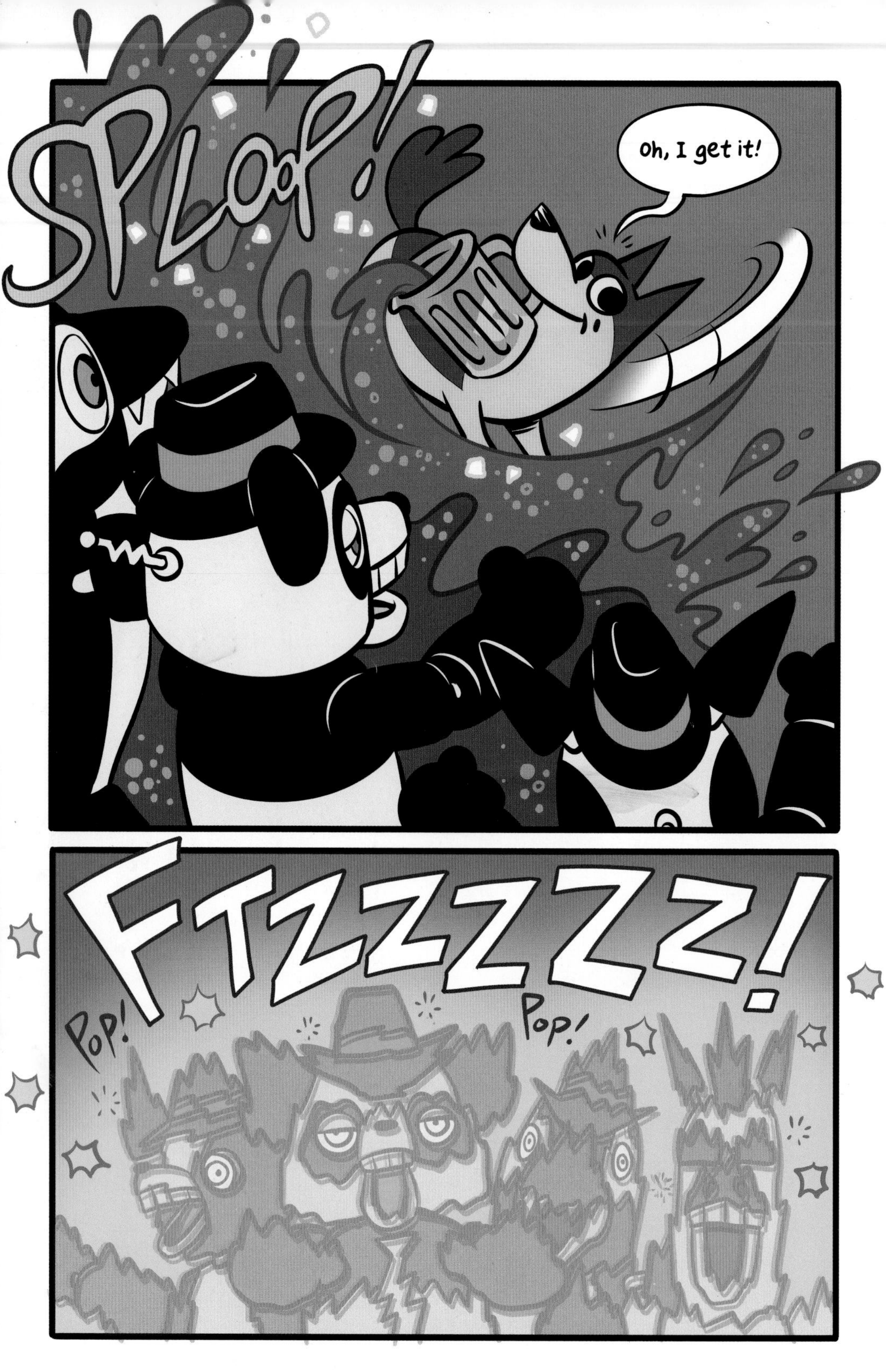
SPLOP!
Oh, I get it!
FTZZZZZ!
POP!
POP!

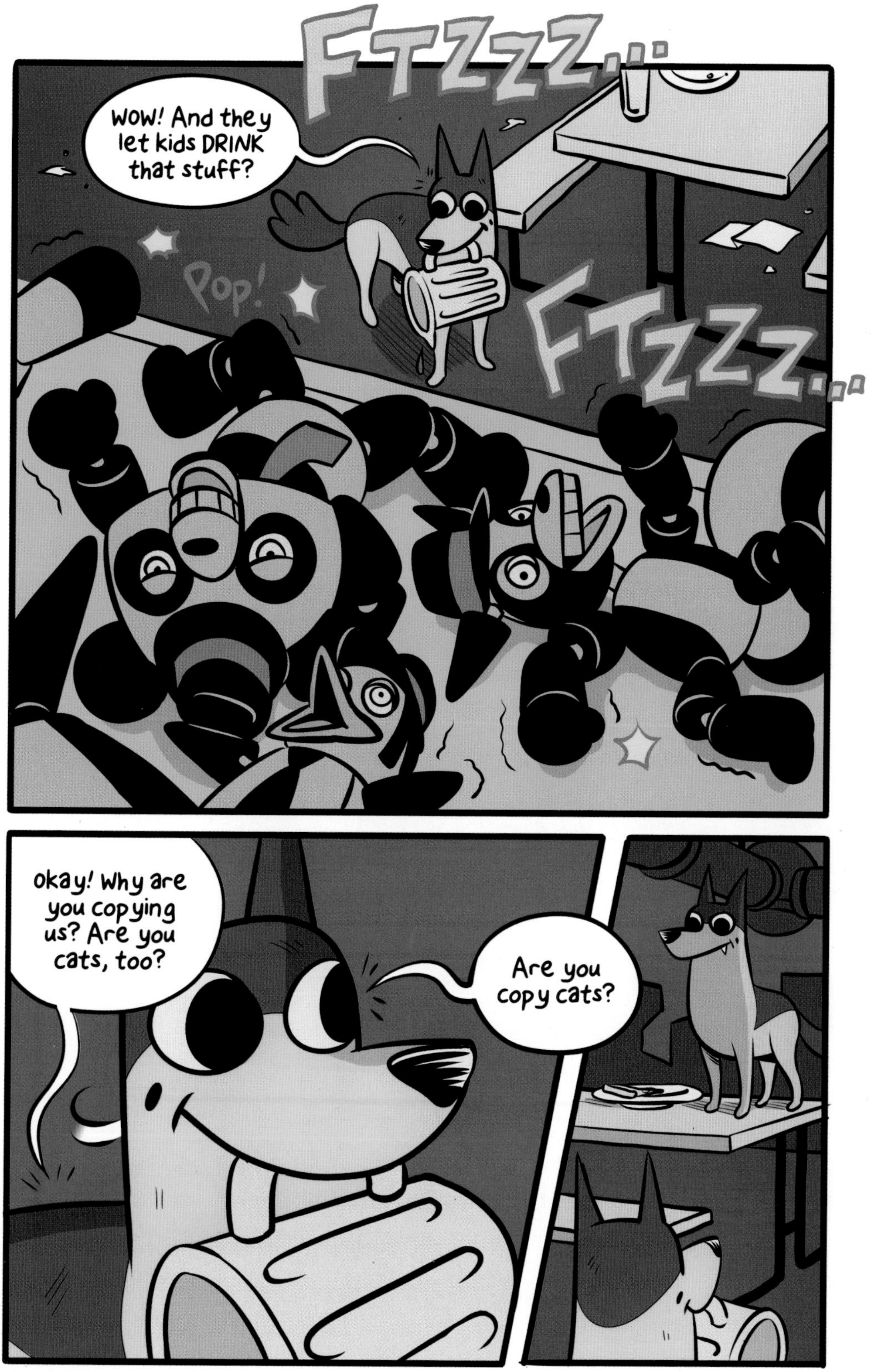
FTZZZ...
WOW! And they let kids DRINK that stuff?
POP!
FTZZZ...
okay! Why are you copying us? Are you cats, too?
Are you copy cats?

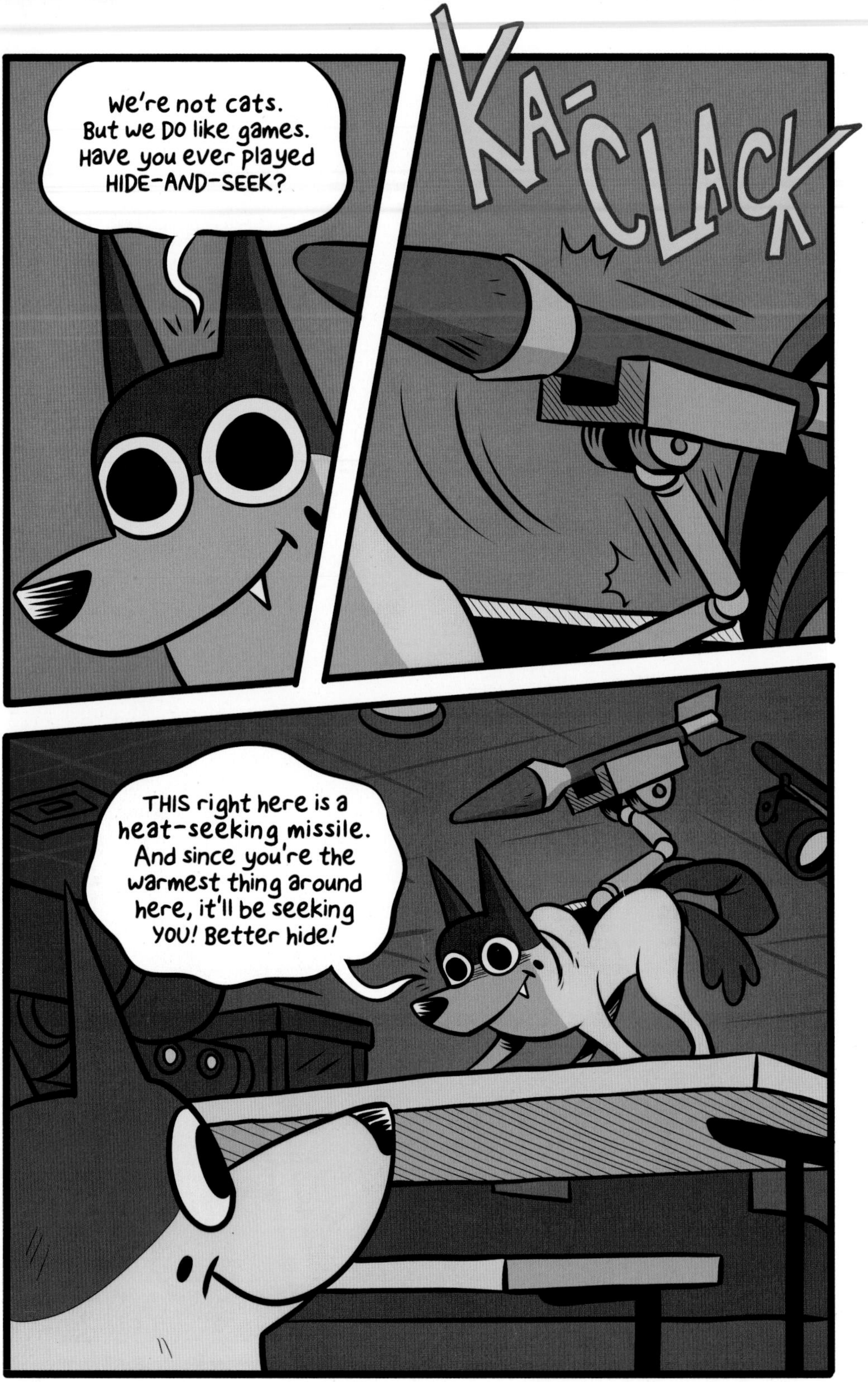
We're not cats. But we DO like games. Have you ever played HIDE-AND-SEEK?
KA-CLACK
THIS right here is a heat-seeking missile. And since you're the warmest thing around here, it'll be seeking YOU! Better hide!

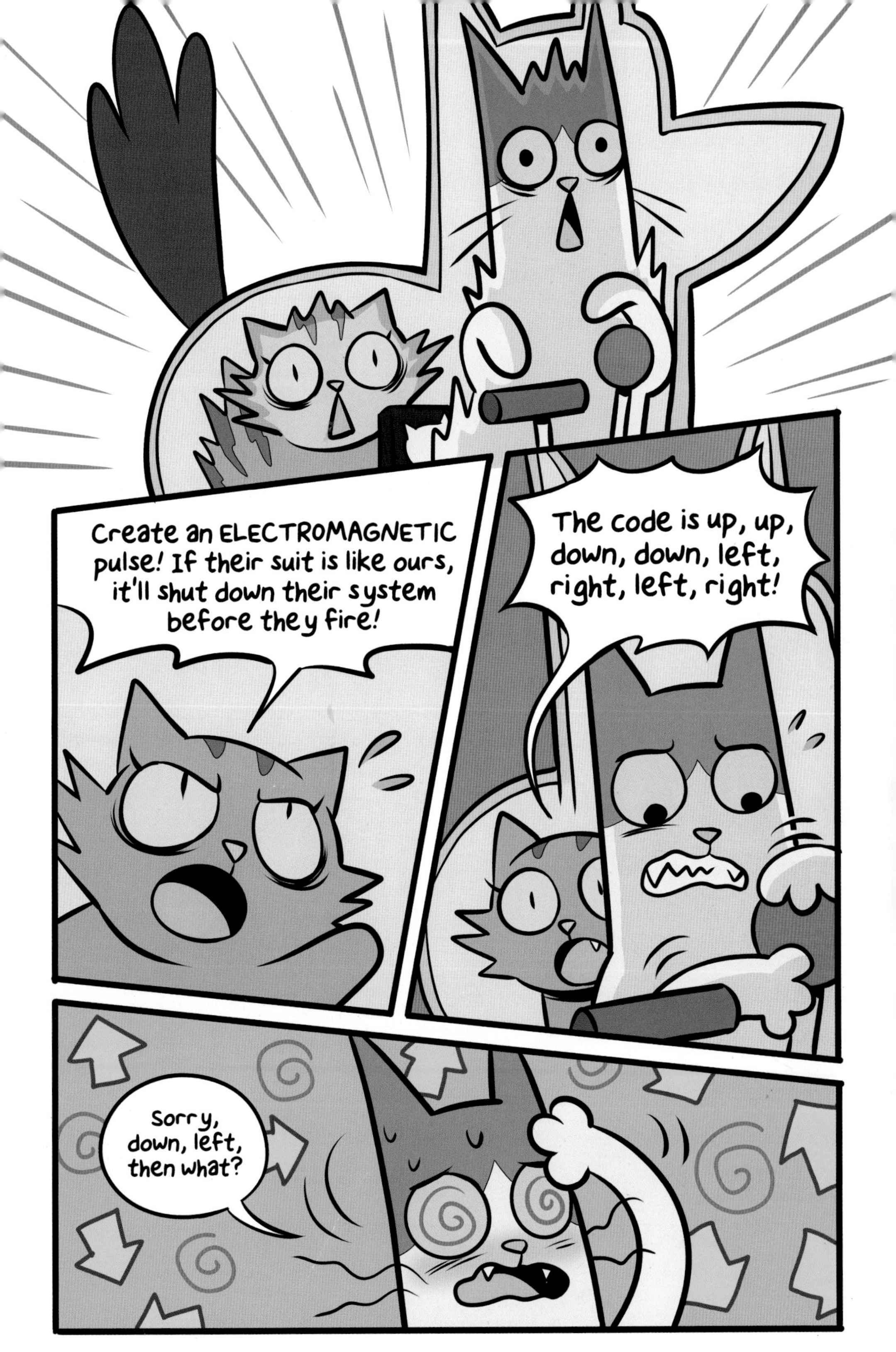
Create an ELECTROMAGNETIC pulse! If their suit is like ours, it'll shut down their system before they fire!
The code is up, up, down, down, left, right, left, right!
Sorry, down, left, then what?

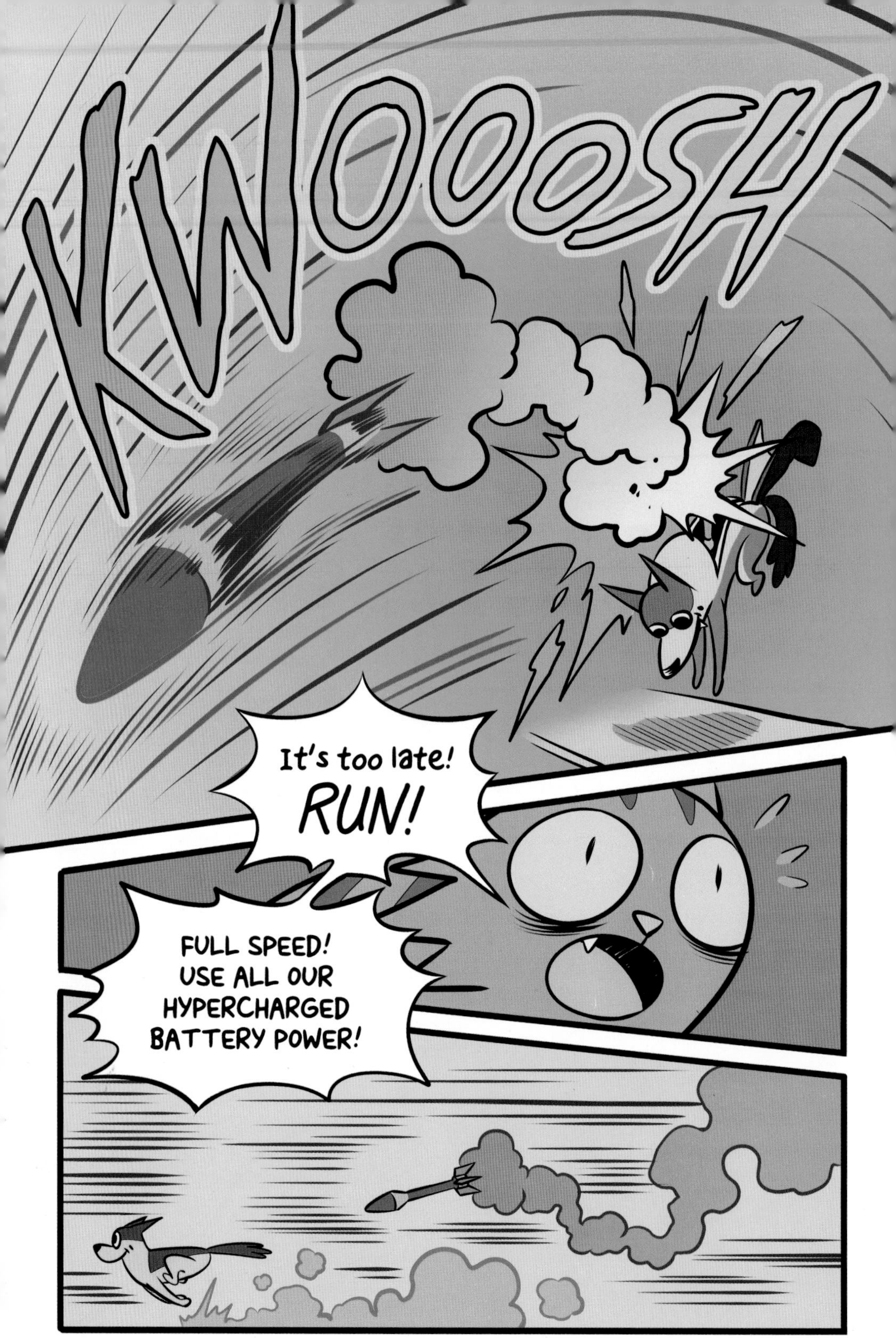
KWOOOSH
It's too late! RUN!
FULL SPEED! USE ALL OUR HYPERCHARGED BATTERY POWER!

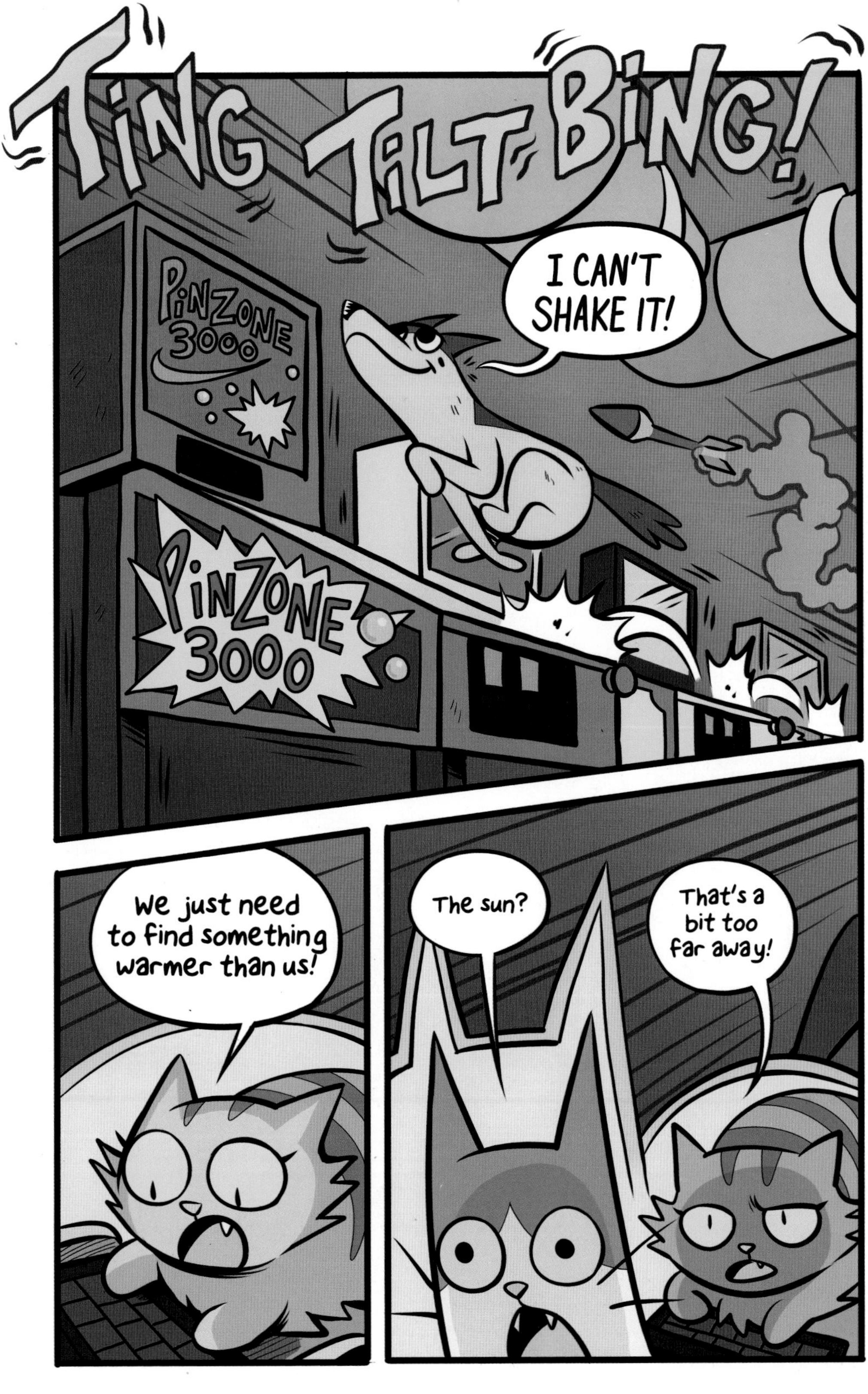

TING TILT BING!
PINZONE 3000
I CAN'T SHAKE IT!
PINZONE 3000
We just need to find something warmer than us!
The sun?
That's a bit too far away!

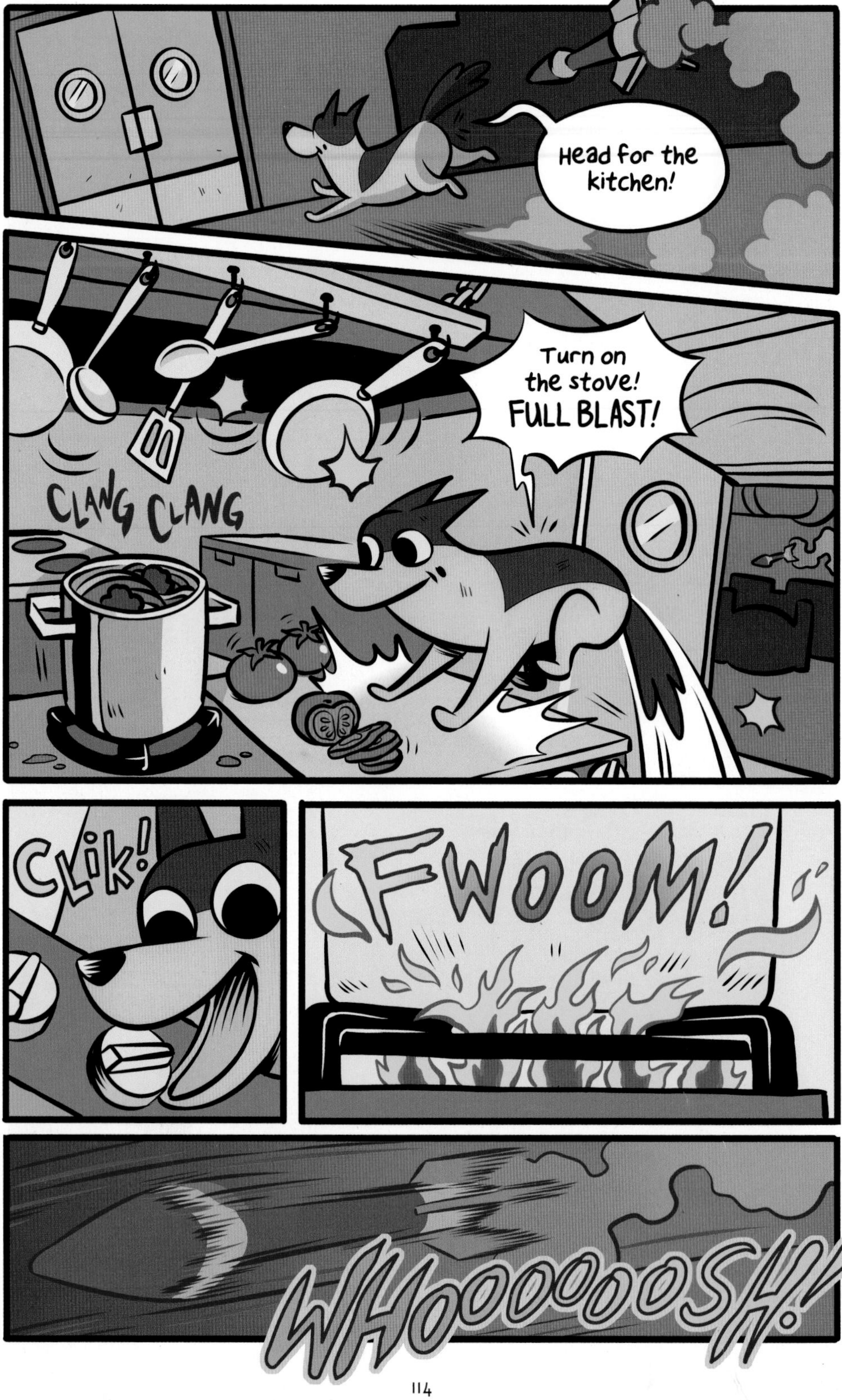
Head for the kitchen!
Turn on the stove! FULL BLAST!
CLANG CLANG
CLIK!
FWOOM!
WHOOOOOOOSH!

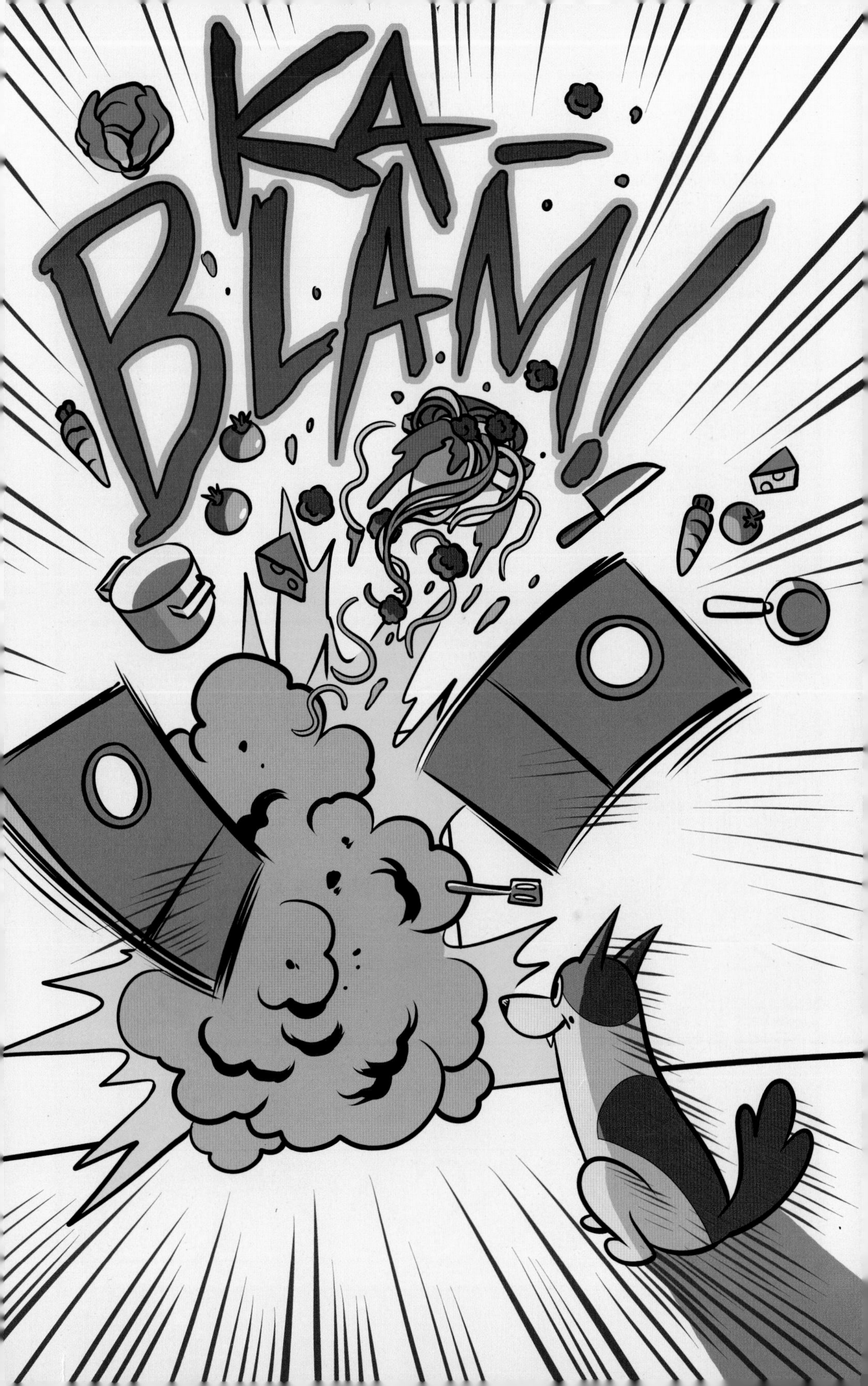
KA-BLAM!

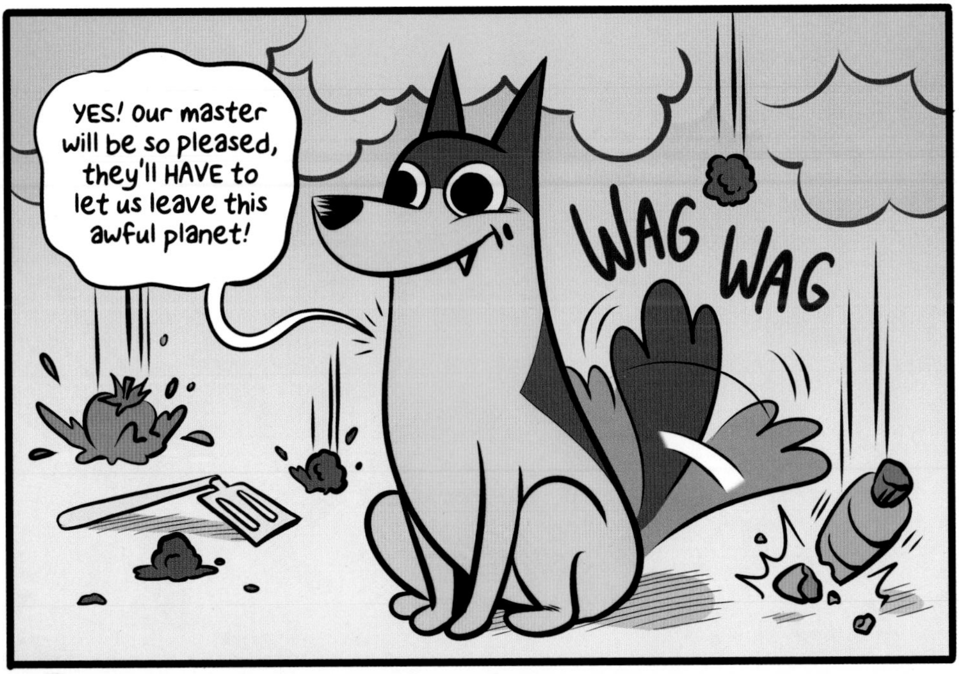
YES! Our master will be so pleased, they'll HAVE to let us leave this awful planet!
WAG WAG

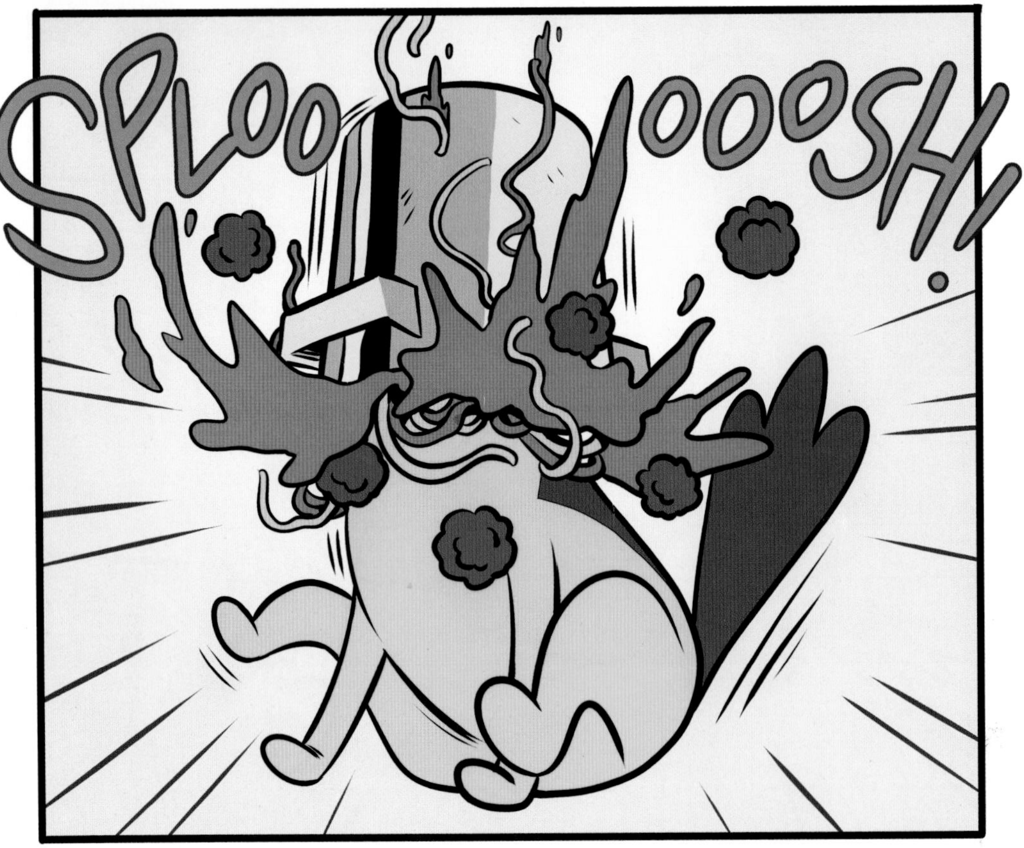
SPLOOOOOSH!

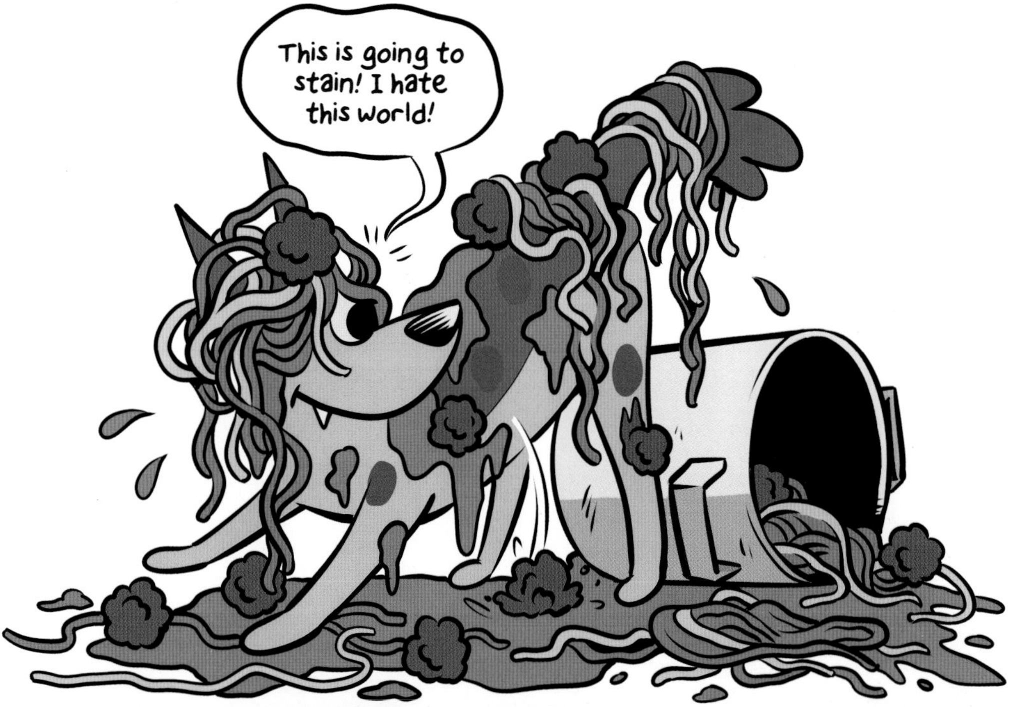
This is going to stain! I hate this world!

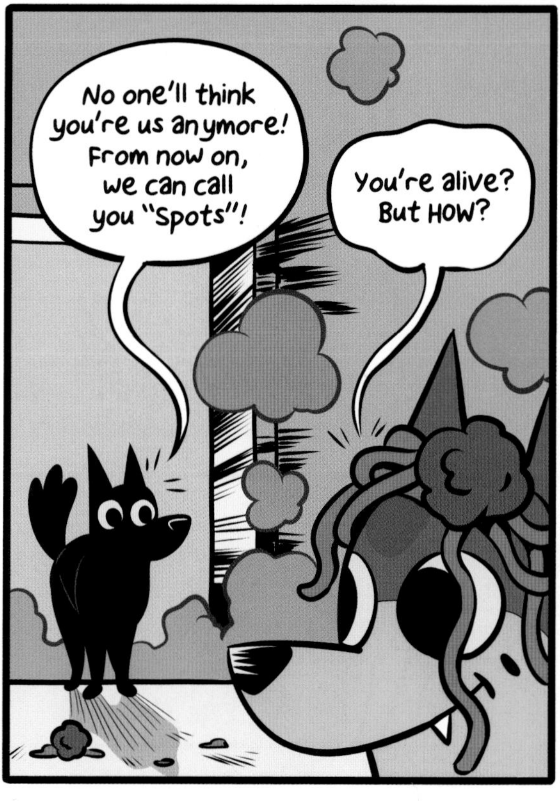
No one'll think you're us anymore! From now on, we can call you "Spots"!
You're alive? But HOW?

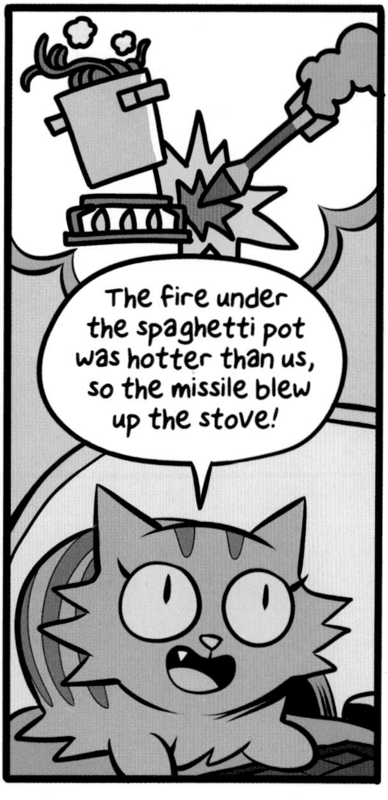
The fire under the spaghetti pot was hotter than us, so the missile blew up the stove!

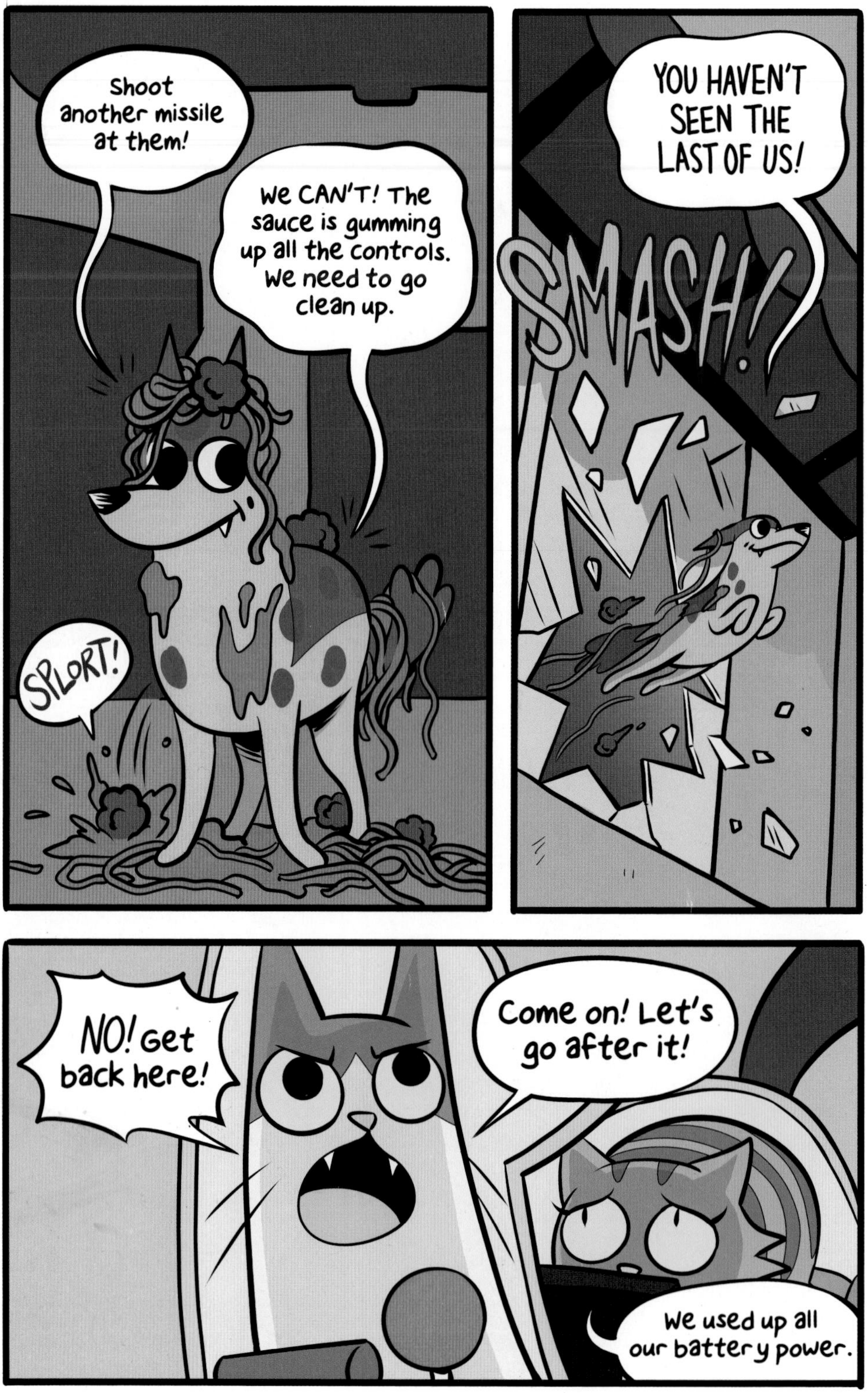

Shoot another missile at them!
We CAN'T! The sauce is gumming up all the controls. We need to go clean up.
SPLORT!
YOU HAVEN'T SEEN THE LAST OF US!
SMASH!
NO! Get back here!
Come on! Let's go after it!
We used up all our battery power.

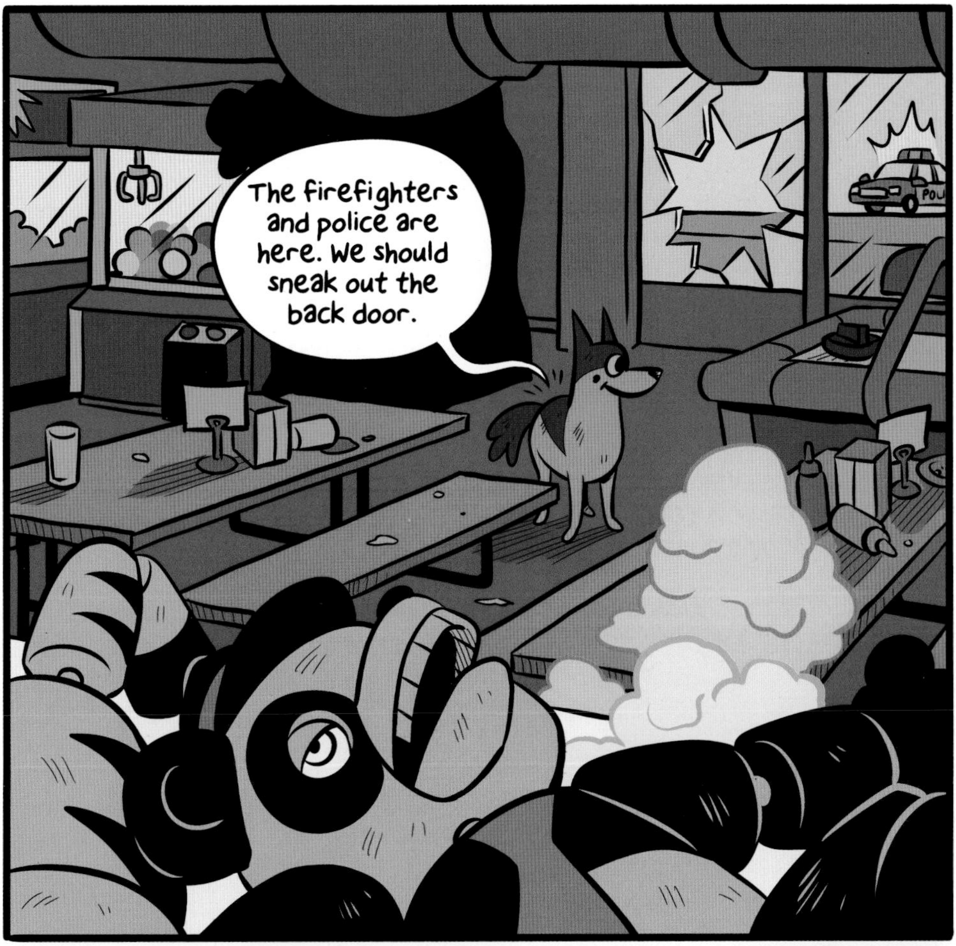
The firefighters and police are here. We should sneak out the back door.

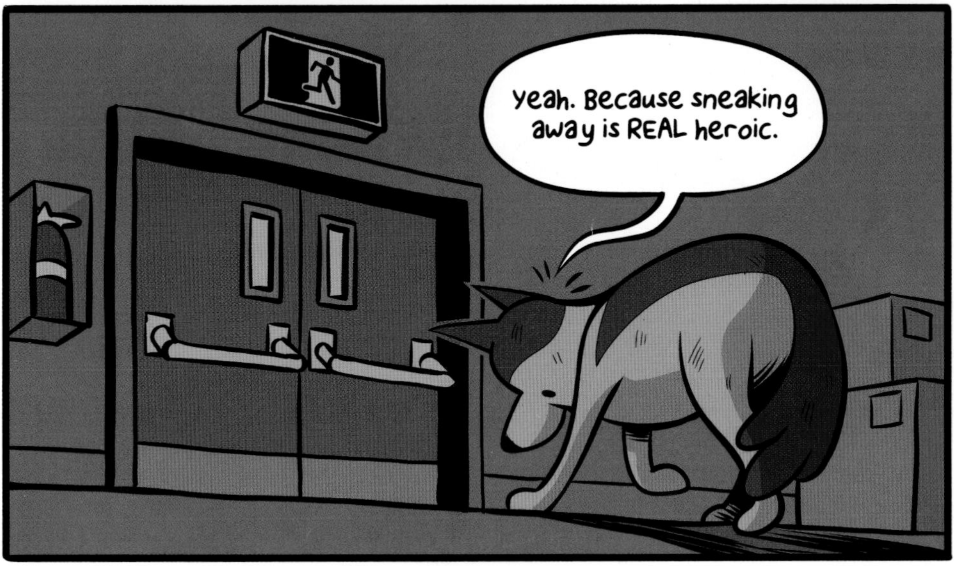
Yeah. Because sneaking away is REAL heroic.

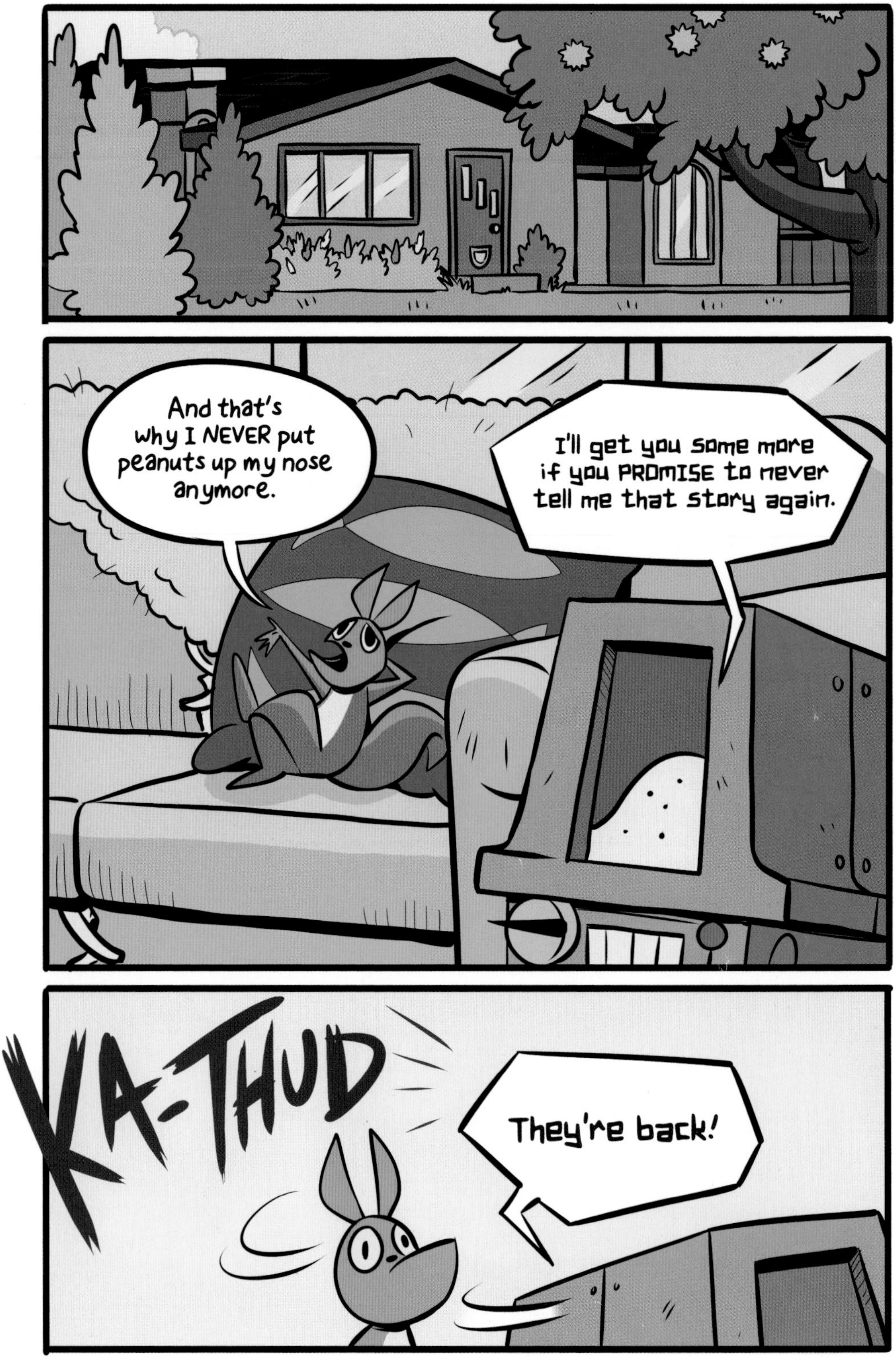
And that's why I NEVER put peanuts up my nose anymore.
I'll get you some more if you PROMISE to never tell me that story again.
KA-THUD
They're back!

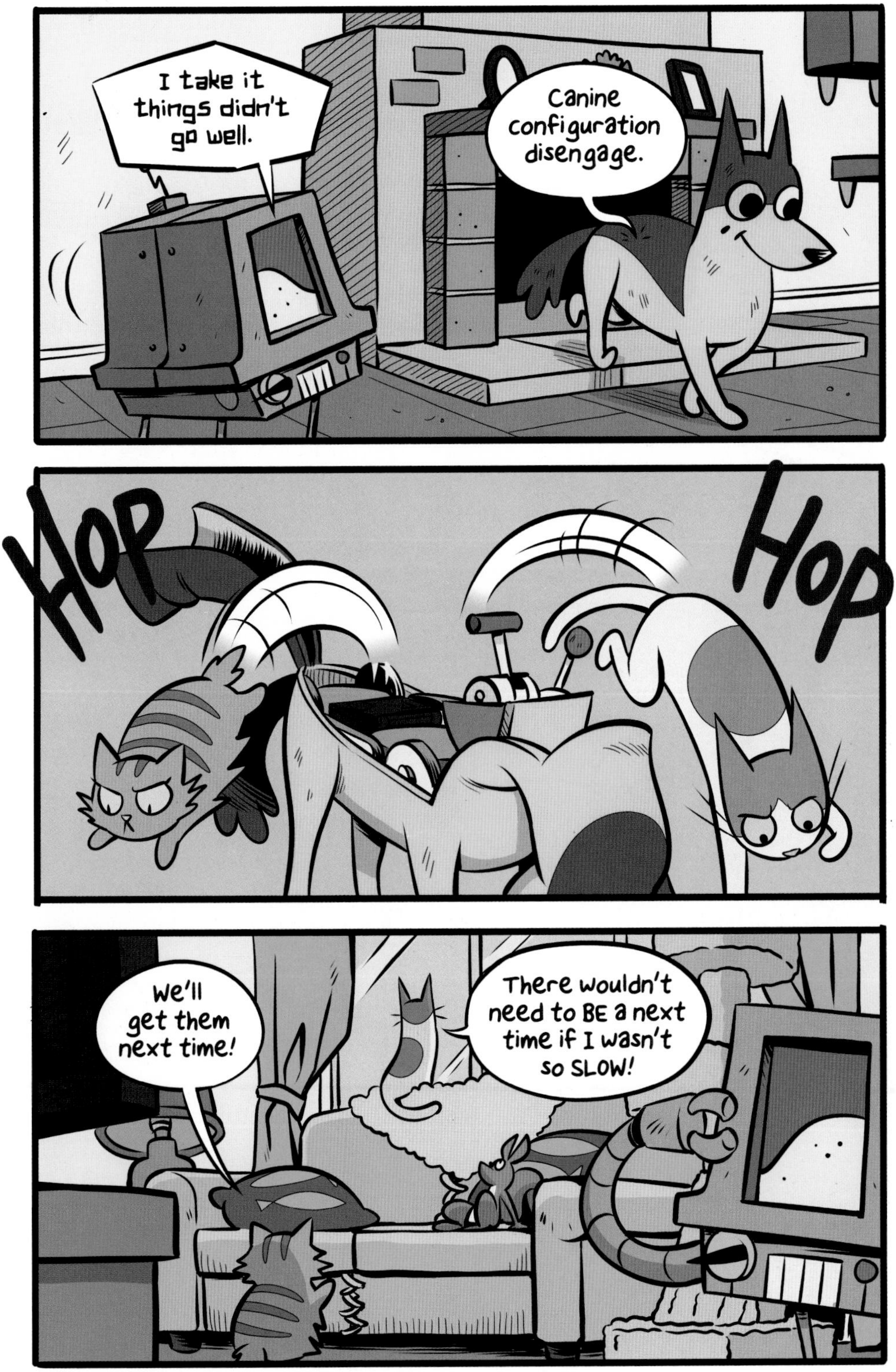
I take it things didn't go well.
Canine configuration disengage.
HOP
HOP
We'll get them next time!
There wouldn't need to BE a next time if I wasn't so SLOW!

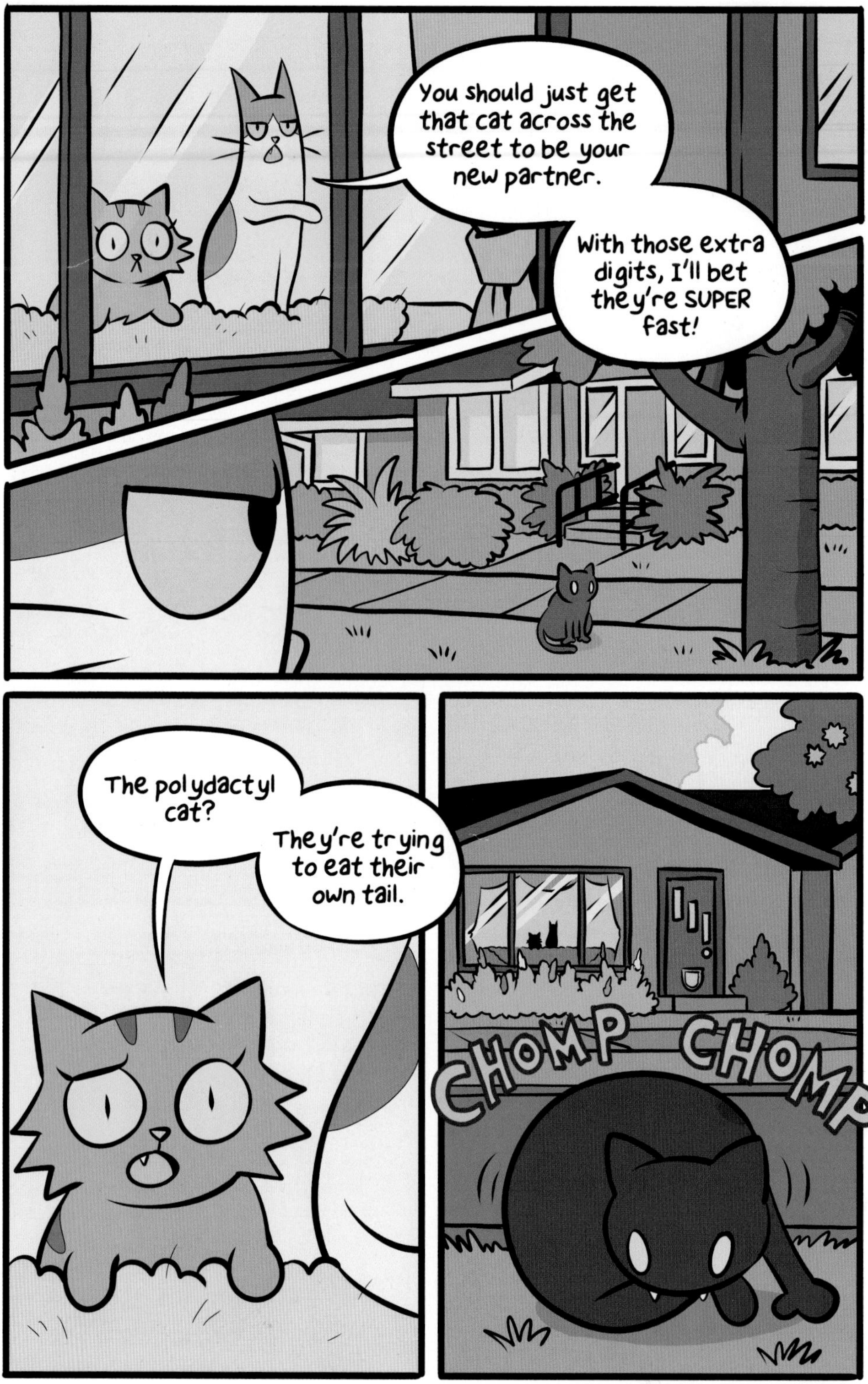

You should just get that cat across the street to be your new partner.
With those extra digits, I'll bet they're SUPER fast!
The polydactyl cat?
They're trying to eat their own tail.
CHOMP CHOMP

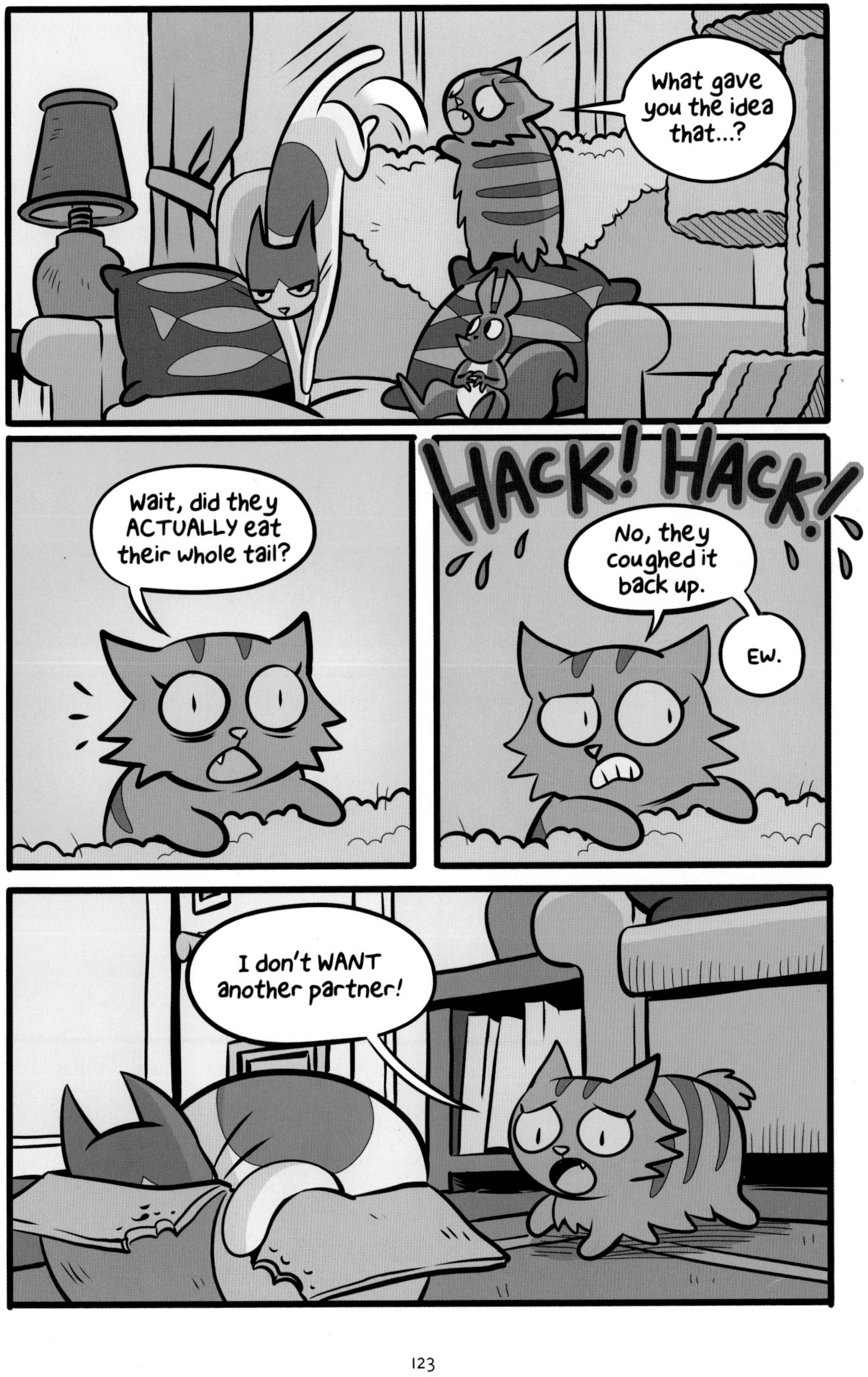
What gave you the idea that...?
Wait, did they ACTUALLY eat their whole tail?
HACK! HACK!
No, they coughed it back up.
EW.
I don't WANT another partner!

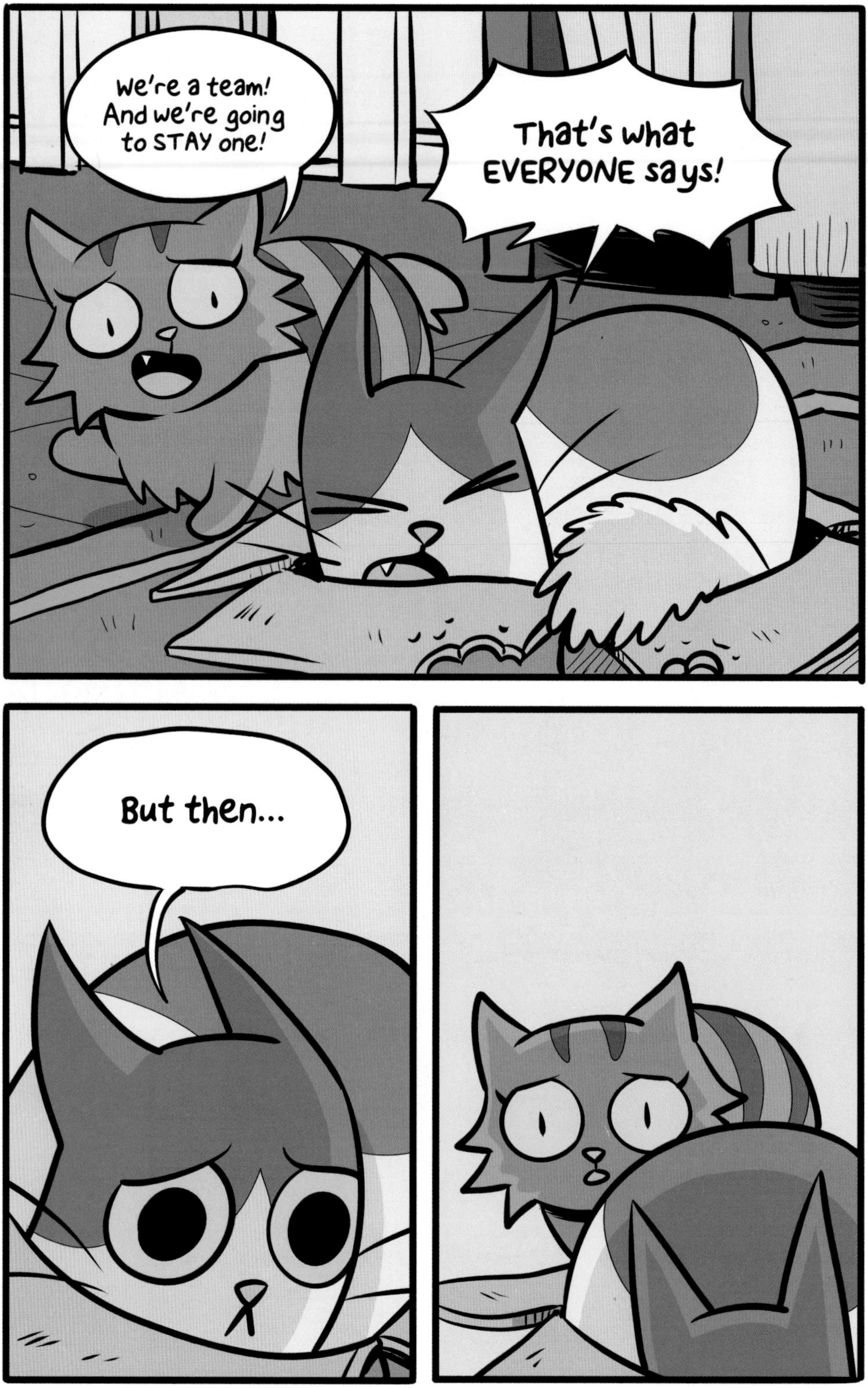
We're a team! And we're going to STAY one!
That's what EVERYONE says!
But then...

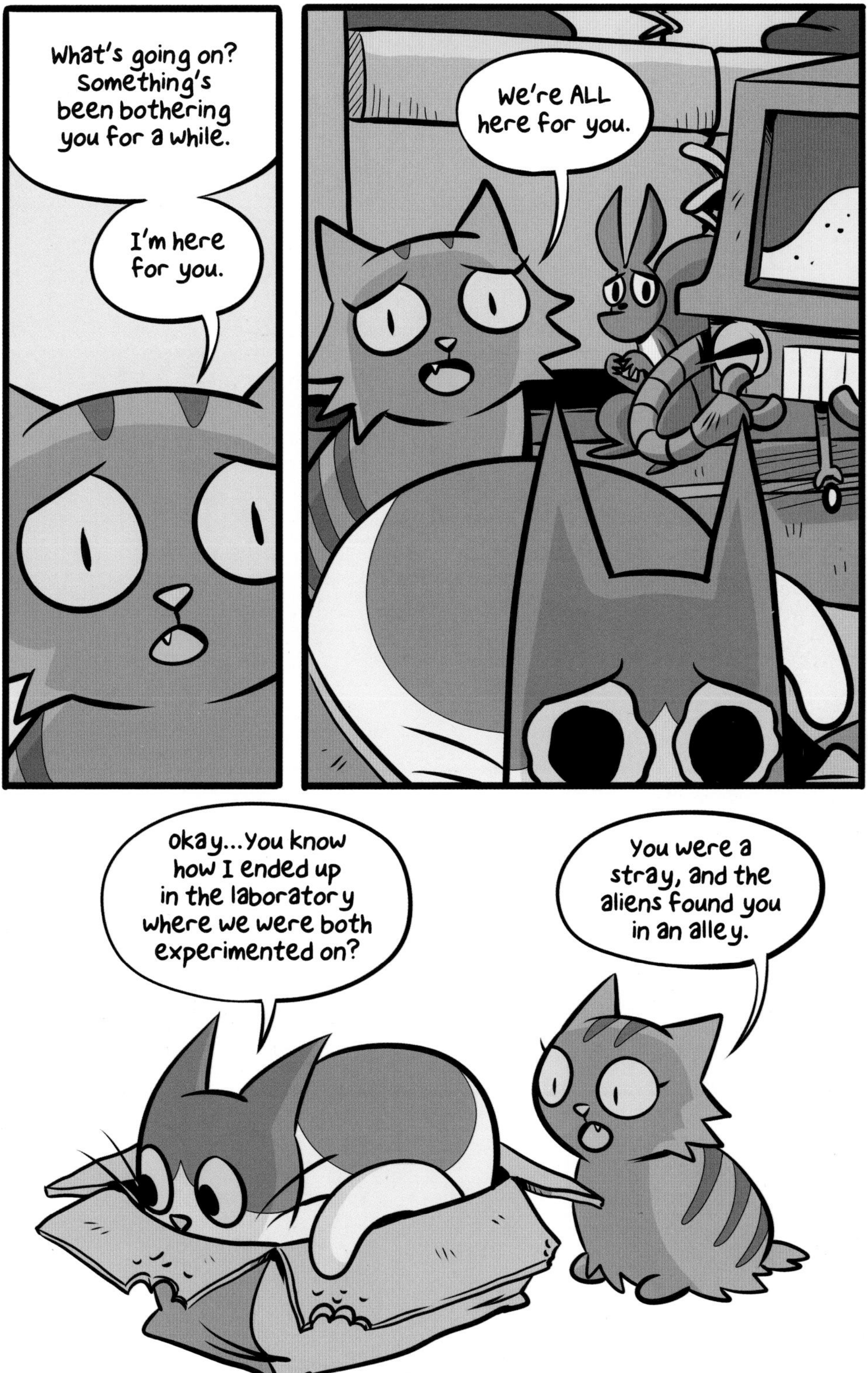
What's going on? Something's been bothering you for a while.
I'm here for you.
We're ALL here for you.
Okay... You know how I ended up in the laboratory where we were both experimented on?
You were a stray, and the aliens found you in an alley.

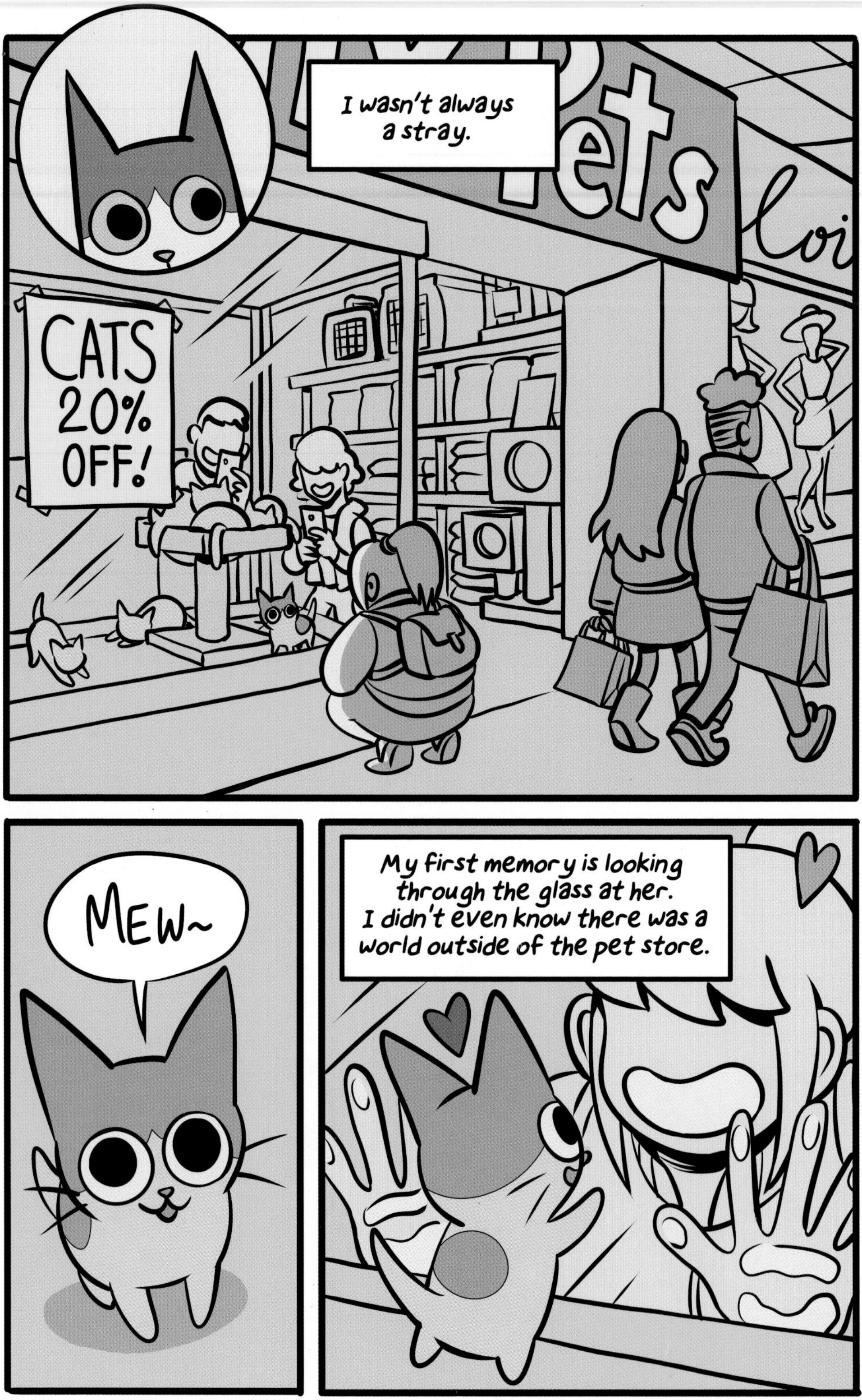
I wasn't always a stray.
Pets
CATS 20% OFF!
MEW~
My first memory is looking through the glass at her. I didn't even know there was a world outside of the pet store.

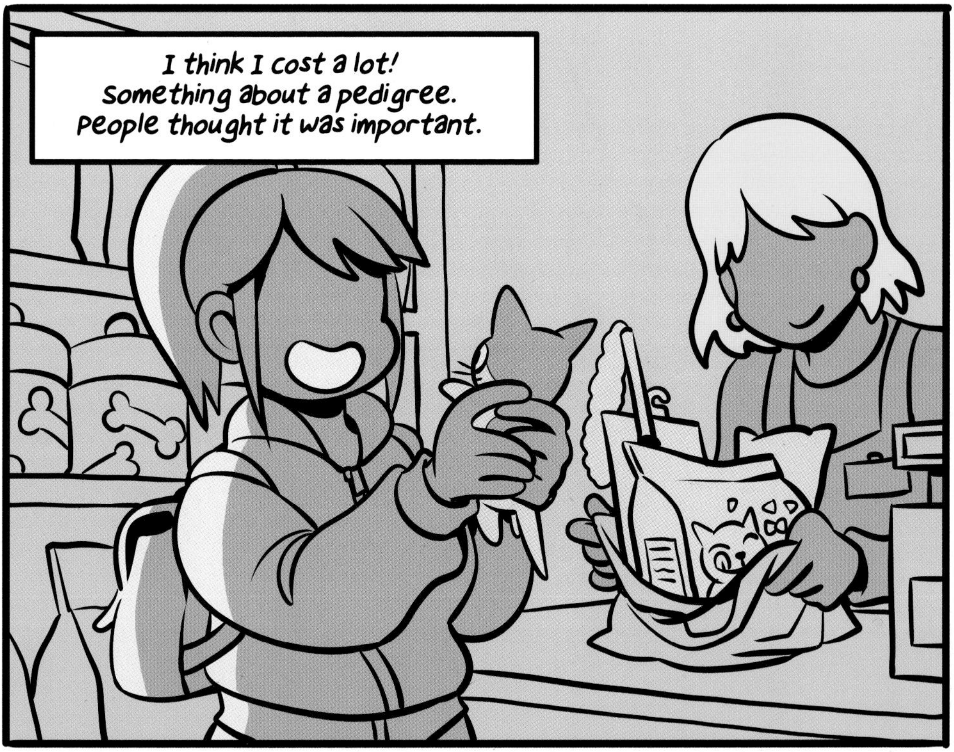
I think I cost a lot! Something about a pedigree. People thought it was important.

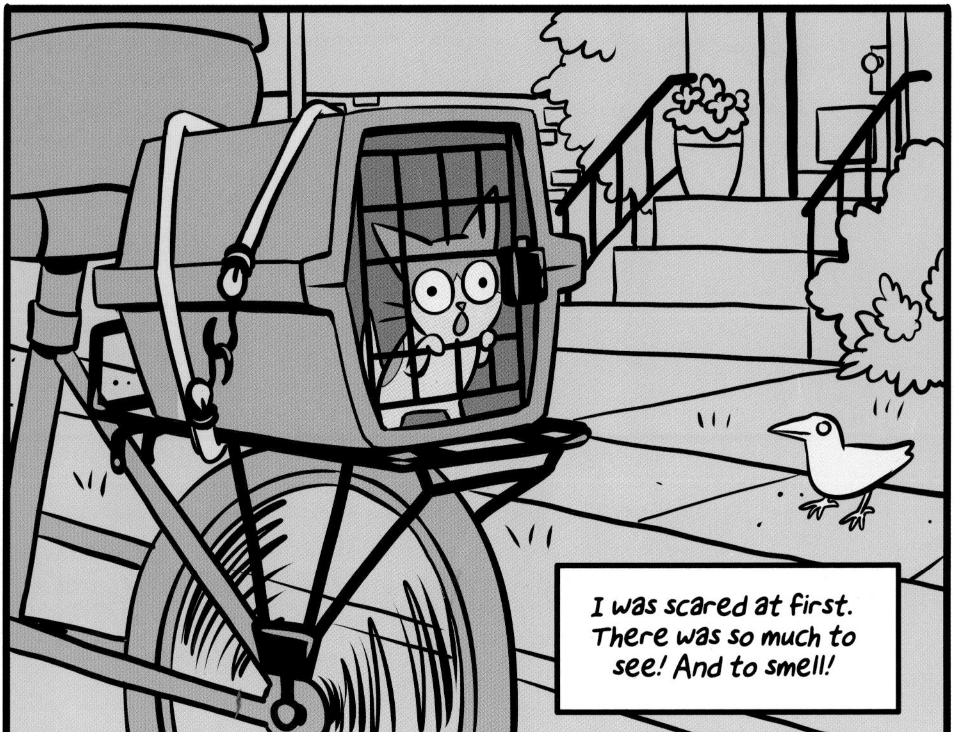
I was scared at first. There was so much to see! And to smell!

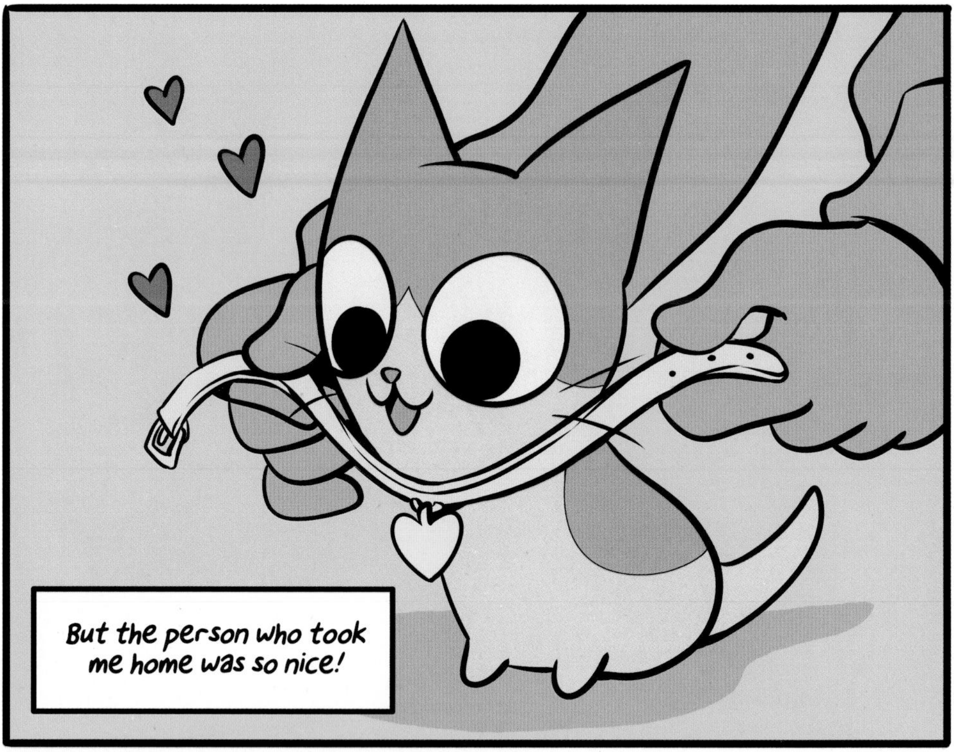
But the person who took me home was so nice!

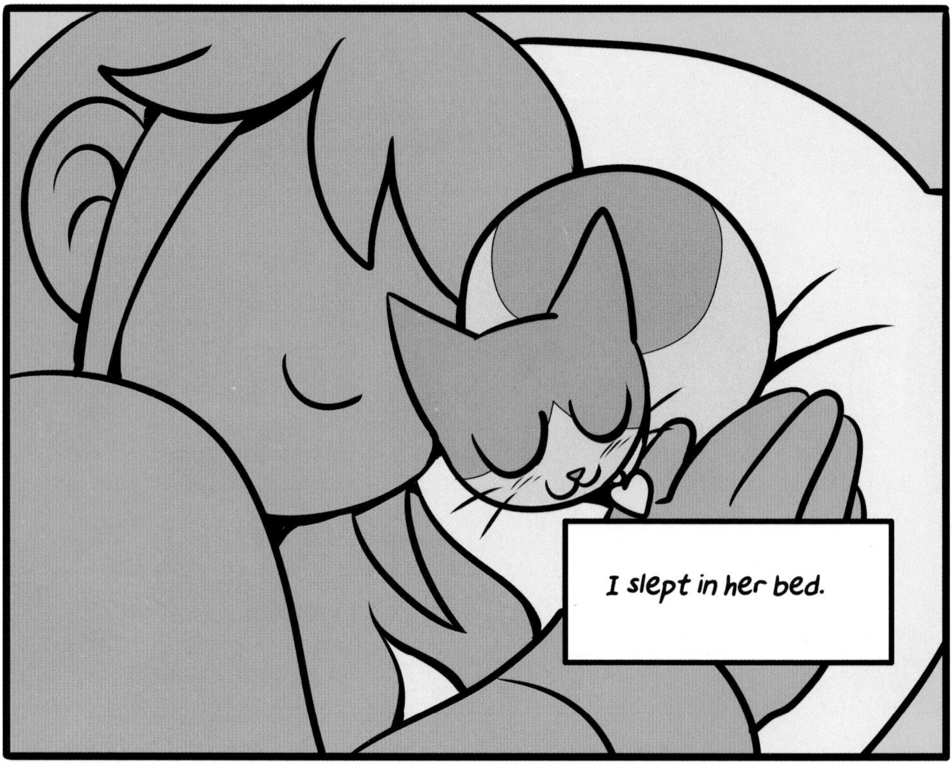
I slept in her bed.

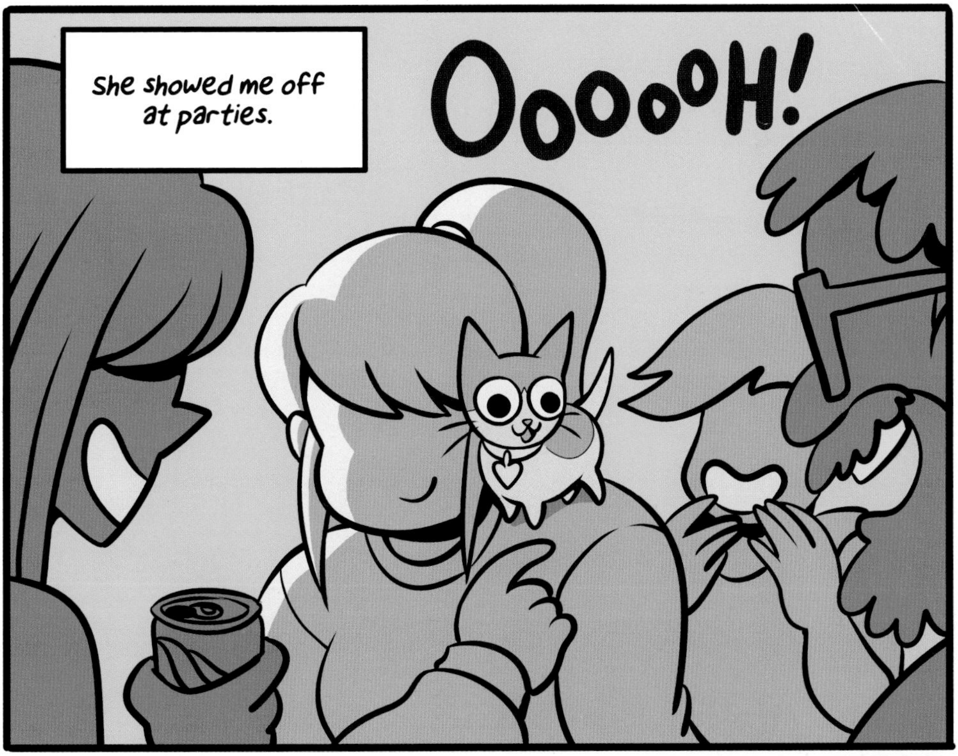
She showed me off at parties.
OooooH!

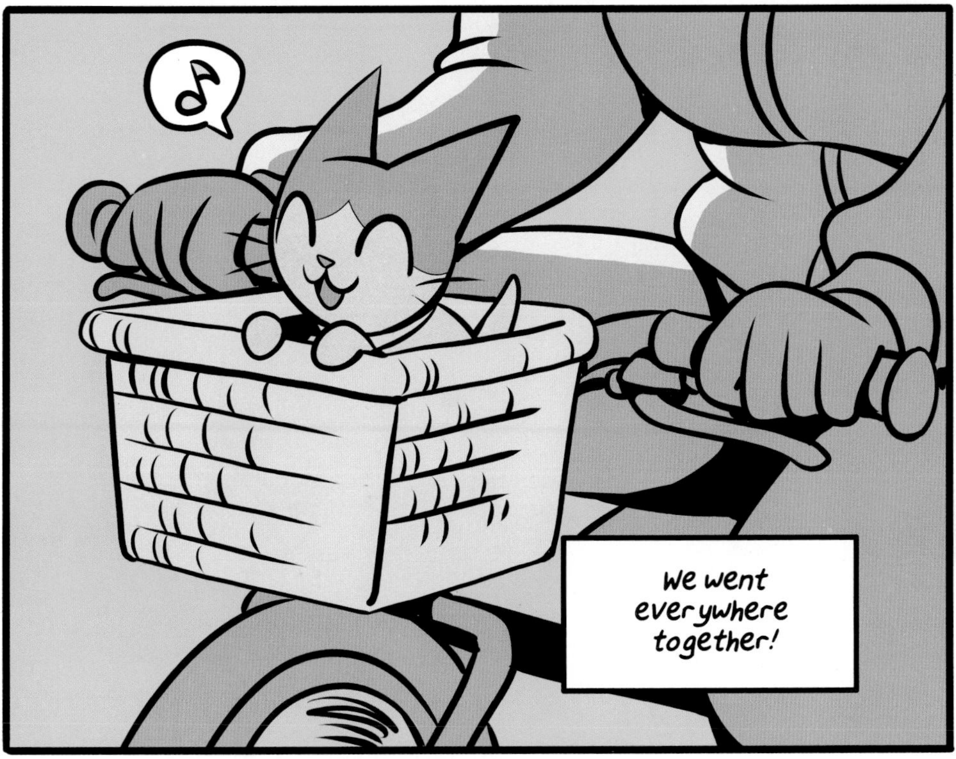
We went everywhere together!

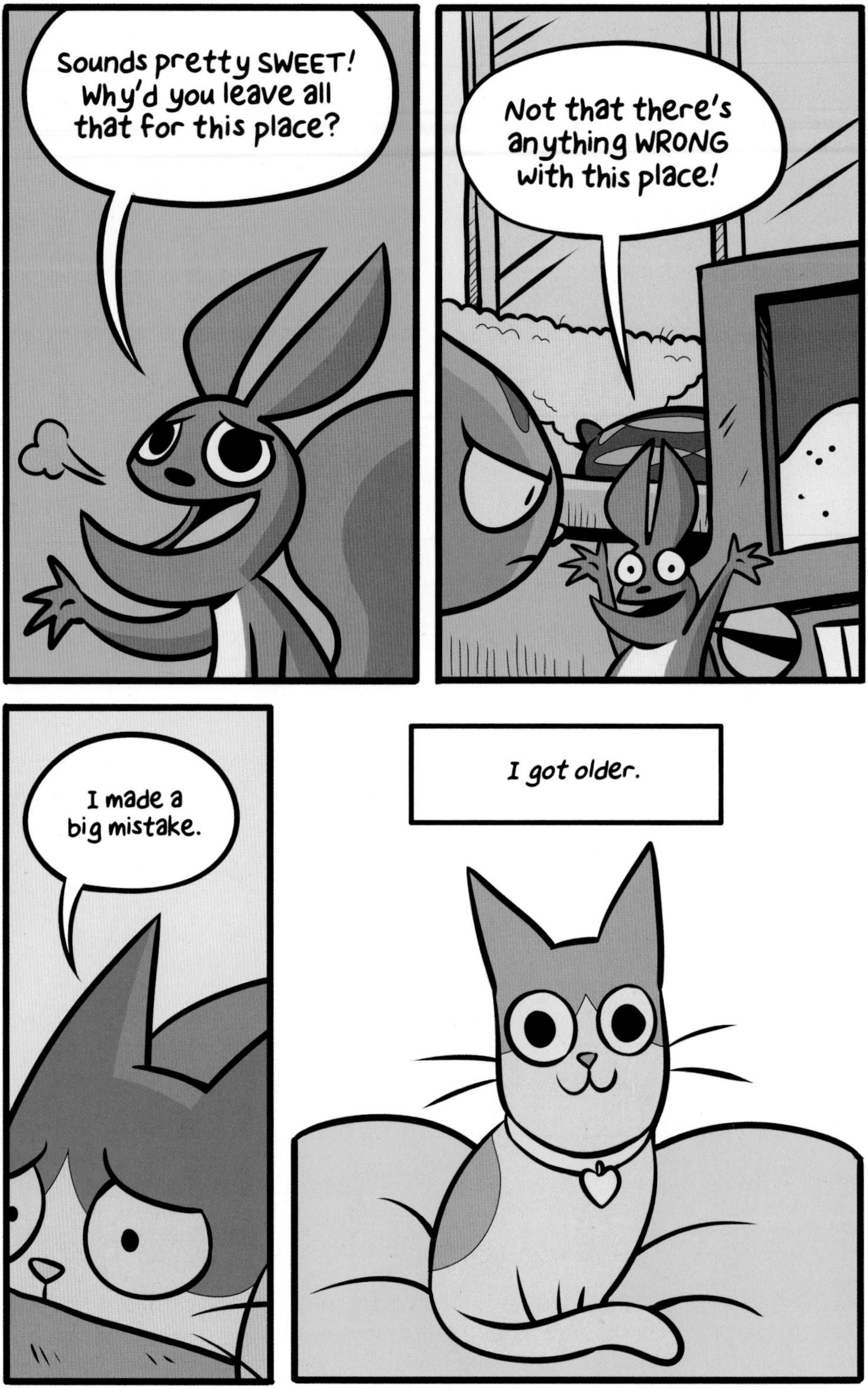
Sounds pretty SWEET! Why'd you leave all that for this place?
Not that there's anything WRONG with this place!
I made a big mistake.
I got older.

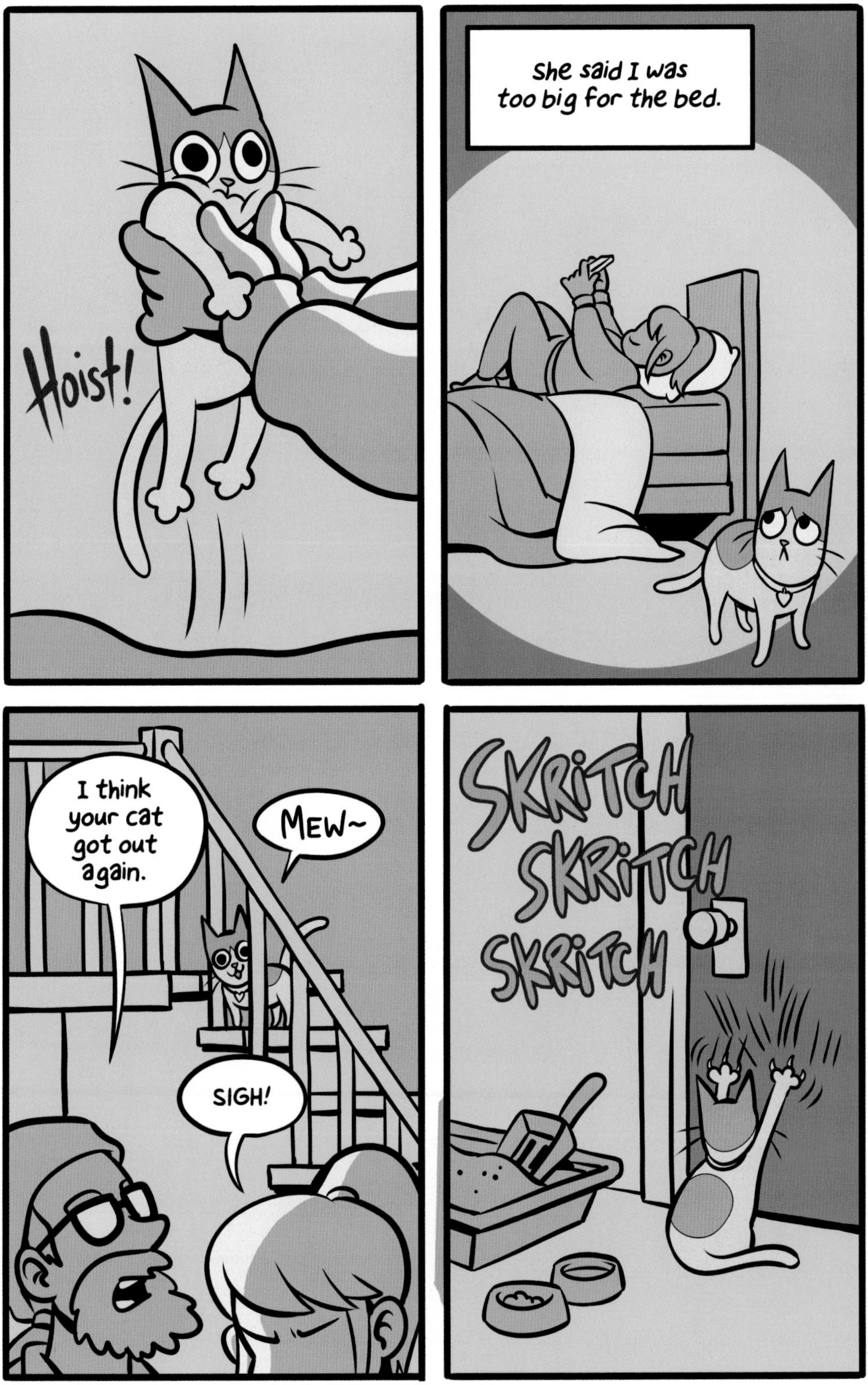
Hoist!
She said I was too big for the bed.
I think your cat got out again.
MEW~
SIGH!
SKRITCH
SKRITCH
SKRITCH

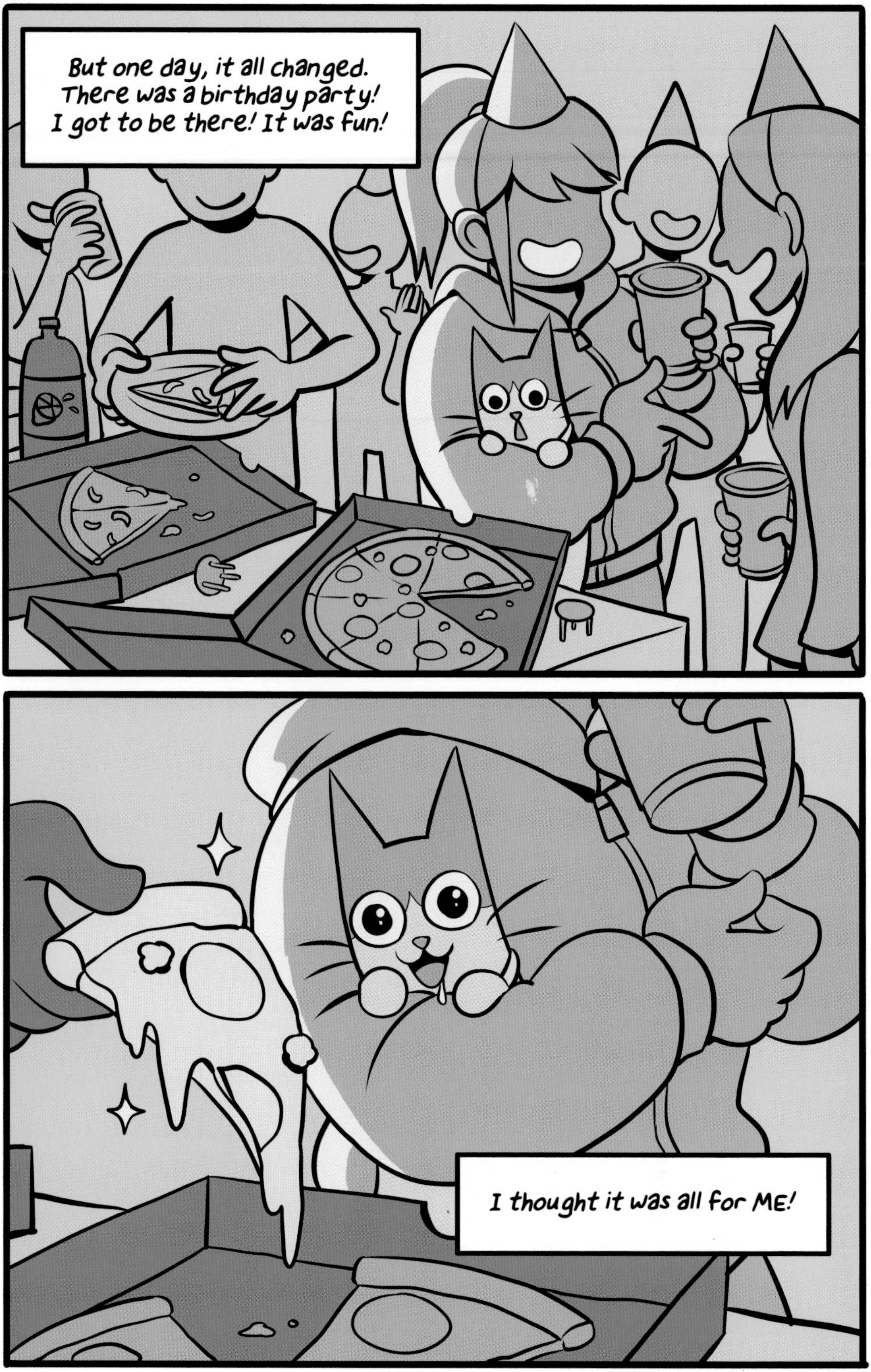
But one day, it all changed. There was a birthday party! I got to be there! It was fun!
I thought it was all for ME!

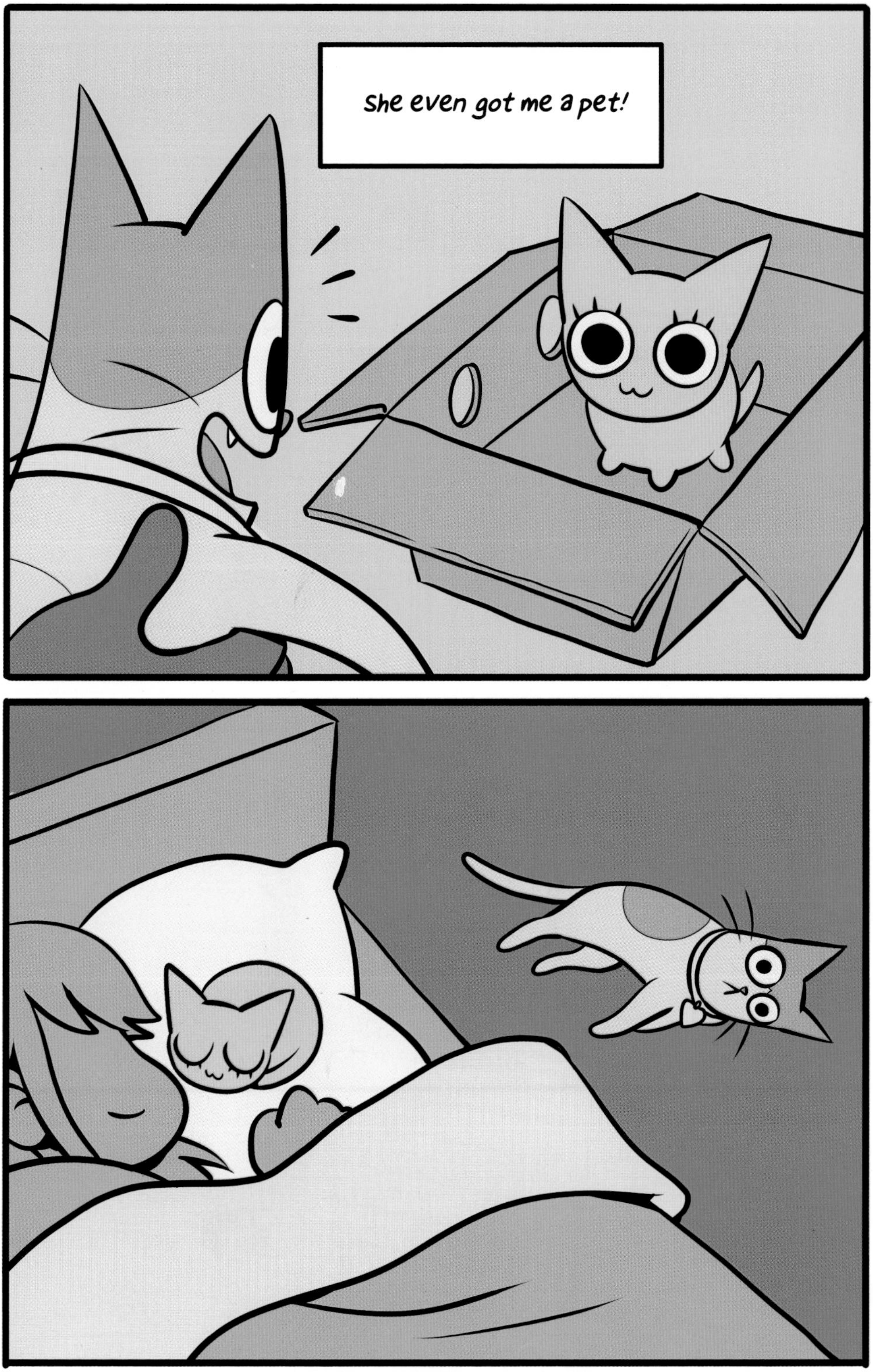
she even got me a pet!

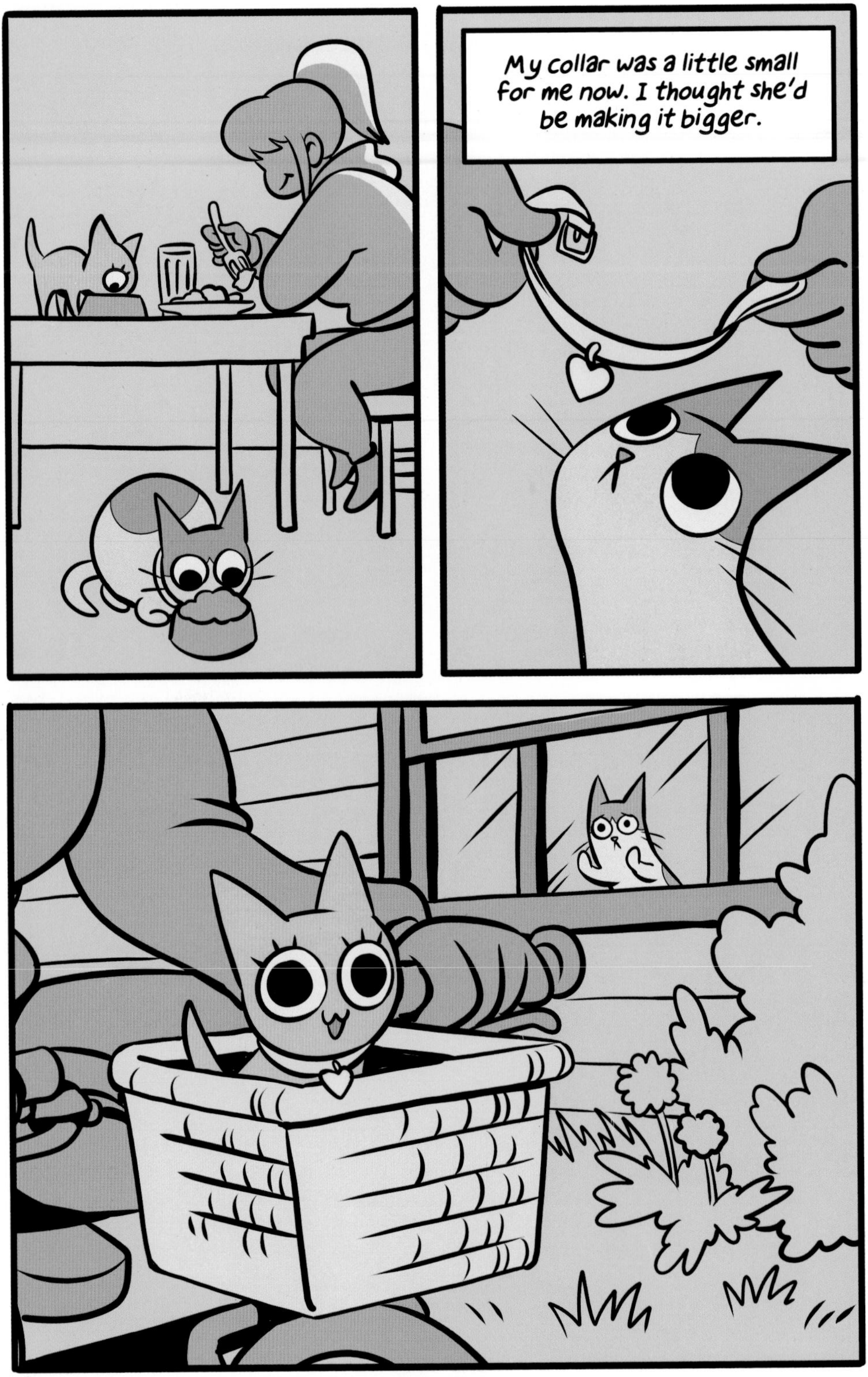
My collar was a little small for me now. I thought she'd be making it bigger.

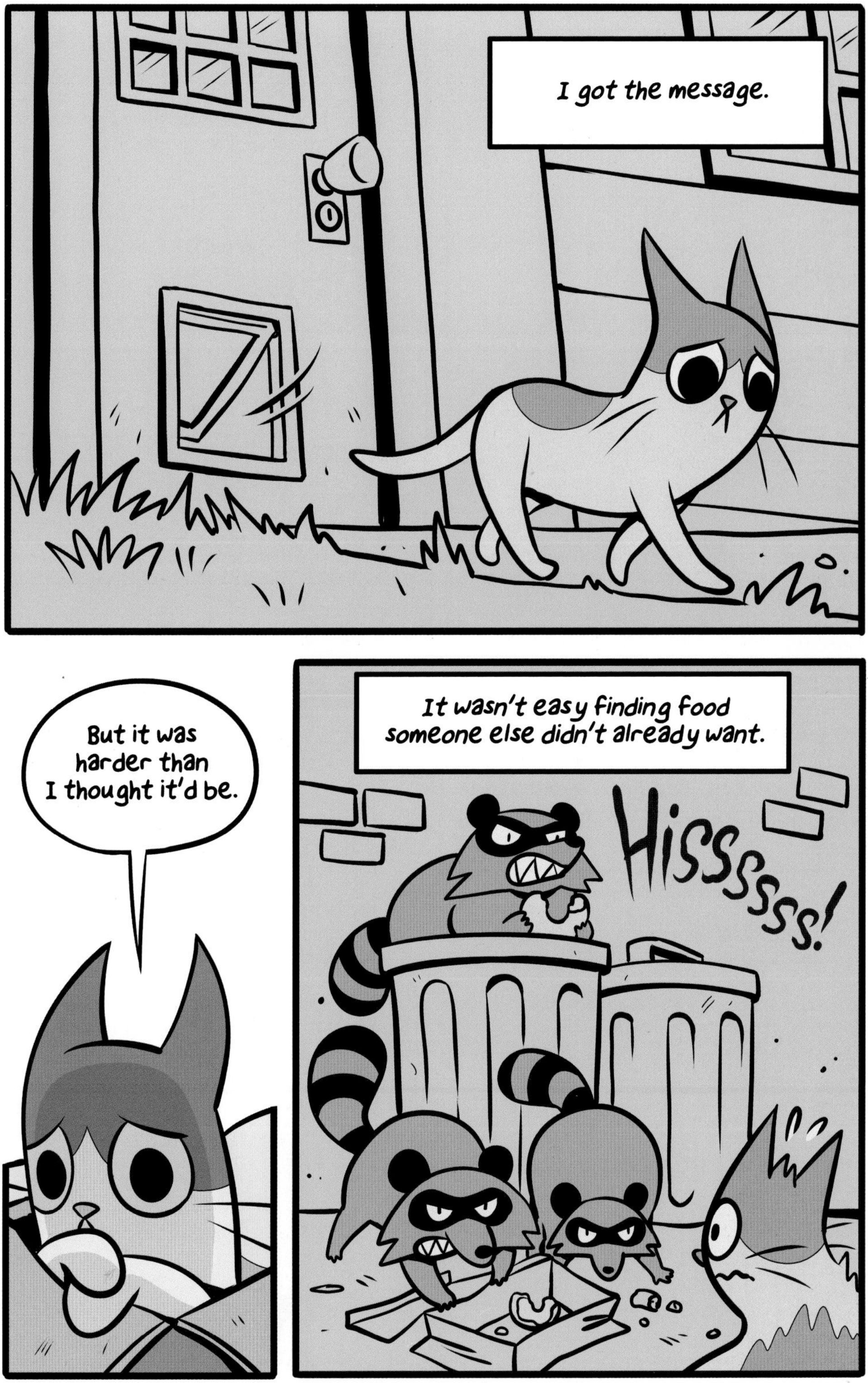
I got the message.
But it was harder than I thought it'd be.
It wasn't easy finding food someone else didn't already want.
HISSSSSS!

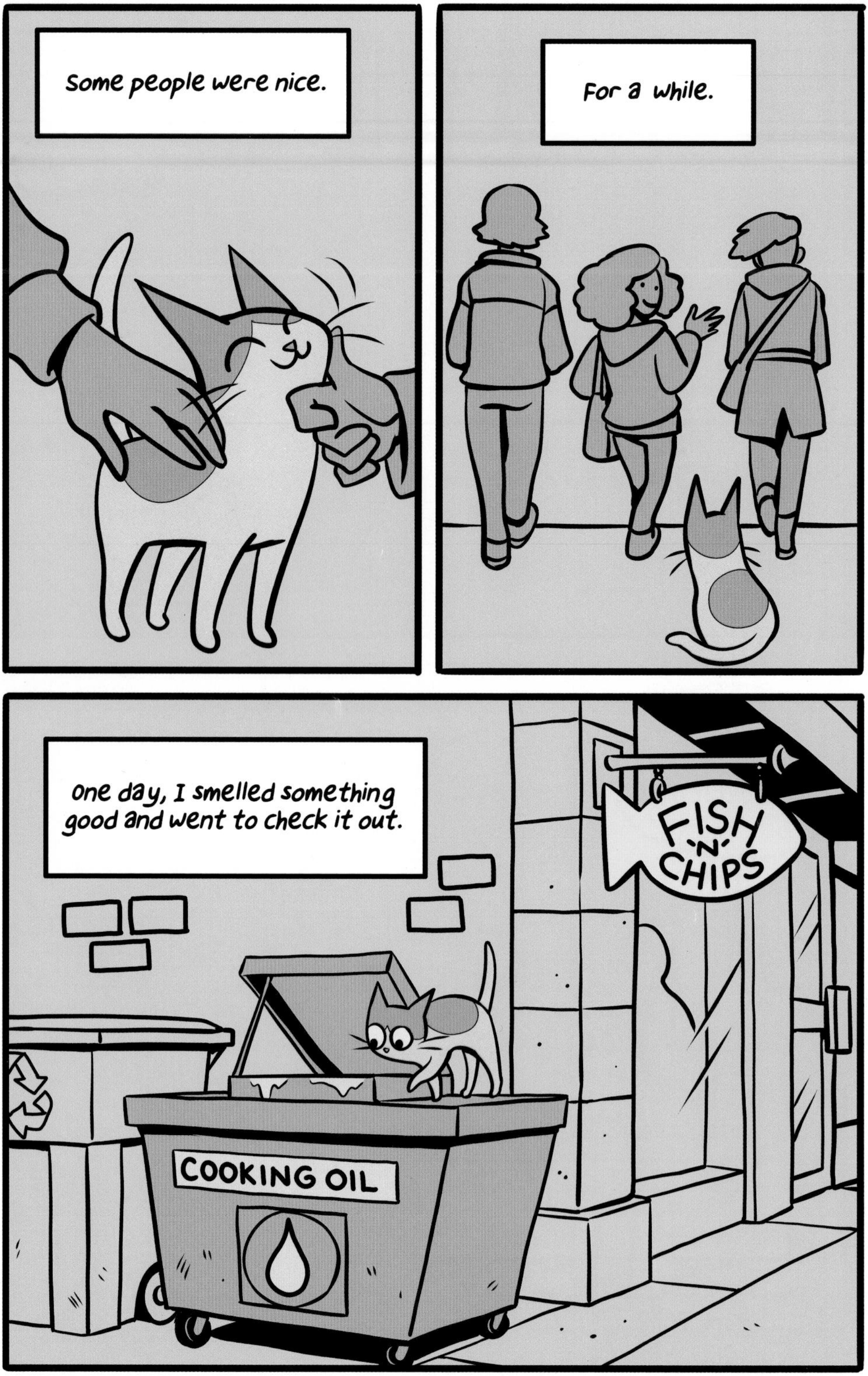
Some people were nice.
For a while.
One day, I smelled something good and went to check it out.
FISH -N- CHIPS
COOKING OIL

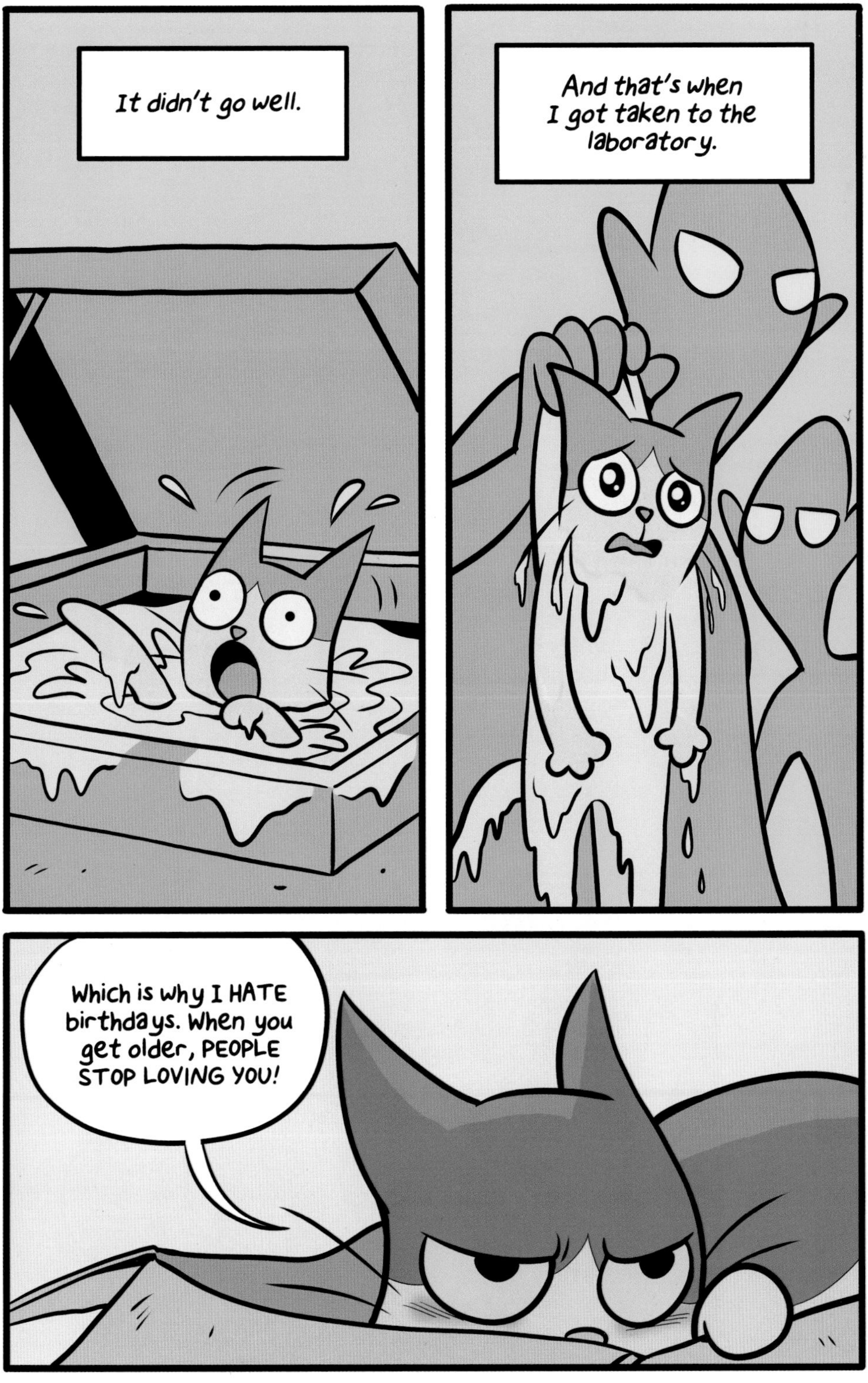
It didn't go well.
And that's when I got taken to the laboratory.
Which is why I HATE birthdays. When you get older, PEOPLE STOP LOVING YOU!

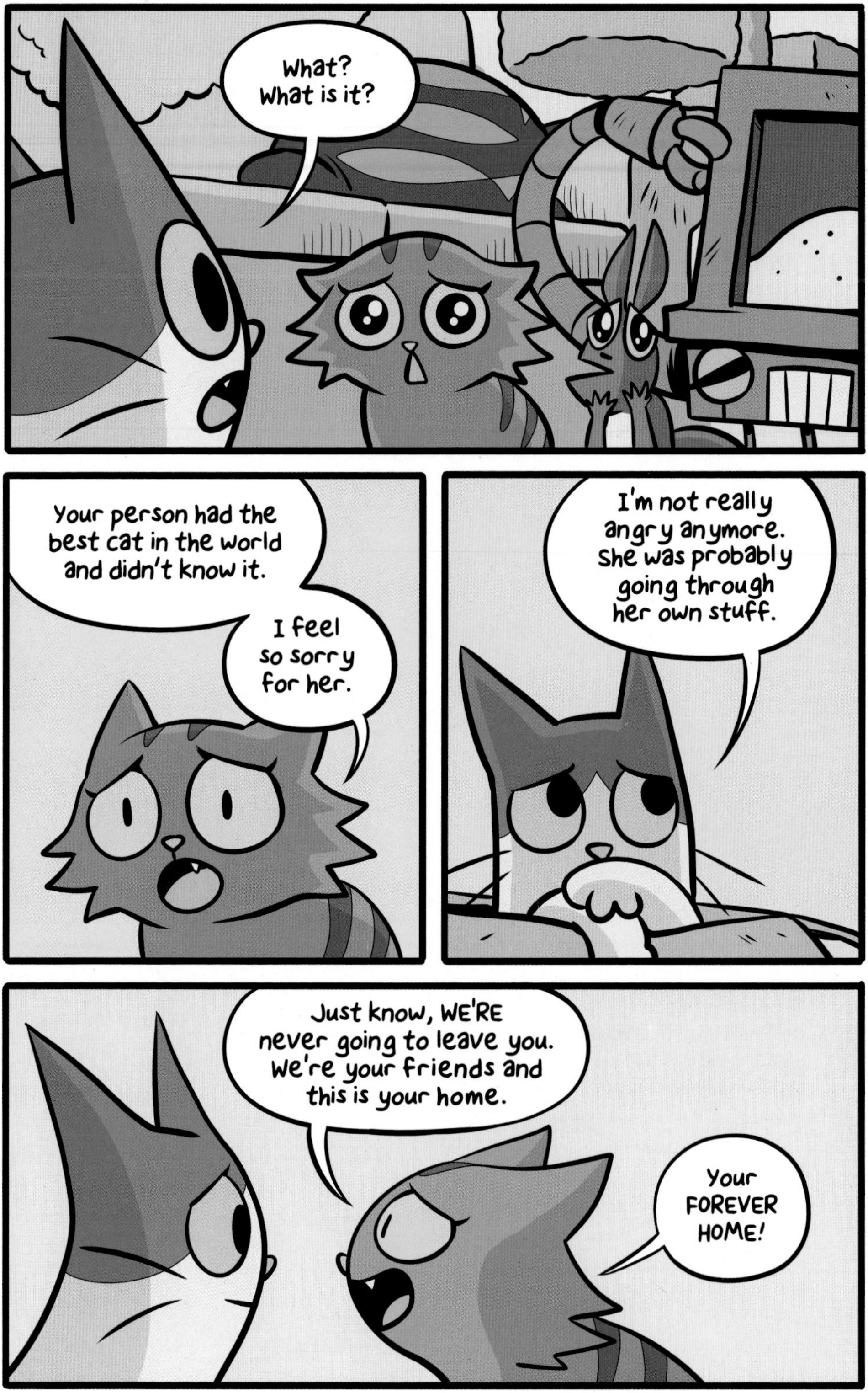
What? What is it?
Your person had the best cat in the world and didn't know it.
I feel so sorry for her.
I'm not really angry anymore. She was probably going through her own stuff.
Just know, WE'RE never going to leave you. We're your friends and this is your home.
Your FOREVER HOME!

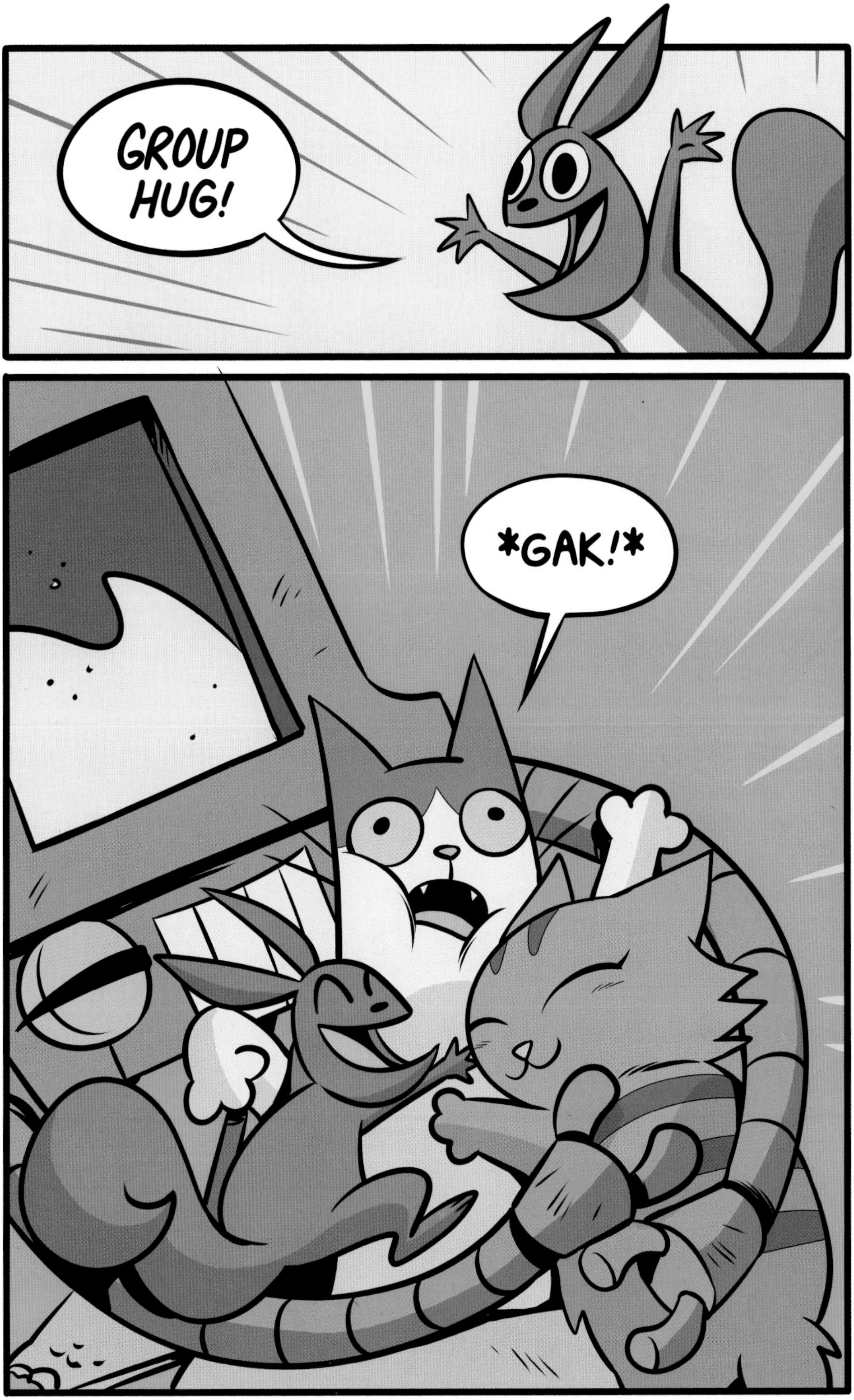
GROUP HUG!
GAK!

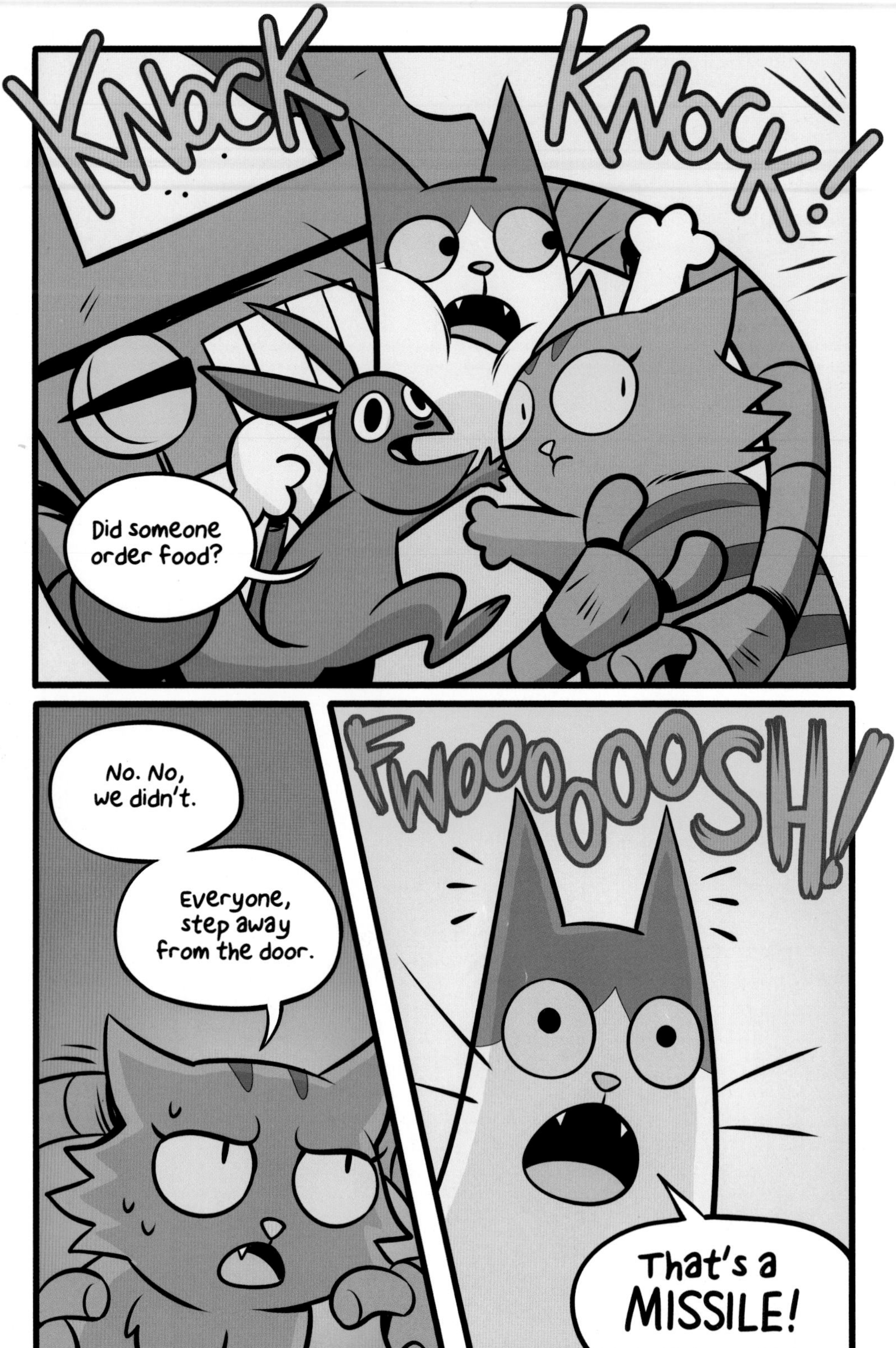
KNOCK
KNOCK!
Did someone order food?
No. No, we didn't.
Everyone, step away from the door.
FWOOOOOOSH!
That's a MISSILE!

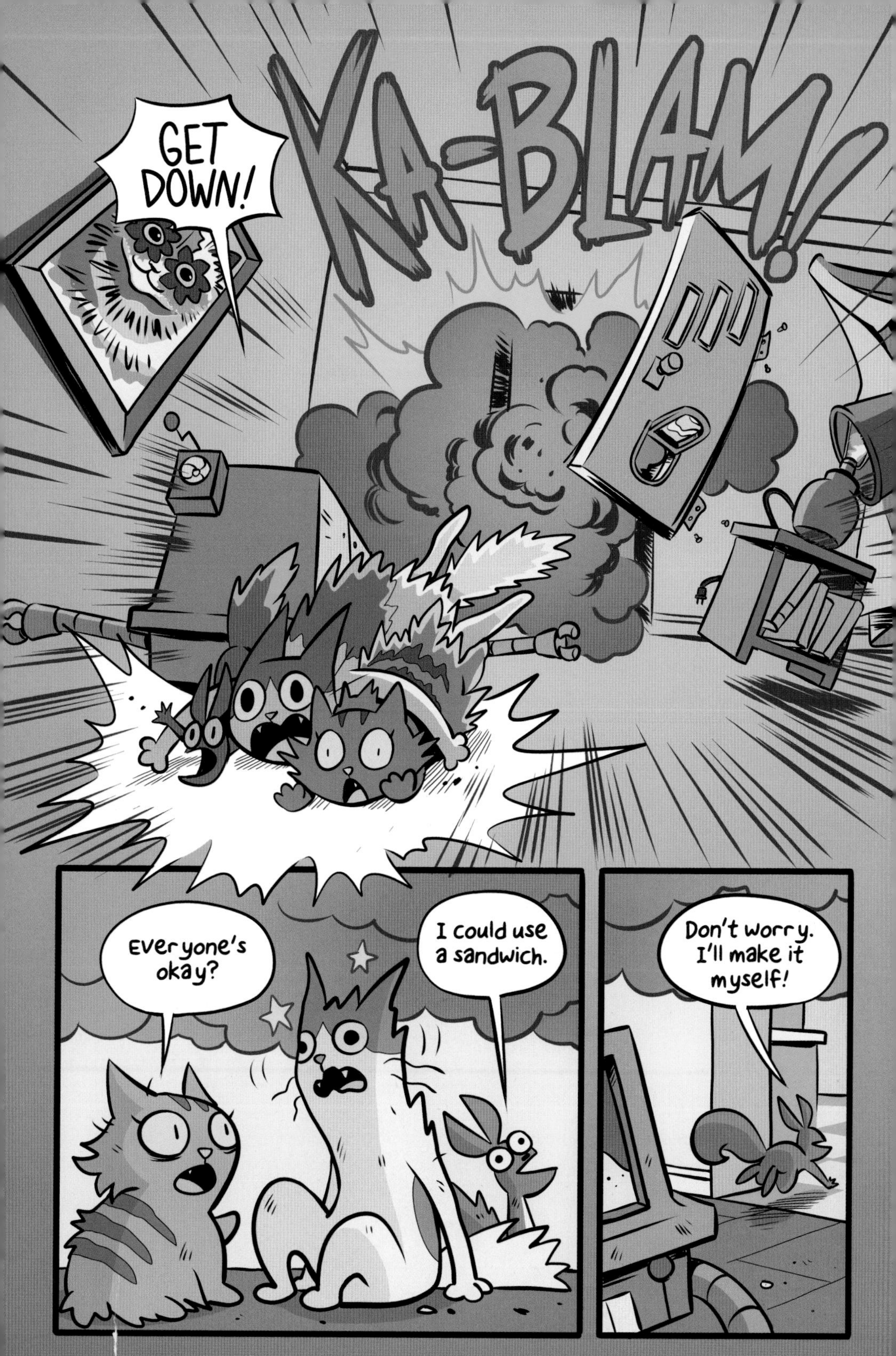
GET DOWN!
KA-BLAM!!
Everyone's okay?
I could use a sandwich.
Don't worry. I'll make it myself!

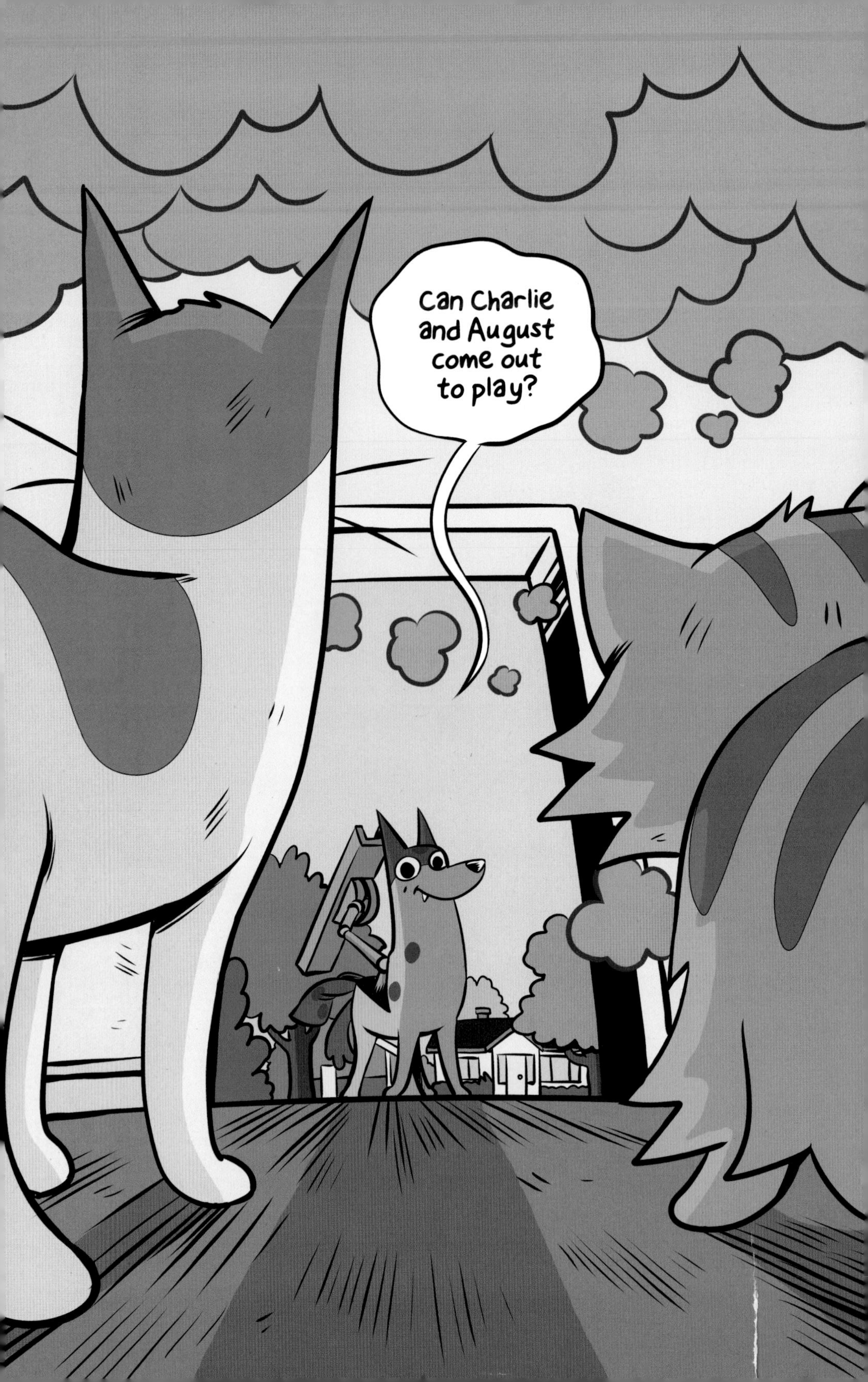
Can Charlie and August come out to play?

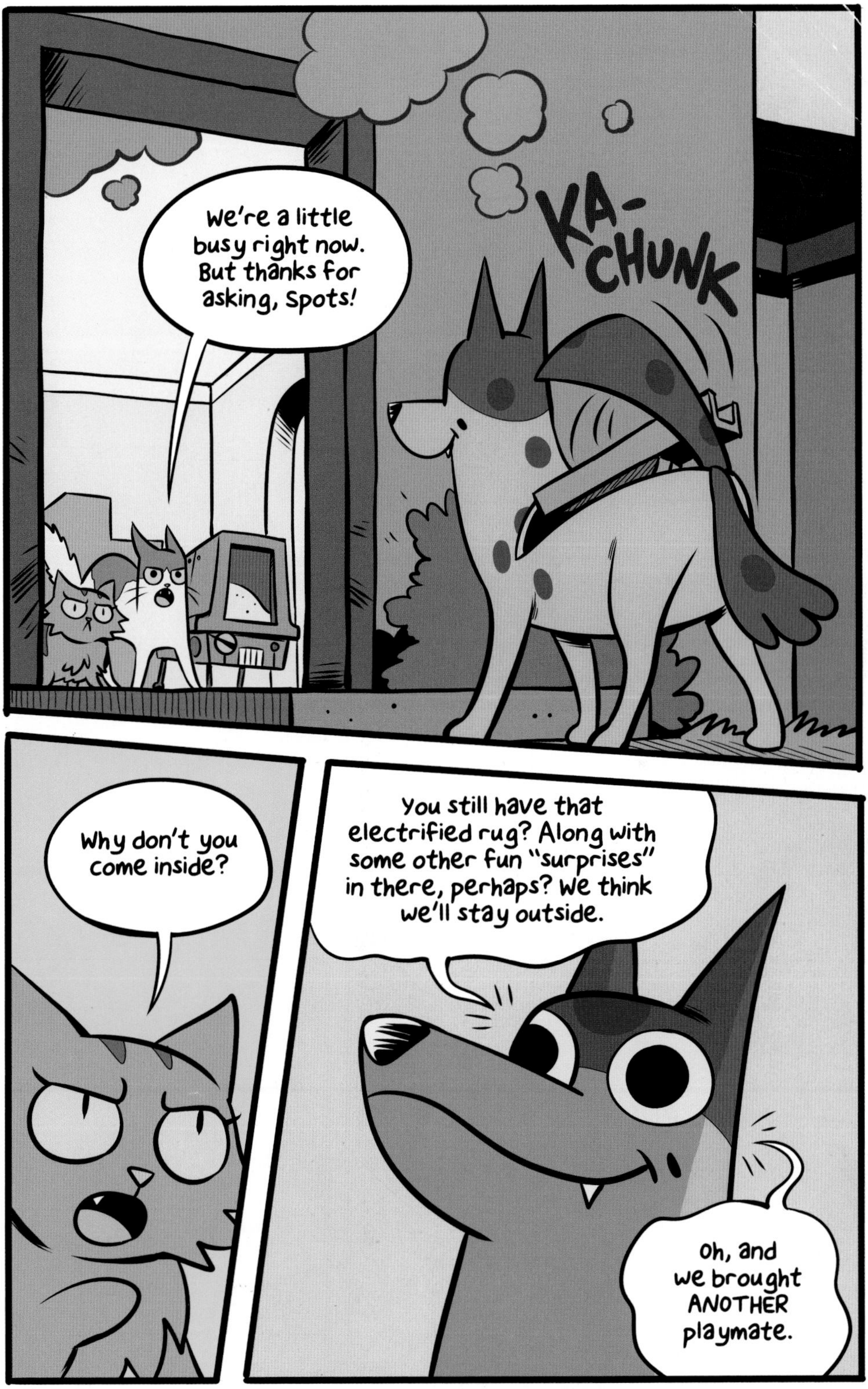
We're a little busy right now. But thanks for asking, Spots!
KA-CHUNK
Why don't you come inside?
You still have that electrified rug? Along with some other fun "surprises" in there, perhaps? We think we'll stay outside.
Oh, and we brought ANOTHER playmate.

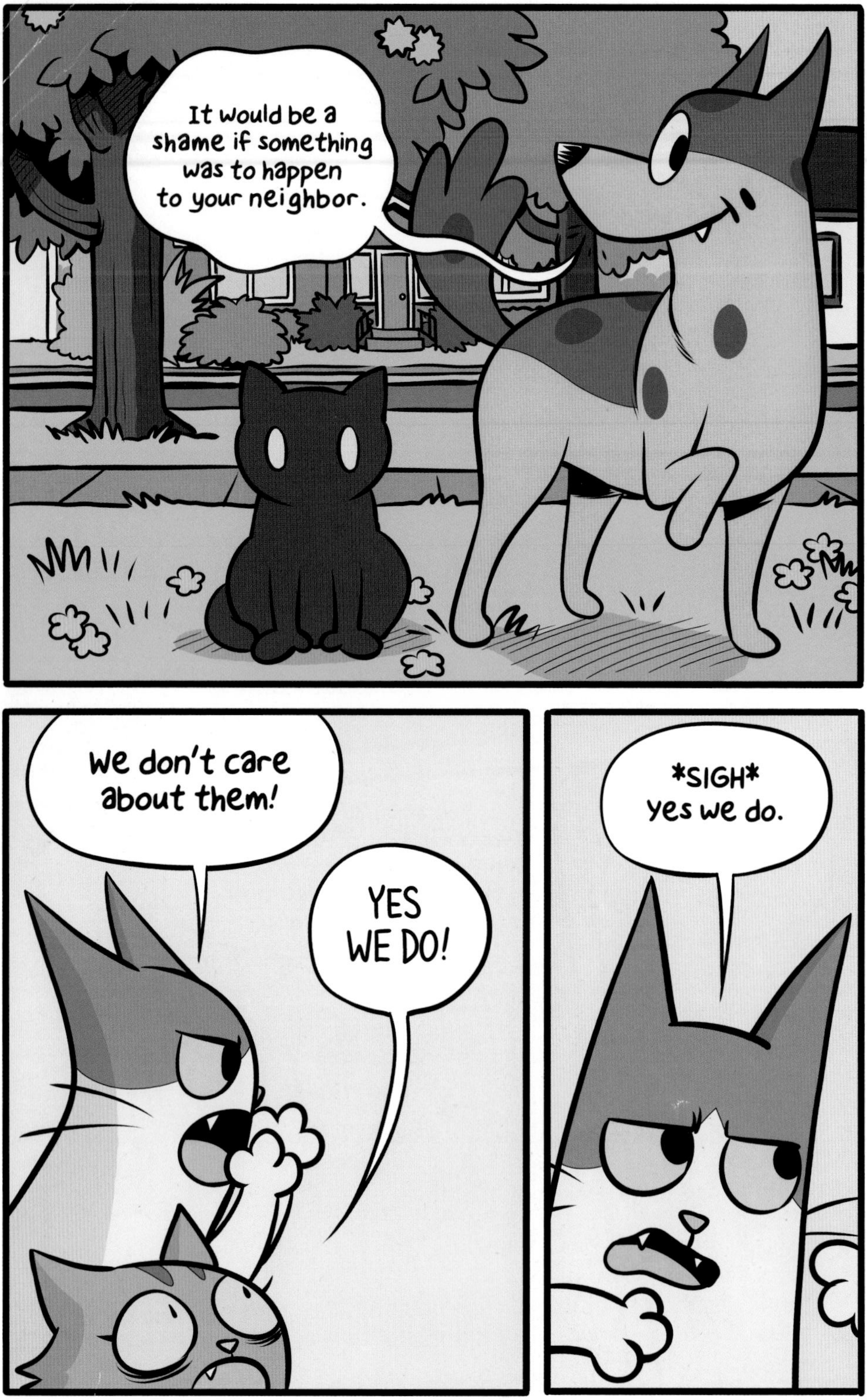
It would be a shame if something was to happen to your neighbor.
We don't care about them!
YES WE DO!
SIGH yes we do.

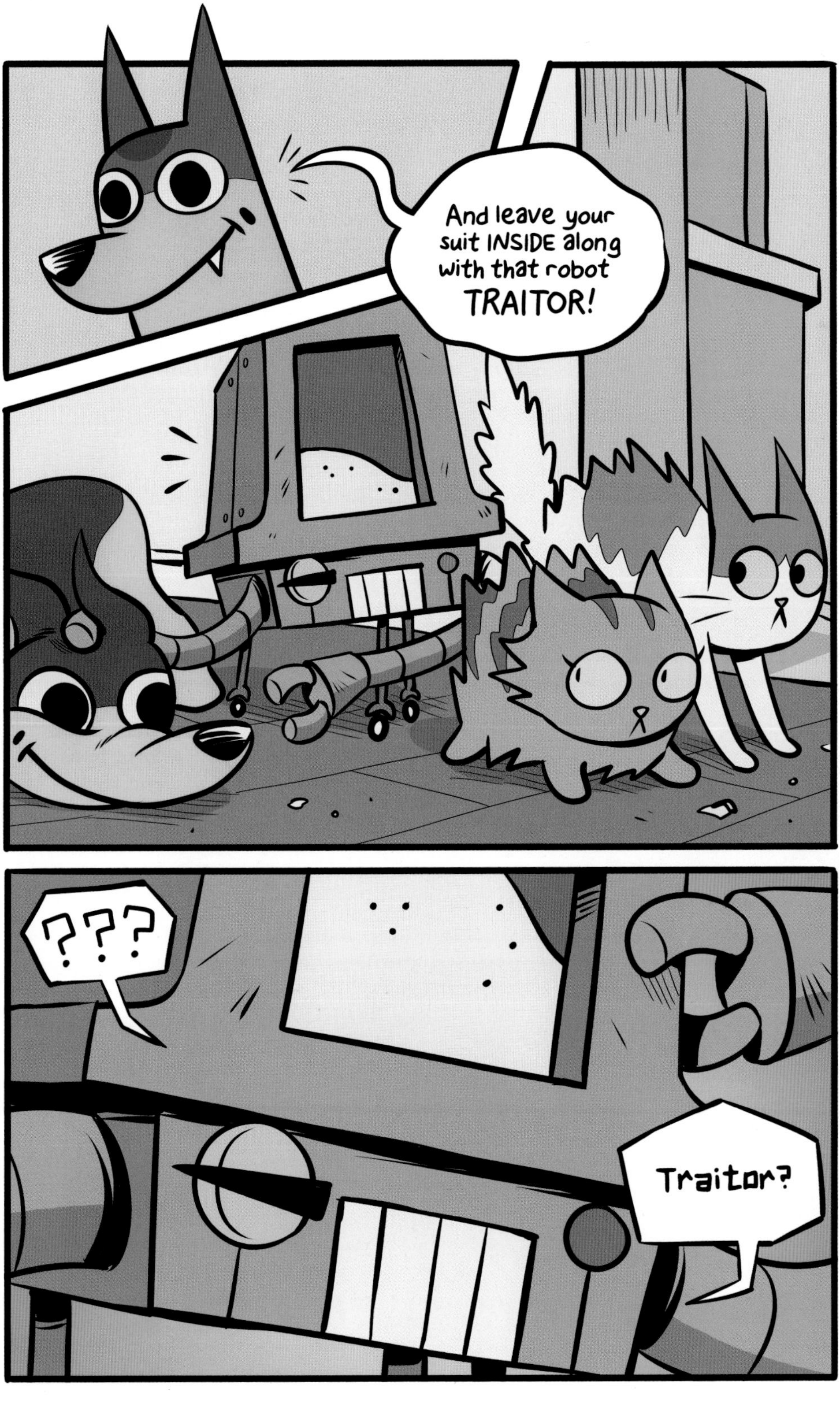
And leave your suit INSIDE along with that robot TRAITOR!
???
Traitor?

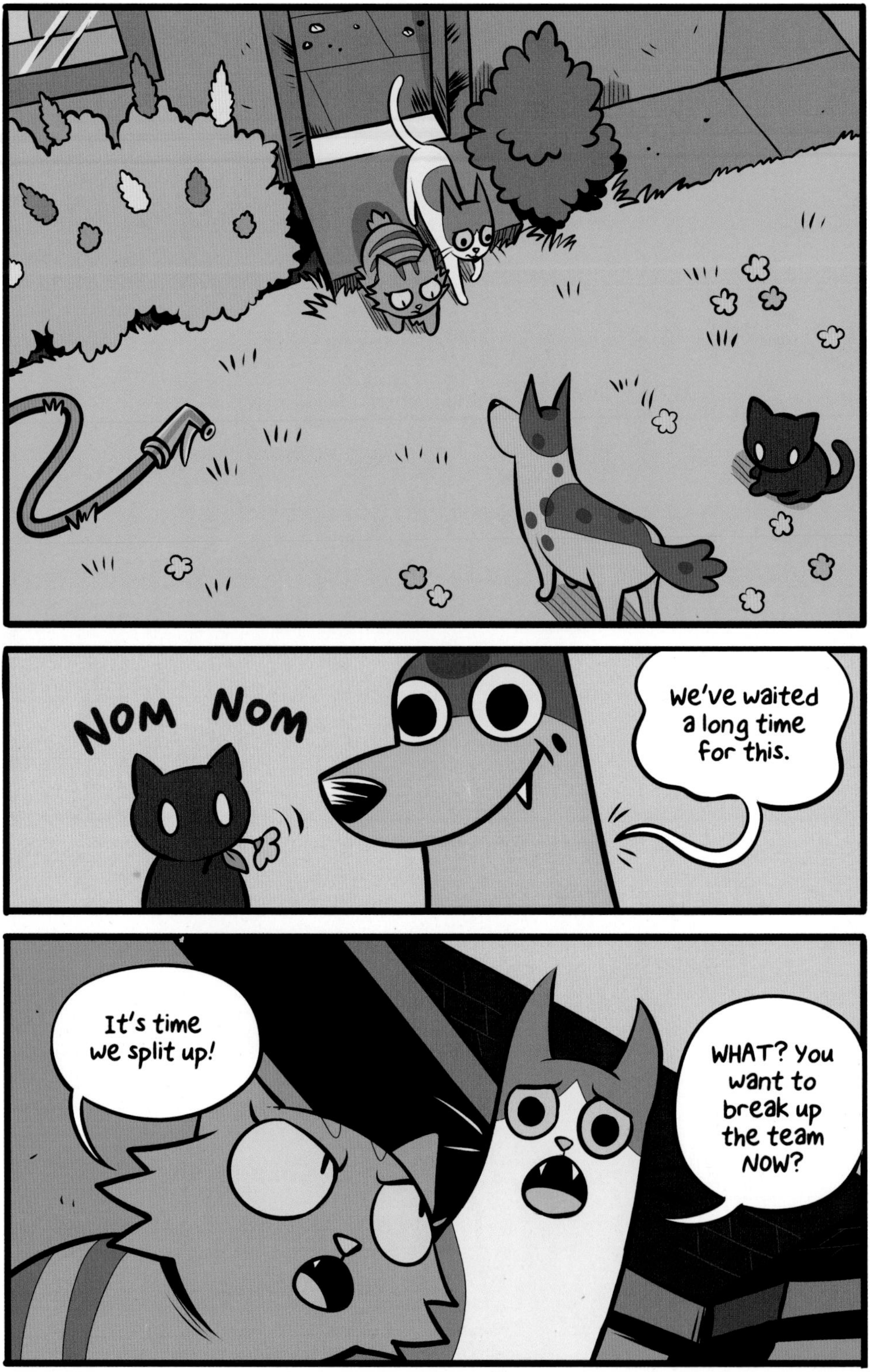
NOM NOM
We've waited a long time for this.
It's time we split up!
WHAT? You want to break up the team NOW?

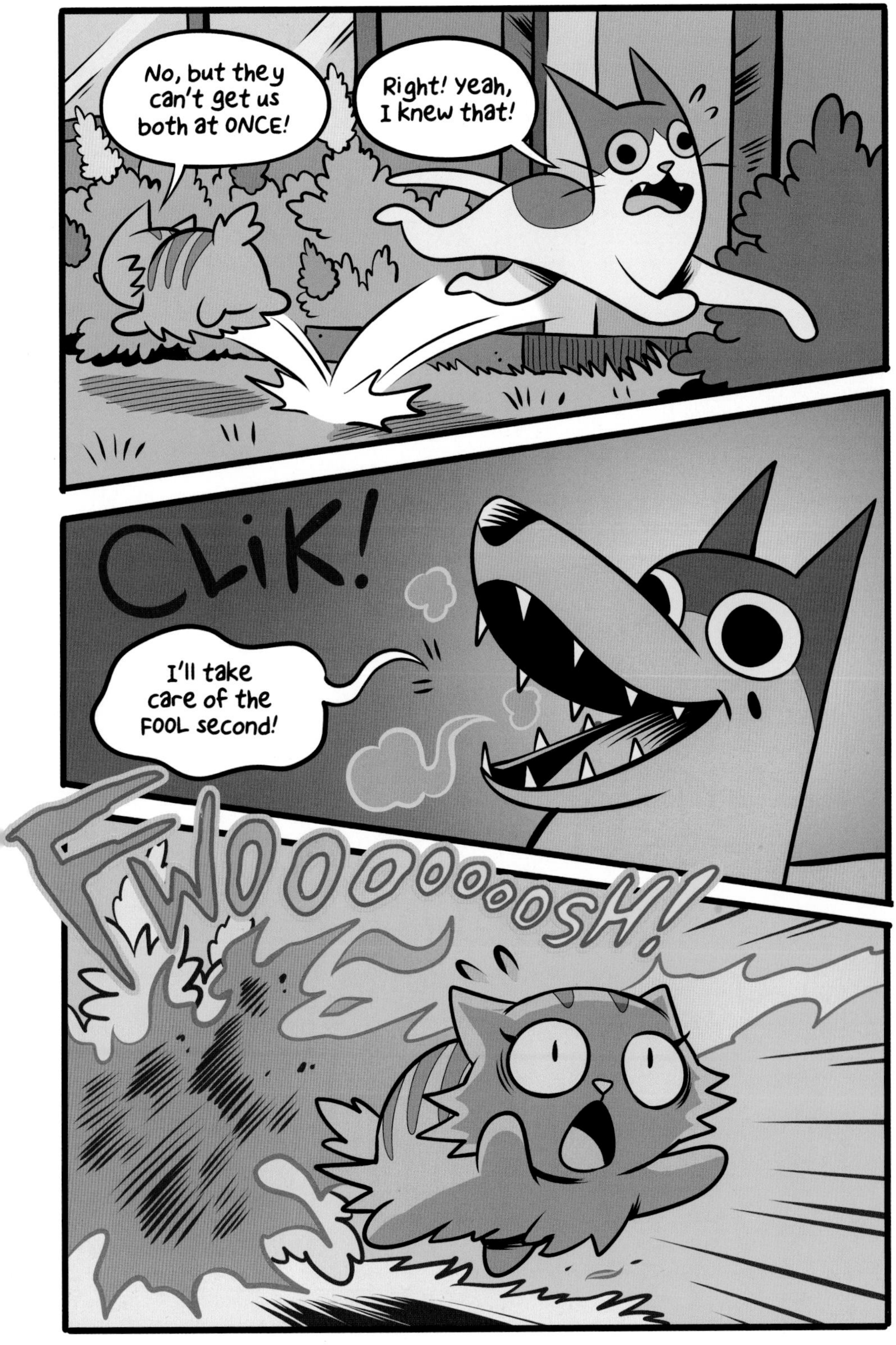
No, but they can't get us both at ONCE!
Right! yeah, I knew that!
CLIK!
I'll take care of the FOOL second!
FWOOOOOOOSH!

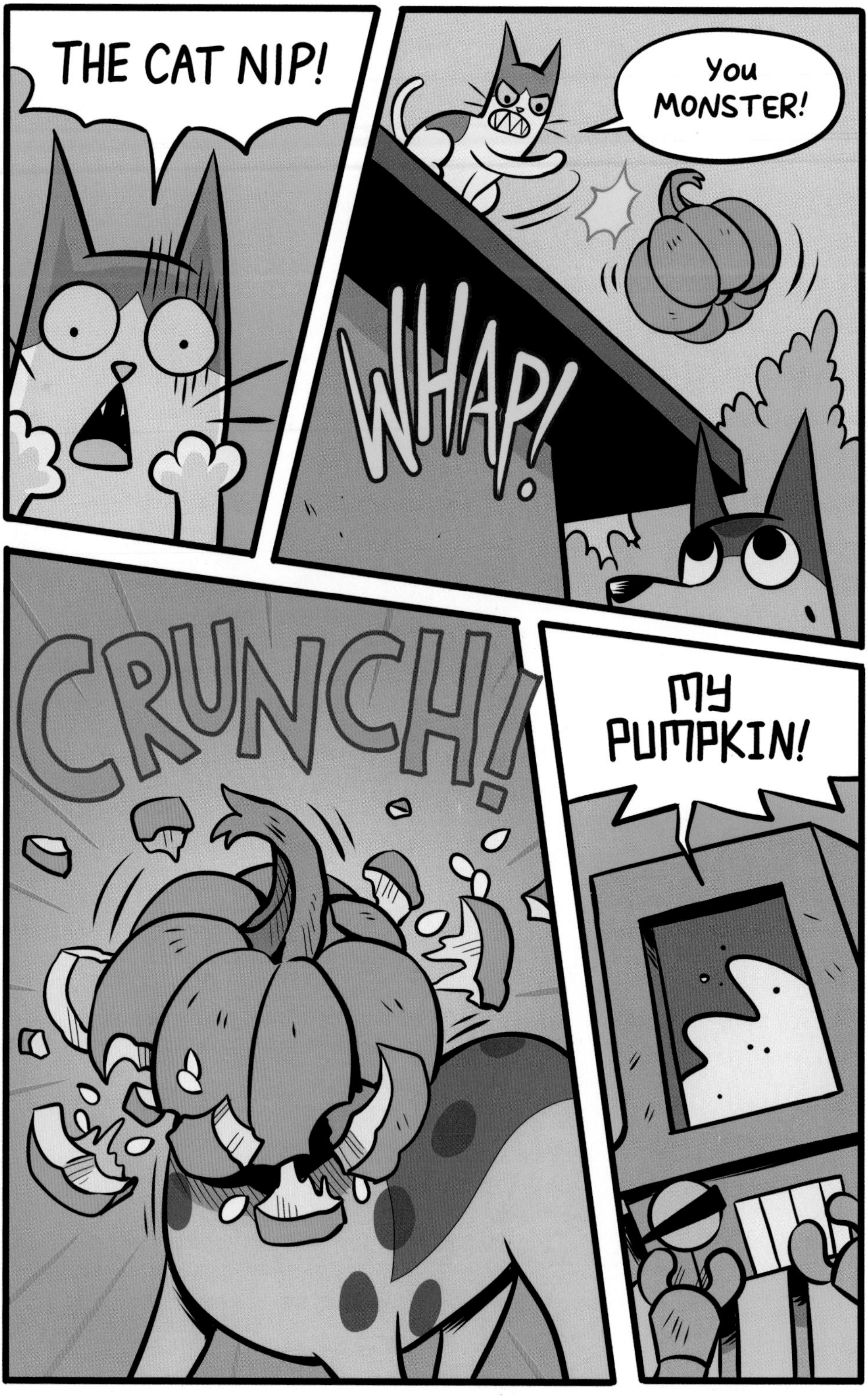
THE CAT NIP!
You MONSTER!
WHAP!
CRUNCH!
MY PUMPKIN!

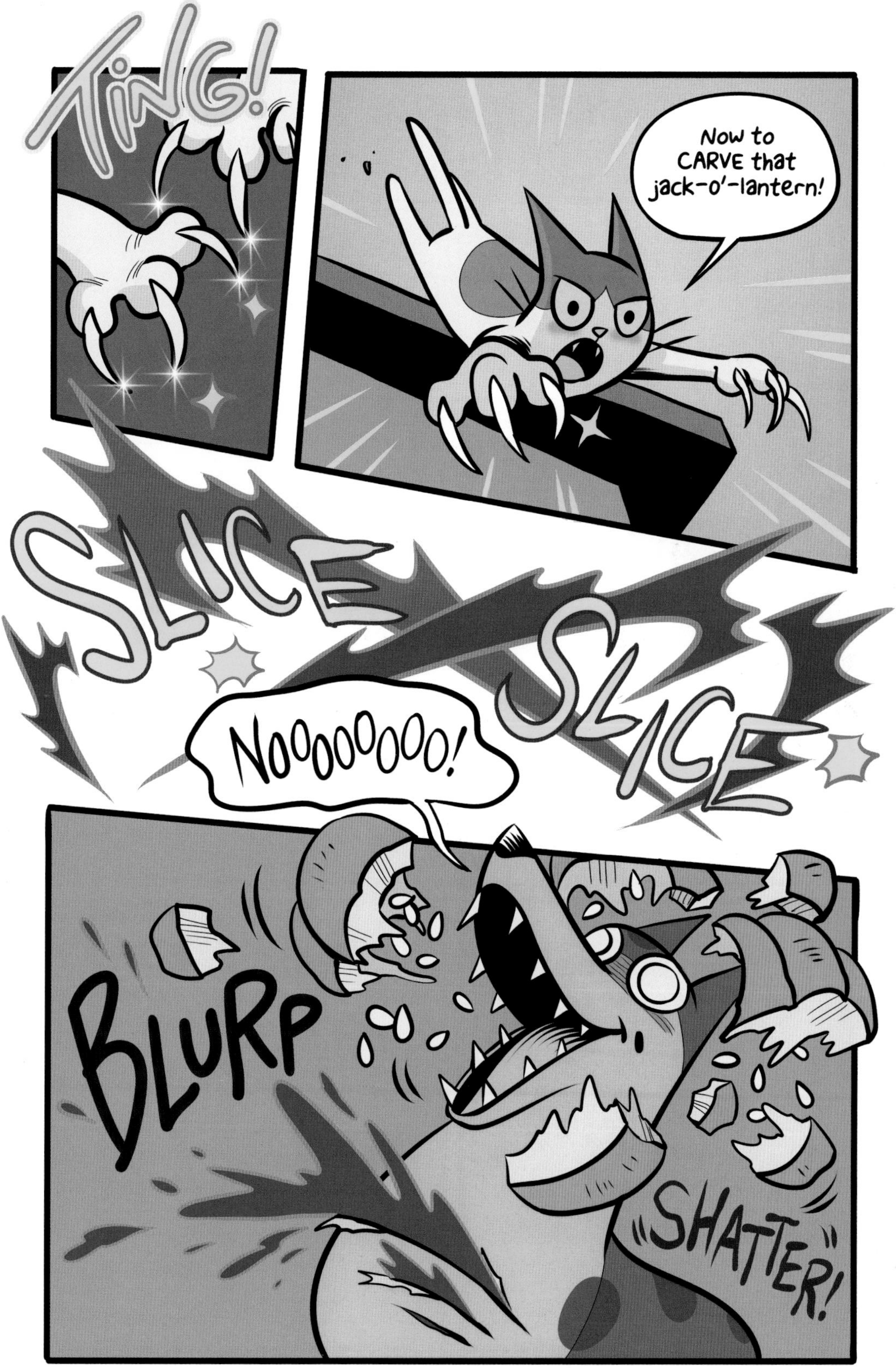
TING!
Now to CARVE that jack-o'-lantern!
SLICE
SLICE
NOOOOOOOO!
BLURP
SHATTER!

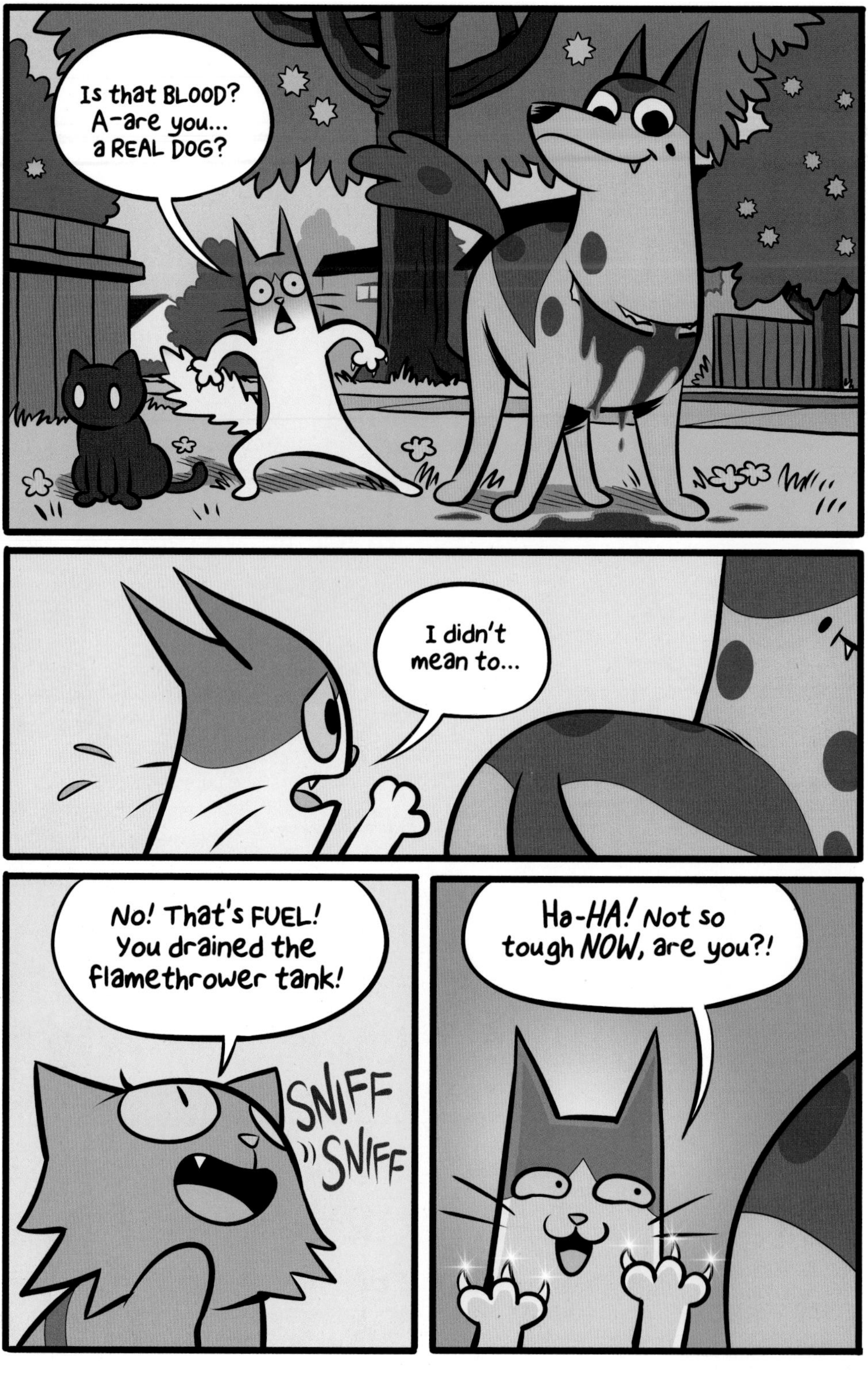
Is that BLOOD? A-are you... a REAL DOG?
I didn't mean to...
No! That's FUEL! You drained the flamethrower tank!
SNIFF
SNIFF
Ha-HA! Not so tough NOW, are you?!

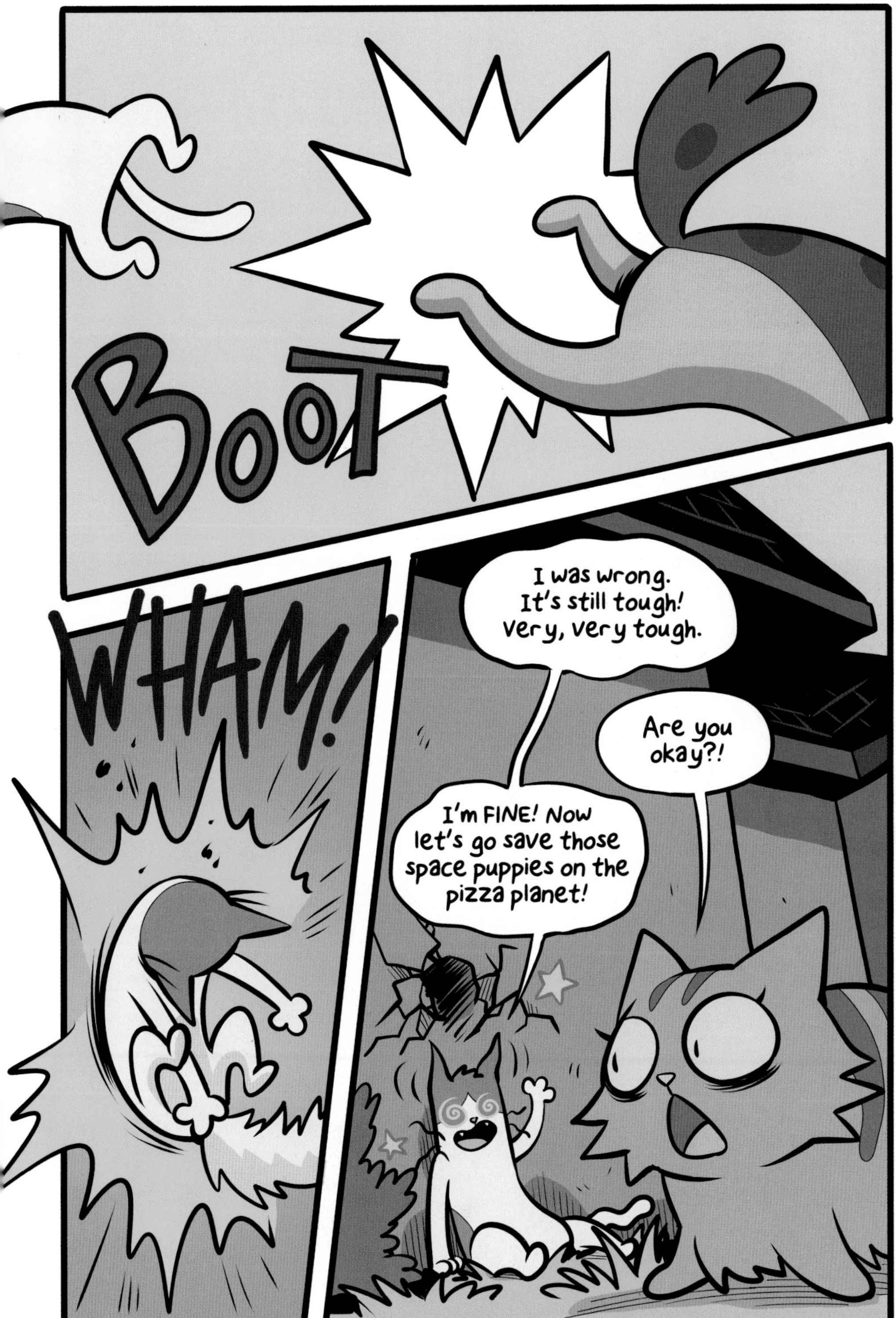
BOOT
WHAM!
I was wrong. It's still tough! Very, very tough.
Are you okay?!
I'm FINE! Now let's go save those space puppies on the pizza planet!

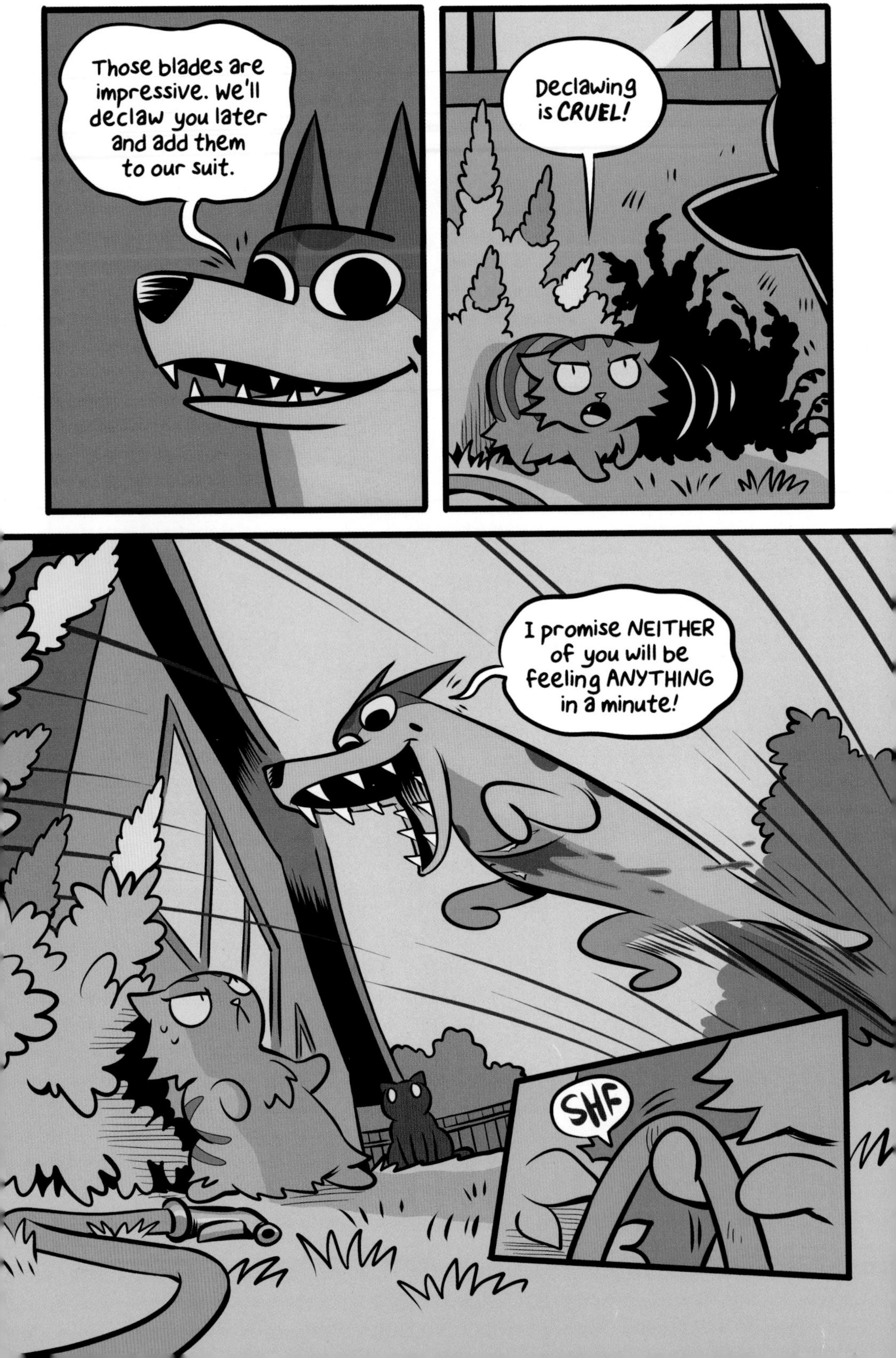
Those blades are impressive. We'll declaw you later and add them to our suit.
Declawing is CRUEL!
I promise NEITHER of you will be feeling ANYTHING in a minute!
SHF

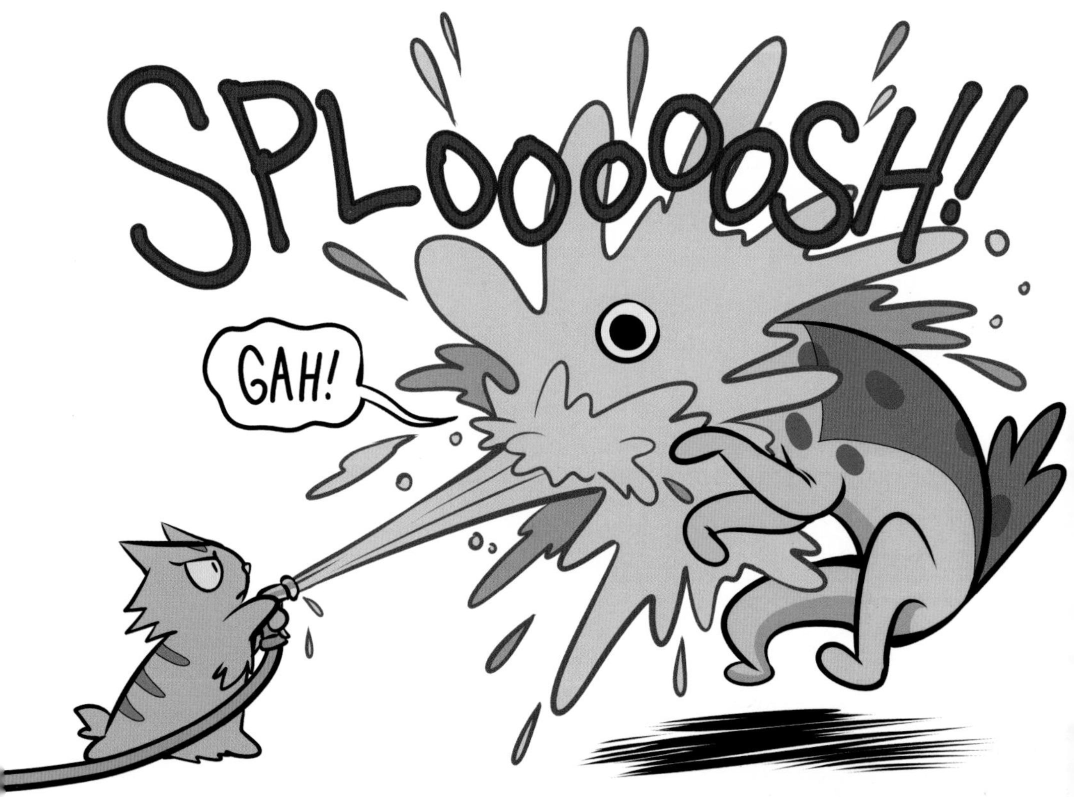
SPLOOOOOSH!!
GAH!

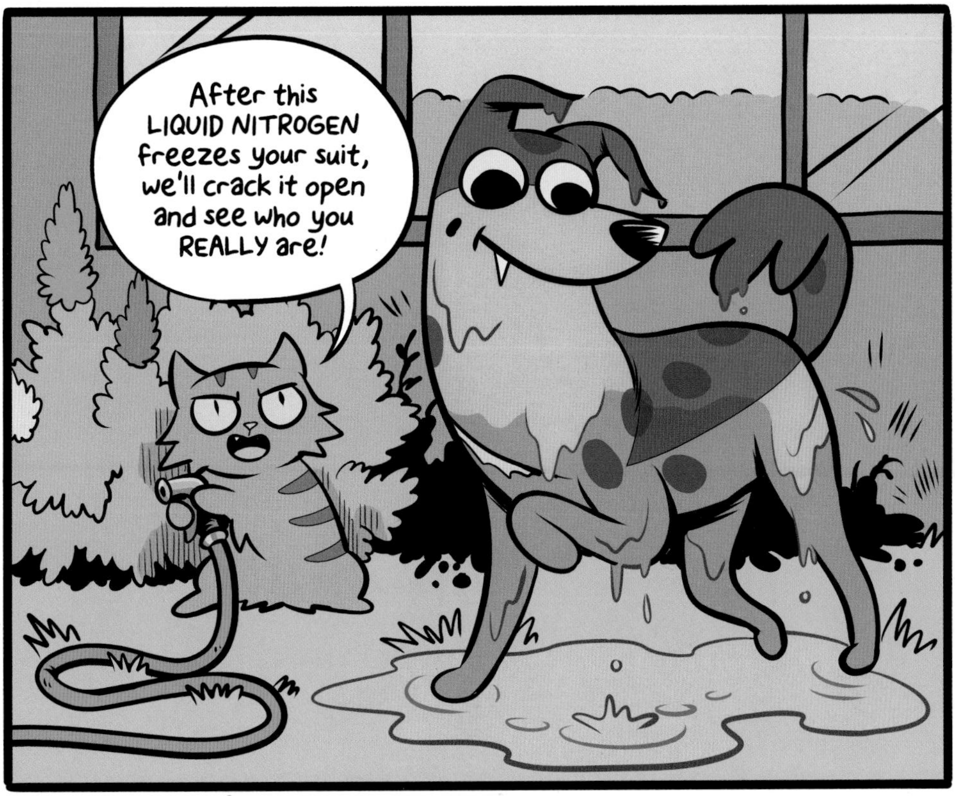
After this LIQUID NITROGEN freezes your suit, we'll crack it open and see who you REALLY are!

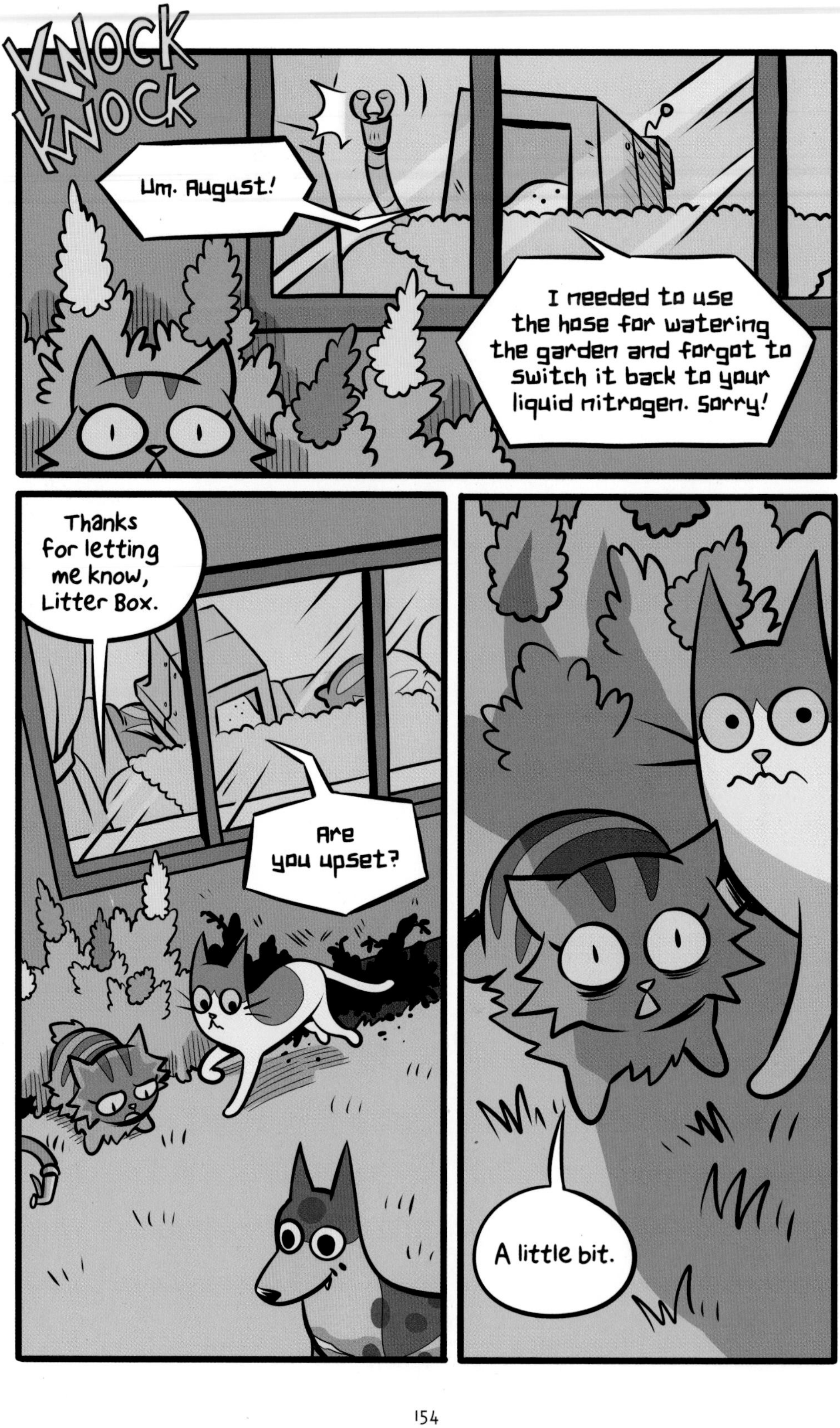
KNOCK KNOCK
Um. August!
I needed to use the hose for watering the garden and forgot to switch it back to your liquid nitrogen. Sorry!
Thanks for letting me know, Litter Box.
Are you upset?
A little bit.

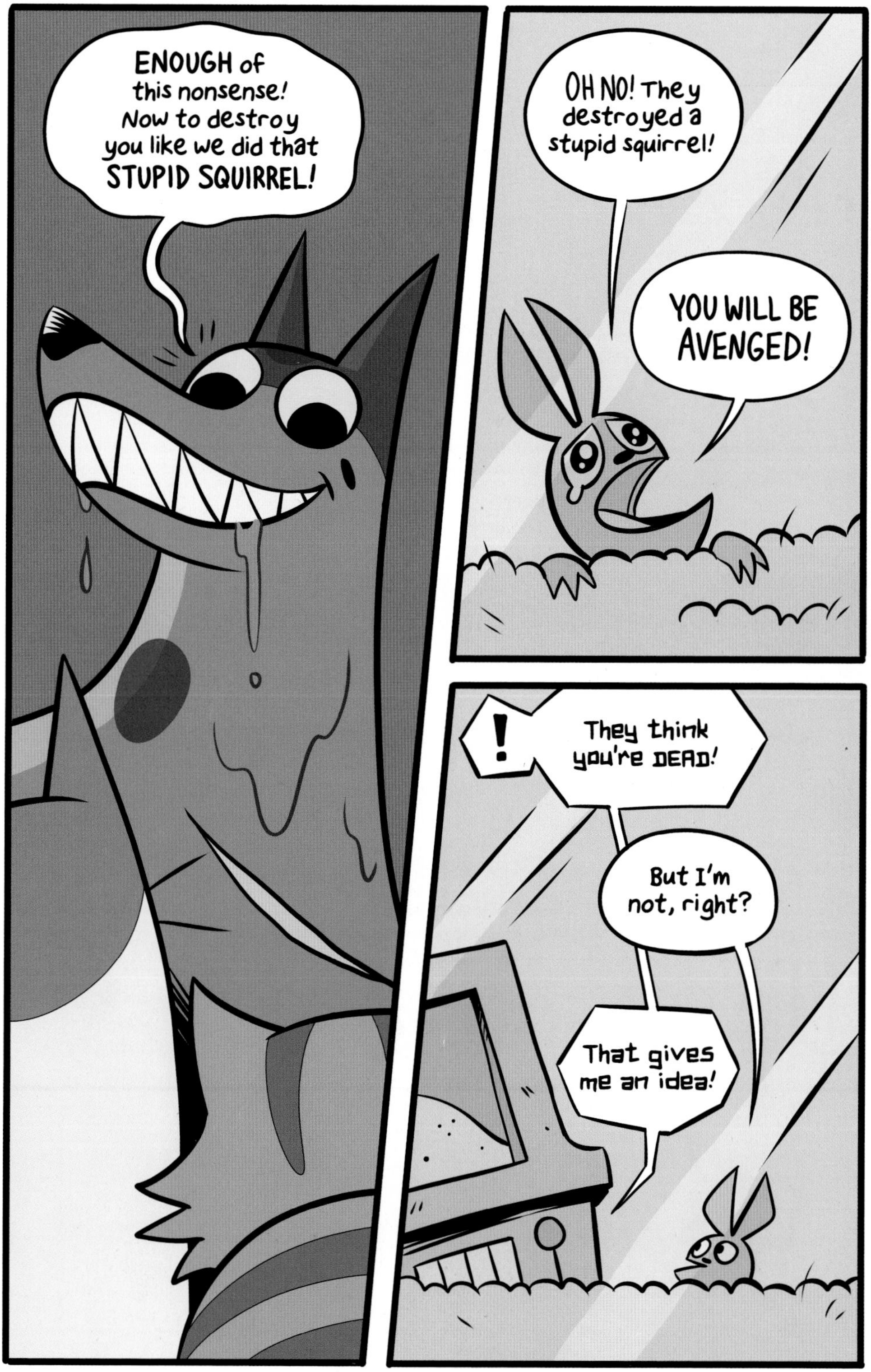
ENOUGH of this nonsense! Now to destroy you like we did that STUPID SQUIRREL!
OH NO! They destroyed a stupid squirrel!
YOU WILL BE AVENGED!
!
They think you're DEAD!
But I'm not, right?
That gives me an idea!

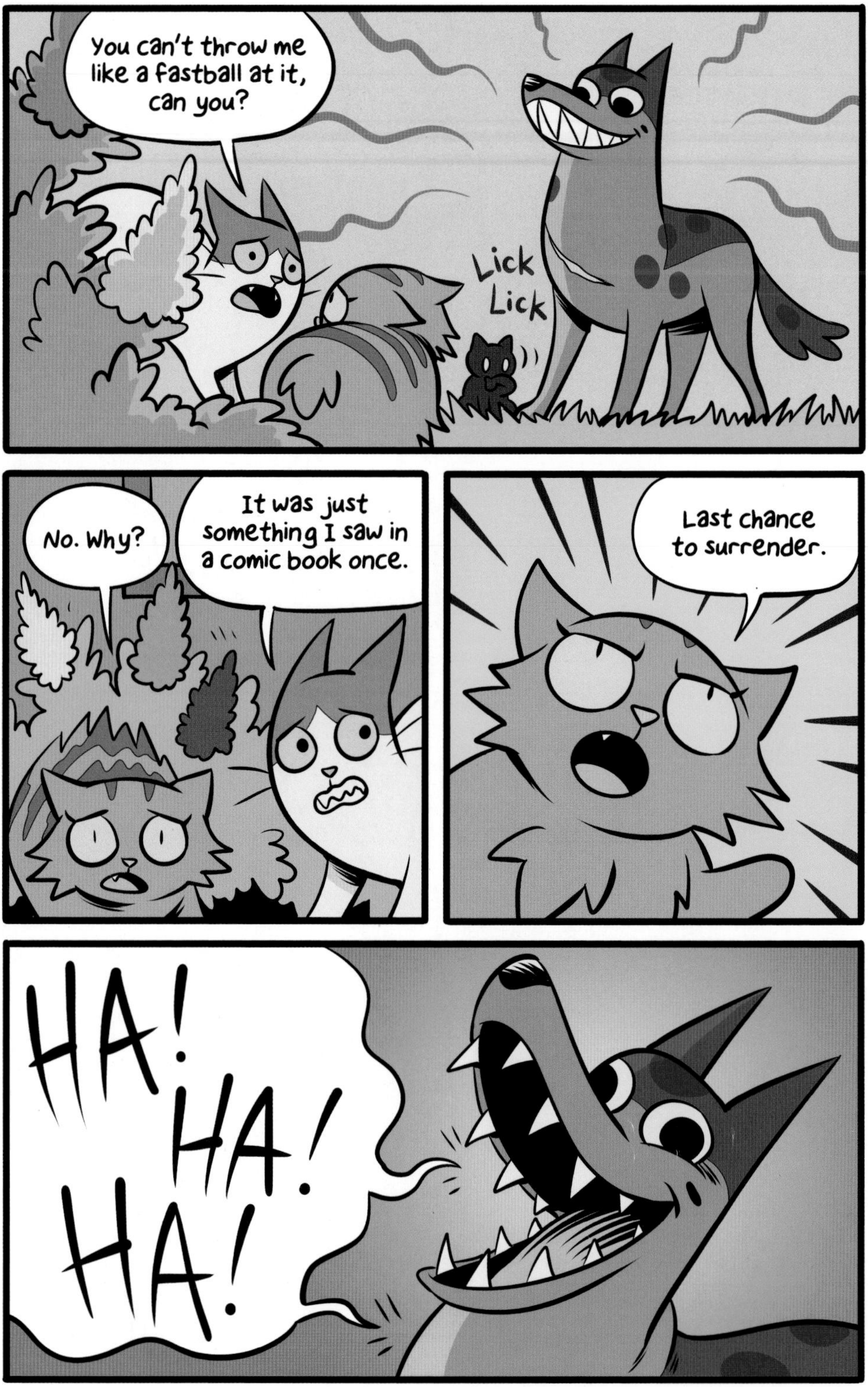
You can't throw me like a fastball at it, can you?
Lick Lick
No. Why?
It was just something I saw in a comic book once.
Last chance to surrender.
HA! HA! HA!

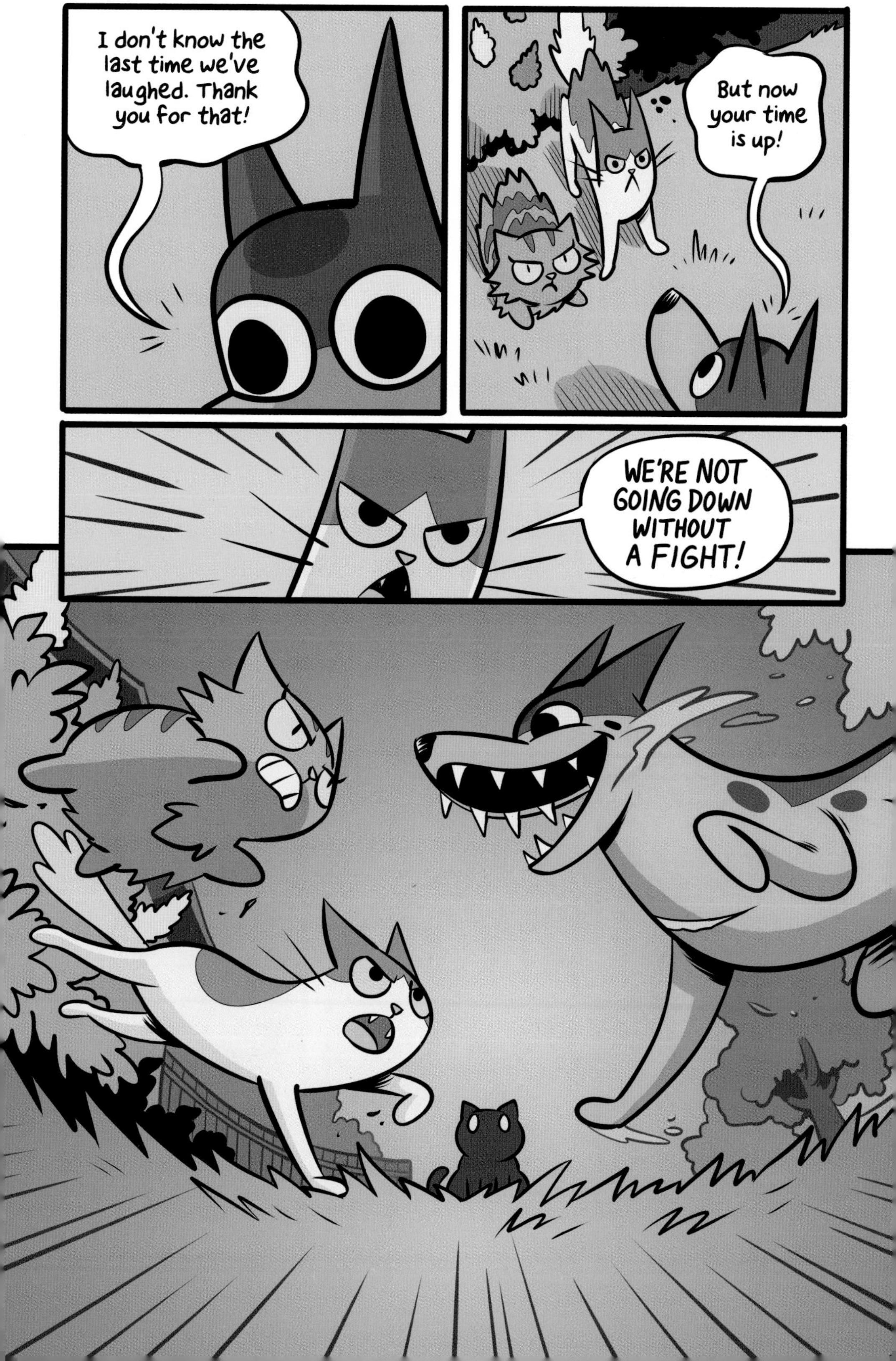
I don't know the last time we've laughed. Thank you for that!
But now your time is up!
WE'RE NOT GOING DOWN WITHOUT A FIGHT!

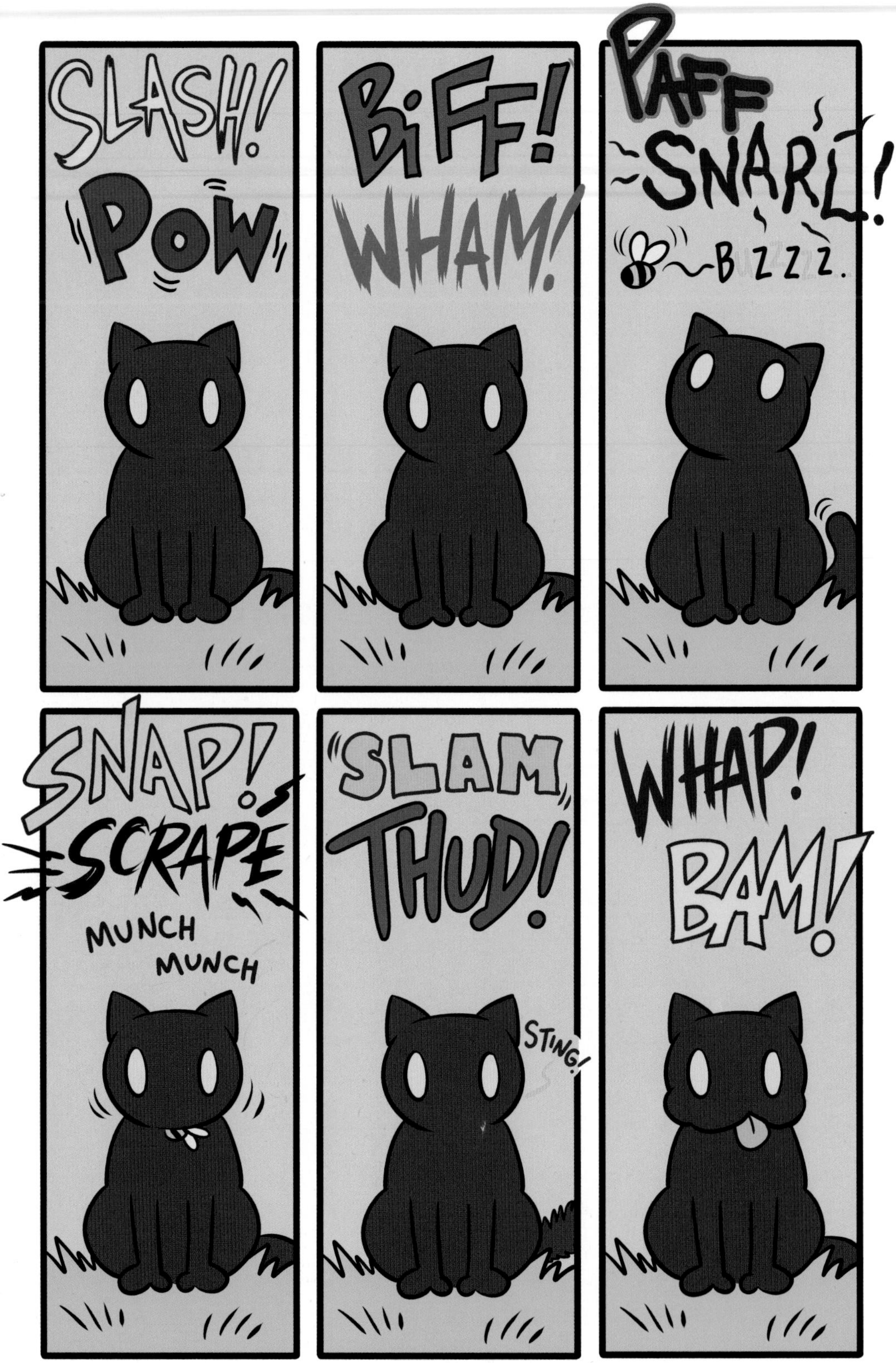
SLASH!
POW
BIFF!
WHAM!
PAFF
SNARL!
BZZZZ..
SNAP!
SCRAPE
MUNCH
MUNCH
SLAM
THUD!
STING!
WHAP!
BAM!

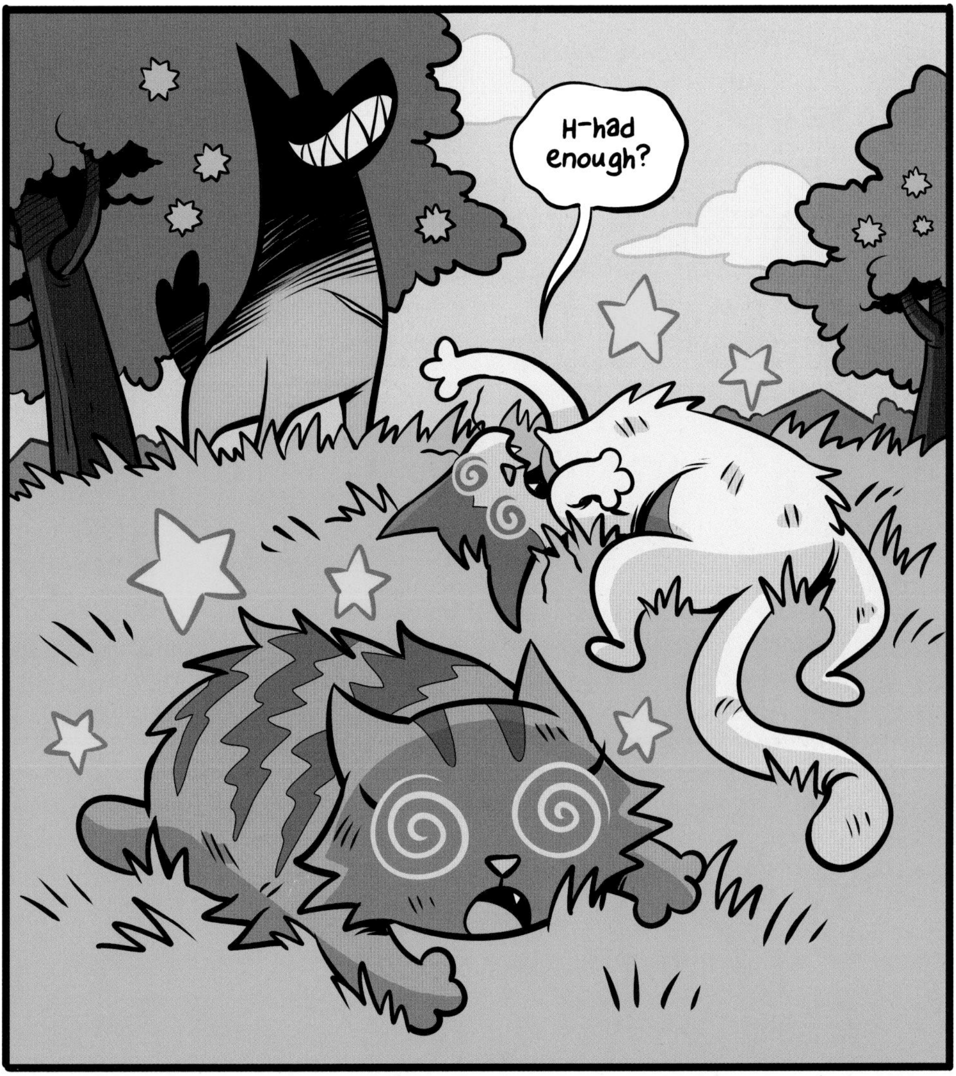
H-had enough?

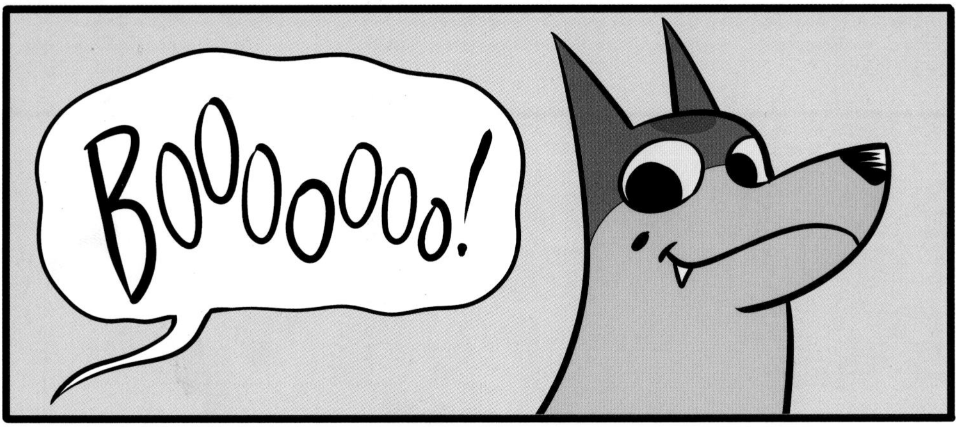
BOOOOOOO!

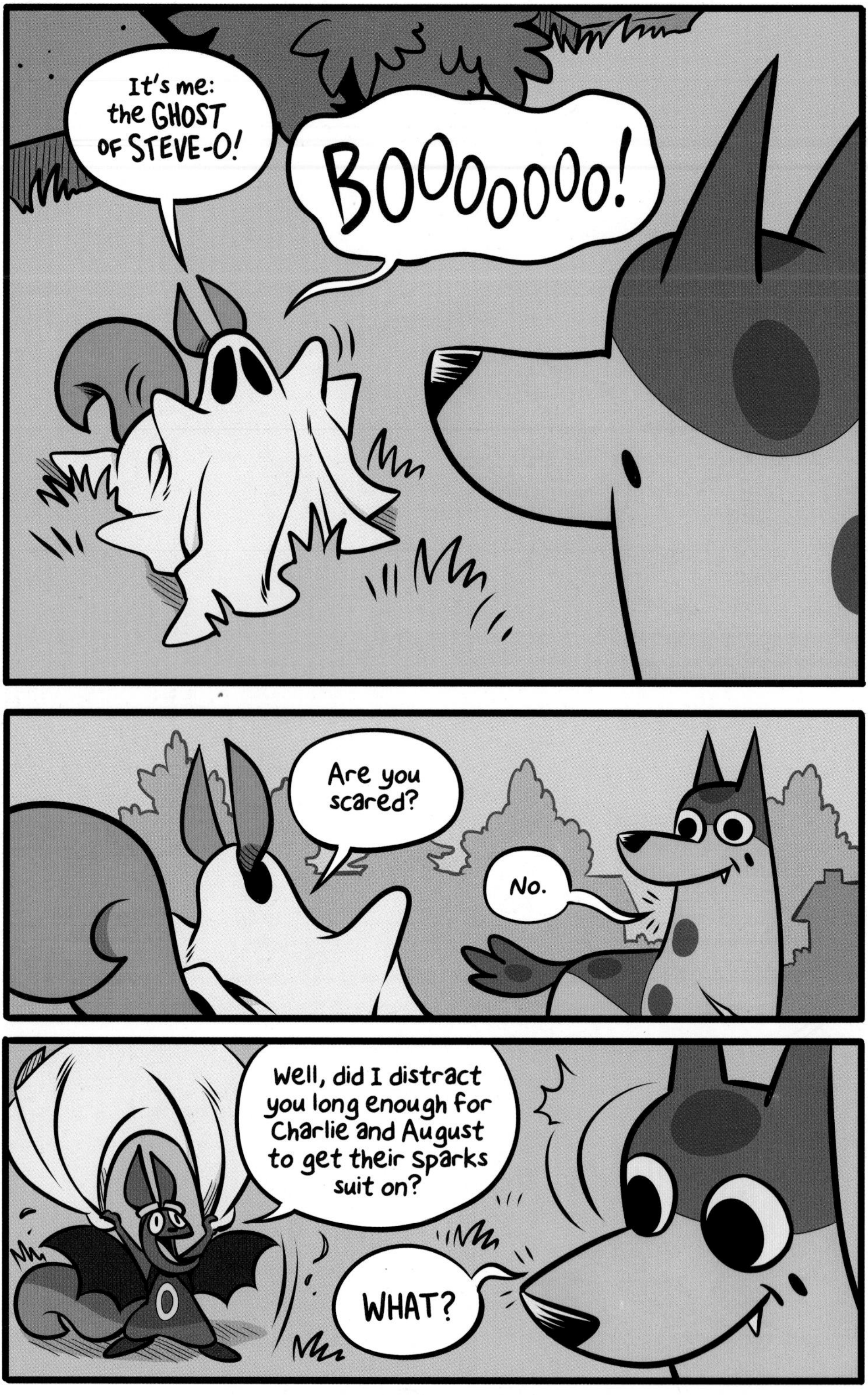

It's me: the GHOST OF STEVE-O!
BOOOOOOO!
Are you scared?
No.
Well, did I distract you long enough for Charlie and August to get their Sparks suit on?
WHAT?

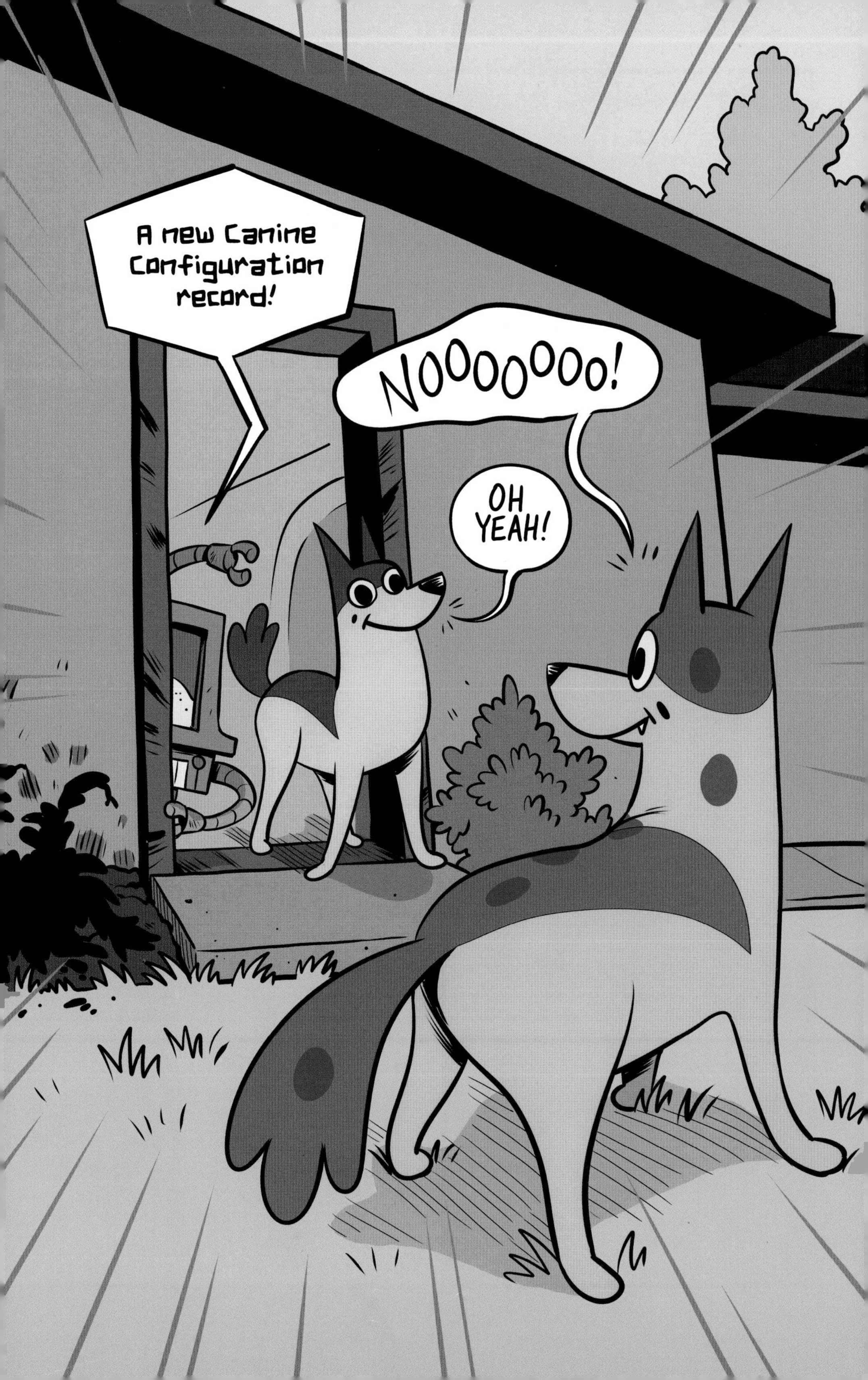
A new Canine Configuration record!
NOOOOOOO!
OH YEAH!

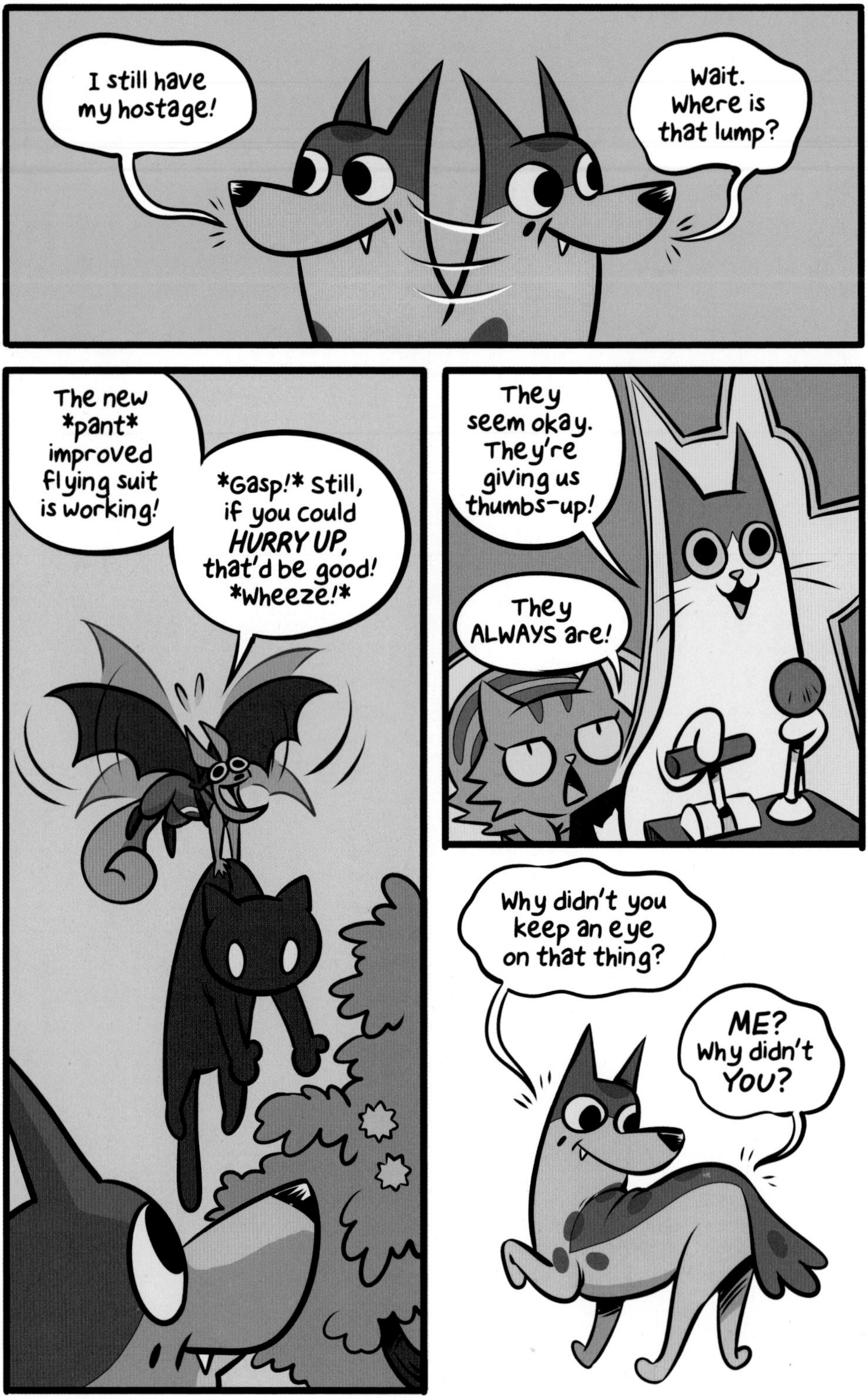
I still have my hostage!
Wait. Where is that lump?
The new *pant* improved flying suit is working!
Gasp! Still, if you could HURRY UP, that'd be good! *Wheeze!*
They seem okay. They're giving us thumbs-up!
They ALWAYS are!
Why didn't you keep an eye on that thing?
ME? Why didn't YOU?

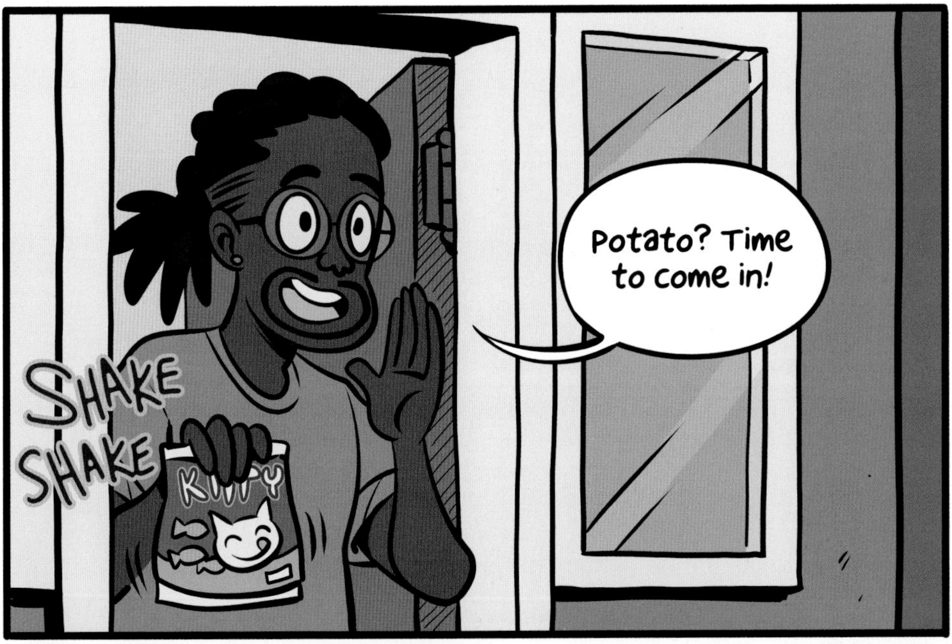
Potato? Time to come in!
SHAKE SHAKE
KITTY

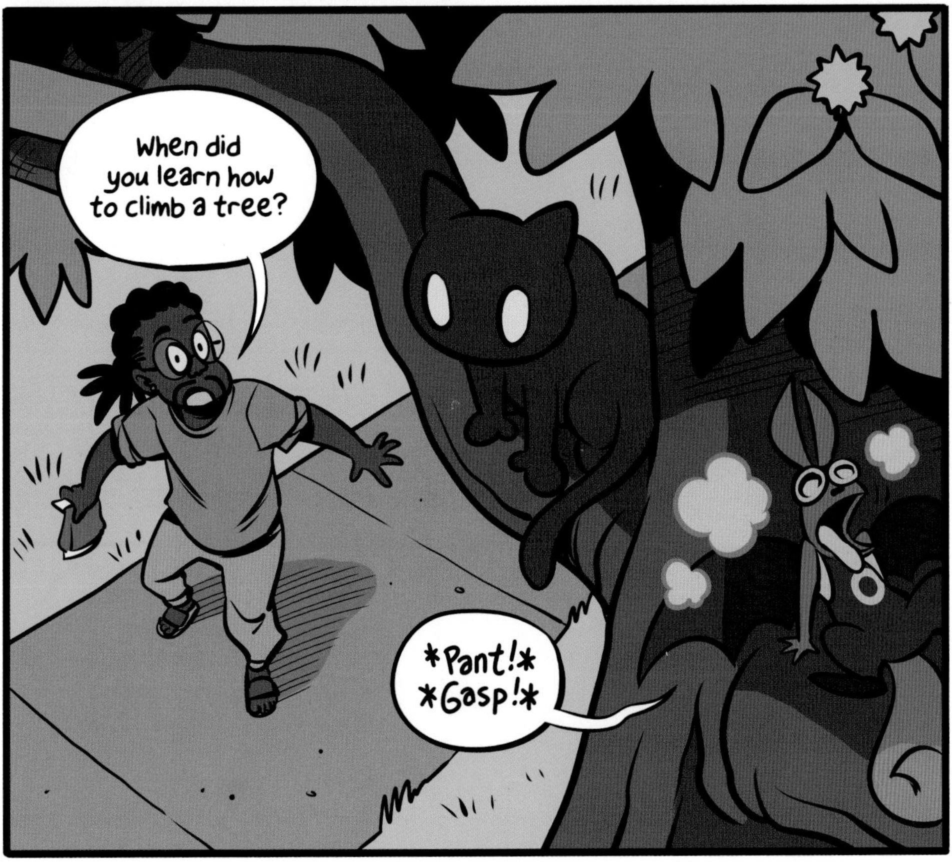
When did you learn how to climb a tree?
Pant! *Gasp!*

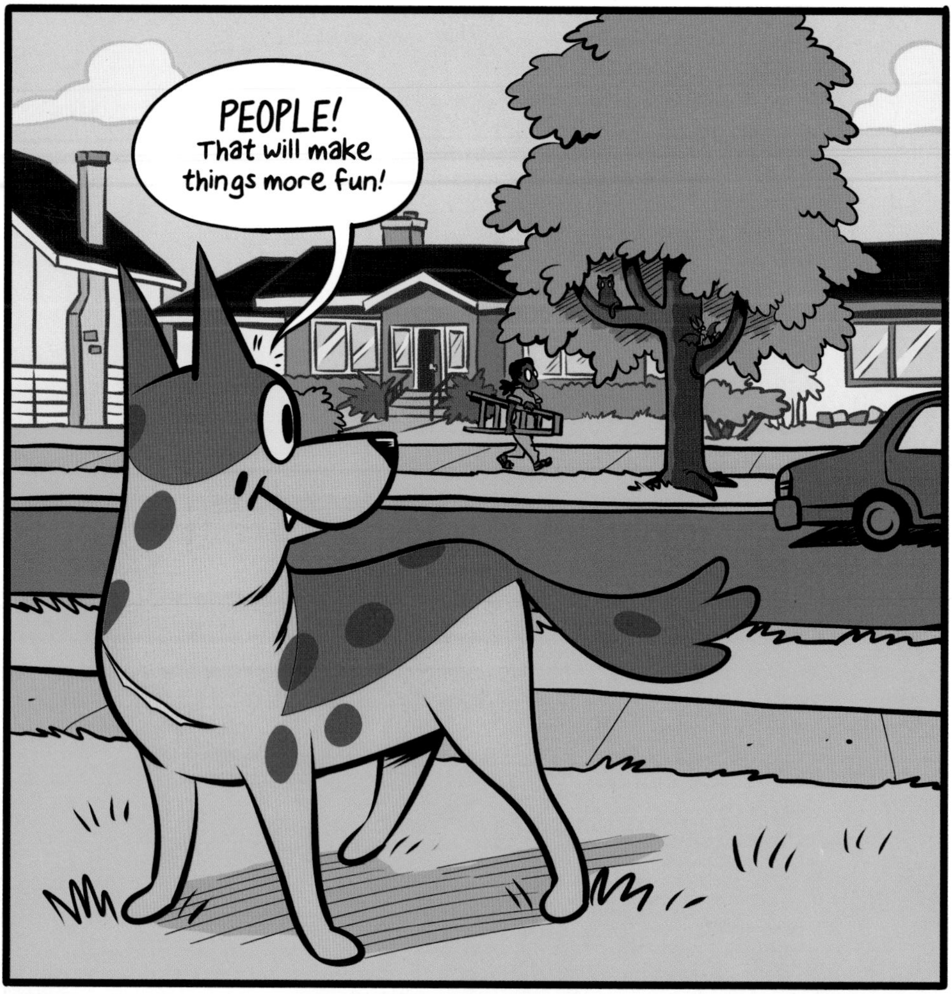
PEOPLE! That will make things more fun!

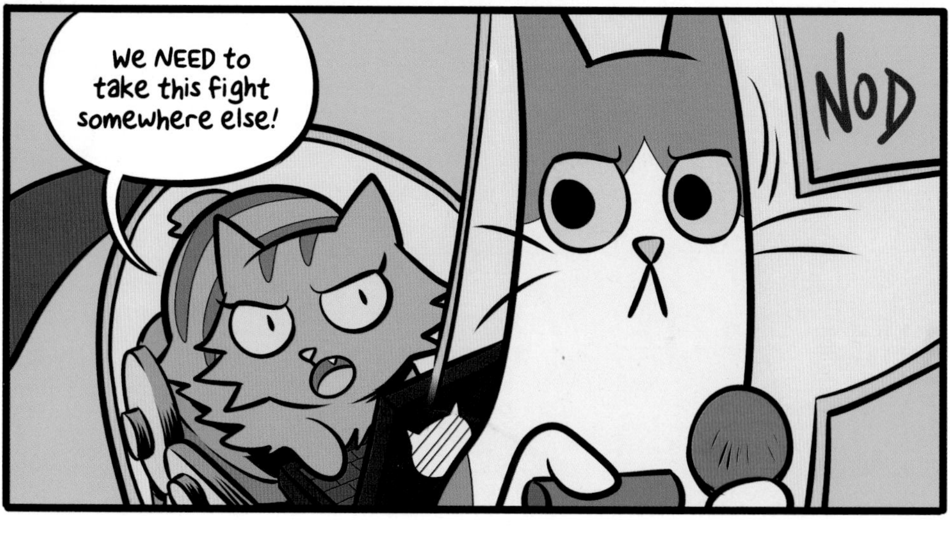
WE NEED to take this fight somewhere else!
NOD

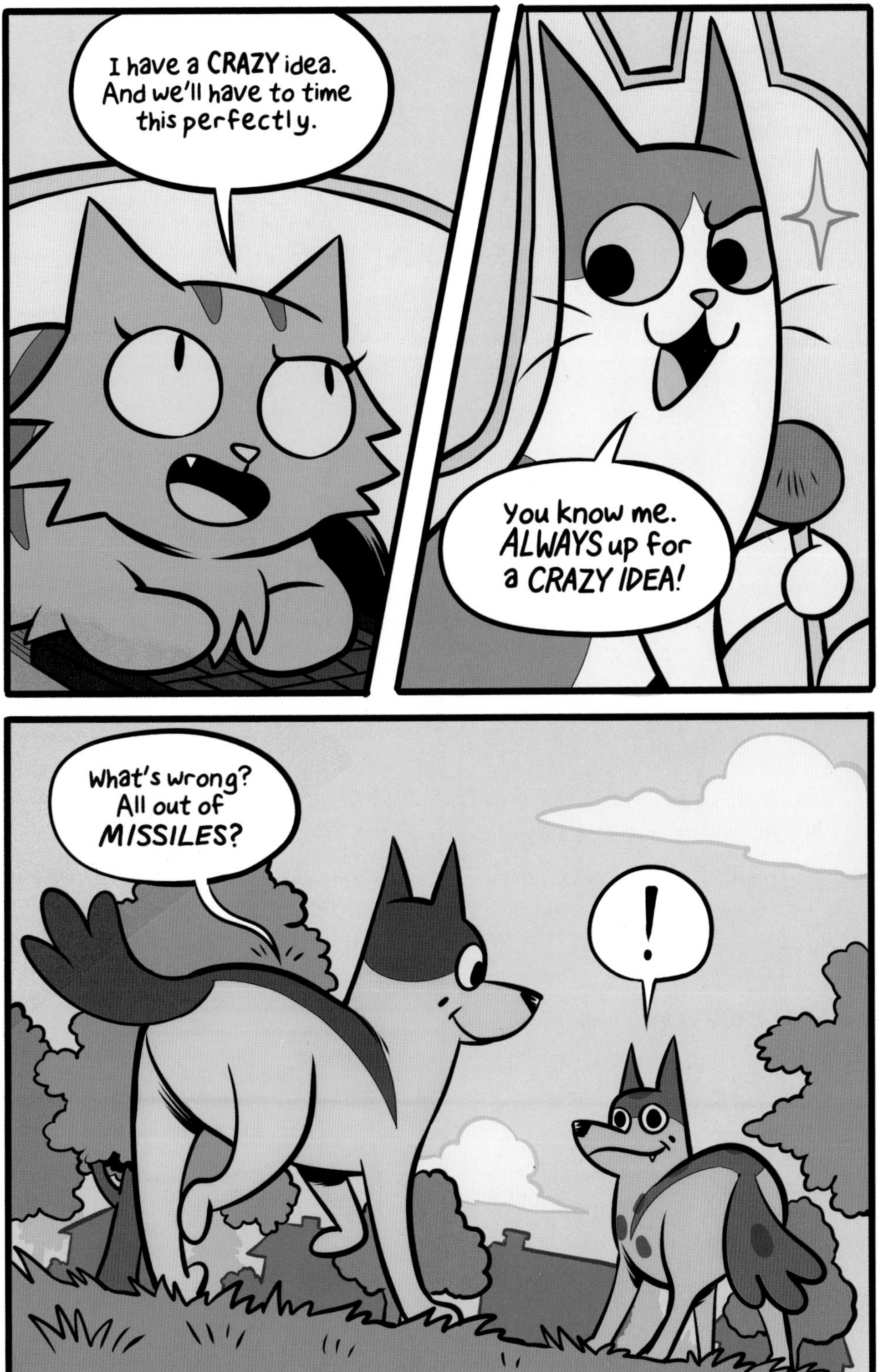
I have a CRAZY idea. And we'll have to time this perfectly.
You know me. ALWAYS up for a CRAZY IDEA!
What's wrong? All out of MISSILES?
!

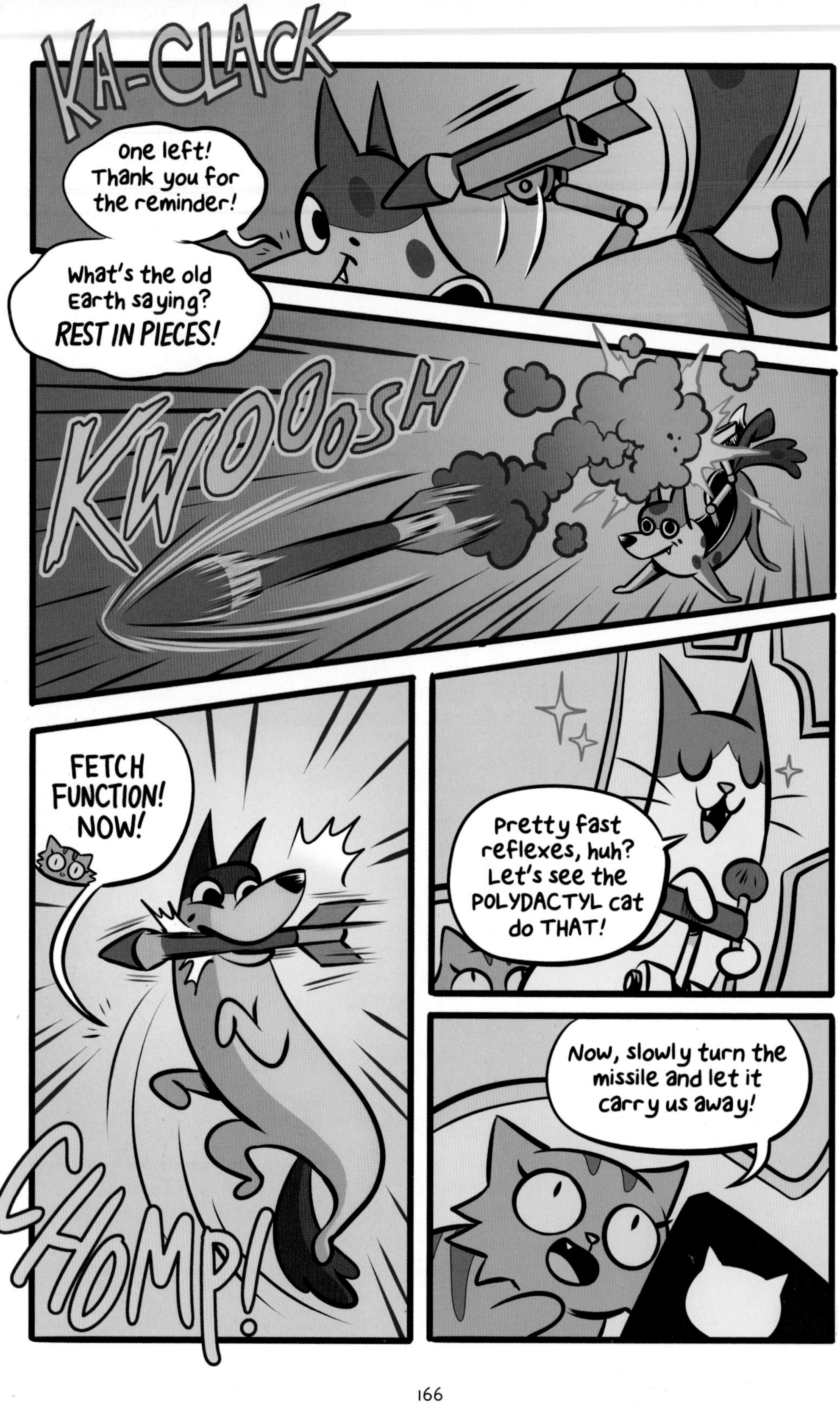
KA-CLACK
one left! Thank you for the reminder!
What's the old Earth saying? REST IN PIECES!
KWOOOOSH
FETCH FUNCTION! NOW!
CHOMP!
Pretty fast reflexes, huh? Let's see the POLYDACTYL cat do THAT!
Now, slowly turn the missile and let it carry us away!

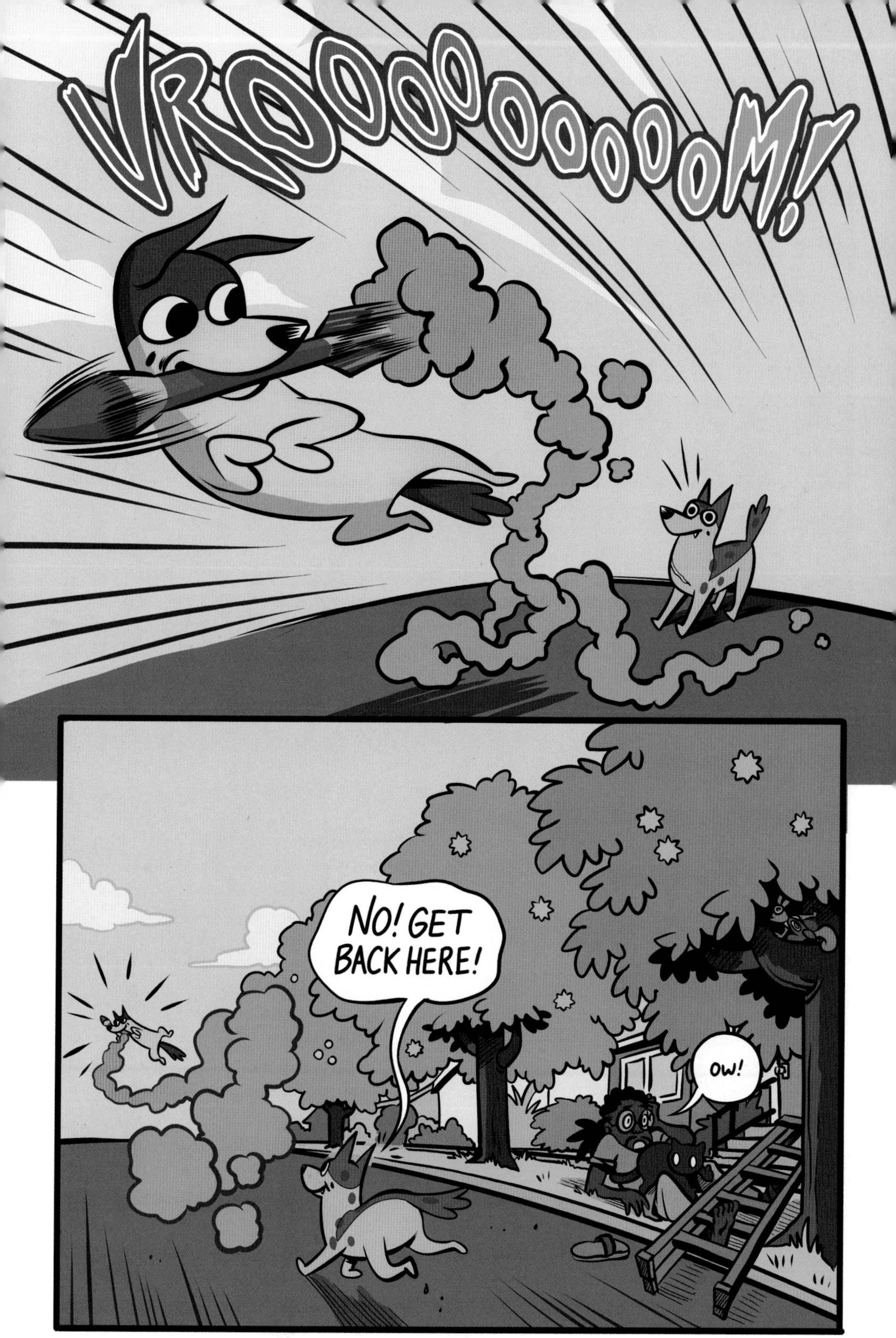
VROOOOOOOOOOM!
NO! GET BACK HERE!
OW!

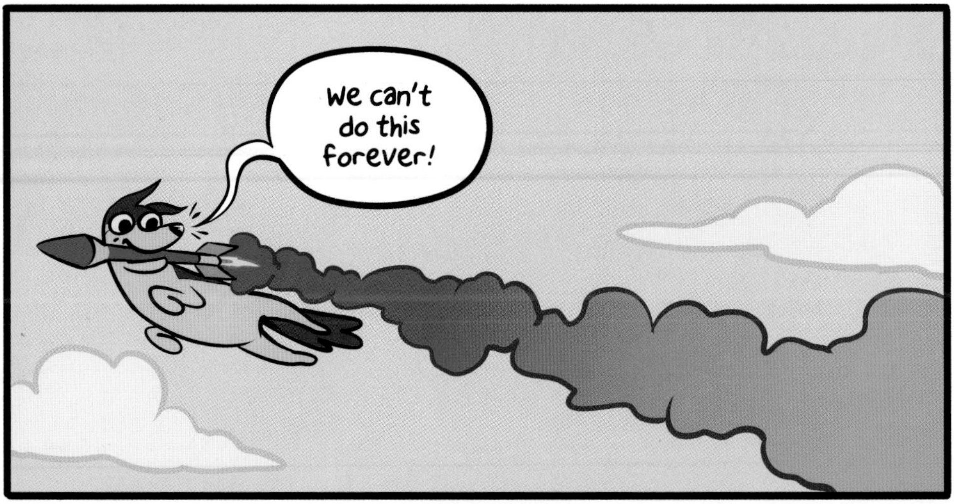
We can't do this forever!

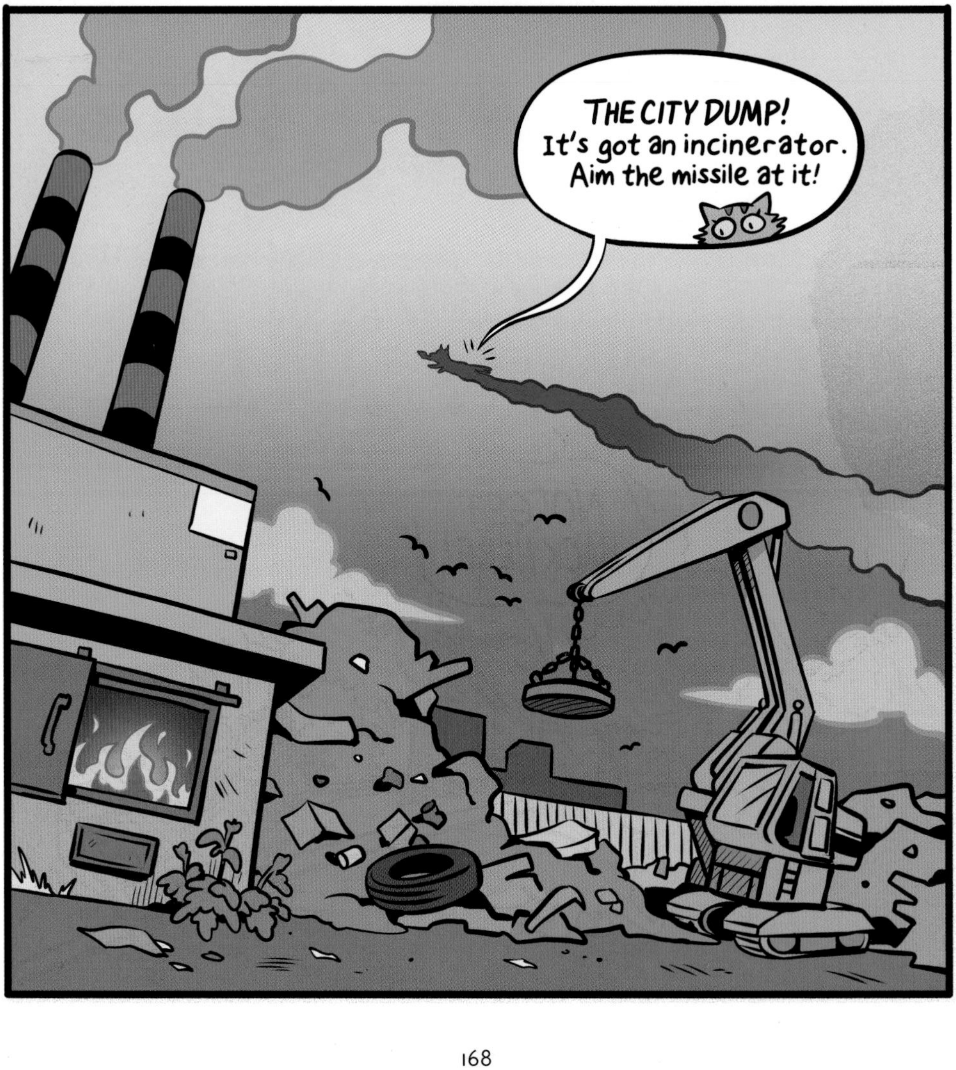
THE CITY DUMP! It's got an incinerator. Aim the missile at it!

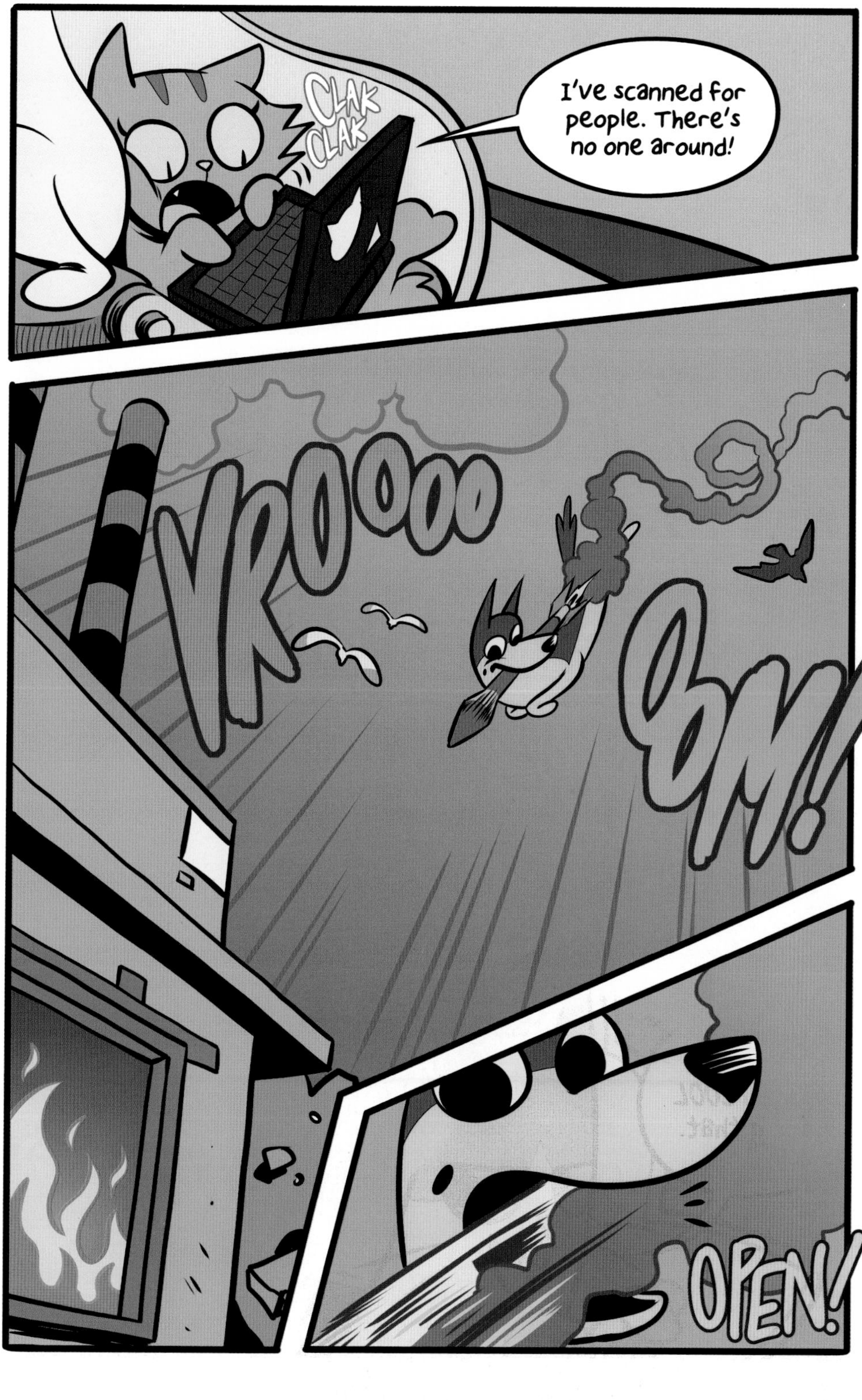
CLAK CLAK
I've scanned for people. There's no one around!
VROOOO
OOM!
OPEN!

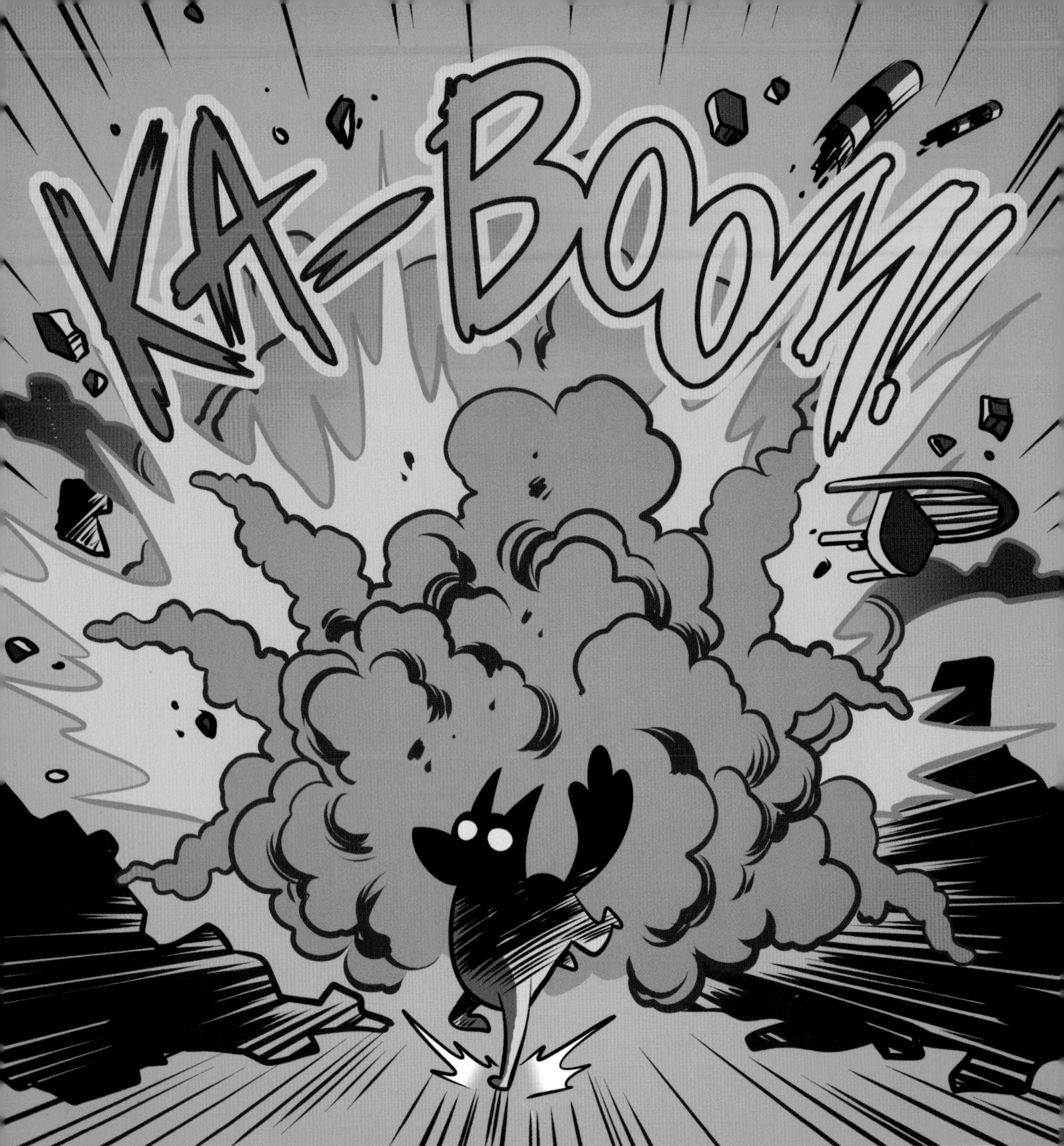
KA-BOOM!

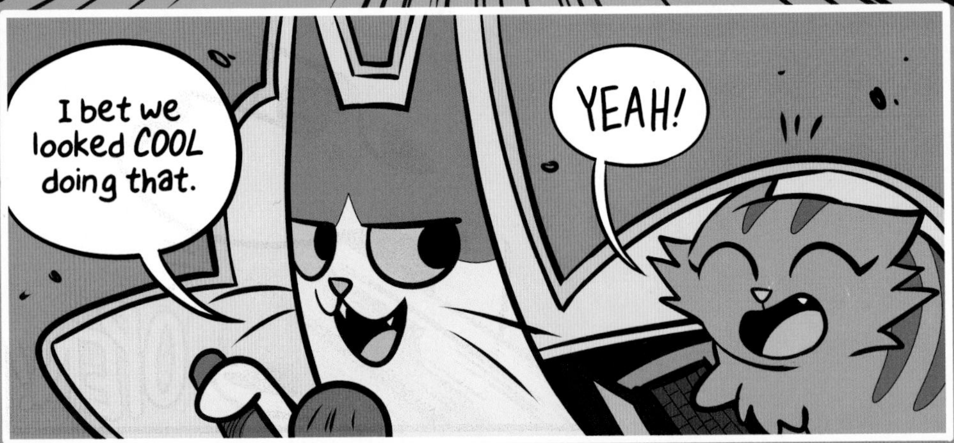
I bet we looked COOL doing that.
YEAH!

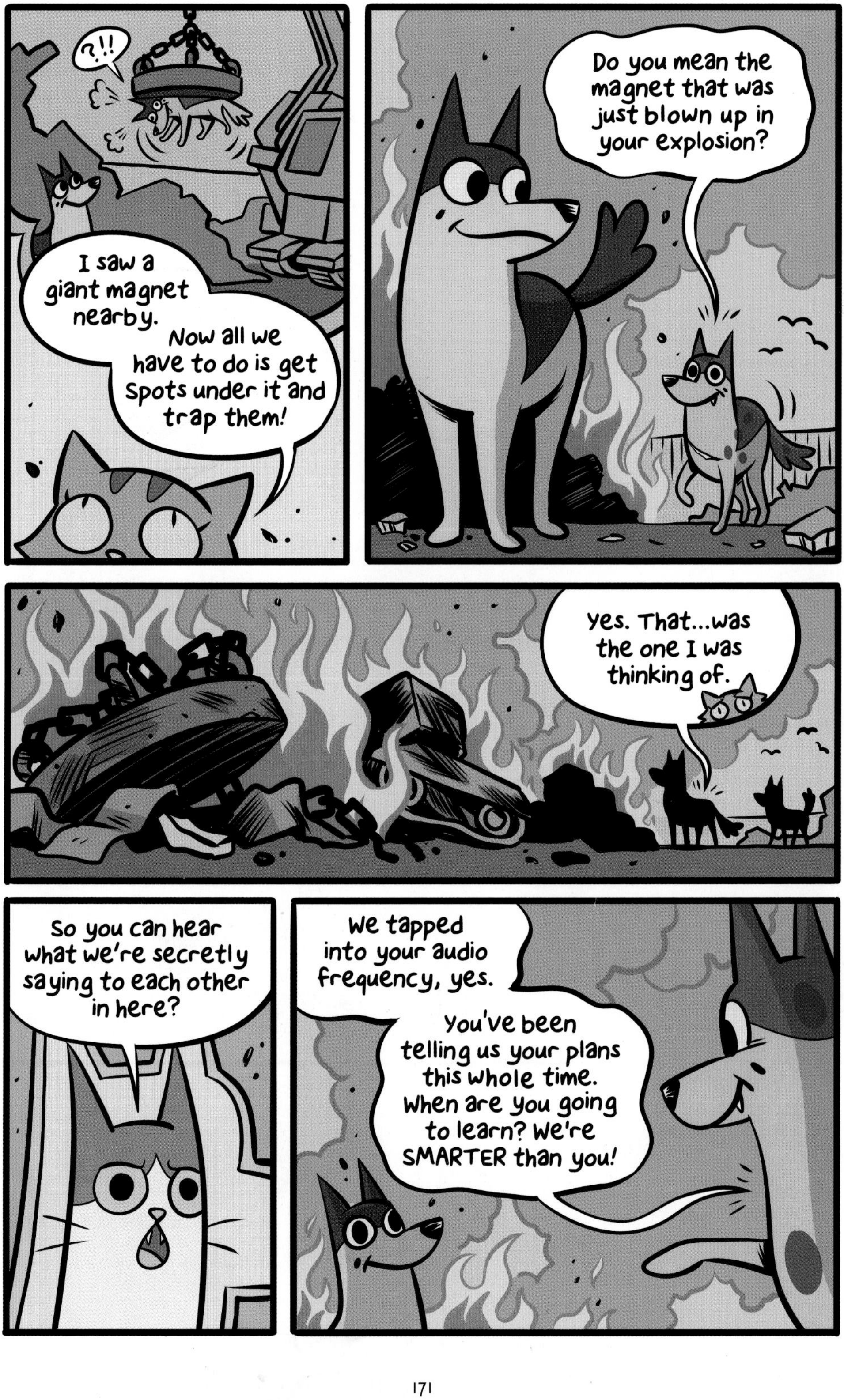
?!!
I saw a giant magnet nearby.
Now all we have to do is get Spots under it and trap them!
Do you mean the magnet that was just blown up in your explosion?
Yes. That...was the one I was thinking of.
So you can hear what we're secretly saying to each other in here?
We tapped into your audio frequency, yes.
You've been telling us your plans this whole time. When are you going to learn? We're SMARTER than you!

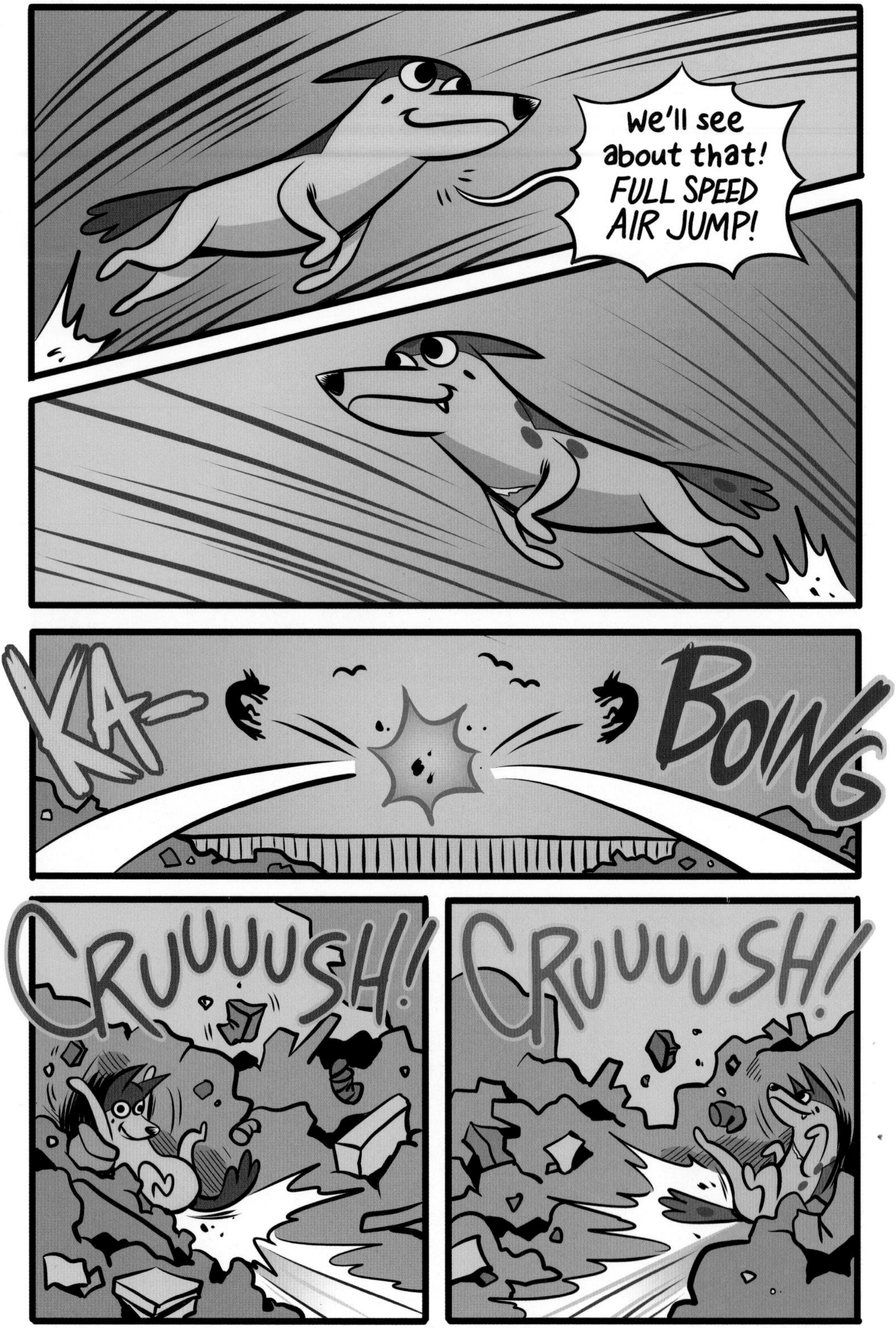
We'll see about that! FULL SPEED AIR JUMP!
KA-BOING
CRUUUUSH!
CRUUUUSH!

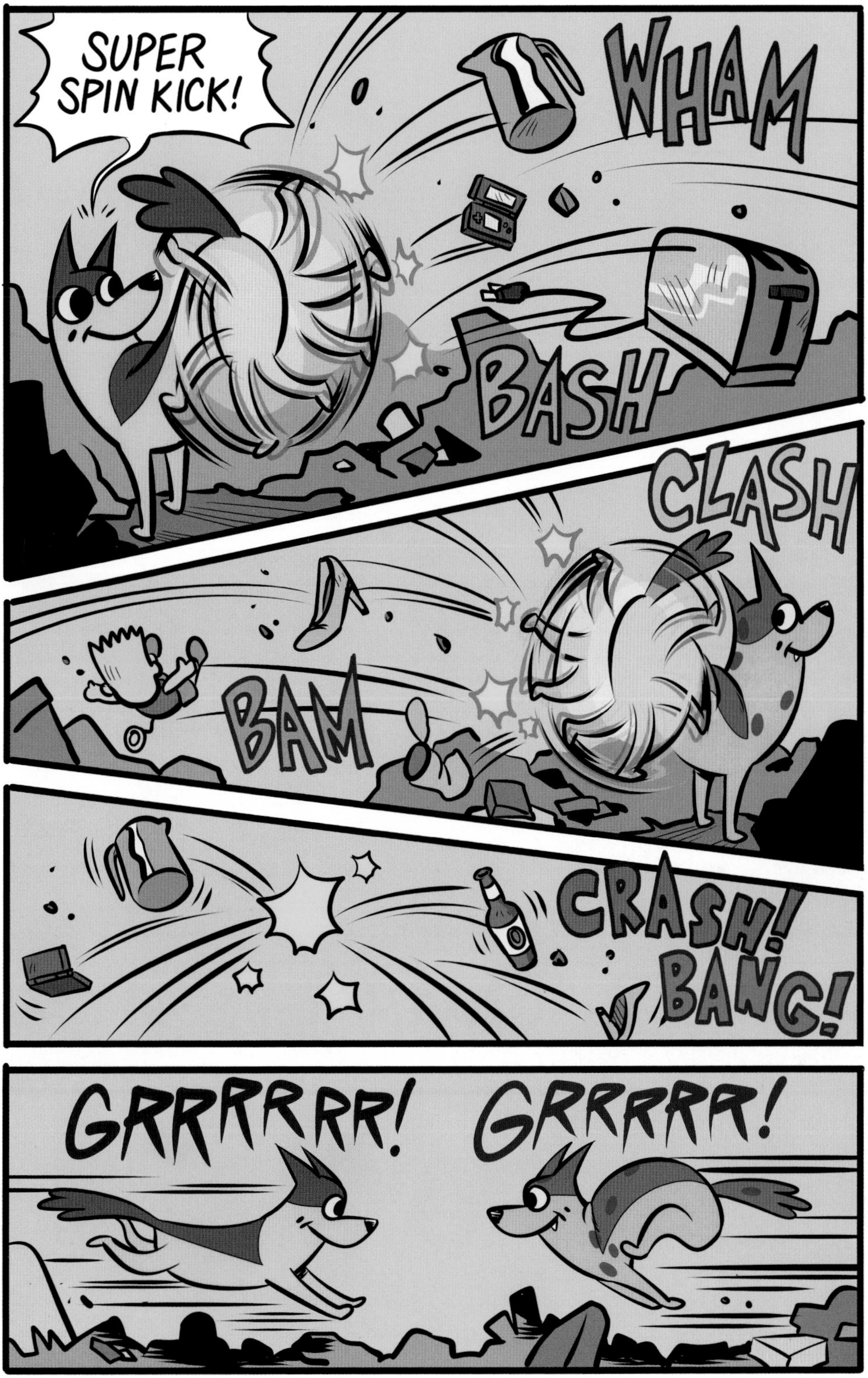
SUPER SPIN KICK!
WHAM
BASH
CLASH
BAM
CRASH!
BANG!
GRRRRRR!
GRRRRR!

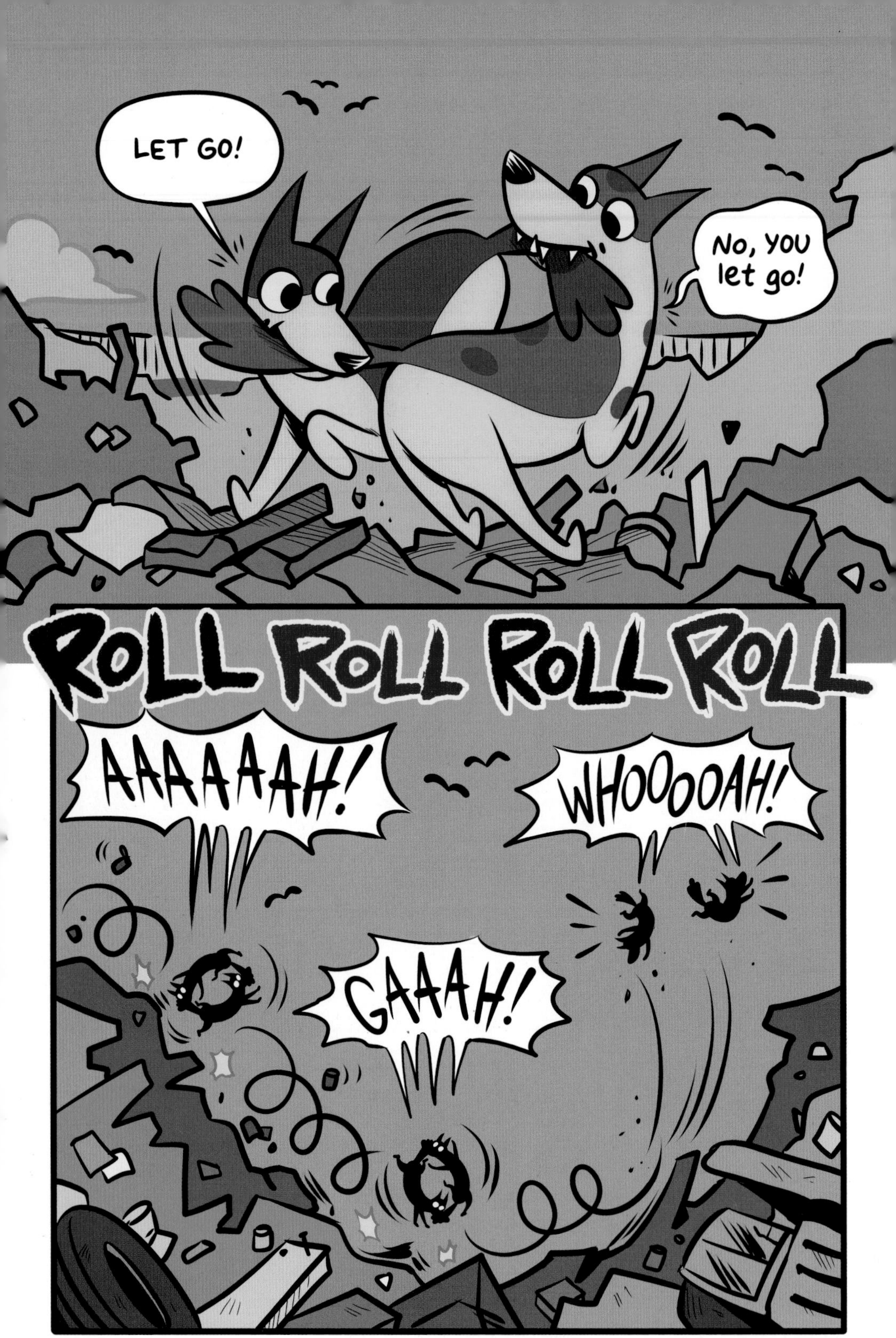
LET GO!
No, YOU let go!
ROLL ROLL ROLL ROLL
AAAAAAH!
WHOOOOAH!
GAAAH!

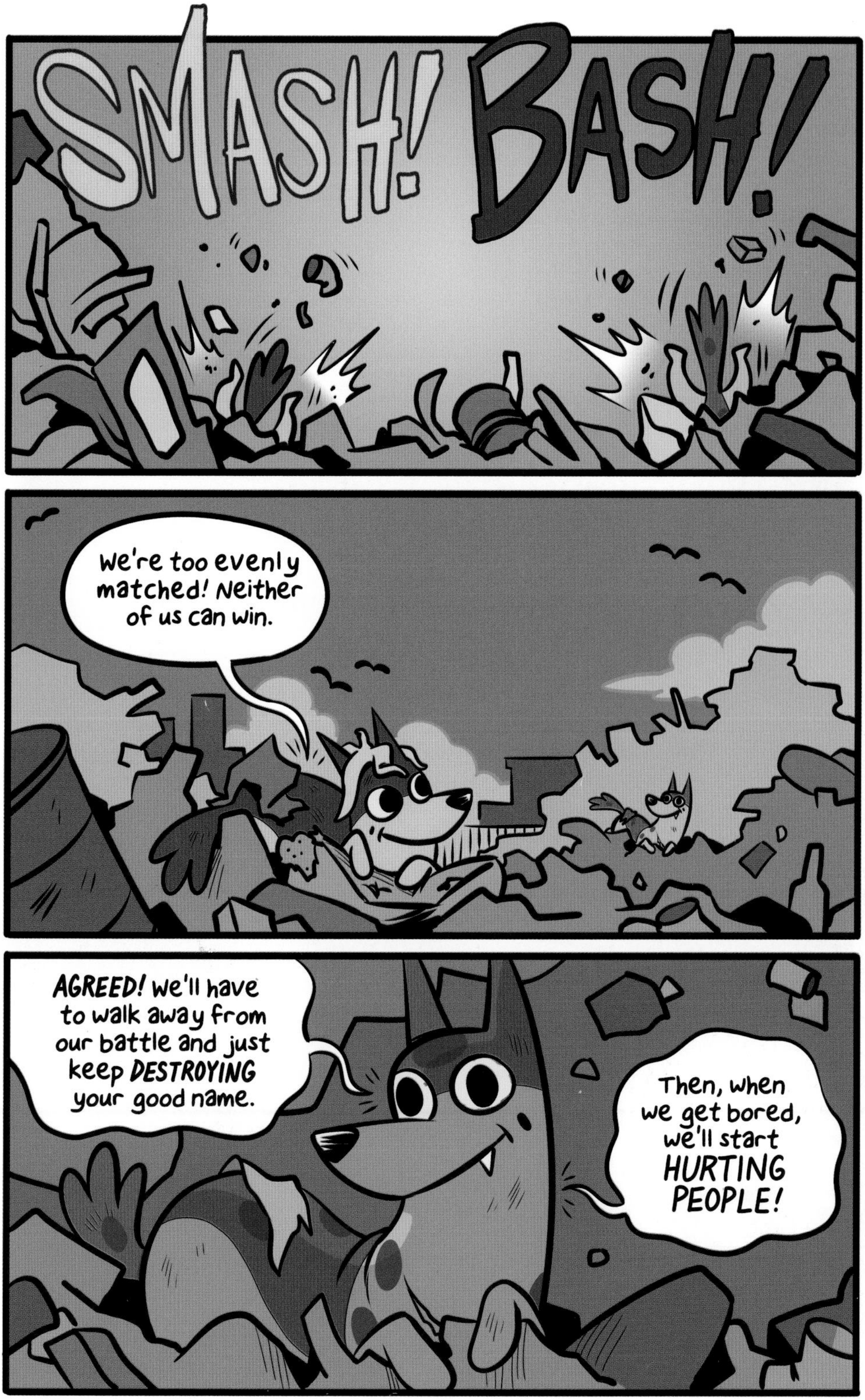
SMASH! BASH!
We're too evenly matched! Neither of us can win.
AGREED! We'll have to walk away from our battle and just keep DESTROYING your good name.
Then, when we get bored, we'll start HURTING PEOPLE!

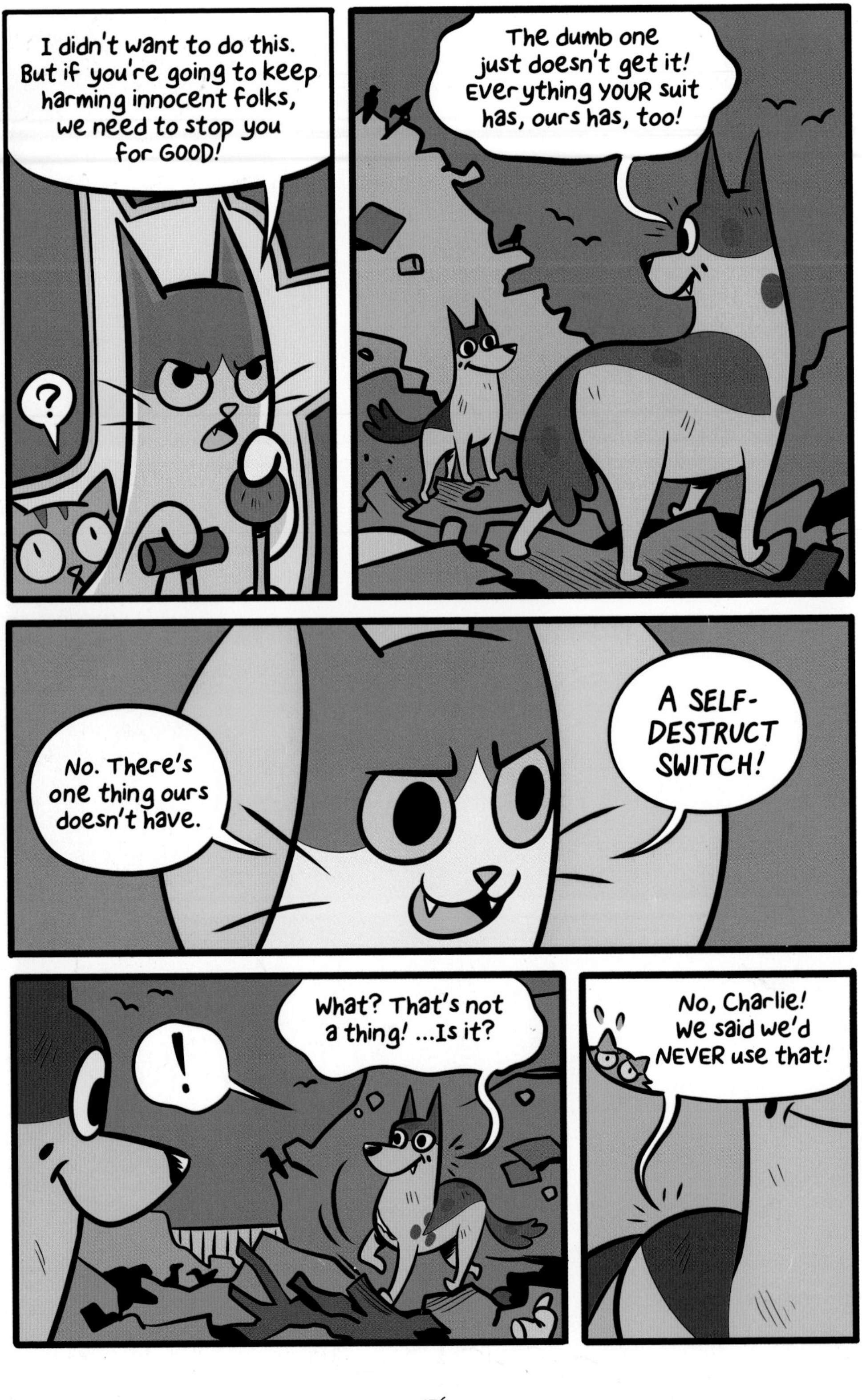
I didn't want to do this. But if you're going to keep harming innocent folks, we need to stop you for GOOD!
?
The dumb one just doesn't get it! Everything YOUR suit has, ours has, too!
No. There's one thing ours doesn't have.
A SELF-DESTRUCT SWITCH!
!
What? That's not a thing! ...Is it?
No, Charlie! We said we'd NEVER use that!

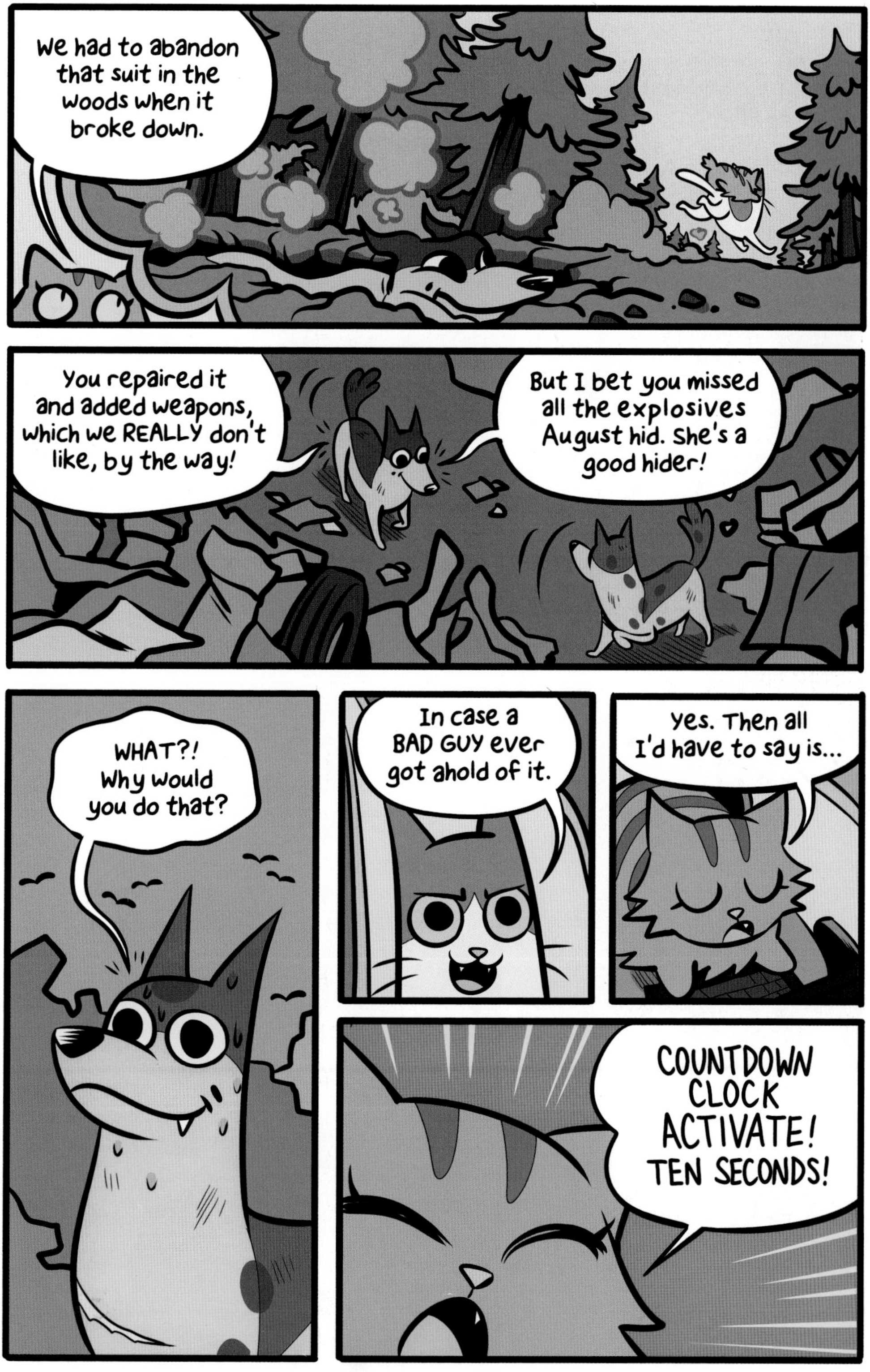
We had to abandon that suit in the woods when it broke down.
You repaired it and added weapons, which we REALLY don't like, by the way!
But I bet you missed all the explosives August hid. She's a good hider!
WHAT?! Why would you do that?
In case a BAD GUY ever got ahold of it.
Yes. Then all I'd have to say is...
COUNTDOWN CLOCK ACTIVATE! TEN SECONDS!

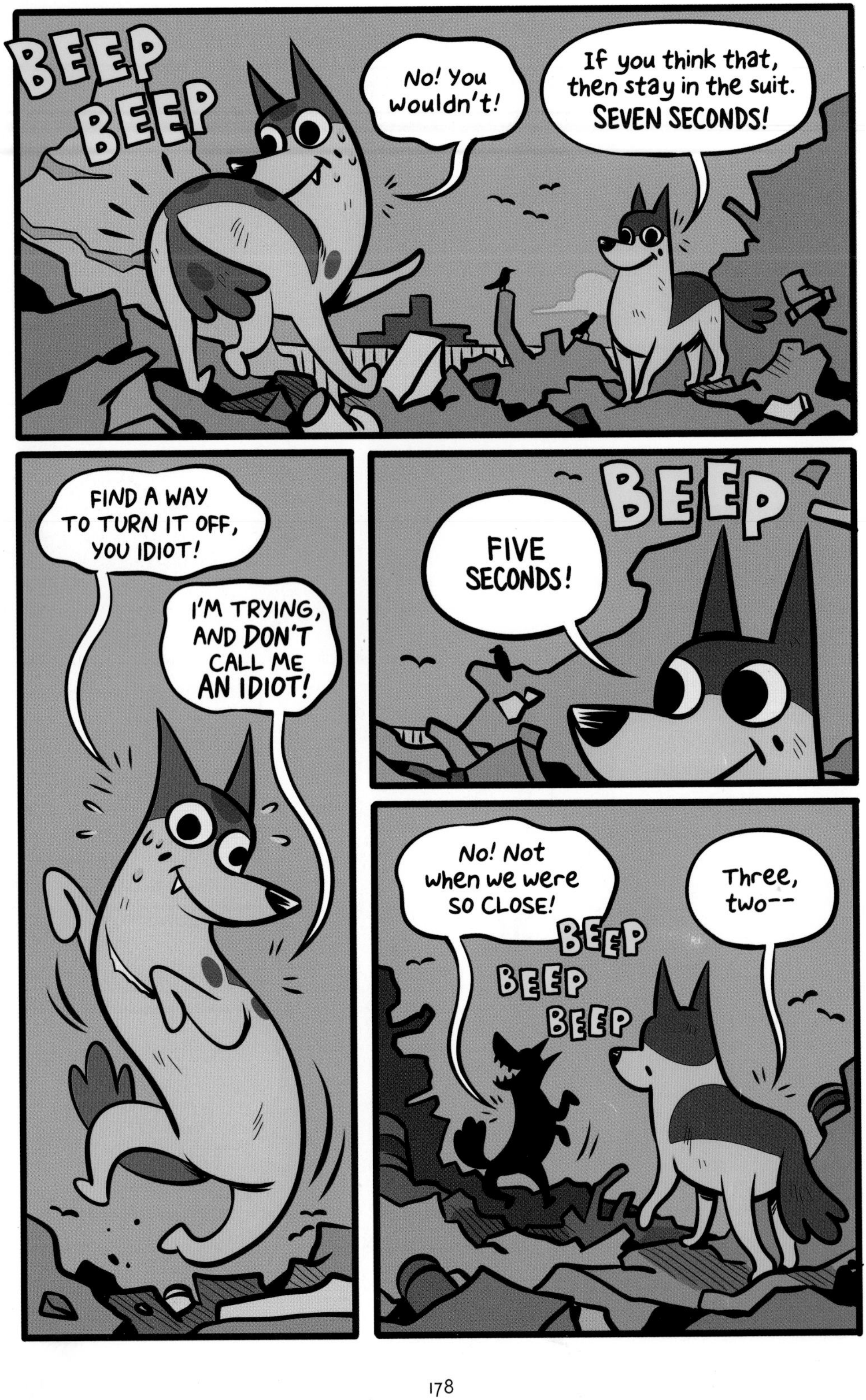
BEEP
BEEP
No! You wouldn't!
If you think that, then stay in the suit. SEVEN SECONDS!
FIND A WAY TO TURN IT OFF, YOU IDIOT!
I'M TRYING, AND DON'T CALL ME AN IDIOT!
BEEP
FIVE SECONDS!
No! Not when we were SO CLOSE!
BEEP
BEEP
BEEP
Three, two--

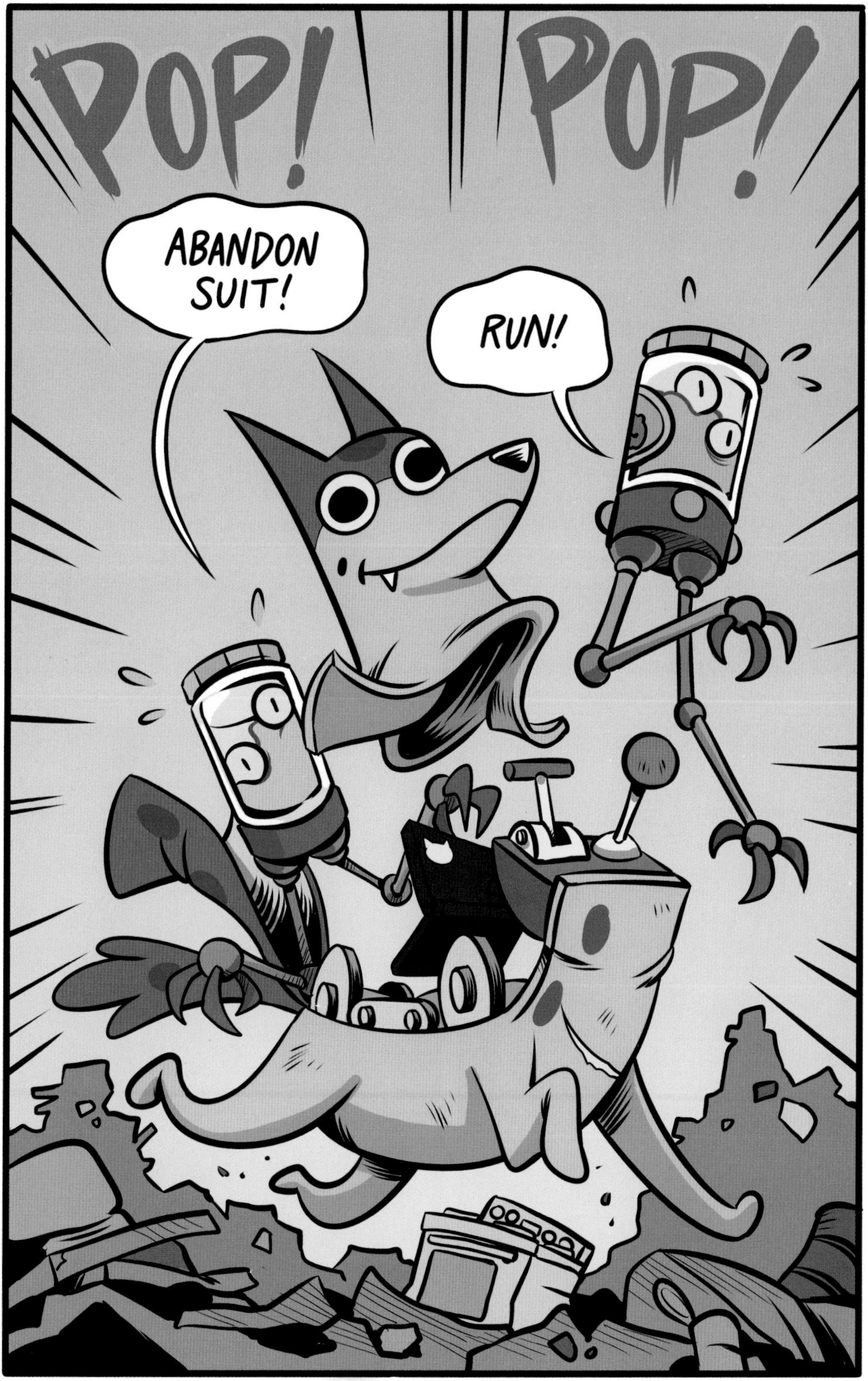
POP! POP!
ABANDON SUIT!
RUN!

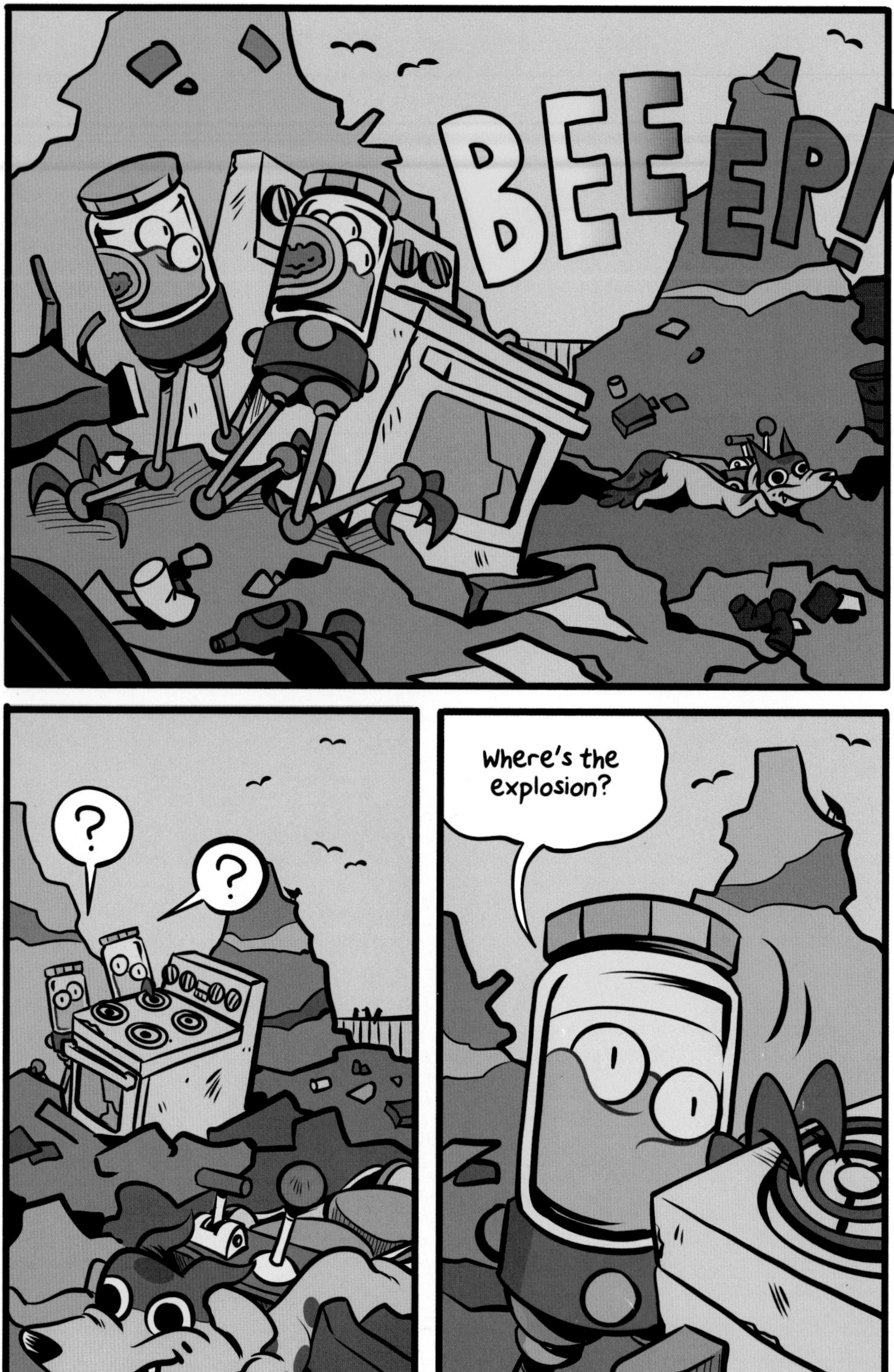
BEEEP!
?
?
Where's the explosion?

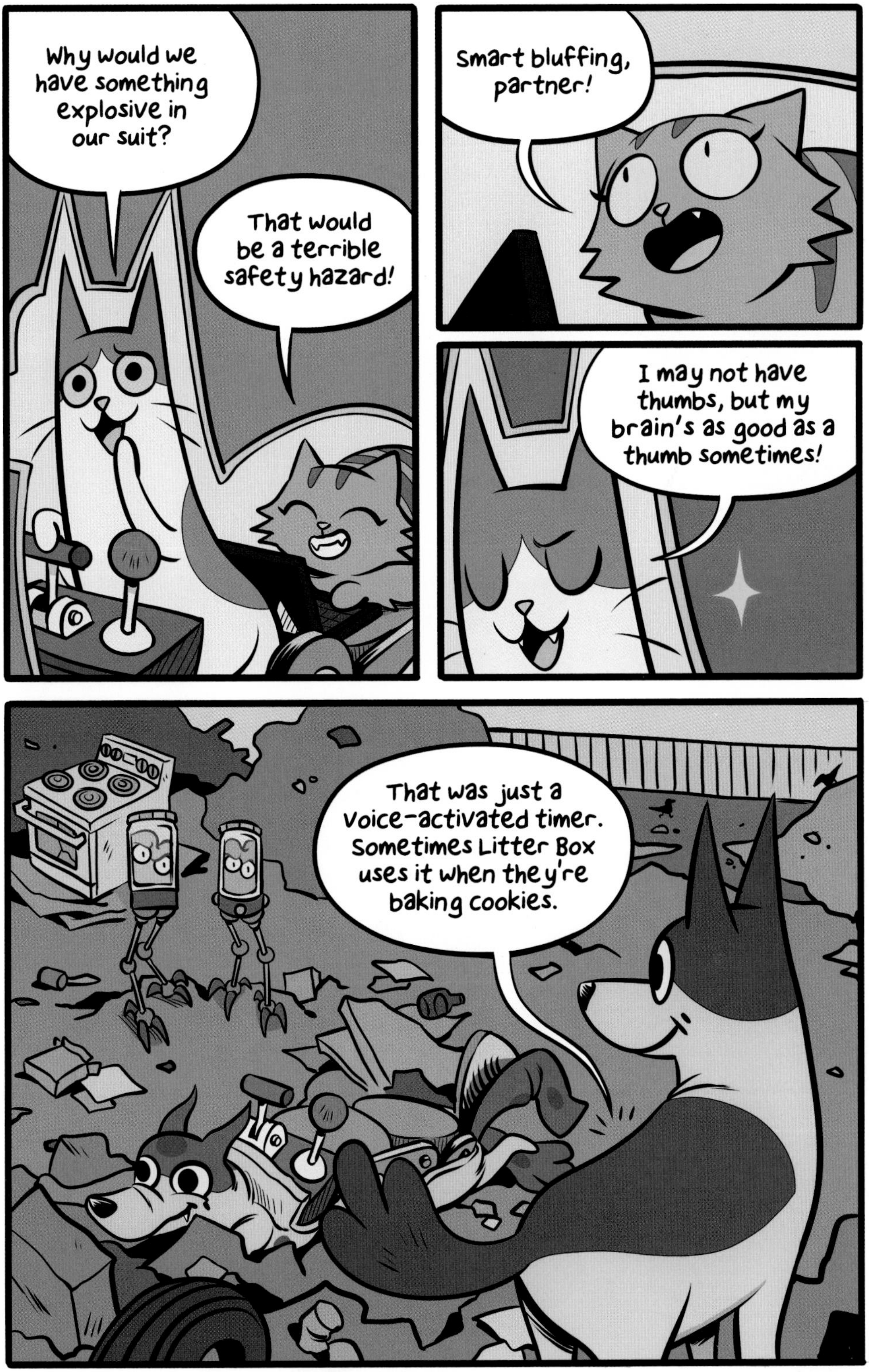
Why would we have something explosive in our suit?
That would be a terrible safety hazard!
Smart bluffing, partner!
I may not have thumbs, but my brain's as good as a thumb sometimes!
That was just a voice-activated timer. Sometimes Litter Box uses it when they're baking cookies.

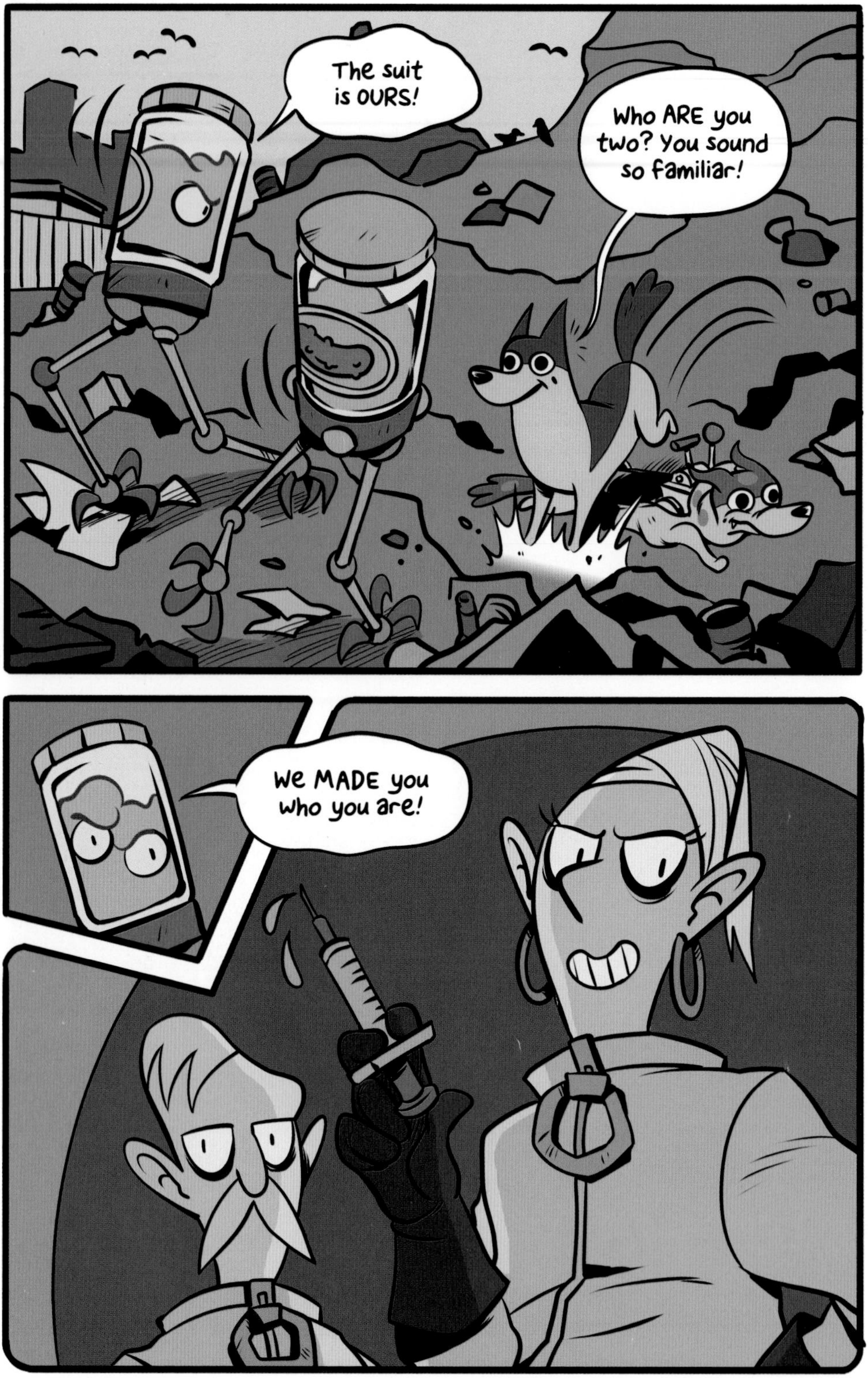
The suit is OURS!
Who ARE you two? You sound so familiar!
WE MADE you who you are!

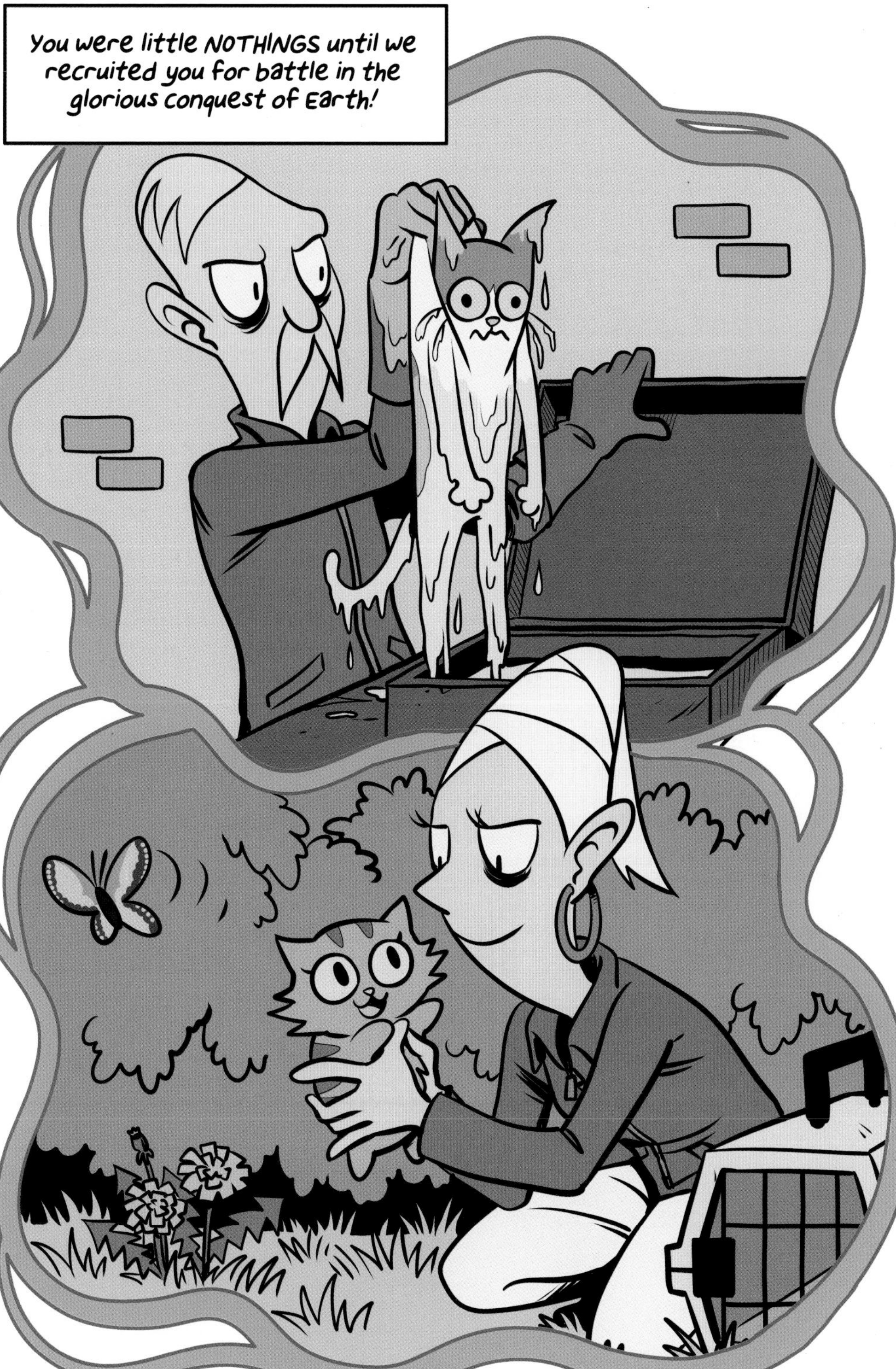
You were little NOTHINGS until we recruited you for battle in the glorious conquest of Earth!

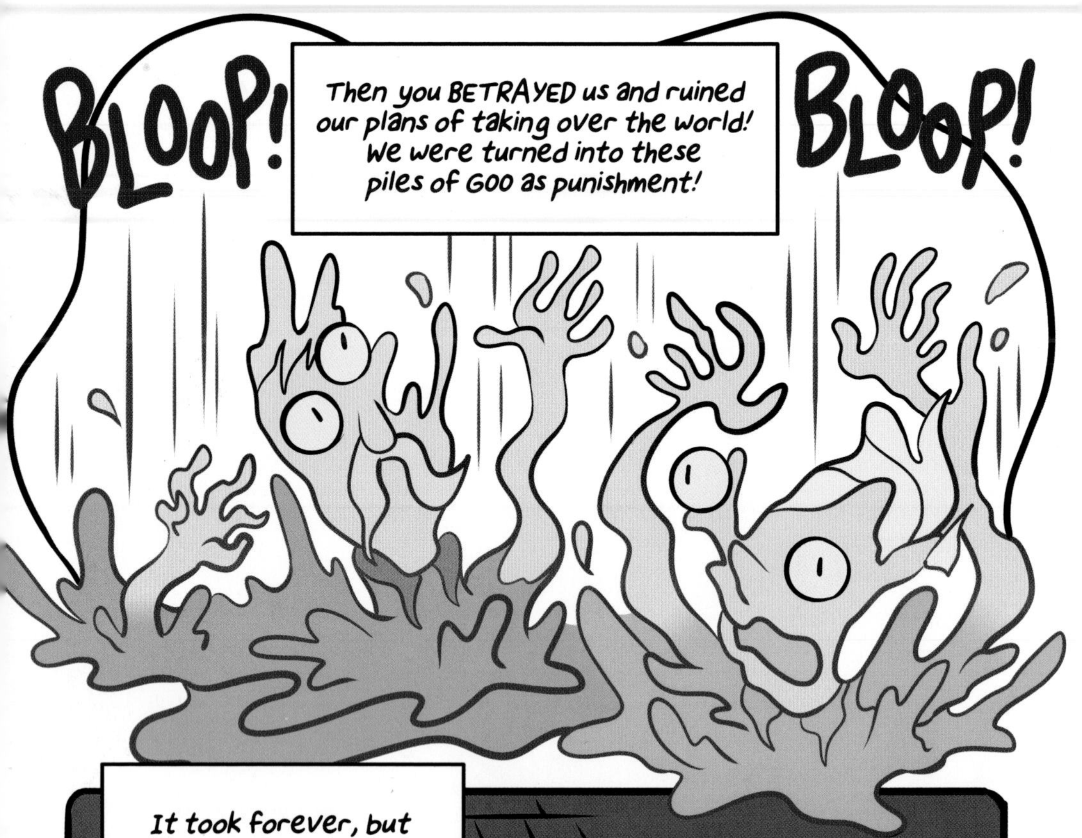
BLOOP!
Then you BETRAYED us and ruined our plans of taking over the world! We were turned into these piles of GOO as punishment!
BLOOP!

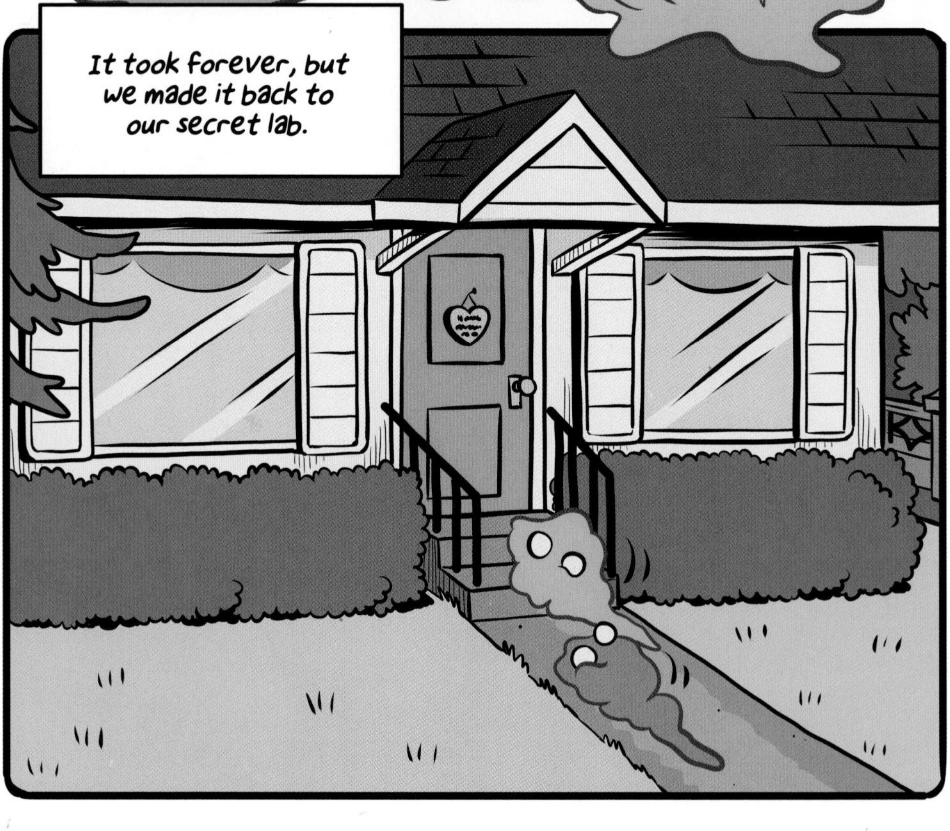
It took forever, but we made it back to our secret lab.

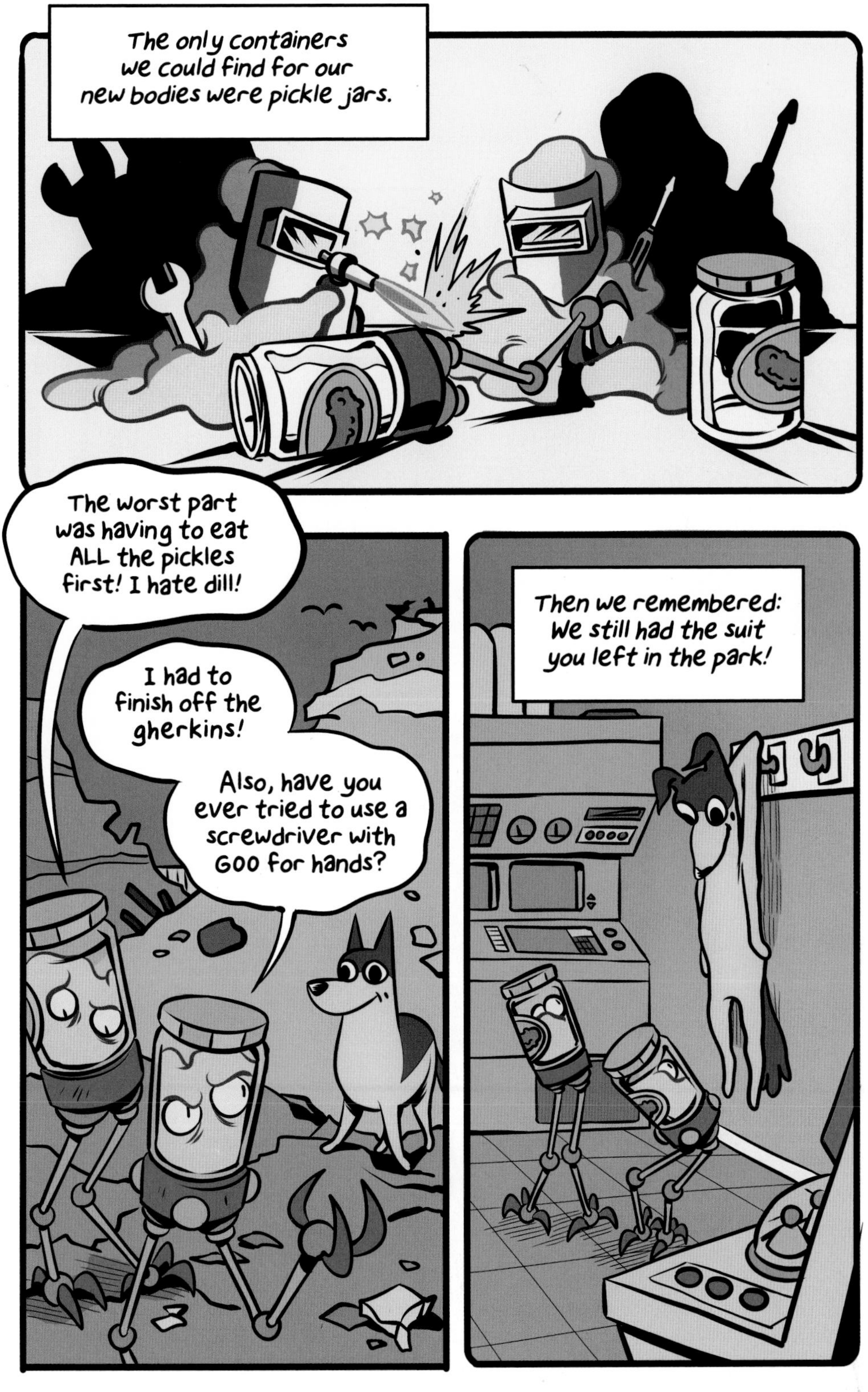
The only containers we could find for our new bodies were pickle jars.
The worst part was having to eat ALL the pickles first! I hate dill!
I had to finish off the gherkins!
Also, have you ever tried to use a screwdriver with GOO for hands?
Then we remembered: We still had the suit you left in the park!

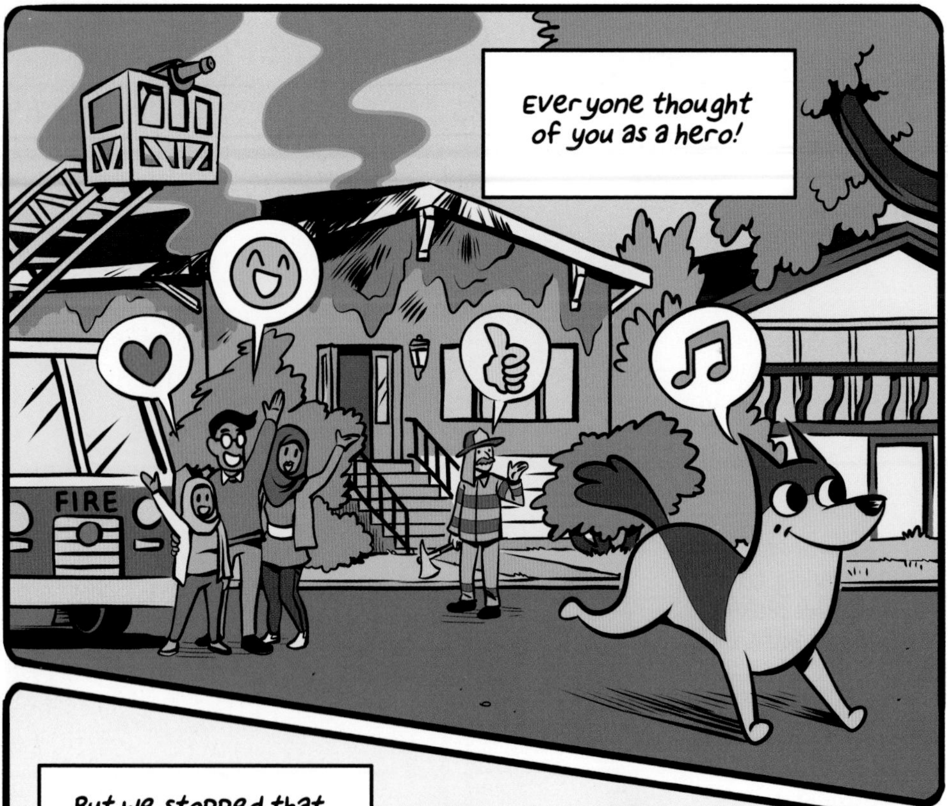
Everyone thought of you as a hero!
FIRE

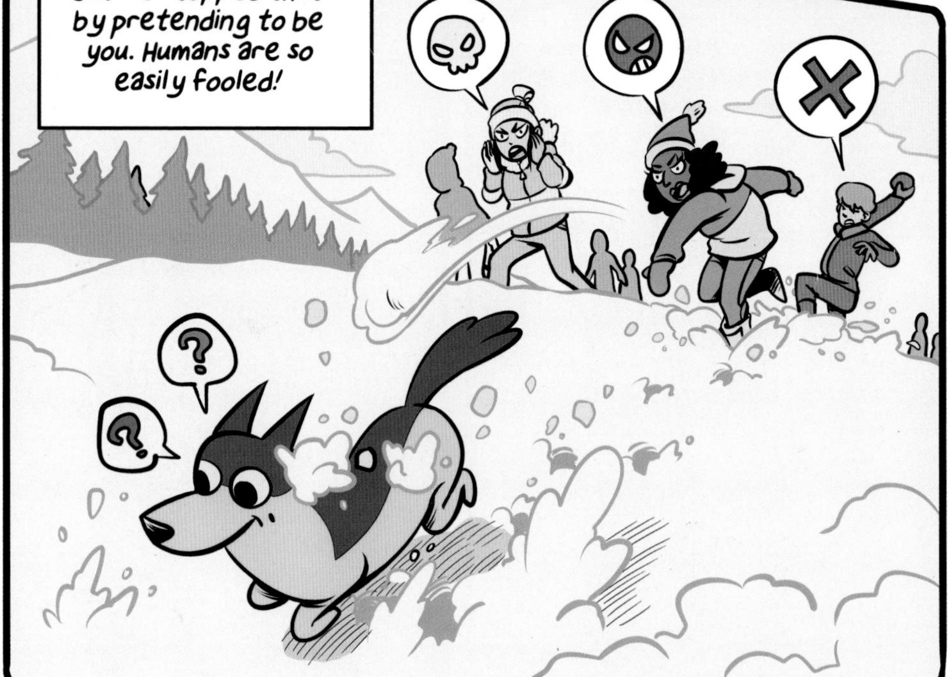
But we stopped that by pretending to be you. Humans are so easily fooled!

So you were endangering all those people's lives just for revenge?

Yes, and we thought the news coverage of it might get the attention of our leader, Princess. She likes watching Earth TV before bed.

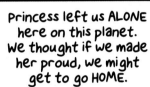

Princess left us ALONE here on this planet. We thought if we made her proud, we might get to go HOME.

So you were abandoned?

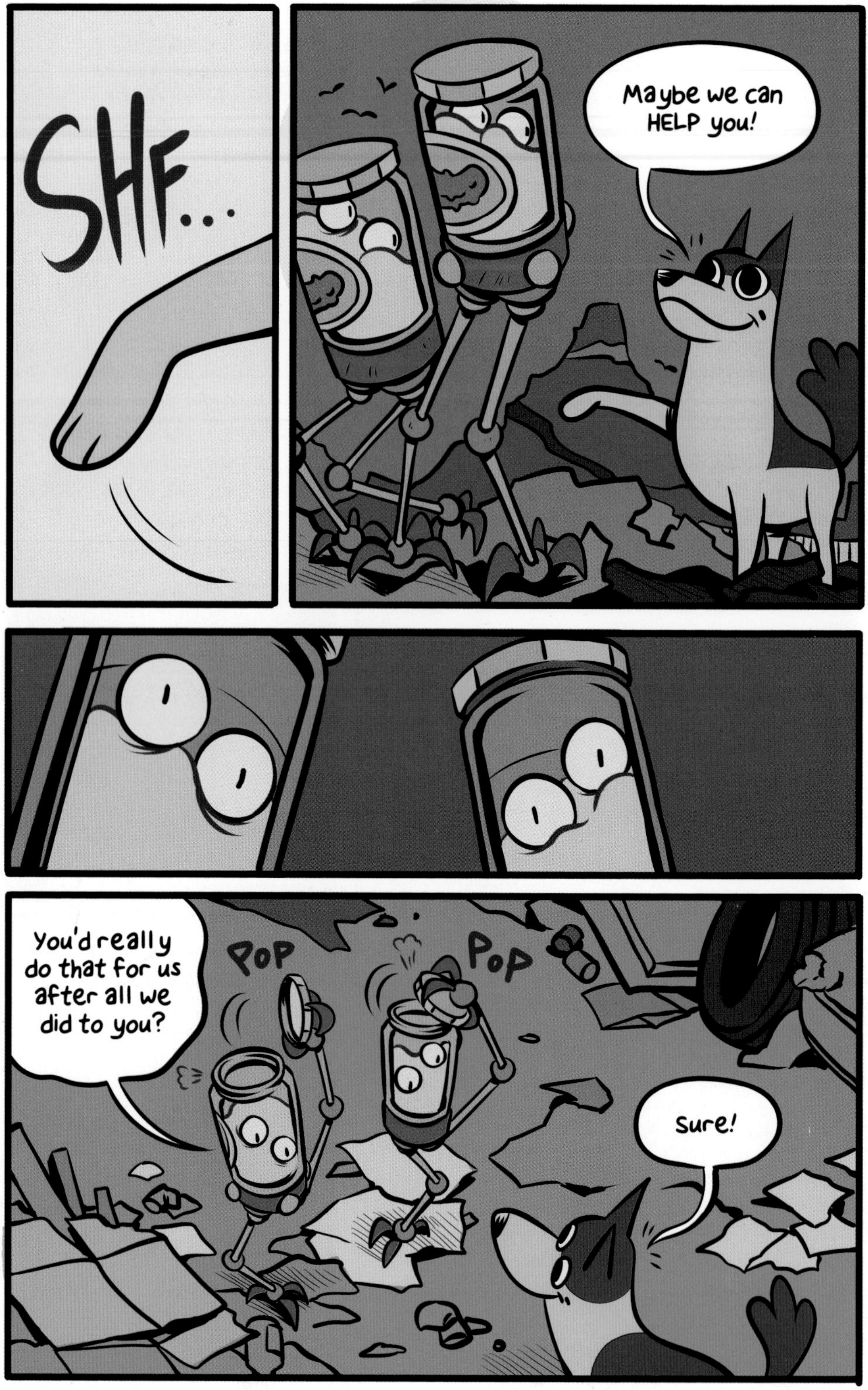
SHF...
Maybe we can HELP you!
You'd really do that for us after all we did to you?
POP
POP
Sure!

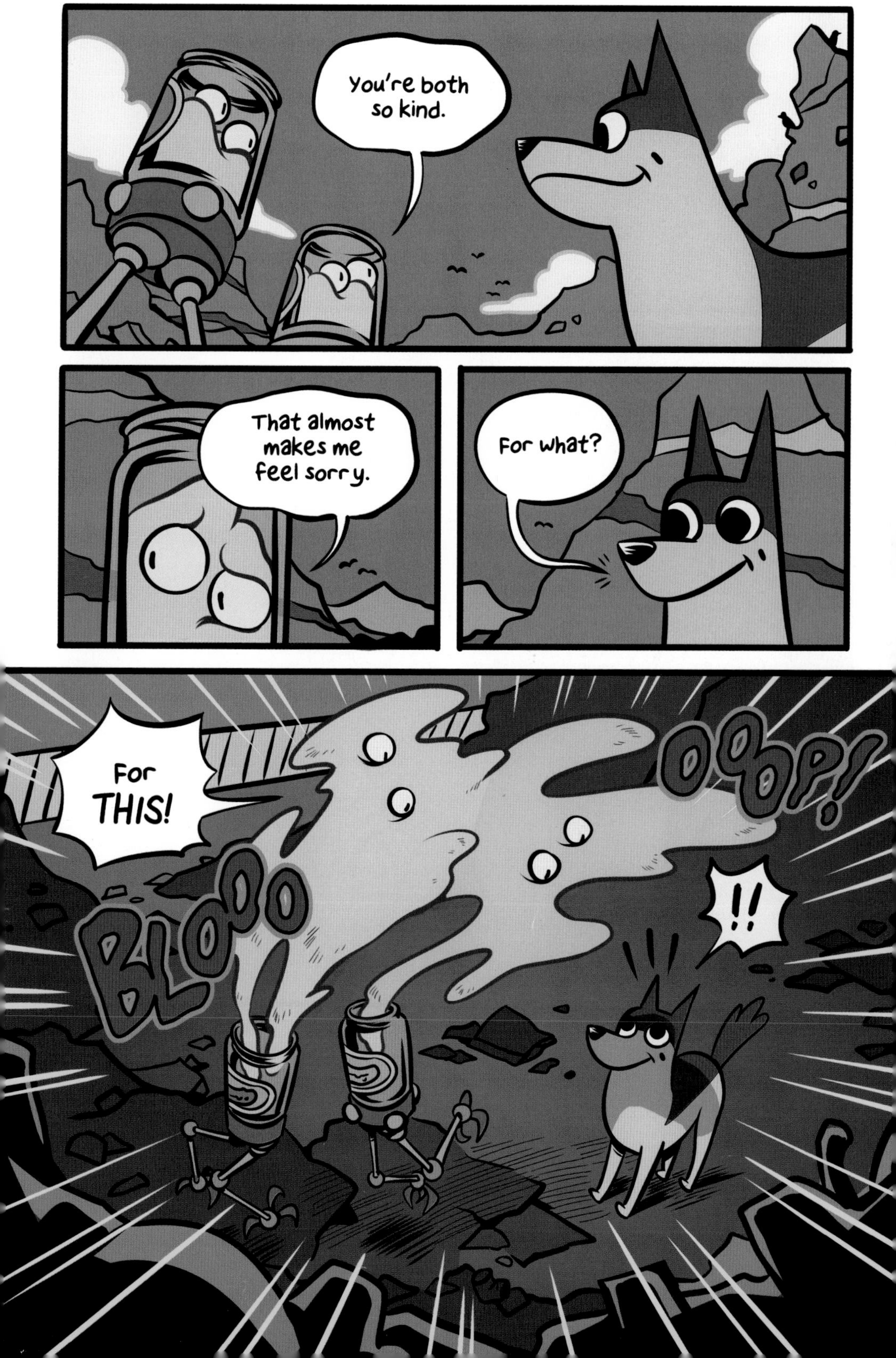
You're both so kind.
That almost makes me feel sorry.
For what?
For THIS!
OOOP!
BLOOO
!!

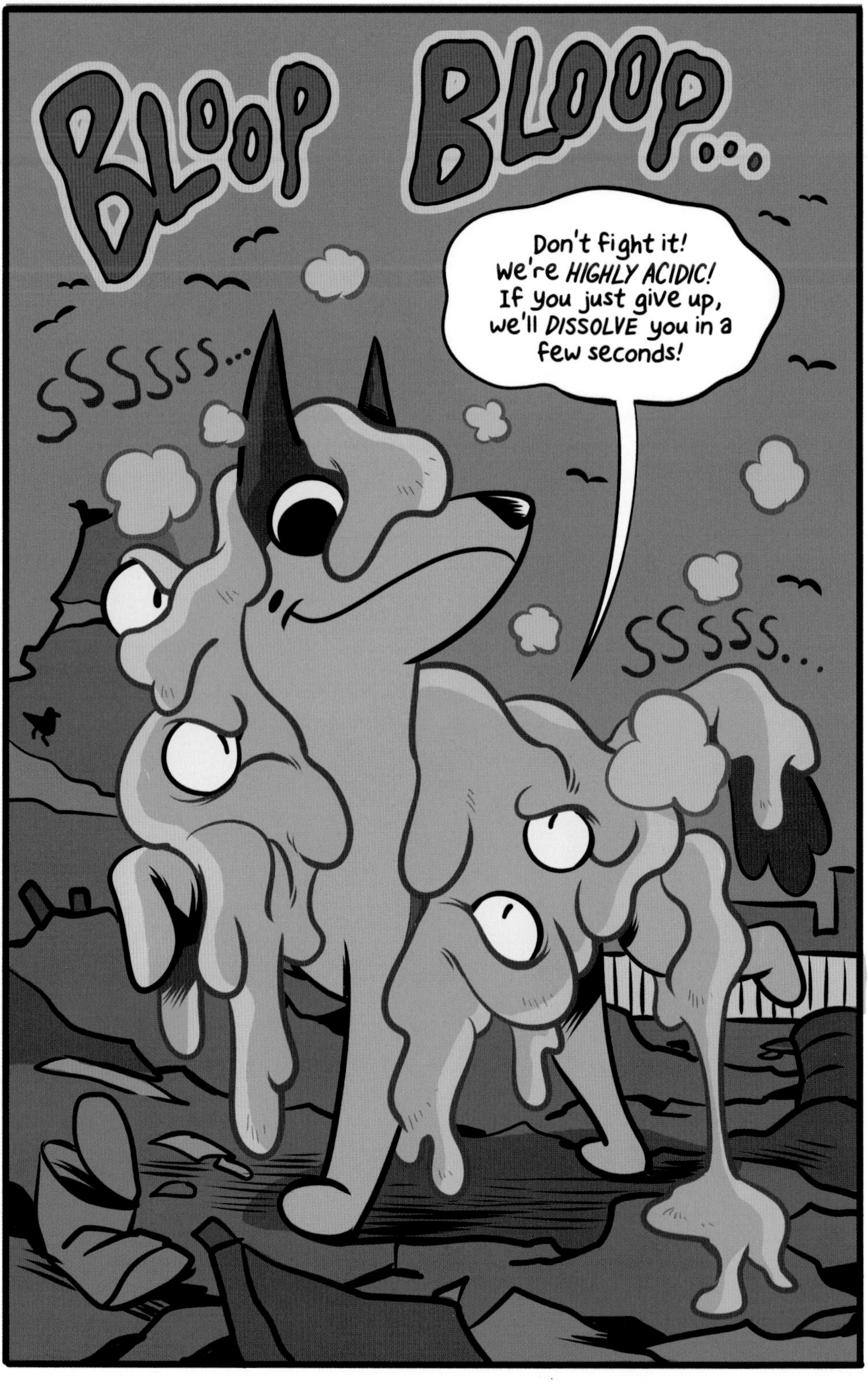
BLOOP BLOOP...
Don't fight it! We're *HIGHLY ACIDIC!* If you just give up, we'll *DISSOLVE* you in a few seconds!
SSSSSS...
SSSSS...

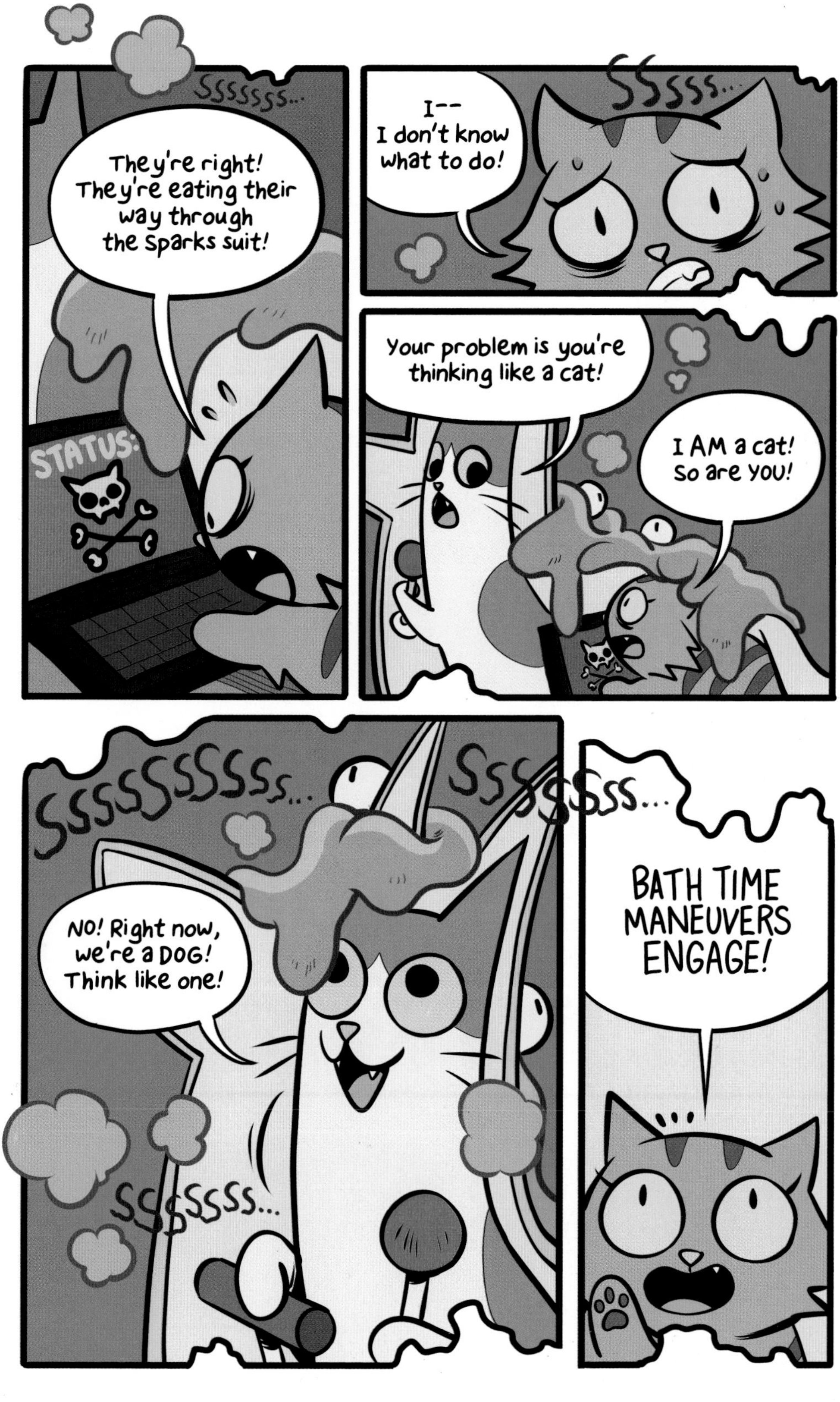
SSSSSSS...
They're right! They're eating their way through the Sparks suit!
STATUS:
I-- I don't know what to do!
SSSSSS...
Your problem is you're thinking like a cat!
I AM a cat! So are YOU!
SSSSSSSSSS...
SSSSSSS...
NO! Right now, we're a DOG! Think like one!
SSSSSSS...
BATH TIME MANEUVERS ENGAGE!
...

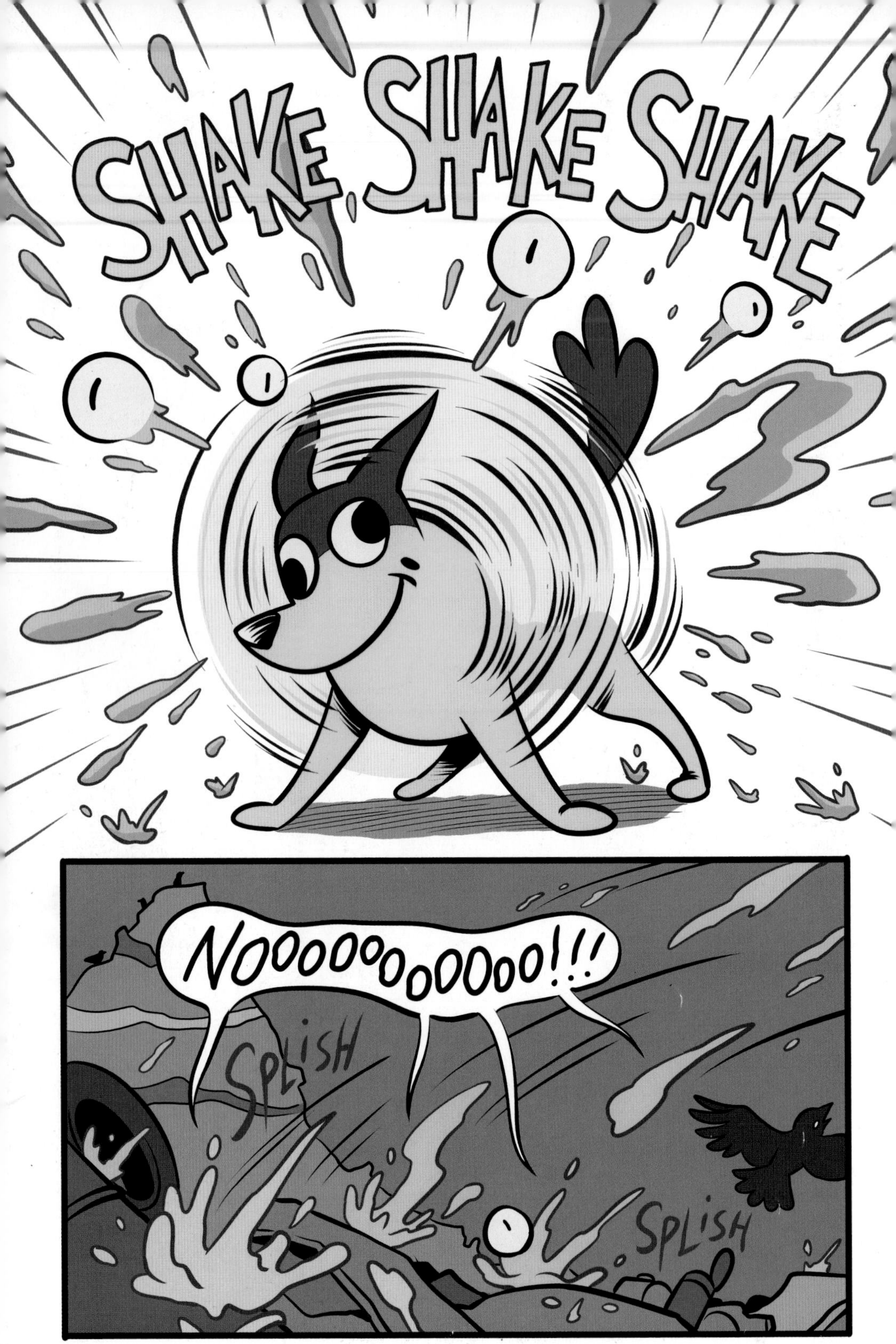
SHAKE SHAKE SHAKE
NOOOOOOOOOOOO!!!
SPLISH
SPLISH

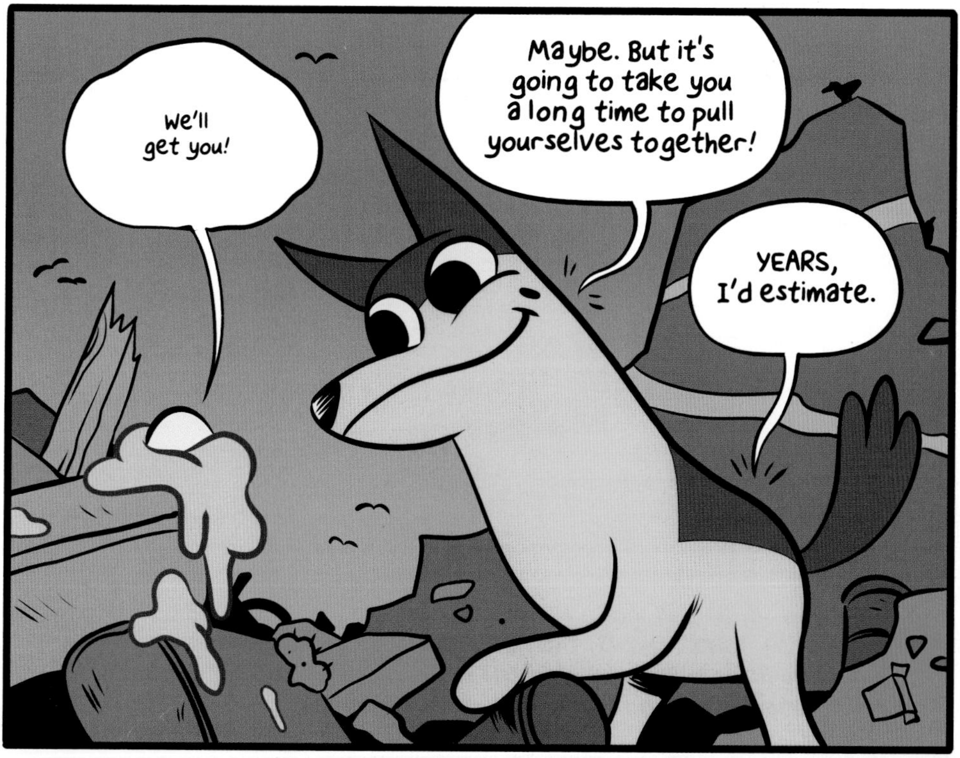
We'll get you!
Maybe. But it's going to take you a long time to pull yourselves together!
YEARS, I'd estimate.

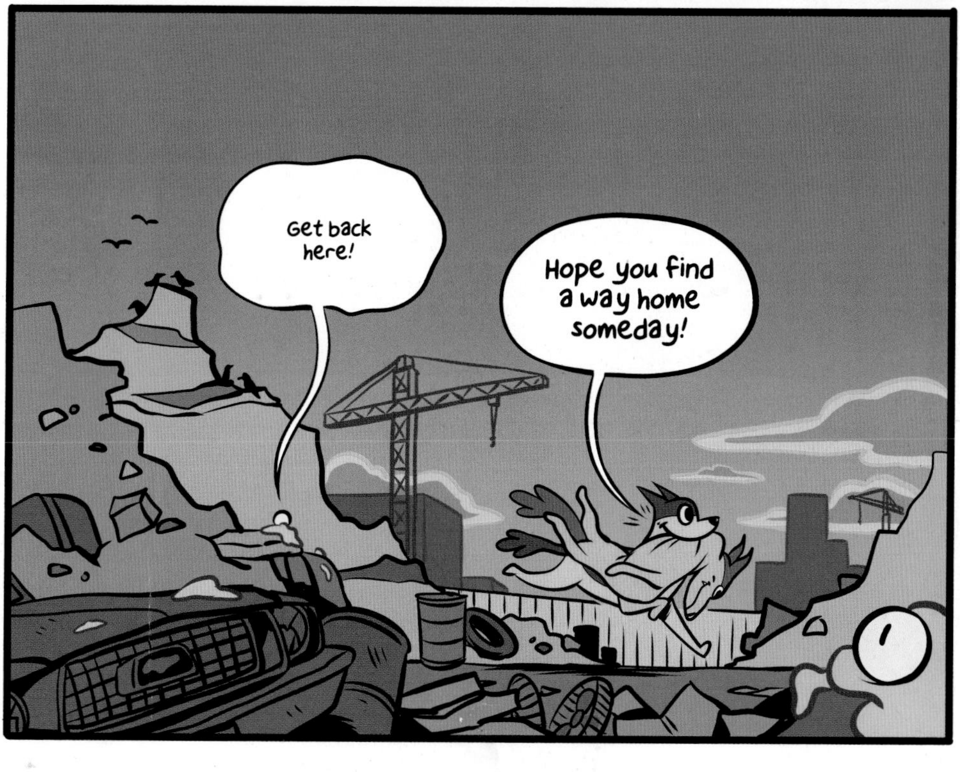
Get back here!
Hope you find a way home someday!

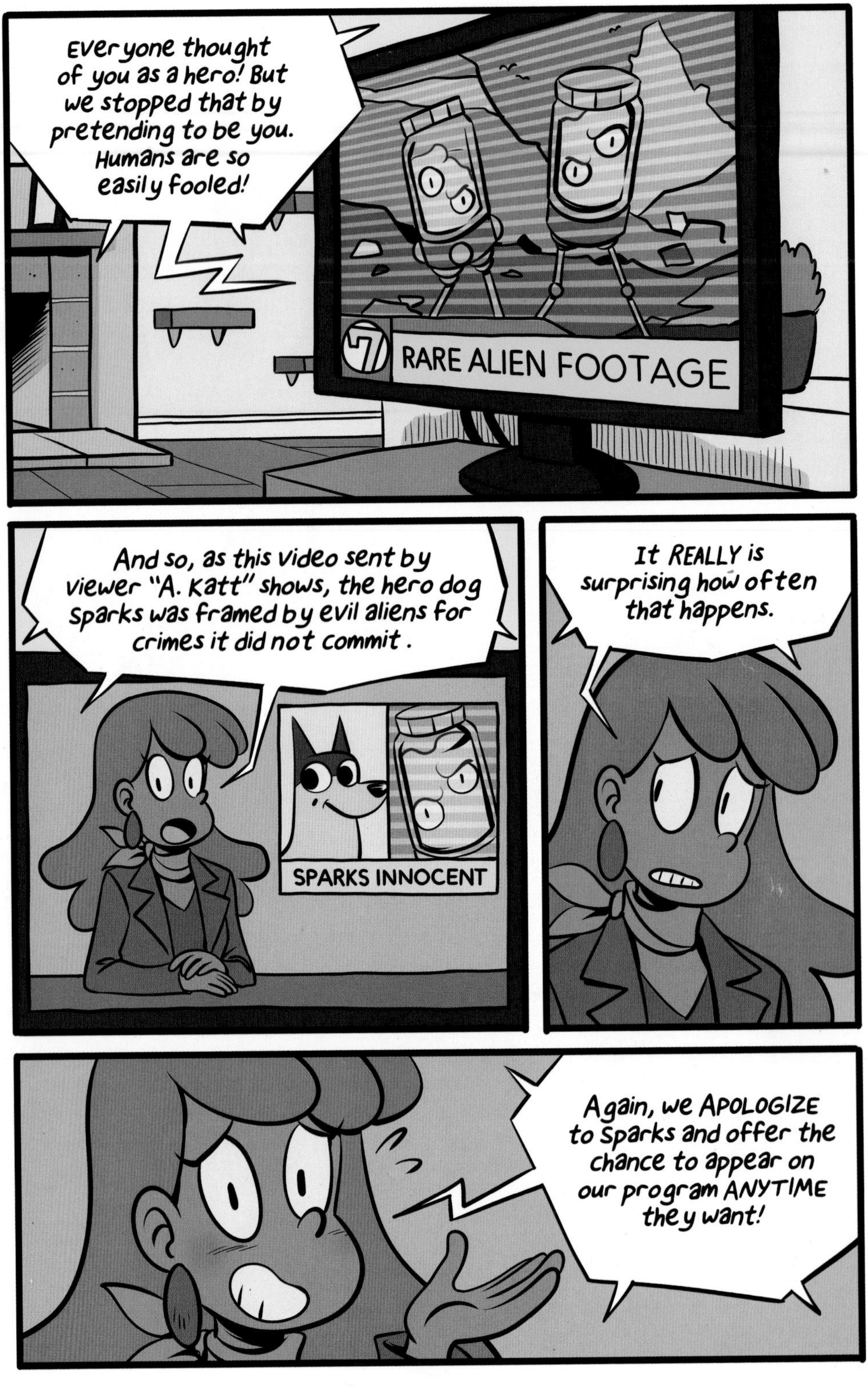
Everyone thought of you as a hero! But we stopped that by pretending to be you. Humans are so easily fooled!
7
RARE ALIEN FOOTAGE
And so, as this video sent by viewer "A. Katt" shows, the hero dog Sparks was framed by evil aliens for crimes it did not commit.
SPARKS INNOCENT
It REALLY is surprising how often that happens.
Again, we APOLOGIZE to Sparks and offer the chance to appear on our program ANYTIME they want!

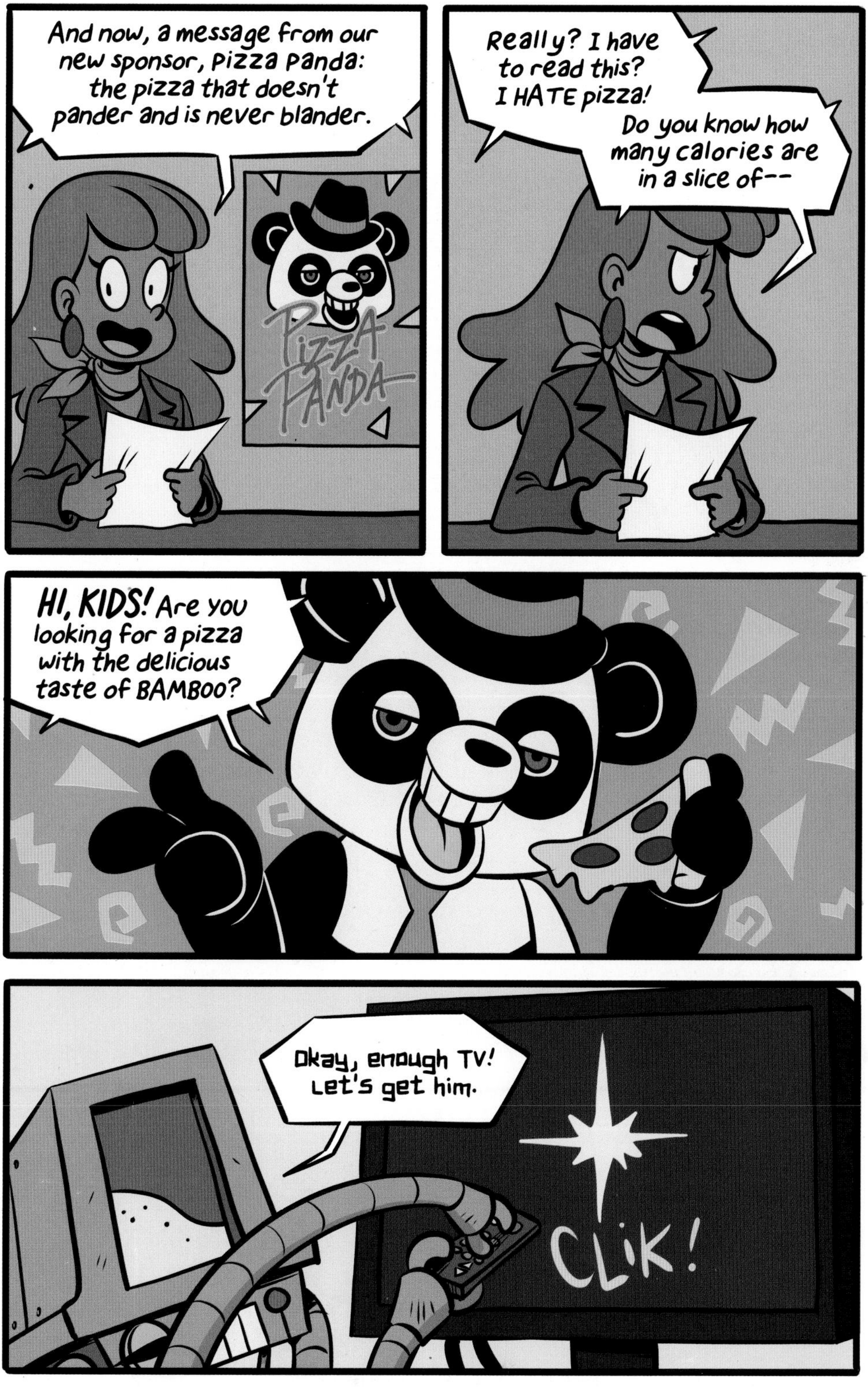
And now, a message from our new sponsor, Pizza Panda: the pizza that doesn't pander and is never blander.
Pizza Panda
Really? I have to read this? I HATE pizza!
Do you know how many calories are in a slice of--
HI, KIDS! Are you looking for a pizza with the delicious taste of BAMBOO?
Okay, enough TV! Let's get him.
CLIK!

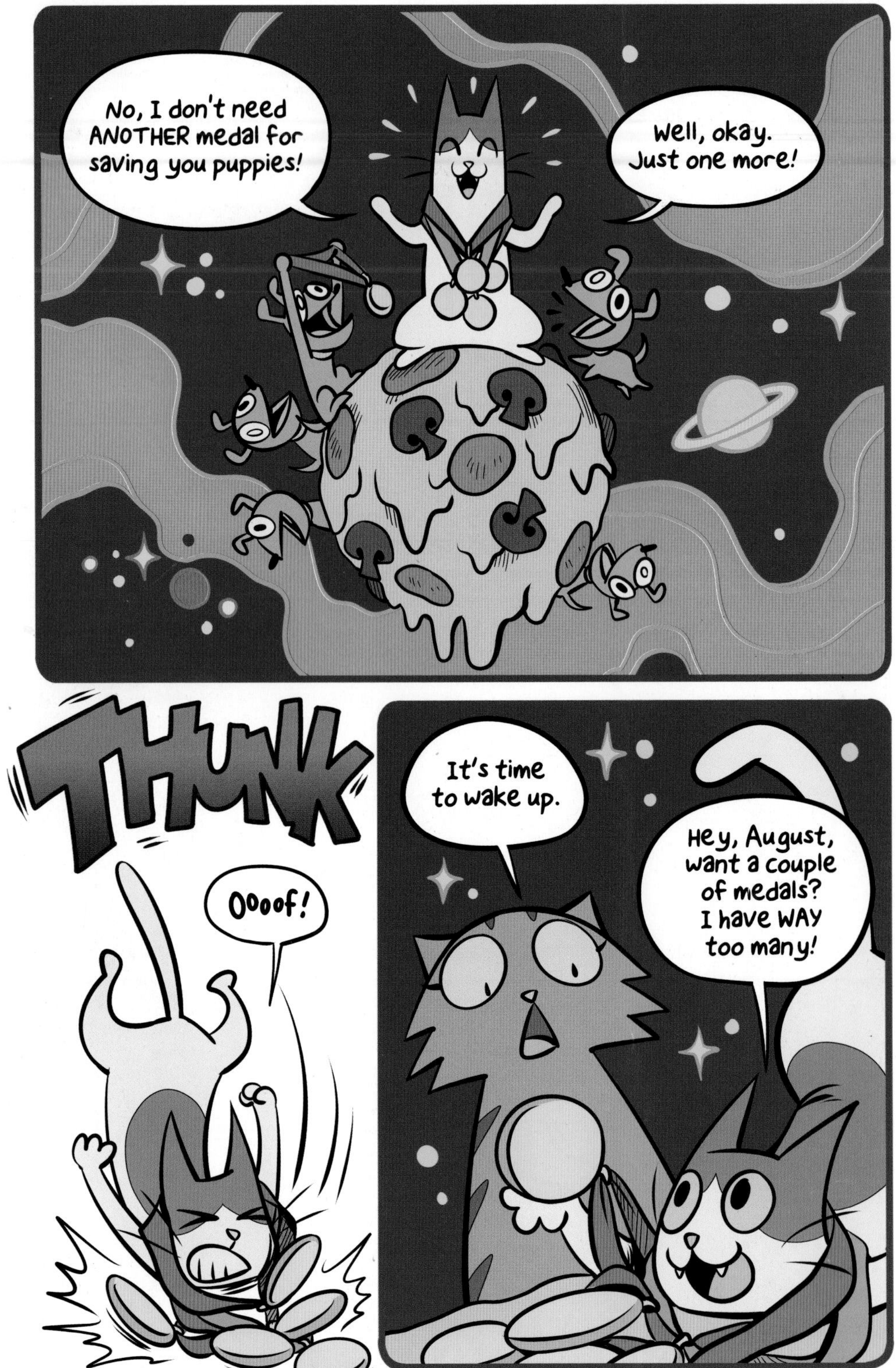
No, I don't need ANOTHER medal for saving you puppies!
Well, okay. Just one more!
THUNK
Oooof!
It's time to wake up.
Hey, August, want a couple of medals? I have WAY too many!

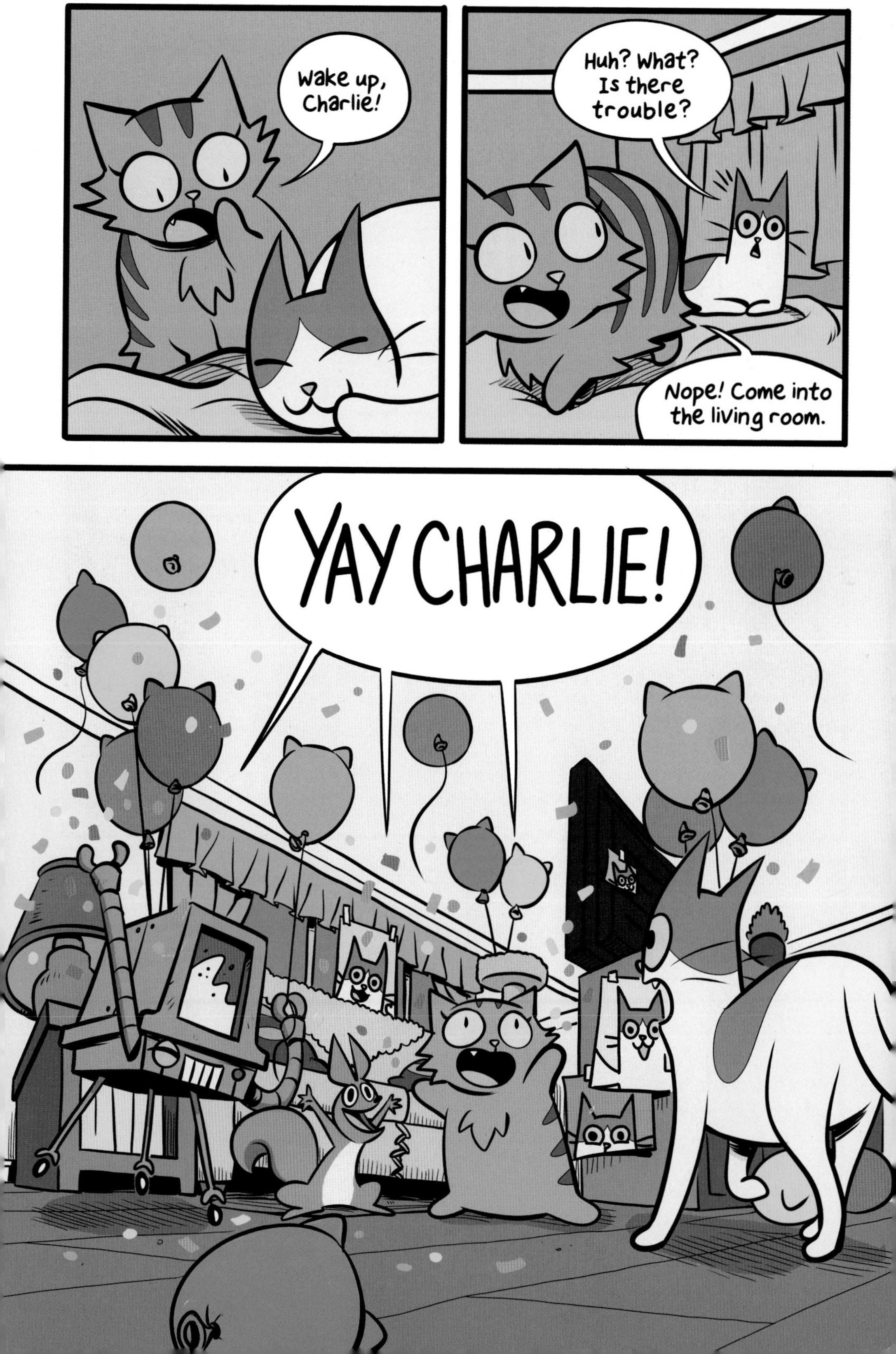
Wake up, Charlie!
Huh? What? Is there trouble?
Nope! Come into the living room.
YAY CHARLIE!

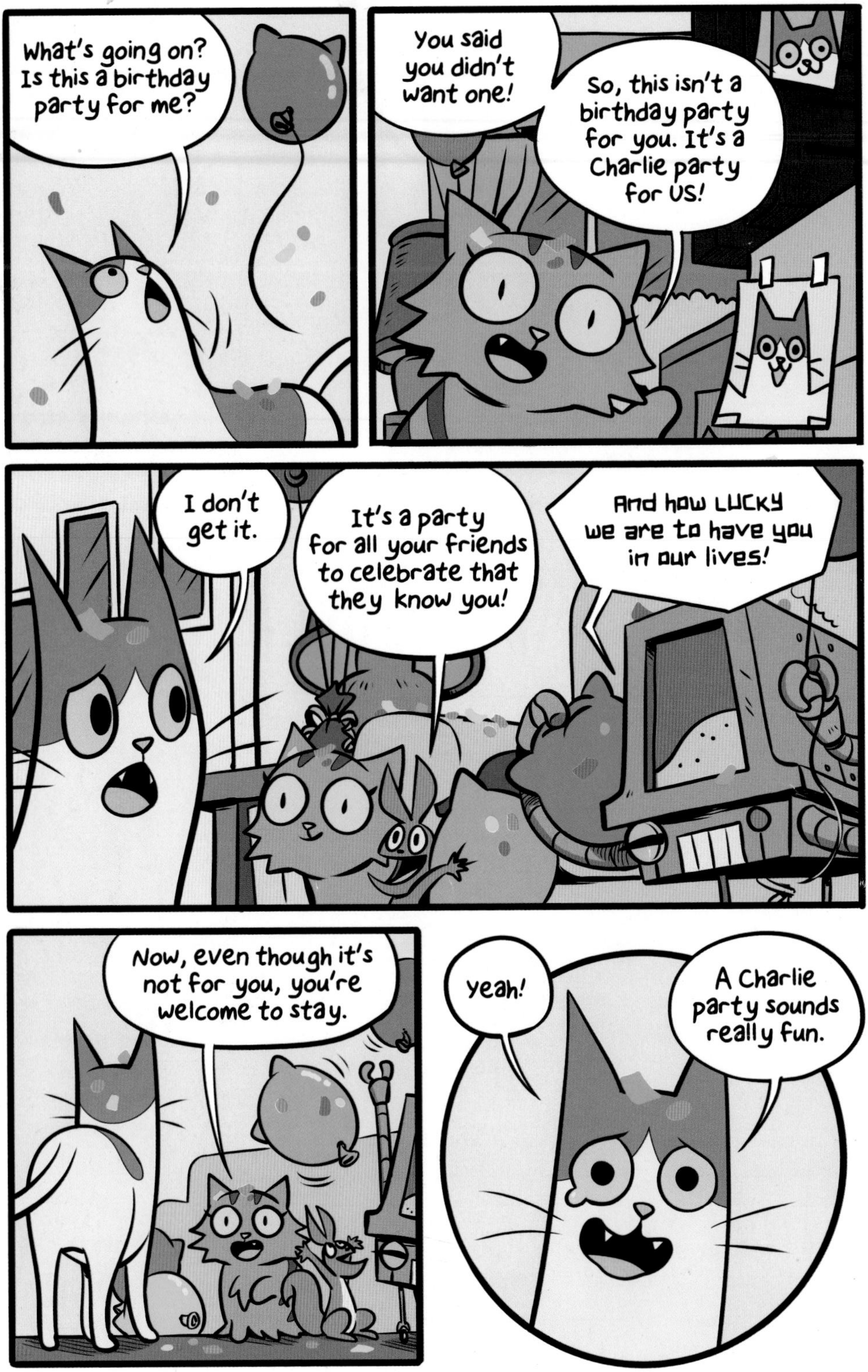
What's going on? Is this a birthday party for me?
You said you didn't want one!
So, this isn't a birthday party for you. It's a Charlie party for US!
I don't get it.
It's a party for all your friends to celebrate that they know you!
And how LUCKY we are to have you in our lives!
Now, even though it's not for you, you're welcome to stay.
Yeah!
A Charlie party sounds really fun.

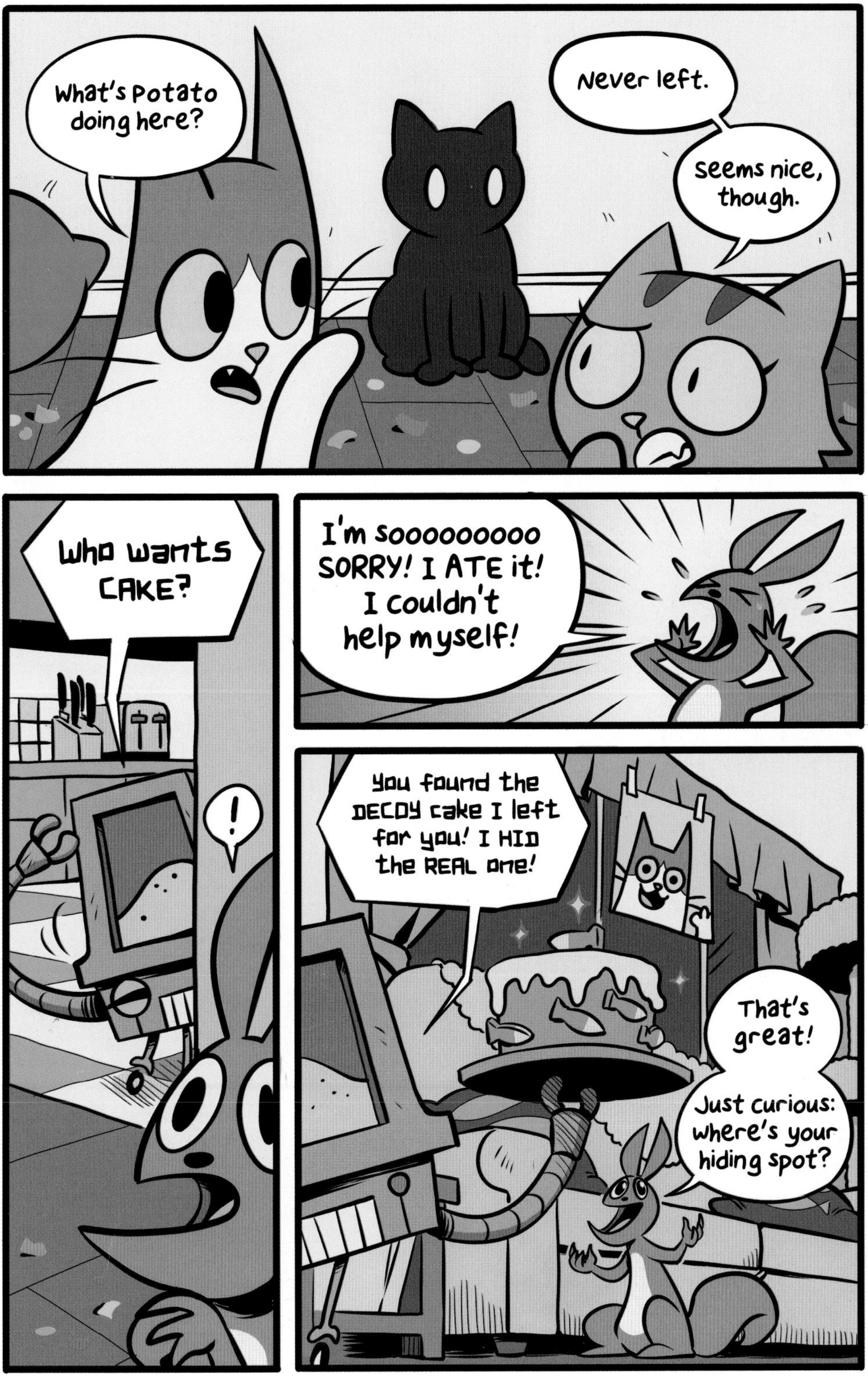
What's Potato doing here?
Never left.
Seems nice, though.
Who wants CAKE?
!
I'm sooooooooo SORRY! I ATE it! I couldn't help myself!
You found the DECOY cake I left for you! I HID the REAL one!
That's great!
Just curious: where's your hiding spot?

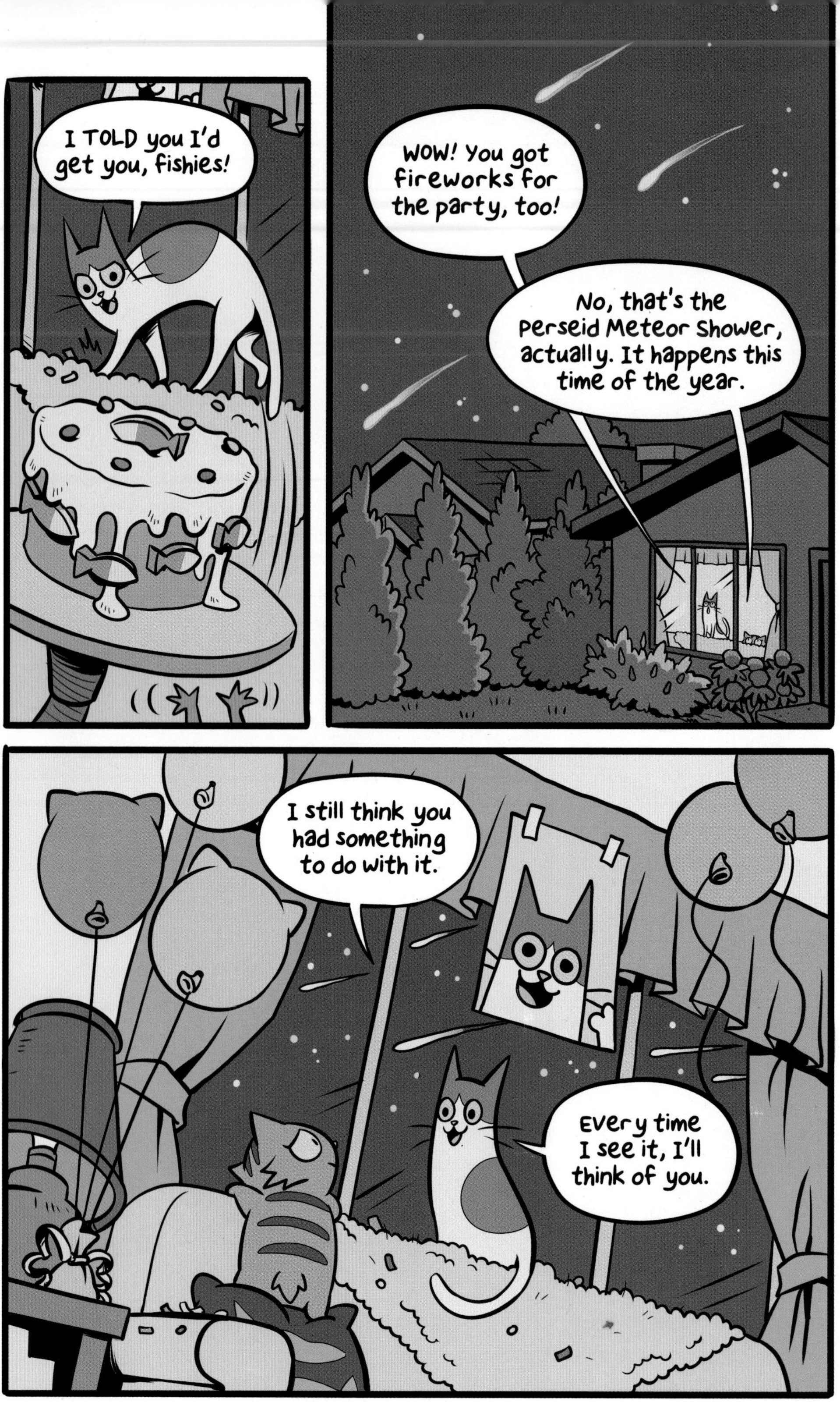
I TOLD you I'd get you, fishies!
WOW! You got fireworks for the party, too!
No, that's the Perseid Meteor Shower, actually. It happens this time of the year.
I still think you had something to do with it.
Every time I see it, I'll think of you.

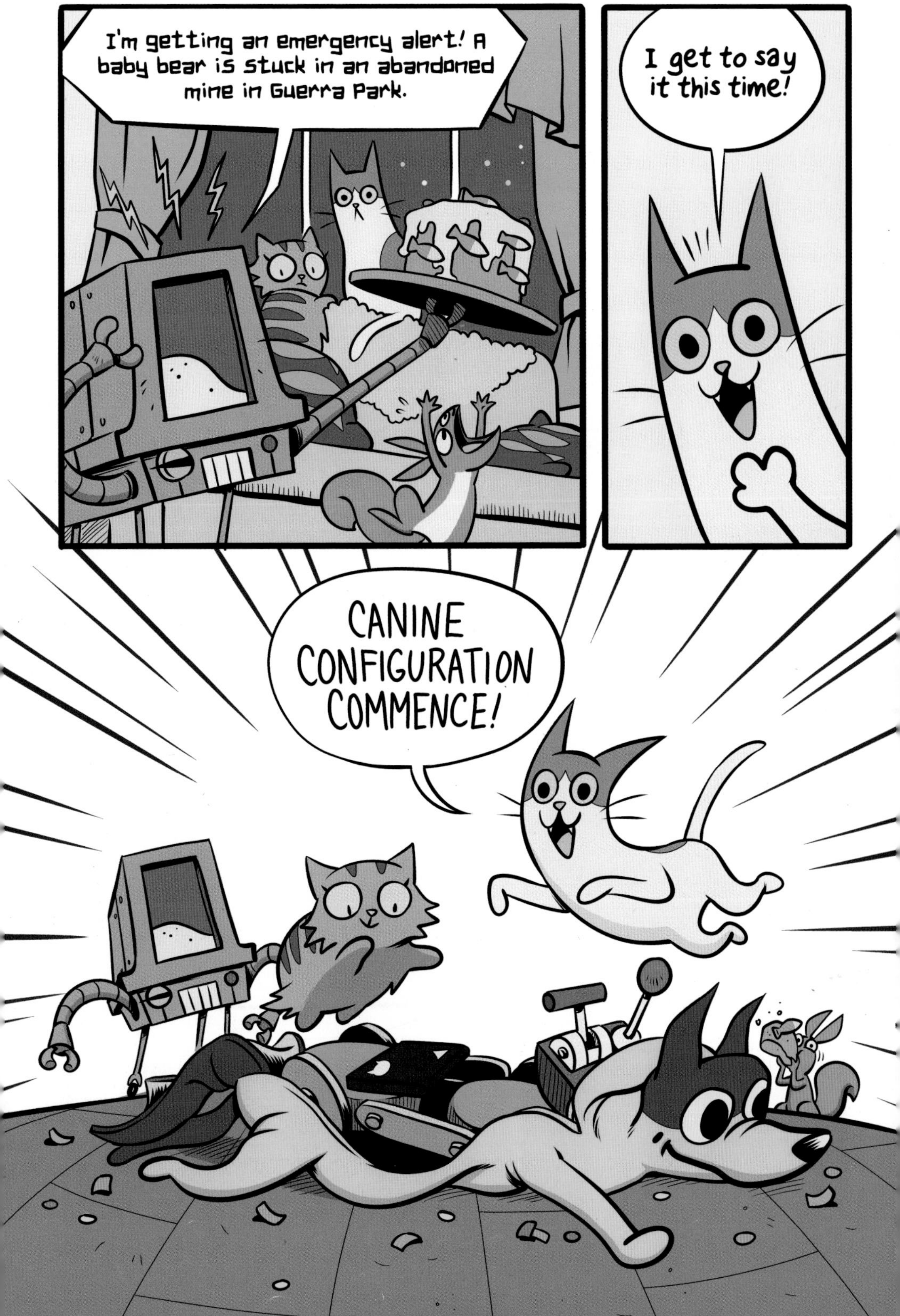
I'm getting an emergency alert! A baby bear is stuck in an abandoned mine in Guerra Park.
I get to say it this time!
CANINE CONFIGURATION COMMENCE!

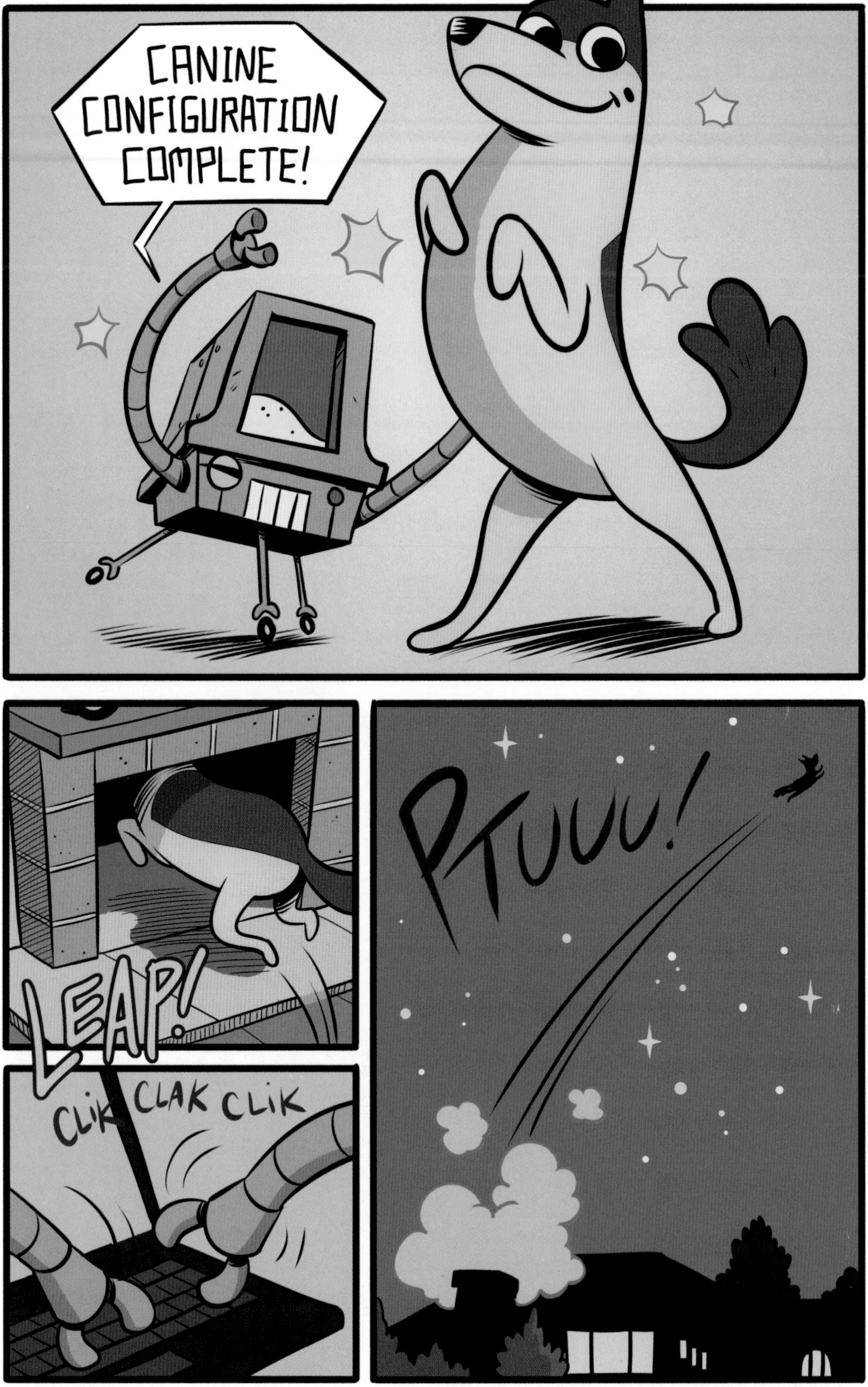
CANINE CONFIGURATION COMPLETE!
LEAP!
CLIK CLAK CLIK
PTUUU!

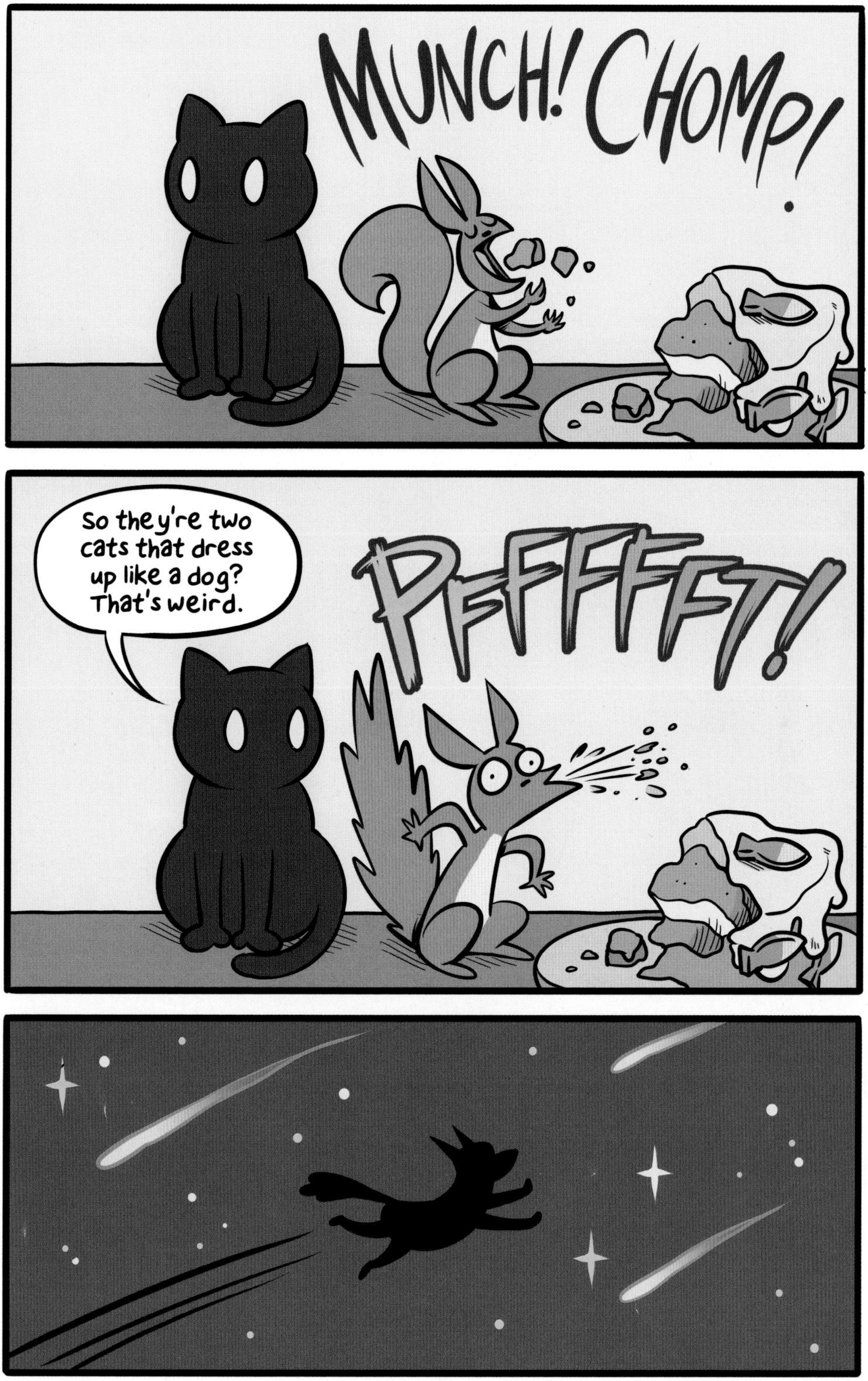
MUNCH! CHOMP!
So they're two cats that dress up like a dog? That's weird.
PFFFFFT!

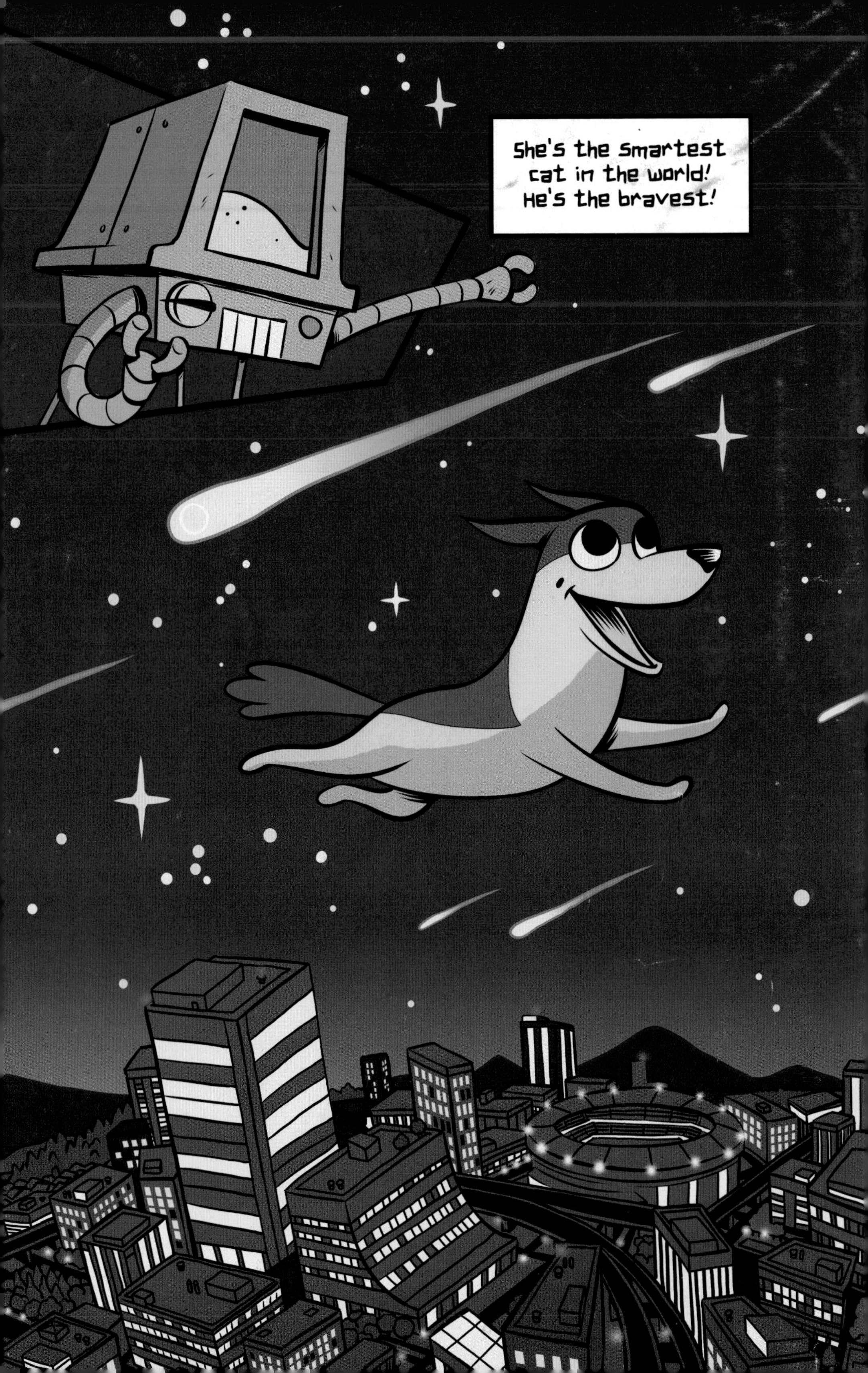
She's the smartest cat in the world! He's the bravest!

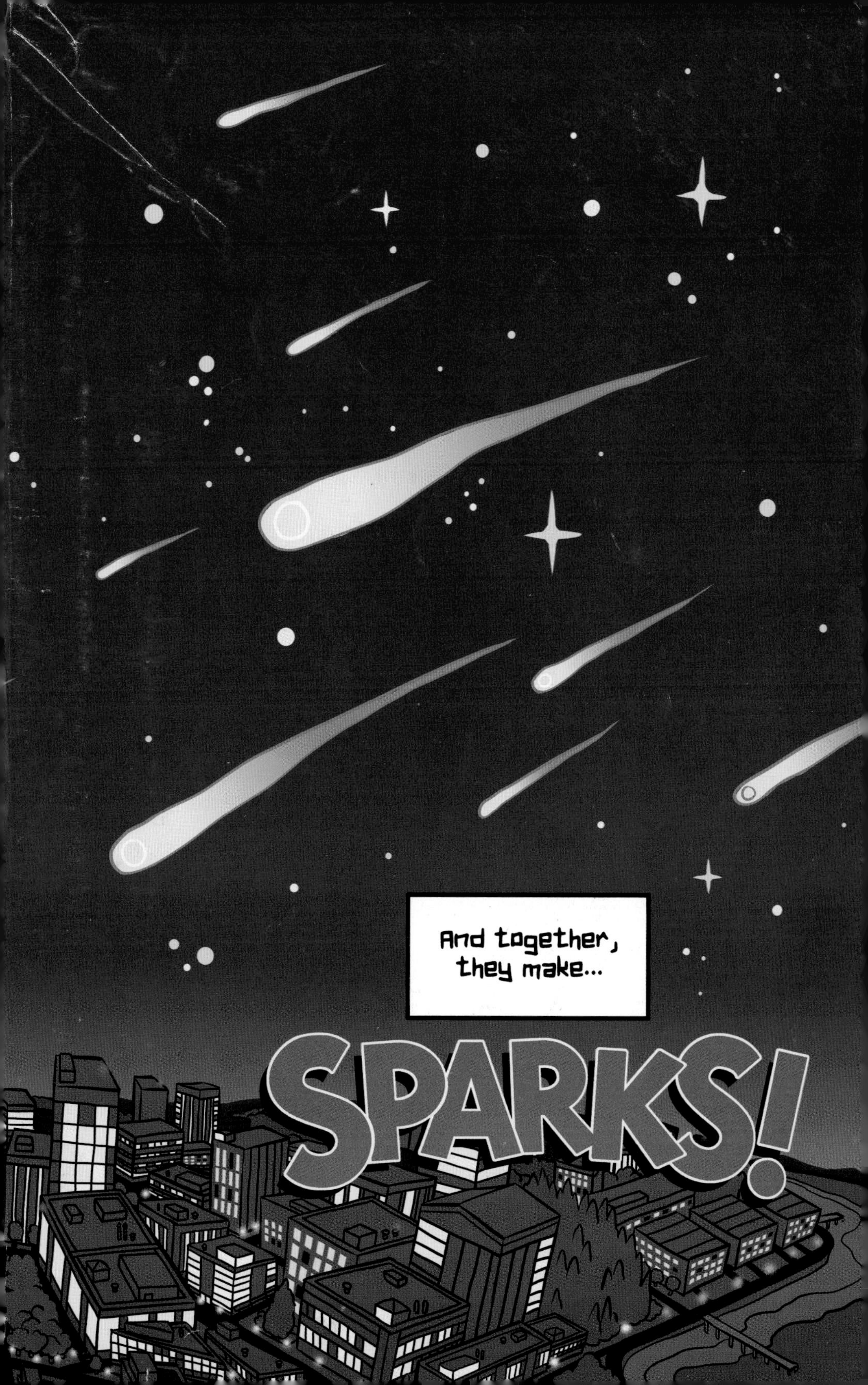
And together, they make...
SPARKS!

IAN BOOTHBY has been writing comedy for TV, radio, and comics since he was thirteen. Ian has written for *The Simpsons* and *Futurama* comics as well as being a regular cartoon contributor to *MAD* magazine and the *New Yorker* with his wife, Pia Guerra. Ian has also won the Eisner Award for Best Short Story with his friend and *Sparks!* cocreator Nina Matsumoto. Ian loves cats but has a hard time drawing them.

NINA MATSUMOTO is a Japanese Canadian who designs video game T-shirts and merchandise for Fangamer. She has been drawing comics for over ten years — most notably for *Simpsons Comics*, which won her an Eisner Award for a story she drew written by Ian. She loves every type of pizza and believes all toppings are valid.

DAVID DEDRICK has been writing and drawing funny pictures his whole life. This is his second time coloring a book. He lives with his wife, two daughters, two dogs, one cat, one horse, one pony, and two chickens — but only some of them actually live in the house!